"You can't have it both ways, Jaron.

Ma-
... had met when his foster
... Sam Rafferty, married Bria Stanton. Back
then Mariah had a crush on him, and although he
had found her attractive, he knew that a nine-year
age difference made him too old for her. But over
the years, he would have had to be as blind as a bat
not to notice that she had grown into a beautiful,
sexy woman.

And that was the problem.

Interested didn't even begin to cover how he felt for
Mariah.

* * *

Tempted by the Texan
is part of The Good, the Bad
and the Texan series—Running with
these billionaires will be one wild ride

You are either interested or you aren't.”

“You're my sister-in-law's kid sister,” he said stubbornly. “I'm just watching out for you.”

“Oh, good grief! Get over it, Jaron,” Mariah rested her hands on her sexy hips. “In case you haven't noticed lately, I'm no longer a naive eighteen-year-old girl. I've grown up. I'm twenty-five and perfectly capable of taking care of myself.”

Jaron took a deep breath. Oh, he'd noticed. Mariah wasn't the teenager he'd once...

TEMPTED BY
THE TEXAN

BY
KATHIE DeNOSKY

First Published in Great Britain 2016
By Mills & Boon, an imprint of HarperCollins*Publishers*
1 London Bridge Street, London, SE1 9GF

© 2016 Kathie DeNosky

ISBN: 978-0-263-91849-6

51-0216

Printed and bound in Spain
by CPI, Barcelona

Kathie DeNosky lives in her native southern Illinois on the land her family settled in 1839. She writes highly sensual stories with a generous amount of humor. Her books have appeared on the *USA TODAY* bestseller list and received numerous awards, including two National Readers' Choice Awards. Kathie enjoys going to rodeos, traveling to research settings for her books and listening to country music. Readers may contact her by emailing kathie@kathiedenosky.com. They can also visit her website www.kathiedenosky.com or find her on Facebook.

This book is dedicated to my family,
Bryan and Nicole DeNosky, David DeNosky,
and Heath and Angie Blumenstock.
You fill my heart with love. It's a joy and
my privilege to be your mother.

One

After working all day on the ranch he'd bought a few months back, Jaron Lambert sauntered into the Broken Spoke looking for three things—a steak dinner; a cold beer; and a warm, willing woman for a night of no-strings-attached fun. But as he sat down at one of the tables and surveyed the dimly lit roadhouse, he knew he would be settling on the steak and beer, then heading back to his place—alone.

It wasn't that there weren't any women in the bar or that they hadn't paid attention to him when he entered. There were a couple playing pool and a few more sitting at two tables shoved together, looking as if they might be having a girls' night out. One of them had even smiled at him with a come-hither expression on her pretty face. But none of them piqued his interest enough for more than a passing glance. Maybe all the hard work to get his ranch in shape was catching up with him. More than likely it was because none of the women were a certain leggy brunette with the greenest eyes he'd ever seen.

Disgusted with himself for wanting a woman he knew damned good and well he could never have, he decided that he'd have been better off calling a couple of his five brothers to see if they wanted to join him for supper. If he had, at least he would have had someone to talk to while he ate. But they all had wives and kids now, and he could appreciate them wanting to spend the time with their families.

"What can I get for you, handsome?" a young, gum-snapping waitress asked, walking up to his table.

"I'll just have a bottle of Lone Star," he answered, deciding to forego the steak and just have a beer. As soon as he finished draining the bottle, he'd head back home to heat up a pizza and spend the rest of the evening in front of the television.

"One beer coming right up," she said, giving him a bright smile. After a minute, she returned, plunked down a napkin on the worn Formica tabletop and set the bottle on top of it. "You're Jaron Lambert, aren't you?" Her smile widened into a flirty grin when he nodded. "You won the World All-Around Championship at the National Finals Rodeo in Las Vegas just before Christmas, didn't you?"

"Yup." When she continued to stand there expectantly, he gave in and asked what he figured she was waiting on. "So you were there?"

"Oh, no," she said, shaking her head. "I couldn't afford a trip to Vegas on what I make here. I watched it on satellite TV." She gave him an enticing smile. "You sure looked sexy when they awarded you that buckle."

He could tell by the look on her face that she was interested in more than just talking about his big win in Las Vegas. Unfortunately for her, he wasn't. He had dodged more than his fair share of buckle bunnies— young women who flirted and hoped to sleep with a cowboy in possession of a championship belt buckle— over the years, and he was glad that part of his life was behind him. Hopefully with his retirement from rodeo after the finals a couple of months ago, that type of woman would lose interest in him and move on to another cowboy who didn't care if he became nothing more than a notch on a groupie's bedpost.

When he didn't respond to her comment and expectant expression, she shrugged one shoulder. "Well, if you need anything else—anything at all—just let me know."

"Thanks," Jaron said, taking a swig of his beer as he watched the waitress move over to another table where three men sat. It was clear one of them was going to get lucky and be invited to join her for a night of fun after she got off work.

After downing his beer, he got several dollars out of his wallet and tossed them on top of the table. There was no sense sitting there paying for more beer when he had a cold twelve-pack in his refrigerator at home.

But just as he started to get up, he noticed a woman walk through the door and up to the bar. He uttered a word under his breath that he reserved for smashed thumbs and card games with his brothers as he settled back down in his chair. What the hell was *she* doing here?

She was wearing a red dress that fit her body like a glove, and there was very little left to the imagination about the size of her breasts or the curve of her slender hips. He swallowed back another curse as his gaze drifted lower. That little red number she wore ended about midthigh and gave him more than a fair idea of how long and shapely her legs were. But it was the shiny black high heels she had on that caused him to grind his teeth. Those four-inch spikes were the kind a man looked at and knew the woman wearing them was just asking for him to take her home and pleasure her throughout the night.

Apparently, he wasn't the only guy in the room to notice. As Jaron watched, a seedy-looking cowboy with a Skoal ring on the hip pocket of his jeans and a leering grin walked up beside her. She glanced at the man, shook her head and turned back to speak to the bartender. It was crystal clear she wasn't buying what the good old boy was selling.

Jaron decided he wasn't going anywhere. At least not while Mariah Stanton was standing there looking for all the world like every man's midnight fantasy.

But as he watched the cowboy try to get her to pay attention to him, Jaron could tell from the look on the man's face that there was going to be trouble. The guy wanted her, and she didn't want any part of him. Unfortunately, the son of a bitch was either too drunk, too stupid or too determined to take no for an answer.

When the jerk reached out and took hold of her upper arm, Mariah recoiled, and that was when Jaron came up out of his chair to cross the room like a bull out of the bucking chute. Without a moment's hesitation, he planted his right fist along the man's jaw and watched the bastard hit the floor in an undignified heap.

"Jaron?" Mariah sounded startled when she looked over her shoulder at him. "What are you doing?"

"Saving your pretty little ass from getting into more trouble than you can handle," he retorted angrily.

"You knocked out Roy Lee!" one of the man's friends shouted, taking a step toward Jaron.

"Do we have a problem?" Jaron growled through clenched teeth as he quickly moved Mariah behind him out of harm's way.

A good six inches shorter than Jaron's six-foot-two-inch height, the man stared at him a moment then hastily shook his head. "I ain't got no quarrel with you, dude," he said, hastily taking a couple of steps in the opposite direction.

"Then, I strongly suggest you pick Roy Lee up off the floor and leave me and the lady alone," Jaron ordered.

As Roy Lee's friends hauled him to his feet, Jaron turned and, putting his arm around Mariah's waist, ushered her out of the place. She tried to pull away from him, but he tightened his arm around her and didn't stop as he guided her out the exit and toward her car in the parking lot.

"Jaron, have you lost your mind?" she asked as he hurried her along.

"What the hell do you think you were doing walking

into a cowboy bar looking for all the world as if you're advertising for a roll in the hay, Mariah?" he demanded when they reached her compact sedan.

"I don't look like I'm advertising for any such thing," she said, jerking away from him. "And what's wrong with the way I'm dressed? I think I look just fine."

Jaron folded his arms across his chest and let his gaze slide from the top of her dark brown hair to the soles of her impossibly high heels. That was the problem. She did look fine. Too fine.

He ignored her question and asked one of his own. "What in the name of Sam Hill did you think you were doing stopping by the Broken Spoke alone?"

"Not that it's any of your concern, but I had a dinner meeting in Fort Worth and on my way back home my car started making an odd noise. I managed to get it into this parking lot just before it died completely, and after I discovered that my cell phone needed recharging, I went inside to call a tow truck."

He watched her emerald eyes narrow as she glared at him. "And even if I had been there for other reasons, it's none of your business. I can handle situations like what happened in there all by myself."

"Oh, yeah? Is that why old Roy Lee put his filthy hands on you?" Jaron asked, doing his best to hold on to his temper. "The minute that bastard grabbed hold of your arm he made it my business."

When he'd seen the man touch her, Jaron had damned near come unglued. Aside from the fact that he took exception to any man forcing his attention on a woman when it was clear she didn't want it, the woman in question had been Mariah. As long as he had a single breath left in his body, nobody was going to treat her with anything but complete respect.

"Really? It's your business? You've made it perfectly clear all these years that you have absolutely no interest in anything I do." She shook her head. "You can't have it both ways, Jaron. Either you are interested or you aren't."

"You're my sister-in-law's kid sister," he said stubbornly. "I'm just watching out for you."

"Oh, good grief! Get over it, Jaron." She rested her hands on her sexy hips. "In case you haven't noticed lately, I'm no longer a naive eighteen-year-old girl. I've grown up. I'm twenty-five and perfectly capable of taking care of myself."

Jaron took a deep breath. Oh, he'd noticed several years ago that Mariah wasn't the teenager he had met when his foster brother Sam Rafferty had married Bria Stanton. Back then Mariah had had a crush on him, and although he had found her attractive, he knew that a nine-year age difference made him too old for her. But over the years, he would have had to be as blind as a bat not to notice that she had grown into a beautiful, sexy woman. And that was the problem.

Interested didn't even begin to cover what he felt for Mariah. He wouldn't call it love. Hell, he'd have to believe in the emotion before he could say that was what it was. But he did find himself thinking about her a lot, and whenever the family got together for birthdays dinners or holidays, he couldn't seem to take his eyes off her.

"I don't care how old you are. There's no sense in putting yourself into a dangerous situation," he insisted.

"Dangerous?" She laughed and the sound sent a shock wave of heat straight through him. She pointed toward the entrance to the bar. "Sam brings Bria here for dinner all the time. For that matter, the rest of your brothers bring their wives here, as well. We both know they wouldn't dream of doing that if they thought they were placing the women in jeopardy."

It was Jaron's turn to laugh. "Do you honestly think that some dust-covered cowboy would have the guts to try putting the moves on one of my sisters-in-law with my brothers right there to knock them flat?"

Continuing to glare at him, she shook her head. "I'm not going to get into a debate with you about your antiquated idea that women need a man's protection whenever they go out." She started to brush past him to go back into the bar. "I've had a trying day, I'm tired and I need to make that phone call."

"Not in there you're not," Jaron said, placing his hands on her slender shoulders to stop her.

"Jaron Lambert, I swear if you don't—"

Before he could stop himself, he pulled her close and brought his mouth down on hers to silence her. But the moment he tasted her perfect coral lips, he lost every ounce of sense he'd ever possessed and gave in to years of temptation and denial.

Wrapping his arms around her, Jaron settled Mariah against him, and the feel of her breasts crushed to his chest, her body touching his from their shoulders to their knees, set a fire in his belly that he thought just might burn him to a crisp. Without a thought to the consequences, he traced the seam of her mouth with his tongue to coax her to open for him. When she did, he slipped inside to explore her inner recesses.

As he stroked and teased her, she grabbed the front of his jeans jacket with both hands for support as she sagged against him. That fueled the fire in his belly to a fever pitch, and his erection was not only inevitable—it caused him to feel light-headed from its intensity. Tightening his arms around her, he held her to him and he knew the second she felt the evidence of his need when she shivered and pressed herself even closer.

His heart stalled as another wave of heat flowed through his veins. He had wanted her for so damned long, if he didn't put some distance between them, and real quick, he wasn't sure he would be able to. But when he tried to ease away from the kiss, Mariah's lips clung to his and he knew it was going to take every ounce of strength he could muster to move away from her.

Forcing himself to take a step back before she made him forget he was a gentleman, he took a deep breath. "What seems to be wrong with your car?"

"I…uh, I'm not sure," she said, sounding as winded as he felt. "I heard a noise and a few minutes later I noticed the lights were dimming. By the time I parked it here, they went out completely and the engine died. When I turned the key to restart it, all it did was make a clicking sound."

"It sounds as if you might have a bad battery or the alternator went out," he said, thankful to focus on something besides the enticing woman standing next to him.

It appeared that neither wanted to mention the kiss, and that was just fine with him. The less said about his lapse of judgment, the better.

"Is that expensive?" she asked, nibbling on her lower lip. She wasn't trying to be provocative, but it was all he could do to keep from kissing her again.

"Don't worry about it," he said, shaking his head. "I'll have my men come and get your car in the morning and see what they can do. I've got a hired hand who can fix just about anything with four tires and a motor."

"That's great, but how am I supposed to get home tonight?" she asked, rubbing her temple with her fingertips as if she might be developing a headache. A sudden rumble of thunder followed by a flash of lightning in the distance caused her to groan. "Great! Just great. I still have ninety miles to drive before I get home, my car won't run and now it's going to start raining. Could this day get any better?"

"It's been a rough one?" he asked, noticing the defeated expression on her pretty face.

She looked at him as though he might be one of the simplest souls she'd ever met. "Let me put it to you this way—I've definitely had a lot better."

As he stood there staring at her, he waged an internal battle with himself. It was getting late and there weren't a lot of choices. He was worn-out from working all day and she sounded as though she was exhausted from whatever had ruined hers. He could drive her down to Shady Grove, but he really wasn't looking forward to making the hour-and-a-half drive back as tired as he was—not when he had a very comfortable, fully furnished six-bedroom ranch house ten miles away.

"Don't worry about how you're going to get home," he said, glancing at his watch. "You can stay at my place tonight and drive back to Shady Grove in the morning after my men get your car fixed."

"I don't want to impose." A sudden gust of wind had her impatiently brushing her long dark brown hair away from her face as she shivered from the February cold. "Could you drive me over to Sam and Bria's?"

It would be the best for all concerned if he could take her to her sister and his brother's ranch. Unfortunately, that option wasn't on the table. "Sam and Bria left this morning to go down to Houston for a stock show."

She looked uncertain for several seconds and he could tell she was trying to think of something— anything—else she could do. When her shoulders sagged in defeat, he knew she'd reached the same conclusion he had.

She sighed heavily. "It doesn't look as though I have a choice, does it?"

He shook his head. "I've got five spare bedrooms and you can take your pick."

"All right," she finally agreed, opening her car door. She retrieved a short black leather jacket from the passenger seat and pulled it on, then used her remote to lock the car.

Neither spoke as they walked the short distance to his truck and he helped her into the passenger side of the cab. What could they say? He had let his guard down and given in to the temptation of kissing her. But it couldn't happen again. Now that she was going to have to spend the night at his place because her car had broken down, another kiss like the one he'd given her a few minutes ago could very easily push him over the edge and cause him to lose what little sense he had left.

When Jaron walked around the front of the truck to slide into the driver's seat, he stared straight ahead as he started the powerful engine. He still wanted her and he could only hope that he'd cool off on the ten-mile drive to the Wild Maverick Ranch, at least enough to get some sleep.

But as he steered the truck out of the parking lot and headed toward his ranch, he knew as surely as the sun would rise in the east tomorrow morning that wasn't going to happen. Now that he had tasted her sweet lips and held her soft body against his, he wanted a whole lot more. And that was something he knew for certain he could never have.

Mariah deserved a man who could offer her a future free of the emotional and physical scars of the past. Unfortunately, he had both.

When Jaron drove his truck beneath the arched entrance sign of the Wild Maverick Ranch, Mariah's heart skipped a beat. She still couldn't believe that he'd kissed her, let alone that she was going to spend the night at his new ranch.

When she was eighteen, she'd had a crush on him and dreamed of nothing more than having him feel as enamored with her as she was with him. He'd known about the infatuation, and instead of teasing her about it as some men might have done, he had been a perfect gentleman. He hadn't encouraged her in order to stroke his ego, nor had he discouraged her. He had simply ignored it and treated her the same as the rest of his brothers. She'd known he thought he was too old for her back then, and he'd been right. She hadn't been mature enough to handle a relationship with a man in his late twenties.

As the years went by and they saw each other at the family gatherings her sister held for the six foster brothers, she'd seen Jaron watch her and known he found her attractive. But to her disappointment, he hadn't asked her out or treated her any different than he had when she was a teenager.

Then as the brothers married and started their families, her relationship with Jaron had turned into a rivalry of sorts. Whenever one of the sisters-in-law became pregnant, Jaron insisted the baby would be a boy, while she just knew it would be a girl. But even as they argued about it, there had been an undertone of tension that had recently become so thick it was impossible to deny.

Mariah glanced at Jaron. But tonight something had changed between them. She'd known it the moment he punched the cowboy at the Broken Spoke. Although any of his brothers would have taken exception to the man grabbing her by the arm, Jaron had been absolutely furious. And if his reaction hadn't given her a hint that things were different between them, the kiss he had given her certainly had.

She had been kissed many times before, and although they'd been pleasant, none of them had been like the kiss Jaron had given her. There had been so much passion in the caress that it had been overwhelming. And what she couldn't get over was the fact that they had both ignored it, as if it hadn't even happened. They had started talking about her car problems and where she was going to stay for the night instead of addressing the fact that after all these years he had finally acted on their mutual attraction.

"Unbelievable."

"What's unbelievable?" he asked as he parked his truck in the four-car garage and pushed the remote on the visor to lower the door.

Unaware that she'd spoken her thoughts aloud, Mariah shrugged. "I was just thinking about my day," she lied.

"Some days are like that," he said, getting out of the truck. "Maybe tomorrow will be better."

"It has to be. I doubt it could get any worse," she said, opening the passenger door. Before she could figure out how to get out of the truck without breaking one of her high heels, or for that matter one of her ankles, Jaron was there to lift her down from the seat. His large hands wrapped around her waist caused her to feel warm all over. "Th-thank you."

"Would you like something to eat?" he asked as they walked through the door to the mudroom. "I've got a couple of frozen pizzas I can toss in the oven."

"No, thank you." She shrugged. "I had dinner after my meeting." She didn't add that she hadn't been able to eat due to the fact that during the meeting she had learned she was out of a job—effective immediately. "If you don't mind, I think I'd like to go on to bed."

"Of course not." He led the way down the hall to the stairs. "Bria and the other sisters-in-law made up all the rooms when they decorated the place, so you can have your pick."

"They did a fantastic job," she said, noticing the original paintings by a popular Western artist hanging on the wall as they climbed the steps. The decor reflected the Wild Maverick's new owner and his cowboy lifestyle.

"They did a better job than I would have done, that's for sure," he commented. When they reached the top floor, he opened the first door they came to and flipped on the light switch to turn on the bedside lamps. "If you don't like this room, there are four more to choose from."

"This will be fine," she said, looking around. Decorated in a cool shade of green and cream, the colors complemented the Native American artwork on the walls and the handwoven area rugs on the hardwood floor. "Bria and the others should consider going into interior decorating."

"I was going to leave the bedrooms empty, but Bria pointed out that I needed to furnish them in case I had guests." He shrugged. "I doubt that I'll ever have that many, since all of my brothers live close by."

"If you don't think you'll need the rooms, why did you buy such a big house?" she asked, unable to see the logic in him paying for something he didn't intend to use.

"I wanted the land," he admitted. "It's close enough to all of my brothers' ranches that we can help each other out when needed and not have to drive more than an hour or so to get there." He gave her a half smile. "The house just came with it."

She wasn't surprised Jaron wanted to live close to his foster brothers. From what her sister had told her, all six of them had been in trouble with the law when they were teenagers and the foster-care system had given up on them as lost causes. They'd been sent to the Last Chance Ranch, and thanks to a special man named Hank Calvert and his unique way of using ranch work and rodeo to teach them life lessons, all of the boys had worked through their troubles and turned their lives around. They had all become honest, productive adults, and because of their similar problems when they were boys and having no families to return to once they were of age, they had bonded into a very close family of their own.

"I wish I could live closer to Bria and Sam," Mariah said wistfully. Living a couple of hours away, she didn't get to see her only sibling nearly as much as she would have liked.

Jaron surprised her, and if his expression was any indication, he might have stunned himself when he stepped closer and brushed a wayward strand of her hair from her cheek. "Maybe one day that real estate place you work for will open a branch office some-where around here and you'll be able to live closer to your sister."

She knew he meant the gesture as comforting, but

his gentle touch and the knowledge that she no longer had a job with the company caused her to blink back tears. "I doubt...that will ever happen."

"What's wrong, Mariah?" His deep baritone was filled with gentle concern.

"Nothing," she lied. "It's been a really tough day. And one that I would just as soon forget."

She didn't want to go into the dismal turn her life had taken. She'd lost a boyfriend, a roommate and her job in less than twenty-four hours, and when she'd left Fort Worth after her meeting, she'd planned on having a good cry once she got home. The boyfriend hadn't really bothered her because they hadn't been seeing each other more than a couple of weeks and their relationship hadn't been serious. In fact, it never would have been. They both knew that one day they'd stop seeing each other and she hadn't even bothered mentioning that she was seeing him to her sister. But the loss of her roommate and her job had been devastating. Her roommate had left without notice, and she was going to have to find a way to pay both halves of the rent. Without her job, she had no way of doing that. But since her car broke down and she couldn't be alone for that cleansing cry, she'd just have to keep her tears at bay for a while longer.

Jaron seemed to hesitate a moment before he wrapped his arms around her and drew her to his broad chest for a supportive hug. "I'm sure you'll feel better after a good night's sleep."

"I doubt it, but thanks for the encouragement." She knew he was only trying to set her mind at ease, but the feel of his strong arms around her was absolutely wonderful, and without thinking she snuggled closer into his reassuring embrace.

She felt him go perfectly still. "Mariah…I think I'd better let you get some sleep."

She nodded but couldn't bring herself to pull away from him. "That would probably be for the best," she agreed.

When neither of them moved, Jaron used his index finger to lift her chin until their gazes met. "Tell me to get the hell away from you and leave you alone, Mariah."

Staring up at him, she knew she should do as he commanded. But without hesitation, she slowly shook her head. "I can't do that, Jaron."

"What I'm feeling right now is wrong," he warned, his expression testament to his inner turmoil. "I'm no good for you."

"That's your opinion," she said softly. "It isn't mine and never has been."

He stared at her a moment before he shook his head. "Don't say that, Mariah."

"I'm just being honest, Jaron," she answered quietly.

He closed his eyes a moment, as if struggling with himself, before opening them to capture her gaze with his. Slowly lowering his head, he kissed her so tenderly it sent shivers of anticipation up her spine. But instead of him releasing her and taking a step back as she thought he would do, his mouth settled more fully over hers for a deeper caress.

When his tongue touched hers, the heat that she'd

felt the first time he kissed her came rushing back and caused her knees to give way. As he caught her to him, he stroked and teased her with precise care and Mariah felt the growing evidence of his need against her lower belly. An answering desire caused an empty ache deep in the most feminine part of her. Her heart skipped a beat when she realized where things were going. She knew without question that if she asked him to call a halt to things, he would do it no matter how difficult it was for him. But that wasn't what she wanted. She had waited for what seemed like an eternity for him to hold her like this and now that he was, she never wanted it to end.

Feeling as if her head was spinning from the intense longing coursing through her, she was vaguely aware that he tightened his arms around her a moment before he lifted his head to stare down at her. "Mariah, kissing is one thing. But it's going to go way beyond that if we don't stop this right now."

"Jaron, I don't care how far this goes," she said honestly. She raised her arms to circle his neck and tangled her fingers in his thick dark brown hair brushing the collar of his shirt. "I've wanted you to hold me like this since the moment we met."

"Don't say that." When he closed his eyes, a muscle twitched along his lean jaw and she knew he was struggling to do what he thought was right. "I'm not the kind of man you need, Mariah."

"That's where you're wrong, cowboy," she whispered, cupping his cheek with her palm. "You're exactly what I've always needed."

Two

Jaron felt as if he'd been struck by a bolt of lightning when Mariah touched his face with her delicate hand. He might have had a chance to harden his resolve and not let things go too far between them if she hadn't admitted that she had always needed him. But her softly spoken words and the feel of her touch sent a flash fire streaking through his veins and made thinking clearly all but impossible. He'd wanted her for years, and not allowing himself to hold her, kiss her, had been his own personal hell.

He knew it was wrong—that he should walk away and leave her alone. But when he looked down at the woman in his arms, he knew in his heart that wasn't going to happen. He needed Mariah more than he needed his next breath, needed to lose himself in her softness and forget for one night that she could never be his.

When she pressed a kiss to the exposed skin at the open collar of his shirt, then looked up at him, the desire in her brilliant green eyes robbed him of breath. She for damned sure wasn't helping him win the battle over the hormones racing through his veins at the speed of light.

"Jaron, I know you need me just as much as I need you."

There was no sense in denying it. Hell, he was certain she could feel the evidence pressed against her. But he had to give her one last chance to save them both from doing something he knew as surely as he knew his own name they would both end up regretting with the morning light.

"Are you sure about this?" he asked. "Once that line is crossed, there's no going back, Mariah."

"I've never been more sure of anything in my entire life," she said without hesitation. "I don't like the way things have been between us recently, and I don't think you do, either."

"I'm not promising anything beyond tonight," he warned her.

She shook her head. "I'm not asking for more."

She might not be asking, but he knew Mariah well enough to know she wasn't a one-night stand kind of woman. If she slept with a man, she would expect it to be the start of a relationship. Unfortunately, he had wanted her for longer than he cared to remember and turning back now just wasn't an option.

Groaning, he buried his face in her silky dark brown

hair and tried to remind himself of all the reasons making love to Mariah would be a bad idea. For the life of him, he couldn't remember a single one. A man had his limits, and Jaron knew that he had reached the end of the line with his.

For the past several years he'd fought against giving in to the attraction between them. But now that he'd finally held her soft body to his and tasted her sweetness, he couldn't seem to stop himself. Maybe it was due to the years of denial or more likely the loneliness that had settled in when he watched his brothers with their families—knowing that due to the fear he had of turning out to be like his father he would never allow himself to have a family of his own. He wasn't entirely sure what the reason was, and it really didn't matter. He'd deal with the guilt and regret in the morning. Tonight he was going to forget about the problems making love to her would cause and love Mariah as if there was no tomorrow.

"Let's go to my room," he suggested, taking her hand in his to lead her down the hall.

As they entered the master suite, Jaron flipped the light switch to turn on the bedside lamps, casting a soft glow over the king-size bed. Closing the door behind them, he immediately took Mariah in his arms and lowered his head to rain kisses along her cheek, down the column of her neck to her collarbone.

"Are you protected, Mariah?" he asked, removing her black leather jacket, then kissing the satiny skin exposed by the dropped shoulder of her slinky red dress.

"I... Um, no," she said, sounding delightfully breathless.

"Don't worry." He continued to nip and taste her. "I'll take care of it."

When he raised his head, the desire clouding her pretty green eyes rendered him speechless. She was without a doubt the most beautiful, exciting woman he had ever known, and unless he missed his guess, she didn't have a clue how hot and sexy she was.

"There's probably…something you should…know," she said, sounding a little unsure.

"Have you changed your mind?" he asked, torn between knowing it would be in the best interest of both of them if she had and at the same time dreading her response.

"No, I haven't changed my mind." There wasn't a moment's hesitation in her answer and, God help him, he was thankful.

"Whatever it is, it can wait until later," he said, bending to remove his boots.

"But I think it's something you'll probably want to know," she said, sounding a little uncertain.

Straightening, he gave her a quick kiss. "Do you want to make love with me, Mariah?" When she nodded, he shook his head. "That's all I need to know."

He didn't want to hear confessions about other men she'd been with. All he wanted to do was focus on bringing her the most pleasure she had ever experienced in any man's arms.

As he kissed his way across her collarbone, she reached up to push her dress down her arms. Stopping her, he shook his head as he lightly skimmed his hands across her bare shoulders then down her arms, taking the stretchy fabric as he went. "I've been thinking about peeling this little number off you since I watched you walk into the Broken Spoke."

When he lowered the knit dress to her waist, then slid it over her shapely hips and down her long legs to lie in a pool around her shiny black high heels, his heart stuttered at the sight of her. Her strapless black lacy bra and matching panties barely covered her feminine secrets and sent his blood pressure up into stroke range. Put a pair of those fancy wings on her back and Mariah could easily model for that famous lingerie company every man with a pulse found so fascinating.

"You're gorgeous," he said, feeling as if all of the oxygen had been sucked from the room as he squatted down to remove her shoes.

"Thank you." When he straightened, she stepped forward to reach for the snaps on his chambray shirt. "But you're a little overdressed for this, don't you think, cowboy?"

As he watched, Mariah unfastened his shirt, pushed it from his shoulders and tossed it aside to place her hands on his bare chest. His pulse sped up and it felt as though he'd been branded where her soft palms rested. How many times had he speculated how her delicate hands would feel when she touched him like this? Nothing he could have imagined came close to the excitement racing through his veins at that moment.

"I knew your body would be beautiful," she said as she traced the valley between his pectoral muscles with her index finger.

"Looks can be deceiving," he said, thankful that she

couldn't see the ugly imperfections he'd spent most of his life trying to hide.

Before she could ask him what he meant, Jaron unbuckled his belt, released the snap at the top of his jeans, then gingerly eased the zipper down over his persistent erection. Shoving his jeans and boxer briefs to his ankles, he quickly stepped out of them and kicked them to the side.

He silently watched as Mariah's gaze traveled the length of his body. He could tell she was trying not to be conspicuous. But when she noticed his arousal, her eyes widened a moment before she lifted them to meet his.

"I'm just a man, darlin'," he said, reaching behind her to unfasten her bra. "You aren't afraid of me, are you?"

"N-no," she murmured. "Being afraid of you has never crossed my mind."

"Good." Tossing the scrap of black lace to the pile of clothes on the floor, he kissed her deeply before cupping her breasts in his palms as he stared into her pretty eyes. "I promise we'll be perfect together, Mariah."

"I—I know," she said, shivering when he kissed each one of the taut peaks, then moved his hands to slip his thumbs into the waistband of her panties.

He slowly lowered them over her slender hips and down her thighs, and when he tossed them aside he stepped back to appreciate her gorgeous body. Everything about her was perfect, and he felt humbled at the knowledge that a woman as stunning as Mariah would want to be with him.

"You're amazing," he said, his voice sounding a lot like a rusty hinge.

When he took her in his arms, the feel of her soft, feminine body pressed to his much harder one sent a shock wave the entire length of him. He had never allowed himself to speculate what it would be like to hold her nude body to his—to have their bare skin touching. But he knew for certain that he never could have imagined anything as erotic or sensual as what he was experiencing at that moment.

When she sagged against him, Jaron swung her up into his arms and carried her over to place her in the middle of his king-size bed. Her long dark brown hair spread across his pillow and her lithe body lying on the black satin sheets was an image he knew he would never forget.

Opening the bedside table's drawer, he removed a small foil packet and, tucking it under his pillow, stretched out beside her to take her in his arms. "Do you have any idea how beautiful you are?" he asked, not really expecting an answer.

"Not as beautiful as you are," she said, raising her arms to his shoulders. From the look on her face, he knew the moment she felt the scars on his shoulder that he normally kept covered. "Are these from participating in the rough stock events for so many years?"

He didn't want to lie to her, but he didn't want to explain, either. "Everyone who competes in rodeo has a few," he said, making sure he kept his answer vague. He did have a couple of scars from riding the rough stock, just not the ones under her fingertips.

To distract her from asking more about them, he fused his mouth with hers and kissed her with all of the need he had denied for almost as long as he had known her. Sweet and soft, when her lips melded with his, Jaron forgot about anything but the woman in his arms and the heat inside him that had built to a fever pitch. He had wanted Mariah for years and he found it damned near impossible to think about anything but burying himself so deep inside her that they lost sight of where he ended and she began.

Unable to wait any longer, he kissed his way down to her collarbone as he moved his hand along her side to her hip and beyond. Caressing her satin skin, he parted her to stroke the soft folds with tender care. The fire inside him threatened to burn out of control at her readiness for him. She needed him as much as he needed her.

"Mariah, I promise next time we'll go slower," he said, reaching for the packet under his pillow. "But right now, I need to be inside you."

"I need that…too," she said, her tone breathless.

He quickly arranged their protection and nudged her knees apart to rise over her. When she raised her arms to his shoulders and closed her eyes, he leaned down for a brief kiss.

"Open your eyes, Mariah," he commanded.

When she did, he captured her gaze with his as he guided himself to her. The desire and the depth of emotion he saw in her rapt expression were humbling, and unable to wait any longer, he slowly, gently moved forward.

The mind-blowing tightness as he carefully entered her robbed him of breath. It felt as if she had never…

He immediately froze. "Mariah…are you a virgin?"

he asked hesitantly. He hadn't even considered the possibility that she'd never been with a man. But he was
for damned sure thinking about it now.

"Y-yes," she answered.

Jaron closed his eyes as he waged the biggest battle
he'd ever fought in his entire life. The logical part of
his brain advised him to get out of bed, send her back
to the guest room, then go downstairs to his game room
and drink himself into a useless stupor. But his body
was urging him to complete the act of loving her—to
make her his and damn the inevitable consequences.

She must have sensed the conflict within him because, wrapping her long legs around him, she captured his face with her soft hands. "Jaron, I want this.
I want you."

He might have been able to win his inner struggle if
he hadn't seen the desire coloring her smooth cheeks or
heard the urgency in her sweet voice. But the combina-
tion of her heartfelt declaration and the feel of her tight
body surrounding his was more than he could resist.

"Forgive me, darlin'," he said, pushing himself forward to breach the thin barrier blocking his way. Her
eyes widened and a soft moan passed her parted lips
when he sank himself completely inside her.

Holding his lower body perfectly still, Jaron kissed
away the lone tear slowly trickling down her cheek. He
hated that in order to love Mariah this first time he had
to cause her pain. But as he felt her body relax around
him, he knew that she was adjusting to his presence
and, easing himself back and then forward, he set a
pace he hoped would cause her the least amount of dis-

comfort. He knew she probably wouldn't derive much pleasure from their lovemaking, but that wasn't going to keep him from trying to give her whatever pleasure he possibly could.

As the driving force of the tension holding them captive increased, Jaron held himself in check until he felt Mariah begin to respond to his gentle movement. Only then did he increase the depth and strength of his strokes.

When he felt her tiny feminine muscles begin to tighten around him, he knew she was close to realizing the satisfaction they both sought and, reaching between them, he touched her in a way he knew would send her over the edge. Her fulfillment triggered his own and, gathering her close, he wasn't sure he wouldn't pass out from the extraordinary sensations of his release.

Collapsing on top of her, Jaron buried his face in her silky hair and tried to catch his breath as he slowly drifted back to reality. He had never experienced anything as intense or as meaningful as being one with Mariah.

As his strength returned, he eased himself to her side and pulled her into his arms. "Are you all right?"

With her head pillowed on his shoulder, she nodded as she rested her hand on his chest. "I'm fine." She yawned. "That was amazing."

He could tell by the sound of her voice that she was drowsy and, remembering that she'd mentioned having a rough day, he kissed the top of her head and reached over to turn off the bedside lamp. "Get some rest, darlin'."

He'd barely finished making the suggestion before he could tell that Mariah had dozed off. Long after he was sure she was sound asleep, he continued to hold her close as he stared up at the ceiling. What the hell had he done?

No matter how much he would like to go back to the way things had been between them in the past, it would never be the same again. He'd not only crossed the line with her, he had taken something that she could give to only one man.

He closed his eyes as he fought the need building inside him once again. He wanted her, and just the thought that he had been the first man to touch her like this sent heat streaking throughout his body with lightning speed.

It hadn't even crossed his mind that she might still be a virgin. Hell, Mariah was twenty-five years old and he knew for certain that over the years she'd dated several men. So why him? Why had he been the one she chose to be the first man she made love with?

Unable to think clearly with Mariah in his arms, Jaron contented himself with simply holding her while she slept until sometime around dawn, when he reluctantly eased away from her and got out of bed to pick up their clothes. Folding hers, he placed them on the bench at the end of the bed, then took a quick shower and got dressed.

As he started to leave the room, he turned to gaze at the beautiful woman sleeping peacefully in his bed. How had he let things get so out of hand with her? Why had he ignored that voice of reason in his head, telling him to walk away before he did something he was sure to regret? And how was he going to be with her at family gatherings without losing his mind from wanting her and not allowing himself to touch her?

Guilt and regret so strong it threatened to choke him settled in his gut and, shaking his head, Jaron headed downstairs for a stiff drink. He needed to shore up his resolve and do what he knew was right and would be the best for Mariah. As soon as his men repaired her car, he was going to send her on her way and hope like hell one day he could forget the most incredible night of his entire life.

When Mariah awoke the following morning to sunlight peeping through a part in the drapes, two things were immediately apparent—she was in Jaron's bed and he wasn't with her. She was a little disappointed, but not really surprised. Bria had told her that ranchers usually started their days before dawn and sometimes worked until well past sundown. Now that Jaron owned the Wild Maverick Ranch, it stood to reason that he would keep those hours, as well.

Lying there surrounded by his clean masculine scent on the black satin sheets, Mariah's heart skipped a beat as she thought about the shift in the direction of their relationship. After all these years, Jaron had finally recognized she was no longer an eighteen-year-old girl with stars in her eyes. He had finally seen her as the woman she had become, albeit almost grudgingly. But she was certain that even he would have to admit that what they had shared was beautiful.

As she thought about his hesitancy, she frowned. Why had Jaron kissed her, made love to her, if he had been so reluctant? She might not be as experienced as a lot of women her age, but she knew beyond a shadow of doubt that it wasn't because he hadn't desired her. In fact, it had been as if needing her was the last thing he wanted. But he hadn't been able to stop himself.

Confused by his reaction, she got up and collected her clothes from the bench at the end of the bed, then she went into the master bathroom for a shower. They needed to talk, and his usual brooding silence wasn't going to cut it this time. She wanted answers and she wasn't going anywhere until she got them. What they had shared last night had been too meaningful to be dismissed. Nor was she going to allow him to ignore their lovemaking as if it never happened the way he'd ignored their first kiss.

Twenty minutes later as Mariah pulled on the clothes she'd worn the night before, she made the bed, then opted to carry her shoes instead of trying to navigate the circular staircase in four-inch heels. As much as she liked the boost the shoes added to her five-foot-five-inch height, she wasn't willing to take the chance of breaking her neck before she confronted Jaron and got the answers she wanted.

Picking up her jacket and purse, she left the master suite to go downstairs in search of Jaron. She was a bit surprised to find him seated at the table in the breakfast nook, drinking a cup of coffee. She had fully expected him to be somewhere outside with his ranch hands, doing whatever ranchers did.

"Good morning," she said, walking over to set her things on one of the chairs.

He gave her a silent, stoic nod as he got up to take a mug from the cabinet above the coffeemaker. "You like cream in your coffee, don't you?"

"I'm surprised you know that," she said, pulling a chair from the table to sit down.

"I've watched you drink coffee with dessert at our family dinners for years. You and Lane's wife, Taylor, are the only ones who don't drink it black." He shrugged one broad shoulder as he reached into the refrigerator to take out a dairy carton. "Will milk be okay? It's the closest thing I have to cream."

"That's fine." She'd known he watched her whenever they were together, but she hadn't taken into consideration that he might have actually paid attention to mundane things like how she took her coffee.

"Would you like something to eat?" he asked as he set the cup in front of her. "I can make you some toast, but that's about it. I haven't hired a housekeeper and I'm not much of a cook."

"No, thank you. I don't usually eat breakfast." She stared at him as he sat back down at the table. There was no easy way to bring up what he was trying to side-step. And knowing him the way she did, there wasn't a doubt in her mind that he would try to avoid discussing the shift in their relationship if he could. "We need to talk about last night," she finally stated.

He eyed her warily for a moment before he asked, "Are you all right?"

"I'm fine," she said, frowning. "Why wouldn't I be?"

"Until last night, you had never made love." His dark blue gaze caught and held hers for several seconds before he added, "I know I hurt you. I'm sorry."

"That's it?" she asked incredulously. "You gave me the most incredible experience of my life and all you can say is you're sorry?"

"What do you want me to say, Mariah?" His even tone and calm demeanor infuriated her.

So angry she found it impossible to sit still, Mariah rose from the chair to pace the length of the kitchen. "How about admitting that our lovemaking meant as much to you as it did to me?" She stopped to glare at him. "And don't you dare give me the excuse of being too old for me, because we both know it would be a total lie."

A fleeting shadow in his dark blue eyes was the only indication that he wasn't as removed from the situation as he would like her to believe. "Last night shouldn't have happened," he said, his stubborn calm irritating her as little else could. "I took something from you that I had no right to take, Mariah."

"My virginity." When he nodded, she shook her head. "You didn't *take* anything," she stated flatly. "It was my call to make. I *chose* to give that to you."

"Last night was a mistake," he insisted.

"No, it wasn't. A mistake is taking it for granted that your roommate isn't going to move out without telling you and leave you owing the entire month's rent. Or believing that you have job security and then suddenly finding yourself out of work," she shot back. "And we won't even go into how big a mistake it is to believe that your car is reliable when it's ten years old and makes more odd noises than you can count." Mariah shook her head. "Last night was the only good thing that happened to me yesterday, and I'm not going to let you dismiss it as if it meant nothing."

Jaron frowned as he got up and walked over to stand in front of her. "You lost your job?"

"Yes, but that's not the issue here." She refused to allow him to divert the conversation. "We're not talking about my work situation. We're discussing what happened between *us*."

"There is no us, Mariah," he said quietly as he rested his hands on her shoulders. The heat from his palms felt absolutely wonderful, but she did her best to ignore it. "I told you I wasn't promising anything past last night," he continued. He shook his head. "That hasn't changed, darlin'."

Staring up at him, she could see the determination in his eyes and the stubborn set of his jaw. She would have about as much luck convincing elephants to roost in trees as she would getting him to admit that what they'd shared was special. It simply wasn't going to happen.

Resigned, she walked over to slip on her high heels and gather her jacket and purse. "I don't suppose your men had a chance to see about my car?"

He dug into the front pocket of his jeans and, producing the keys to her car, handed them to her. "All you needed was a new battery."

When he placed the keys in her hand, his fingers brushed her palm and a streak of electricity zinged straight up her arm. She could tell by the slight tightening of his jaw that he felt it, as well.

"I'll pay you for the repair as soon as I get a new job," she said, walking toward the door.

"Don't worry about it," he said, following her. "It didn't cost that much."

"I most certainly will pay you back for the battery. I may be out of a job right now, but I do have my pride," Mariah said, turning back to glare at him. "I'm not a charity case."

"I never thought you were," he said, looking a little bewildered. "I'm just trying to help you out."

"I don't need your help," she said pointedly. "The only thing I need from you is an explanation of what changed between us and why you're wanting to go back to the way things were. But you refuse to talk to me about it."

She knew she was probably overreacting to the situation. But she was frustrated beyond reason and besides, if she didn't vent in some way, she couldn't be sure she wouldn't bop him on top of his stubborn head with her purse.

"Do you have any prospects of finding another job?" Jaron asked, following her out the door. "Do you need help making the rent since your roommate moved out? I could loan you—"

"Don't you dare offer me money," she warned, her anger rising to the boiling point. "After last night, you would be the last person I—"

"I'd like to do something to help," he interrupted, reaching up to run his hand through his dark brown hair as if he was trying to think of a way to help her out. He hesitated for a moment before he offered, "I still need a housekeeper who cooks. And the job comes with free room and board. You could work here until something better comes along." He didn't sound all that encouraging, and she knew it was nothing more than a token gesture. He didn't want her to take the job and had only offered it to her because he felt guilty.

"You're offering me a job and a place to live?" she asked incredulously. She didn't know whether to laugh out loud at his erroneous assumption that she could cook or be highly insulted that he thought she was so desperate she would accept his offer.

"The job is yours if you want it," he said, looking less than enthusiastic about having her around all the time. She had no doubt he expected her to turn it down and that was exactly what she intended to do.

"No, thank you," Mariah answered as she carefully descended the steps. If her mother hadn't taught her to be a lady, she'd gladly tell him what he could do with that job.

As she navigated her way across the yard to the driveway, hoping that she could keep from breaking an ankle or at the very least one of the expensive four-inch heels, she thought about the opportunity Jaron had inadvertently handed her. It would be poetic justice if she did accept the job. By living under the same roof with him, he certainly wouldn't be able to avoid her, nor would she let him forget the special night they had shared. And as for making his meals, it would serve him right if he had to eat her cooking.

But the more she thought about it, the more sense it made. She needed a job, and he owed her an explanation that she was determined to eventually get from him. What better way to do that than by seeing him every day?

The only drawback she could see about taking the job was the possibility of losing what was left of her sanity from dealing with a man who made a habit of closing himself off. And then there was the problem of her sister accusing her of being impulsive again when Bria learned Mariah was living at the ranch with Jaron. But if she could find out the reason behind his insistence that he was no good for her, it would be worth it.

When she got into her car, she glanced up at the house to see Jaron still standing on the porch, watching her. His arms were folded across his broad chest and he was leaning one shoulder against a support post. He looked so darned good to her it took her breath away.

Mariah worried her lower lip as she weighed her options. If she drove away, she might never get the answers she wanted from Jaron. And if she stayed, she might get an explanation that she didn't want to hear. Unfortunately, she would never know unless she took the chance.

Taking a deep breath, she reached for the door handle. She might be setting herself up for a huge fall, but she just couldn't pass up the opportunity to settle things with Jaron Lambert once and for all.

Jaron frowned when he watched Mariah open the car door. What was she doing? She had rejected his guilt-induced job offer outright, and he had been greatly re-lieved. Why wasn't she leaving and getting on with her life, so he could try to get on with his? He had made it perfectly clear there was nothing to talk over and that they'd never be more than good friends.

Or could she be having more car trouble? That had to be it, he decided. Her car was older and had so many miles on it that he'd been surprised it had only taken a battery to get it going that morning.

By the time she made her way back to the porch in those ridiculously high heels, he was reaching for the cell phone to call Billy Ray to come up from the barn to see about her car again. But when she climbed the steps to stand in front of him, the defiant look on her pretty face stopped him cold.

"I changed my mind. I'm taking the job you offered me until I can find an office management position. I expect you to be in Shady Grove first thing Saturday morning with your truck to help me move," she stated flatly. Turning, she added as she descended the steps to go back to her car, "And don't be late. I want to get settled in before I have to start the job on Monday morning."

Shocked all the way down to his size-twelve Tony Lamas, all Jaron could do was stand there staring as he watched her march back down the steps and out to her car. As she drove away, he couldn't help but won-der what the hell had just happened. He'd only offered her the job of housekeeper and cook as a token gesture because he'd been sure she would turn it down. And she had. So why had she changed her mind?

Rubbing at the sudden tension building at the back of his neck, Jaron watched her car disappear down the lane leading to the main road before he turned and walked back into the house. What was he going to do now? He couldn't rescind the job offer. He'd brought it up and Mariah had accepted it. As far as he was concerned, that was as good as a written contract.

But what was he going to do about living in the same house with her? How was he going to keep from going completely insane from the temptation she posed day in and day out? And why was there a part of him that wasn't the least bit sorry that she had taken the job?

Three

Late Saturday afternoon, Jaron carried the last of Mariah's things into the Wild Maverick ranch house and wondered how one woman could possibly need so much stuff. She had two huge boxes alone that had been marked "shoes." Why did she need so many? All he had were his dress boots, a couple of pairs of work boots and a pair of athletic shoes he wore when he worked out.

For reasons he didn't want to delve into, he had decided to move her into the room he'd shown her the night he brought her home with him from the Broken Spoke, instead of the housekeeper's quarters off the kitchen. And it was just as well that he had. The closet down there was way too small and would have never held all of her clothes and shoes.

"Is that the last of the boxes from my car?" Mariah

asked, sticking her head out of the walk-in closet when he entered the bedroom.

He nodded. "That's the last of it."

"Just be glad I donated a lot of clothes and household items to the crisis center," she said, laughing as she walked out of the closet to get one of the containers of shoes. "If I hadn't, you'd probably be carrying in boxes until well after midnight."

"Do you want this in the closet?" he asked, stepping forward to pick up the big box for her.

"I could have carried that myself," she said, following him.

Setting it in front of the built-in shoe racks, he shook his head. "My foster father would come back and haunt me if I let you do that. If he told us once, he told us a hundred times that a man should never let a woman carry anything unless both of his arms were broken."

"The Cowboy Code?" she asked, smiling.

Jaron nodded. "Hank Calvert had his own set of rules to live by and they're damned good ones."

"Bria told me that Sam and the rest of your brothers feel the same way," Mariah commented as she opened the box and surveyed the contents.

"We wouldn't be the men we are today if not for Hank," he admitted. "Among other things, he taught us what it meant to have integrity and be respectful of others."

She nodded as she picked out a couple of pairs of high heels. "I never got to meet Hank. When Bria started having family dinners, I was away at college, and by the time I graduated, he had passed away."

"He was one of the best men I've ever had the privilege to know," Jaron said, meaning every word of it. "He made everyone around him want to be a better person."

"From everything I've heard about him, he must have been a wonderful man," she agreed, bending over to pluck more shoes out of the box.

As he stood there staring at her pairing up shoes, he completely forgot what they had been talking about. Swallowing hard, Jaron did his best to concentrate on anything but the woman next to him. The light scent of her herbal shampoo, the sound of her soft voice and the enticing sight of her shapely bottom when she bent over to take more shoes from the box were sending him into sensory overload and playing hell with his intention to forget the most incredible night of his life.

When the region south of his belt buckle began to tighten, he decided a hasty departure would be in both of their best interests and, carrying the last box into the closet for her, he turned toward the hall. "I'll let you get the rest of your things put away. If you need me for anything, I'll be downstairs."

Before she had the chance to tempt him further, Jaron went down to his office, walked around the desk and plopped down in his desk chair. What the hell had he gotten himself into?

He couldn't be in the same room with Mariah for more than five minutes without burning to hold her, kiss her and a whole lot more. But he refused to allow that to happen again, even if he did end up in a constant state of arousal for as long as she resided at the ranch.

As he sat there shoring up his resolve, his gaze

landed on the only thing he had kept from his life before being sent to the Last Chance Ranch—the reason
he couldn't allow himself to get involved with Mariah.
Encased in a small acrylic cube, the creased and tat-
tered Dallas bus pass represented his escape and free-
dom from years of physical abuse at the hands of a man
who never should have been allowed to procreate.

Reminded of his dismal childhood, Jaron took a deep
breath. He had been afraid that no one would believe a
thirteen-year-old kid when he'd told them that his old
man had killed his mother. But he had skipped school
that day anyway and used his lunch money to buy a
bus pass to police headquarters downtown. At first,
he'd been right—no one had taken his claims seriously.
Even the rookie patrolman assigned to take his statement had treated him like a child with nothing more
than a grudge against his father.

But when Jaron had shown the officer the scars on
his back and told the man that Simon Collier had threatened to kill him and dispose of his body the way he had
done with his mother, they'd immediately started paying more attention to what he had to say. A caseworker
from Family and Protective Services had immediately
been called, a photographer had taken pictures to document the ugly evidence of the abuse marring his skin
and a warrant for aggravated battery of a child had been
issued for his father's arrest.

Jaron had been upset that they were focused on ap-
prehending his father on charges of child abuse rather
than the murder of his mother. But he needn't have worried. True to form, old Simon had allowed his temper to

get away from him when he'd seen that Jaron had been the one who'd turned him in to the law. During his tirade, he'd shouted that he should have done away with him at the same time he killed Jaron's mother. Unfortunately, during the ensuing investigation and trial, DNA evidence had linked his father to at least four more homicides of women with the probability that there were several more. But DNA analysis hadn't been as developed back then and what evidence they'd collected for some of the other murders had either been destroyed or contaminated.

But his dad had been convicted for the murder of Jaron's mother, and the only other good that had come out of the trial was the judge had allowed Jaron to legally have his last name changed to his mother's maiden name.

Unfortunately, that hadn't been enough to erase his connection to the bastard who spawned him. Every foster family he had been placed with had looked at him as if he'd killed those women himself, and it hadn't been long before he'd got in trouble with the system for running away. But when he'd been sent to the Last Chance Ranch he'd had no reason to run. He'd been accepted for himself, and not rejected for what his father had done.

Hearing Mariah start down the stairs, Jaron clenched his teeth and vowed not to bring that kind of ugliness into anyone's life, and especially not hers. He'd never intentionally been cruel to anyone, but how could he be certain that he hadn't inherited something from his father that would rear its menacing head at some point in the future? He couldn't. And unfortunately, he didn't see any way that would ever change.

"Do you have anything else in your freezer besides frozen pizza?" Mariah asked, laughing as she reached for another slice. She was still frustrated with him, but her anger had cooled enough that she could see the humor in his choice of convenience food.

When she'd finished arranging her shoes on the built-in racks in the closet, she'd come downstairs to ask if he wanted her to make them sandwiches for dinner. But Jaron had suggested that she put together a salad while he popped a pizza in the oven for their dinner. She'd offered to bake it, but he'd pointed out that her job as cook and housekeeper didn't start for another couple of days and until then she was his guest.

"Pizza and burritos are about the extent of what's in the freezer," he said, shrugging. "The first thing you'll have to do is go shopping for whatever you need."

"I'm good at shopping," she said, smiling. She failed to add that her kind of shopping didn't include produce or anything else that couldn't be zapped in the micro-wave or didn't have directions on the side of a box.

"I've already added you to the approved users on the credit card I've designated for household expenses," he said, taking a drink of his beer. "Buy whatever you need for the house."

"Do I have a household budget to go by?" she asked. "I don't want to overspend."

Her statement drew a rare chuckle from him. "Spend as much as you want." He named an amount that was more than she'd earned in a year working at the real estate management company. "If you need to go over that, let me know and I'll have the card limit increased."

"Unless it's for a state dinner at the White House, I can't imagine anyone needing that much for groceries," she said incredulously. She'd known Jaron was wealthy, the same as his brothers were, but she'd had no idea. "Is there anything specific that you would like for me to buy?"

"I like pizza," he said as he picked up another slice.

"What man doesn't?" she asked, smiling.

"Hey, it's easy and doesn't require a lot of cooking skills," he said, giving her a smile that sent heat streaking all the way through her. "I also really liked that apple pie you made a few years back for my birthday. One of those once in a while would be nice."

"I'm surprised you remembered that," she said, wishing that he hadn't. There was no way under the sun that she could make another one without Bria standing beside her telling her step by step what to do.

"It was really good," he said, nodding. "That was the closest I've ever had to something that tasted as good as Bria's apple pie."

"I'll put that on the list," she said, deciding to call Bria as soon as she and Sam got back from the stock show tomorrow evening. She not only needed her sister's help making an apple pie, she needed the title of a really good, really easy-to-follow cookbook and help with a comprehensive grocery list of things to stock the pantry and freezer. "What else do I need to get besides food?"

He looked thoughtful a moment. "Well, you might want to get whatever you'll need for cleaning the house. I've got a few things, but when I moved in Bria suggested that I wait until I hired a housekeeper so whoever it was could buy the products they preferred."

More comfortable talking about cleaning than she was cooking, Mariah nodded. "Is there anything else I need to pick up while I'm in town?"

"I don't think so." He finished his beer then got up from the table to put the can in the recycle bin under the sink. "Really whatever you see that you think we need for the house or you want for cooking or cleaning is fine."

How was she supposed to know what she needed in the kitchen when she didn't know how to cook?

Deciding it was time for a change of subject, Mariah rose to clear the table. "Besides cooking, cleaning and shopping, is there anything else I'm supposed to do?"

He stared at her for a moment before he slowly shook his head. "Not that I can think of. Why?"

"I'm just trying to make sure I understand the job description," she said, rinsing their plates and loading them into the dishwasher.

"You didn't say, but what happened with your job?" he asked, his tone a little hesitant.

"Cutbacks," she answered as she wiped off the table. "The company decided to concentrate on the more lucrative rental properties in cities like Dallas and Houston than smaller towns like Shady Grove."

"Were you offered a job if you were willing to relocate?" he asked, frowning as he leaned back against the counter.

"They offered, but I turned it down." She shook her head. "I didn't want to move that far away from Bria, Sam and little Hank. They're the only family I have."

Walking over to stand beside her, he raised his hand as if he intended to touch her cheek, then quickly lowered it to his side. "That's not true, darlin'. You have the rest of us."

A shiver of excitement slid up her spine when she realized he was fighting the urge to touch her. But she did her best to ignore it. He was probably trying to make her feel better and nothing more. "Thanks."

"It was pretty rough losing your parents in that car accident in your junior year in college, wasn't it?" he asked, his tone sympathetic.

Nodding, she had to clear her throat before she could answer. "It was pretty rough, but it would have been worse if I'd been younger."

"Yeah, I lost my mom when I was six," he said, surprising her. In all the years she had known him, she had never heard him mention his biological family before.

"What happened?" she asked.

"I'm not sure." He stared at her a moment, then shook his head. "It doesn't matter. One day she was gone and I knew I'd never see her again."

"I'm so sorry, Jaron," she said, placing her hand on his arm. "At least I got to have my parents with me until I was grown."

He shrugged. "I survived."

"What about your father?" she asked.

His jaw tightened a moment before his expression turned to blank indifference. "He...went away when I was thirteen and I haven't seen him since."

She could tell it bothered him more than he was letting on, but she wasn't at all surprised that he dismissed losing his parents as if it wasn't a big deal. If there was one thing she had learned over the course of the past several years it was that Jaron Lambert didn't talk about himself. Ever.

As they stood there staring at each other, she realized her hand still rested on his arm. But it was the spark that had ignited in his striking blue eyes that took her breath away.

"I...um, probably should get back to putting my things away," she said, thinking quickly as she started to pull away from him.

He placed his hand over hers to hold it in place as if he had found comfort in the gesture. "You've got all day tomorrow to get your things organized," he reminded. "I'm sure you're tired from packing the past few days and all the other things you had to do to get ready for your move to the ranch. Why don't you take the evening off and we'll catch a movie on one of the satellite channels?"

His suggestion surprised her, but what shocked her more was the tension surrounding them. The slight abrasion of his callused palm on her skin and his heated gaze holding her captive was more sensual than she could have ever imagined. But she did her best not to show she was affected by it in any way. If she did, it would give him the perfect excuse to shut her out the way he'd done the morning after they'd made love.

"I think you might be right about taking a break." She laughed to cover her reaction to him. "There was so much to do the past few days, I am pretty tired. I just hope I can stay awake long enough to watch the entire show."

He suddenly dropped his hand and took a step back as if he realized he was still touching her. "In other words the movie needs to be fast paced?"

"Yes, but I'm not a big fan of movies that will scare the stuffing out of me," she admitted.

"I'll keep that in mind," he said, standing back for her to precede him down the hall to the media room.

Once she and Jaron were seated on opposite ends of the big brown leather couch, he turned on the biggest television she'd ever seen and they settled back to watch five unlikely characters defend the galaxy from an evil warlord. Resting her head against the buttery-soft leather, Mariah thought about the bizarre turn her life had taken. Never in a million years would she have dreamed that what seemed to be the worst day of her life had worked out to be the best or that it would lead to her living with Jaron on his ranch.

Yawning, she felt her eyes growing heavy and did her best to focus on the television screen. The next thing she knew, Jaron was touching her arm.

"Mariah, it's time to go upstairs to bed," he said gently.

Blinking, she sat up. "But I'm watching the movie."

The sound of his deep laughter enveloped her like a

comfortable quilt and sent a warm feeling all through her. "Darlin', the movie is over."

She glanced at the TV to see the movie credits scrolling up the screen. "I must have been more tired than I thought."

He nodded. "You fell asleep about fifteen minutes into the story."

"Why didn't you wake me?" she asked, rising to her feet.

"You were sleeping so peacefully, I figured you needed the rest." He switched off the television and got up from the couch. "It's no big deal. If you want to know how it ends we can watch the movie another time."

"I'd like that. What I saw was entertaining," she said, covering a yawn with her hand.

"I think it's time we turn in for the night," he said, placing his hand on the small of her back to guide her toward the door. "You're exhausted and I have to be up early to ride the fence in the south pasture."

"You don't have your men do that?" she asked as they climbed the stairs.

"In winter, they have Sundays off after they get the morning chores finished," he answered, stopping at the door to her room. "I'm going to check out what needs to be done and let them know so they can make the needed repairs before they move a herd of steers to that pasture in a couple of weeks."

From what Bria had told her, any rancher worth his salt knew everything that was going on around his ranch and worked in conjunction with his hired hands to get things done and keep the operation running smoothly.

"It sounds as though we'll both be busy tomorrow. After I finish organizing my things, I plan on taking an inventory of the pantry and starting my shopping list."

He looked thoughtful for a moment. "Since we both have a lot to do and I'm not in the mood for pizza two nights in a row, why don't we plan on going out for supper tomorrow evening?"

"I'll take you up on that offer," she said, smiling. The more time they spent together in a relaxed setting, the better the chance of him letting down his guard and opening up to her.

As they stared at each other, her breath caught at the longing she detected in his steady gaze, and when he lifted his hand like he was going to cup her cheek, she thought he was going to kiss her. But as if he realized what he was about to do, he let his hand drop to his side and took a step back.

"Good night, Mariah. Sleep well." His low, intimate tone sent a shiver of desire straight up her spine.

"Good night, Jaron."

After entering her room, she closed the door and released the breath she had been holding. Just when she thought he was going to give in to the magnetic pull drawing them together, he'd stopped himself.

Mariah sighed heavily as she got a nightshirt from the dresser and headed into the bathroom to change. She had always been told that patience was a virtue. But whoever came up with that old saying had never dealt with Jaron Lambert. He was without a doubt the most frustrating, controlled individual she had ever met.

But that was about to change. She had seen a slip

in his ironclad restraint the other night when he hadn't been able to resist making love to her. And if it happened once, it could happen again.

With renewed determination, she stared into the mirror at the woman staring back at her. "It's past time Mr. Lambert's self-contained little world is shaken up. And you're just the woman to do it."

As he followed Mariah and the hostess through the restaurant to a table at the back of the room the following evening, Jaron looked around and hoped they didn't run into one of his brothers and their wives. That was unlikely, since he'd chosen a roadhouse outside Waco instead of having supper at the Broken Spoke in Beaver Dam. But meeting up with his family would open a whole can of worms that he'd just as soon keep sealed for a while longer.

His brothers had been after him for the past few years to ask Mariah out, and he would just as soon avoid having to explain that they weren't dating but she was living with him at the Wild Maverick. The situation was complicated and he wasn't entirely sure he understood his reasons for offering her a job himself. As for trying to explain it to his brothers, the interrogation that was sure to follow would make a military tribunal look like a walk in the park.

"I didn't realize they have a live band and dancing," Mariah said as he held the chair for her to sit down. Her delight was evident and he knew she was going to want to stick around for the dancing after they ate.

Taking his seat on the opposite side of the small

table, he shrugged. "What the house band lacks in talent, they make up for in enthusiasm."

"I can dance to just about anything," she said happily.

He barely managed to stifle a groan as the sweet sound of her voice wrapped around him. Mariah was without a doubt the most beautiful, exciting woman in the entire restaurant and she was letting him know that she wanted him to dance with her later. Unfortunately, she was with a man who hadn't been born with the dancing gene, like his foster brother Nate. To say that Jaron had two left feet would be an act of kindness. But as awkward as he felt on a dance floor, he wasn't about to let some other guy touch Mariah. If he had to, he'd pay the band a week's pay to play nothing but slow songs, then stand in one spot, hold her close and sway in time to the music the way his brother Ryder had always done.

He wasn't going to examine his decision too closely. If he did, he would have to admit that the thought of another man holding her close caused him to feel as though someone had punched him in the gut. It wasn't something he was the least bit comfortable with, nor was he happy about it.

"Did you find a lot of things that need to be repaired while you were out riding the pastures today?" she asked as they looked over the menu.

"More than I would have liked," he admitted, relieved to focus on something else. "The previous owner was older and lost interest in keeping things in good repair."

"The house seems to be in good shape," she said,

closing the menu and placing it on the table. "Did you have to make a lot of changes before you moved in?"

Jaron shook his head. "His daughter had the house remodeled before she put the ranch up for sale." When their server came to take their order, Jaron told him what they wanted, then waited for the man to walk away before he continued, "There are a few things I'd still like to change, but for the most part, I'm pretty happy with the house."

"The house is beautiful." She looked puzzled. "I can't imagine what you'd want to change about it."

"I'd like to take down the wall between the family room and media room," he answered, taking a sip of his water. "The house already has a formal living room, but it isn't big enough for the whole family to get together. I want a room big enough for us to gather and not be crowded."

Mariah nodded. "I love when your family has a party or dinner."

He frowned. "You're part of the family, too."

"Not really." She shrugged one slender shoulder. "I'm only included because I'm Bria's sister and have nowhere else to go for holidays."

Her statement surprised him, and without thinking, Jaron covered her hand with his where it rested on the pristine tablecloth. "You're just as much a part of the family as any of us, and I don't want to hear you say otherwise, Mariah."

"Th-thank you," she said, her eyes dewy with unshed tears. "That means a lot."

He hated seeing the sadness in her eyes, and at that

moment he knew he would do anything to make her happy, even if that meant making a fool of himself on the dance floor later. "Why don't we concentrate on finishing supper and then stick around for the dancing?"

"I'd like that, Jaron. Thank you."

Her sweet smile sent heat streaking through every vein in his body, and as he stared into her emerald eyes, he suddenly realized that he still held her delicate hand in his. For the life of him, he couldn't bring himself to let it go, nor did he seem to be able to look away.

What the hell was wrong with him? He didn't want to lead her on, nor did he want to fuel the need that burned in his gut every time he was close to her. Why couldn't he stop himself from touching her?

Thankfully, the server arrived with their food, breaking the tension building between them, and Jaron took a deep, fortifying breath. He was going to have to be extremely careful or else he was going to make the same error in judgment he'd made a few nights ago—something he couldn't allow himself to do. No matter how much he wanted to make love to Mariah, he had to stay strong and resist the temptation. He wasn't right for her and no amount of lovemaking would ever change that.

They both remained silent while they ate, and by the time they were finished with the meal, Jaron couldn't have said whether he'd had a rib-eye steak or a piece of worn boot leather. Through the entire meal all he'd been able to think about was holding her while they danced, and he knew as surely as he knew his own name he was in for a night of frustration, ending with a shower cold enough to freeze the tail feathers off a penguin.

When the band started warming up, he glanced over at Mariah, and the twinkle of excitement in her eyes was enough to convince him that he'd endure whatever hell came his way. There was no way he was going to disappoint her.

"I think I'll go freshen up before the dancing starts," she said, rising from her chair.

He waited until she disappeared down the hall leading to the ladies' lounge before he rose from the table, walked up to the bandstand and pulled five one-hundred-dollar bills from his jeans pocket. Handing it to the band's front man, he explained what he wanted, then with the man's assurance that the majority of the songs during the first set would be slow ones, Jaron walked back to the table and waited for Mariah to return.

"Are you ready to kick up your heels, cowboy?" she asked, smiling as she sat down on the chair beside him.

"I think I'd better warn you that I'm not much for dancing," he said, wondering if he'd ever seen her look more beautiful.

"I know," she said, grinning. "I've been attending family parties for years and I've never once seen you dance."

He shrugged. "That's because I'm not of a mind to make a fool of myself."

She cupped his cheek with her soft palm and sent his blood pressure up a good fifty points. "You're not going to make a fool of yourself, Jaron. If you'd like, we can dance the slow dances and if someone asks, I'll save the faster ones for him."

Her long, dark brown hair framed her pretty face and hung over her shoulders to cover her breasts. It made him want to run his fingers through the silky strands. But it was what she was wearing that sent his pulse into overdrive. Dressed in tight-fitting designer jeans with rhinestones on the hip pockets and a shimmery dark purple top, she had to be revving the engine of every guy in the place. The thought of another man holding her while they two-stepped around the dance floor caused him to grind his teeth. Even though he had no claim on her and had no right to make one without entering into a relationship with her, Jaron made a vow right then and there that he'd be damned before he watched her dance with anyone else.

"Like hell," he muttered as the band broke into the first notes of a popular slow country song.

"What was that?" she asked, leaning close.

Fortunately she hadn't heard him, and he didn't intend to enlighten her on his inner struggle. "I can't believe I'm going to say this, but let's dance, darlin'."

Rising to his feet, Jaron reached for her hand to lead her out onto the dance floor. As he took her into his arms, he surveyed the restaurant and caught several men watching Mariah. The appreciative looks on their faces did little to improve his dour mood.

But he quickly forgot about the other male patrons in the restaurant as he pulled Mariah a little closer. The feel of her lithe form rubbing against him as they swayed in time to the music caused him to react in a very predictable, very male way. All he could think about was the night he'd made love to her and how her soft body had felt as they moved together in perfect unison.

Telling himself to move away before he did something stupid, he made the mistake of glancing down at her delicate hand resting on his chest. Even through his chambray shirt, the warm feel of her palm sent a shock wave of need to the core of his being. Without another thought to the consequences, he lifted her chin with his forefinger and covered her mouth with his. Her sweet lips clung to his, fueling the rapidly building fire within him, and he couldn't have stopped himself from deepening the kiss if his life depended on it.

Forgetting where they were, he coaxed her to open for him and slowly, thoroughly savored her. He had a feeling he could quickly become addicted to Mariah's sweetness, and if that wasn't enough to scare him senseless, the fact that she could make him forget where they were and what they were doing was.

"This was a bad idea," he said, breaking the kiss and putting a little space between them.

"Why do you say that?" she asked as she looked up at him.

Jaron could tell by the awareness in her green gaze that she'd felt the evidence of his need and knew exactly what he'd meant by the comment. "Mariah, I'm not what you—"

"Save it, Jaron," she interrupted him. "I've heard it all before. You're too old for me. Or you're not right for me. Or whatever else you've come up with to use as an excuse to put distance between us." She pulled away from him. "I'm ready to leave."

As he followed her back to their table for her to collect her jacket, Jaron took a deep breath. He had been fooling himself to think he could be that close to her without wanting more. The magnetic pull between them was too strong for that to ever happen.

As he watched her walk briskly toward the restaurant's exit, he cursed his weakness and the need for her he couldn't seem to keep under control. He hadn't intended to piss her off, but it was probably just as well that he had. Maybe if she was mad at him, she'd be able to do what he couldn't seem to do himself. And that was to make him keep his hands off her.

By the time they reached the parking lot, Jaron practically had to trot to keep up with Mariah—a good indication of just how upset she was with him. Before he could reach her to help her into his truck, she climbed up into the passenger seat and slammed the door.

So much for dancing with her to make her happy, he thought as he got into the truck and started the engine. The ten-mile ride back to the Wild Maverick was an uncomfortably silent one, and by the time he parked the truck in the garage, he figured she would get out of the truck and go straight upstairs to her room.

But when they entered the kitchen she turned to face him. "Jaron, don't you think it's past time that you were honest with both of us?" she asked point-blank.

He wasn't going to insult her intelligence by asking her what she meant, but he wasn't going to talk about it, either. Instead of answering, he chose to remain silent.

After a few tense moments, Mariah shook her head. "We both know you have feelings for me. But you can't or won't allow yourself to admit that. I want to know why."

"I've told you before," he stated.

"Not good enough." She held up her hand to stop him from responding. "I don't want your standard excuses. I want the truth, Jaron. And until you can give me that, I'd just as soon you don't say anything at all." Without giving him a chance to respond, she turned and walked down the hall toward the stairs.

As he watched her go, Jaron knew she was right. She deserved his honesty. But as much as he would like to tell Mariah about himself, he'd much rather endure her anger than to have her look at him the way some of the foster families had—with a mixture of fear and suspicion.

Four

As Mariah tried to organize the things she had bought at the grocery store on the pantry shelves, she couldn't help but think about what had happened with Jaron at the restaurant the evening before. They'd had a nice dinner and he had suggested they stay afterward to dance, even though it was something he didn't like doing. He had even kissed her while they were dancing. Then, just when she thought he might be ready to admit that there was more going on between them than friendship, he'd stopped himself and reverted back to keeping her at arm's length.

Why did he have to be so darned stubborn? And why couldn't he at least give her an explanation for why he felt the way he did?

She had no idea what could be holding him back. But

telling her he was too old for her or that he wasn't right for her were excuses, not reasons. There was more to it than their age difference and she was determined to find out what it was and if he'd let her, help him move past it.

Deciding there was no easy way to get him to open up to her, she sighed and turned her attention back to the task at hand. She checked the list she had printed from the website of a popular cooking show. She had bought every spice they suggested, even if she didn't have a clue what she was supposed to do with them.

In hindsight, she probably should have called Bria for advice on what to get to stock the pantry and freezer. Her sister would know what all the spices were used for. But she had decided not to bother Bria. For one thing, she was busy chasing after a very active two-year-old and didn't have a lot of free time. And for another, Mariah was reluctant to tell Bria about accepting Jaron's offer to be the housekeeper and cook for the Wild Maverick Ranch.

Aside from the fact that her sister would have reminded her that she didn't know the first thing about cooking, Bria would have probably felt compelled to be the concerned big sister and warn her not to get in over her head or to count on things working out the way she wanted. But Mariah had accepted the job with her eyes wide-open and wasn't expecting anything more than getting the answers she wanted from Jaron.

"It looks as if you have enough food here to feed an army," Jaron commented from the doorway.

Startled by the unexpected interruption, Mariah jumped and placed her hand over her racing heart. After carrying in the groceries for her, he had gone outside to help his men with some repairs to one of the barns and she hadn't heard him reenter the house.

"Good heavens, Jaron! You scared me…out of a year's growth," she said, trying to catch her breath.

"I called your name when I stopped in the mudroom to take off my boots," he said, motioning over his shoulder with his thumb toward the kitchen.

"I must have been concentrating on getting all of these things put away and didn't hear you," she said, brushing past him to enter the kitchen. Glancing at the clock, she walked over to the sink to wash her hands. "After you brought in the groceries for me, I started putting everything away and lost track of time. I'll have your lunch ready in a few minutes. Will a sandwich and chips be okay?"

"That's fine," he said, nodding. "I'll help."

"Did you and your men get the repairs made in the barn?" she asked as she gathered the things she needed to make them ham-and-cheese sandwiches.

"Yes and no," he said, taking plates from the cabinet to set the table.

"How does that work?" she asked, laughing. "You either did or you didn't get things fixed."

His low chuckle sent a warm feeling throughout her body. "We got everything done on the list of things that needed repairing, then we found one of the stall doors has a broken hinge and another stall that needs a few boards replaced."

"It sounds as though keeping things in good shape

is a never-ending job," she said, setting a small platter of sandwiches on the table.

"Welcome to the world of ranching, darlin'," he said, holding her chair for her. When she sat down, he took a seat at the opposite end of the table. "Our foster father always told me and my brothers that if we couldn't find something that needed to be done, we weren't looking."

She laughed. "From everything I've heard about Hank Calvert he was a wonderful, very wise man."

"I don't know of any better," he agreed. "I don't even want to think about where my brothers and I would be if we hadn't been sent to the Last Chance Ranch. He saved us from ourselves and we wouldn't be where we are today without him."

They fell silent for several minutes as they ate before Jaron spoke again.

"I…want to talk to you about last night," he said, his voice hesitant.

Mariah stared at him a moment, wondering what he wanted to say. Had what she'd said to him the night before gotten through to him? Was he finally going to open up to her?

"All right." Her appetite suddenly deserting her, she placed her half-eaten sandwich on her plate. "What do you want to discuss, Jaron?"

"I want to apologize for kissing you." He shook his head. "It shouldn't have happened."

"Oh, good grief, Jaron!" She picked up her plate, got up from the table and carried it over to scrape the remainder of her lunch into the garbage disposal. Putting the plate into the dishwasher, she added, "If I hear you say that one more time, I think I'm going to be sorely tempted to throttle you." She turned to glare at him. "Get a clue, cowboy. Kissing me is something you obviously want to do or it wouldn't keep happening. And as for your apology, there is absolutely no reason for it. I wanted you to kiss me, and the night we made love, I wanted that, too. So keep your 'I didn't mean to do that' or 'it won't happen again' to yourself, because we both know better."

Before she could stop herself, she marched over to the table, placed her palms on his lean cheeks and, leaning down, kissed him for all she was worth. His firm lips immediately molded to hers, and when she traced them with the tip of her tongue it took very little coaxing to get him to allow her entry. Treating him to the same delightful exploration that he had treated her to each time he'd kissed her, Mariah stroked and teased his inner recesses until a groan rumbled up from deep in his chest. Only then did she raise her head to stare into his dark blue eyes. She might have laughed at his startled expression if she hadn't still been so frustrated with him.

"And you want to know something else, cowboy?" She didn't wait for him to respond. "I wanted to kiss you and I'm not one tiny bit sorry that I did. The only difference between us is that I readily admit that I want to kiss you until your boots fly off and a whole lot more."

When she turned to walk away, his voice sounded strained when he asked, "Where are you going?"

"I have things I need to do," she said as she walked

toward the pantry on shaky legs to resume putting things on the shelves.

He cleared his throat. "You can't just kiss me like that and then walk away."

"Why not?" she asked, turning to give him a pointed look. "That's what you do."

Before he had a chance to say anything else, she went into the pantry and, picking up a couple of boxes of snack crackers, stared at the labels without really seeing them. She had never done anything like that in her entire life. But it was time to treat Mr. Jaron Lambert to a dose of his own medicine. If he could kiss her and walk away as if it meant nothing, so could she. And if he thought he was going to convince her there was nothing between them, he was sadly mistaken. She might not be as experienced as he was, but she wasn't that naive. There was something holding him back, and she wasn't even contemplating trying to find another job until she discovered what it was.

Several hours later, Mariah put bags of noodles and pasta in lined sea-grass baskets and placed them on the shelves. Standing back, she proudly surveyed the labels she'd made and how organized everything looked.

"Don't worry about making supper tonight," Jaron said, causing her to jump.

"I wish you'd stop doing that," she said, catching her breath.

"Do what?" he asked, looking puzzled.

"Sneaking up on me like that," she retorted. Lost in thought, she hadn't realized he had come back into the house again.

"I'll try to make more noise from now on," he said, smiling. "I wanted to tell you not to worry about making supper tonight. After I take a quick shower, I'll drive over to Beaver Dam and get a couple of steak dinners for us."

"Why? I thought part of my job description is to cook your meals," she said, frowning.

"You've worked hard all afternoon getting the pantry organized and all this food put away," he said, leaning one shoulder against the door frame as he crossed his arms over his wide chest. "You have to be tired. You can start cooking tomorrow."

"Suit yourself," she said, breathing a little easier as he turned to leave.

At least Jaron buying dinner would give her one more night without having to prepare a meal. He was going to learn soon enough that she had no idea what she was doing in a kitchen, and the longer she could put that off, the better.

Walking back into the kitchen, she watched him disappear down the hall to go upstairs. She was going to do her best and try to make things that he could actually eat. But she wasn't overly confident that would happen for a while. The poor man thought he had hired a woman who could make delicious meals with little or no effort like her sister. He had no idea that Mariah hadn't been born with the cooking gene.

"Hey, Jaron! We didn't expect to see your sorry hide in here tonight."

When Jaron turned to see who was calling to him, he

groaned. He hadn't expected to see two of his brothers at the Broken Spoke either when he went to pick up his and Mariah's supper. But sure enough, there were Ryder McClain and T. J. Malloy sitting at a table toward the back of the room, grinning at him like a couple of fools.

Giving his order for the steak dinners and a bottle of beer to the bartender, Jaron took his beer and walked over to sit down in one of the empty chairs at their table. "I assume I'm doing the same thing you two are doing. Along with this beer, I just ordered a couple of steak dinners for supper."

T.J. grinned as he cut into the steak in front of him. "A couple? You must be real hungry."

"And you're doing carryout? I'd say you're going to be entertaining a lady tonight," Ryder speculated, laughing.

"Anyone we know?" T.J. asked without missing a beat.

Jaron could have kicked himself for mentioning he had ordered two dinners. He should have known that his brothers would want to know who would be eating the other steak.

"I hired a housekeeper," Jaron said, hoping to avoid an inquisition. "She spent the day shopping and stocking the pantry. I figured I'd give her a break and have her start cooking tomorrow."

He watched T.J. and Ryder glance at each other for a moment before their gazes swung back to him. "Okay, what is it that you aren't telling us?" Ryder asked. "And don't try saying there isn't something, because we know you better than that. A seasoned housekeeper would be able to juggle grocery shopping and making supper with her eyes closed."

Jaron had wanted to wait until he and his brothers were all together to tell them that he had hired Mariah to be his housekeeper. He knew they were all going to needle him to death for details, and if he waited until they were together he would only have to endure their questions and comments once and get it over with. But it didn't appear that was going to happen.

He took a deep draw on his beer bottle before he set it down and met his brothers' suspicious gazes head-on. "I hired Mariah."

T.J. choked on the piece of steak he had just put in his mouth. Reaching over, Ryder pounded on T.J.'s back several times without his piercing gaze wavering from Jaron's. "How the hell did that happen? And when?"

"About a week ago, I came here for supper and Mariah walked in," Jaron said. Explaining what had happened with the hapless Roy Lee and about her car breaking down, he finished, "Because it was late and Sam and Bria were down in Houston at the stock show, I took her home with me for the night."

"Any one of us would have done the same," Ryder agreed. "But how did you get from helping her with her car troubles to giving her a job?"

"Over breakfast the next morning, I found out that she had lost her position at the real estate management company and she couldn't afford rent because her roommate moved out." He carefully omitted the fact that if he hadn't felt so damned guilty over making love to her and taking her virginity the night before, he might not have even thought of offering her the job.

Recovered from choking on his steak, T.J. shook his head. "You're playing with fire, bro. Are you sure you can handle it and still keep up your 'I'm too old for her' line of bull?"

Ryder nodded. "You know damned good and well that girl has been moon-eyed over you for years and still is. Although for the life of me I'm beginning to wonder why."

"And you've had a thing for her almost as long," T.J. added. "Have you finally decided that you aren't Methuselah after all?"

"I'm still too old for her," Jaron insisted, stubbornly shaking his head.

"I never thought I'd be saying this, but you better not be leading her on, bro," Ryder warned. "I'd hate to have to kick your ass from here into the next county."

Jaron glared at this brother. "You know me better than that."

They might be irritating the hell out of him, but he wasn't the least bit surprised that T.J. and Ryder were cautioning him about playing with Mariah's affections. She was their sister-in-law's younger sister, and that made all of them protective of her. But it also went back to their days of growing up on the Last Chance Ranch. Besides the obvious talk about using protection if their hormones got the better of them, one of the first things their foster father had told them when they all started dating was to respect a woman and not to lead her on if there wasn't any chance of something working out between them.

But as he sat there staring at his brothers, Jaron couldn't help but feel guilty. By giving Mariah a job and moving her into his home, was he giving her hope where there was none? When he'd made love to her, he'd known that Mariah had assumed it was the beginning of a shift in their friendship, even though he had told her up front that he wasn't promising her anything beyond that one night. In trying to help her out with her employment problems, was he only hurting her more than he already had?

"I'd rather drop dead right here and now than ever hurt Mariah in any way," he said aloud.

"You sound like a man in love," T.J. observed, as if he was some kind of expert on the subject.

Grinding his teeth, Jaron shook his head. "I don't want to hurt anyone, except maybe you right now."

He wished whoever was working in the Broken Spoke's kitchen would get his steaks ready so that he could bid his brothers farewell and leave. He loved all of his brothers, but T.J. and Ryder were reminding him of the war he was waging within himself—a battle that Mariah wasn't doing a thing to help him win. That kiss she'd given him at lunch had damned near sent him into orbit and left him wanting her more than he ever wanted anything in his entire life.

"What's really stopping you with Mariah, Jaron?" Ryder pressed, nailing Jaron with a piercing look. "And let's try the truth this time. We all know the nine-year age difference has nothing to do with the reason you won't give in to your feelings for her."

Jaron loved his brothers and would lay down his life for any one of them. But the major drawback of having them know him so well was they all knew when he wasn't being entirely honest with them.

Taking a deep breath, Jaron stared at the droplets of condensation running down the beer bottle in his hand. "I care too much for her to saddle her with a past like mine."

"We all have pasts," T.J. reminded him. "We weren't sent to the Last Chance Ranch because we were little angels."

"T.J.'s right," Ryder said, nodding. "We all did things when we were young that we regret and aren't proud of. But we found women who love us for the men we became and overlooked the stupid mistakes we made when we were growing up. All you did was run away from foster homes. What the rest of us did to get our asses in trouble was a lot worse than that."

"I understand that," Jaron argued. "But this is Mariah. She deserves the best and I'm not it."

T.J. grunted. "Bro, that's the dumbest thing I think I've ever heard you say. Remember, Hank always told us that we can't change the past, so we might as well leave what we did to land us in trouble back there where it belongs and make the most of the future. And the last I knew, you had done that."

Ryder nodded. "There isn't one of us who thinks we're good enough for our wives. But there's not a day goes by that we don't thank the good Lord above the women disagree."

"In case you haven't noticed, that's the way Mariah feels about you, bro," T.J. said, finishing his steak. "She may not know what happened with your old man or why you ran away from every foster home they put you in, but she knows you have a past and she overlooks it because of the man you are today."

"I'll think about it," Jaron said to placate them. Maybe if they thought he was giving what they said some thought, they'd shut up and leave him alone.

"Now that we've covered what's happening in my life, let me ask you both something," Jaron said, deciding that a change of subject was in order. "Why are you here and not at home with your wives and kids?"

T.J. grinned. "The kids are playing while Summer helps Heather go through designs and options for decorating our new baby's nursery. Once Heather and I find out what we're having, we'll start painting and decorating with cowboys or ballerinas."

"They suggested we come here because they know we're pretty useless when it comes to that kind of thing," Ryder added, laughing.

When Jaron heard the bartender call his name, he breathed a sigh of relief. "It looks as if supper's ready," he said, rising to his feet. As an afterthought, he added, "I'd appreciate it if you'd keep Mariah's working for me to yourselves." He knew that both Ryder and T.J. would keep their mouths shut and respect his wishes.

Both of his brothers nodded their agreement. "You intend to tell the others when you and Mariah show up for Sam's birthday dinner?" Ryder asked, sitting back from the table.

"I figure it's easier to tell everyone at one time and get it over with, instead of having to be asked the same questions over and over," Jaron explained.

"You're probably right," Ryder agreed.

"See you next weekend," T.J. called as Jaron walked over to the bar to get the carryout he'd ordered.

After he paid for the food, Jaron walked out of the bar to his truck and drove back to the Wild Maverick Ranch. His brothers had brought up a couple of things that he needed to give some serious thought.

Although she didn't know what had happened to land him in the foster-care system and eventually get him sent to the Last Chance Ranch, Mariah had always known he had been a troubled kid. And T.J. was right about one thing—she didn't seem to care. Mariah accepted him for who he was now, as opposed to who he'd been back then.

But unlike his foster brothers, he had been labeled a problem because of what his father had done more than for running away from foster homes. Foster families didn't want a serial killer's son living with them— probably because they feared he would turn out like his old man. And the few who had opened their homes to him had made his life so miserable with their accusing looks and constant questions about his father and what he knew about the murders that Jaron had ended up taking off. The last time the authorities had found him, the caseworker had contacted Hank Calvert and it had turned out to be the luckiest day of Jaron's life.

Their foster father had stressed that Jaron and his foster brothers should view their time at the Last Chance
Ranch as a fresh start and had helped all of them grow
up to be productive, upstanding men. He'd counseled
them with his sage advice, and for the most part they
had moved on and left their troubles in the past. So why
hadn't Jaron been able to do that as completely as the
others? If he could find a way to come to terms with
what had happened in his childhood, would he finally
feel free to try having a relationship with Mariah?

As he parked his truck in the garage, he glanced over
at Mariah's car. He wasn't sure what the answers were.
And until he figured it out, it was best just to leave
things the way they were.

"Thank you for dinner," Mariah said as she and Jaron
walked into the family room to watch television after
they ate. "It was delicious, but I'm positively stuffed."

The carryout food that he'd brought back from the
Broken Spoke had been very good, but the portions had
been double the size of those at any restaurant she'd
ever been to and more than she could possibly eat. She
hadn't even been able to take a bite of the delicious-
looking apple pie he'd bought for their dessert. Knowing how much he loved it, she'd insisted he eat her slice
as well as his own.

"You've eaten there before, haven't you?" he asked,
reaching for the remote.

"The other night when my car broke down was the
first time I've ever been in the place," she admitted.

"Normally when I'm in the area, I'm at one of your family's dinners or parties."

"Speaking of family dinners, we have one coming up," he said, turning the television to a popular crime show. "Next weekend we'll be getting together for Sam's birthday."

"I'm looking forward to it," she said, slipping off her shoes to curl up in the corner of the couch. "I haven't seen the babies since Christmas." Bria and Sam's little boy was her only biological nephew, but she loved all of the foster brothers' children as if they were related by blood.

"It won't be long before there are two more." Jaron gave her a wary look. "We know Nate and Jessie are having a girl. I assume you think T.J. and Heather will have a girl, too."

Mariah smiled. "Of course." Every time one of the men's wives became pregnant, she had been positive the baby would be a girl, while Jaron had insisted it would be a boy. "I suppose you think Heather will have a boy."

"To tell you the truth, it really doesn't matter that much anymore." He shrugged. "I'd never been around little girls until Ryder and Summer had Katie. Now all it takes is one of her cute grins and I turn into a damned fool."

"That's the way I feel about all of them," she admitted. "The boys and Katie are all absolutely adorable and I couldn't love them more if I tried."

"Then, why do you keep insisting when one of the sisters-in-law learns she's pregnant that the baby is going to be a girl?" he asked, raising one dark eyebrow.

"You haven't figured it out yet?" she asked, laughing.

Looking confused, he shook his head. "Why don't you let me in on what you think I should have figured out."

"I just like arguing with you," she answered, grinning.

"That's it?" When she nodded, he frowned. "Why?"

Leaning toward him, she whispered, "Because I wanted to get your attention."

"Well, you did that." The lines on his forehead deepened. "I thought you were pissed off at me most of last year after I mentioned that I was right when Lane and Taylor found out they were having a boy."

"No woman likes for a man to gloat on the rare occasion she's wrong," Mariah warned.

"So you *were* mad at me?" he asked.

"I wasn't happy, but I was more miffed than I was angry."

He grunted. "What's the difference?"

"Miffed is unhappy," she explained. "Angry is what I was last week when you went Neanderthal on that poor man and escorted me out of the Broken Spoke because you thought I was incapable of handling the situation myself."

"I'd do it again in a heartbeat if the need arose," he said stubbornly. "And if I were you, I wouldn't feel too sorry for old Roy Lee. He needed a lesson in what it means to respect a woman, and I had no problem giving him a crash course on the subject."

She wanted Jaron to admit what she had suspected all along—that his strong reaction to the situation had been because of her and not just his sense of gallantry. "You'd have done the same if it had been any other woman?" she pressed.

"It wasn't." He clamped his mouth shut and stared at her for a moment before he slowly nodded. "Probably."

"But it wasn't just any woman, was it?" she said, moving closer to him. She couldn't believe her audacity. But if she was going to get to the bottom of things, she had to start somewhere. "It was me."

"Yeah." He didn't look happy about his admission.

"You want to know what I think?" she whispered close to his ear.

He went as still as a marble statue. "You're going to—" he cleared his throat "—tell me no matter what I say, aren't you?"

"Of course." Kissing the side of his neck, she smiled when she felt him shudder. "You're fighting a losing battle, cowboy."

"Mariah, I don't think—" He stared at her as if he waged war within himself. He closed his eyes for a moment, then opened them and wrapped his arms around her. "Oh, hell, I give up."

Before she could ask what he meant, Jaron pulled her onto his lap and fused his mouth with hers. Bringing her arms up to his wide shoulders, she held on to his solid strength as she kissed him back.

Tiny sparkles of light danced behind her closed eyes as his lips moved over hers, and when he coaxed her to allow him entry, she couldn't think of anything she wanted more than for him to deepen the kiss. At the first touch of his tongue to hers, a warmth like nothing she'd ever felt before settled in the most feminine part of her. Apparently he was experiencing the same kind of heat, because there was no denying the evidence of his hard arousal pressing insistently against the side of her hip.

Keeping his arms wrapped tightly around her, he shifted them to a more comfortable position and Mariah found herself stretched out on the couch with Jaron lying partially on top of her. With one of his thighs nestled snugly at the apex of her legs, desire streaked through her veins and caused a flutter of anticipation deep in the pit of her stomach. She wanted him, hadn't stopped wanting him since the night they made love. With sudden clarity, she knew she always would.

As he continued to explore her with a tenderness that robbed her of breath, he moved his hand from her shoulders down to cup her breast. The delicious sensation of his gentle touch as he teased the tip with the pad of his thumb caused her to feel as if her insides had been turned into hot wax. When he broke the contact to nibble kisses down the column of her throat to her collarbone, the tiny moan she'd been holding back escaped her parted lips.

"Does that feel good?" he asked as his lips skimmed her sensitive skin.

"It feels…amazing," she gasped.

"We shouldn't be doing this, Mariah," he said against her sensitive skin.

Placing her palms on either side of his face, she raised his head to meet her determined gaze. "I swear, if you stop…I'll never speak to you…again," she warned breathlessly.

His low chuckle sent a wave of energy to her core and she pressed herself more fully into him. As he continued to tantalize the tight peak through the layers of her clothing, Mariah shivered from the feel of his hard arousal against her thigh. He wanted her as much as she wanted him.

"I have something that I need to go check on down at the barn, darlin'," he said suddenly, sounding as if he had run a marathon. Getting up from the couch, he pulled her up to stand in front of him and softly kissed her forehead. "I'll be back a little later," he added, stepping away from her.

"After you cool off?" she asked point-blank.

He stared at her a moment before he silently nodded.

"Jaron, I want you to do something for me while you're out in the barn," she said as she brushed her hair from her eyes.

"What's that?"

"I want you to think about what I told you earlier," she replied, picking up her shoes to go upstairs. "You're fighting a battle you can't win. You can deny it all you want, but you want me as much as I want you and this is going to continue to happen as long as I'm living here." She shook her head. "And unless you fire me, I'm not going anywhere."

"I'm not firing you," he said without a moment's hesitation.

"Then, I suggest you come to terms with what's going on between us," she advised. "Because there's always been more than just friendship, and we both know it."

Five

After a miserable night, Jaron waited until the star-filled sky gave way to the pearl-gray light of dawn before he finally lost hope of getting any sleep and sat up on the side of his bed. Mariah had given him a lot to think about yesterday evening—as if having her around all the time hadn't been the *only* thing on his mind for the past week.

Resting his forearms on his knees, he stared down at his loosely clasped hands. Between what she had told him and what his brothers had mentioned about her knowing and not caring that there was some kind of trouble in his background, he had given serious thought to the possibilities, as well as the consequences.

There had been something going on between him and Mariah for several years. But whether she could accept his past or not, he wasn't sure he ever would. The stigma of being the son of someone the world considered to be pure evil wasn't something that went away that easily, and he had no intention of bringing that kind of repulsive reality into her life.

Unfortunately, it was becoming impossible to resist the temptation of having Mariah with him all the time and keep his hands to himself. He would like nothing more than to be free to hold her to him, kiss her until they both gasped for air and make love to her for as long as she wanted to stay with him. And she wasn't helping him to resist those needs. She'd let him know in more ways than one that she wanted that, too.

But he had to think of what was best for her and put that ahead of his own desires. She might not think his past was a problem, but he knew better. When he was young he'd had too many people look at him as if they thought he might murder them in their sleep once they learned who his father was. That wasn't something he would ever forget, nor was it anything he wanted Mariah to even consider. He hoped she never learned the revolting secrets he tried so hard to protect her from. He couldn't bear the thought of seeing the disillusionment in her eyes if she ever found out.

Jaron sighed heavily. He should probably fire her and send her on her way. But she needed the job and it was the only way he could think of to help her without hurting her pride or pissing her off to the point of her never speaking to him again.

Now, if he could just figure out a way to keep his hands to himself...

When he heard her close her bedroom door and start down the stairs, he abandoned his troubling thoughts, took a quick shower and got dressed. She would have breakfast ready soon and he had a full day's work ahead of him repairing fence with his men. Besides, there was no sense wasting time thinking about things that he couldn't change.

As he pulled on his boots, a keening wail suddenly split the air, raising the hair on the back of his neck and sending an icy chill straight up his spine. Jumping up from the bench at the end of the bed, Jaron ran out into the hall and headed for the stairs. While the smoke alarm screeched relentlessly, the acrid smell of something burning stung his nostrils and caused his eyes to water.

When he reached the kitchen, he immediately looked for Mariah. She was frantically opening cabinet doors, and he assumed she was looking for something to put out the fire. Fairly certain she was all right, he reached into the cabinet under the sink, pulled out the fire extinguisher and, removing the pin, aimed the hose at the flaming skillet on the ceramic stove top. As soon as he was sure the blaze was out, he went straight to the screaming smoke detector and removed the battery to stop the incessant noise.

"Are you all right?" he asked, going over to put his arm around her shoulders to guide her out onto the back porch.

Coughing, she nodded. "I'm okay, but I'm afraid breakfast is going to be late."

He hugged her close for a moment to reassure himself she was okay, then released her to reach for the door. "Stay here and catch your breath while I go open the windows to air out the kitchen."

When he returned, she was standing there shivering with her arms wrapped around her waist. He wasn't sure if she was cold or if she was having a nervous reaction to the fire. It didn't matter. Without giving it a second thought, he drew her to him to keep her warm.

"It's okay, darlin'," he said, gently rubbing her back. "All that matters is that you weren't hurt." When she nodded, he asked, "What was in the skillet?"

"I was trying to fry a couple of eggs, but they suddenly burst into flames," she answered, holding on to him as though he was her lifeline. "I think the oil might have been too hot."

He couldn't help but chuckle. "You may have just come up with a new recipe. I don't think I've ever heard of eggs flambé before."

"I suppose there's something I should tell you about my ability to cook," she said, her voice muffled from her face being buried in his chest.

"I'm listening," he said, doing his best not to laugh. He had a good idea what she was about to tell him.

"I don't know the first thing about cooking unless it's reading the back of a box to find out how many minutes to program the timer on a microwave," she admitted.

"But that apple pie you made for my birthday a couple of years ago tasted great," he reminded her.

"If Bria hadn't stood beside me and told me step by step what to do, it wouldn't have been edible." She shook her head. "I should have told you I can't cook."

"Oh, I kind of got that cooking might not be in your skill set when the smoke alarm went off. And if that hadn't tipped me off, I think the blazing skillet would have." Using his finger to lift her chin so their gazes met, he grinned. "Until a few minutes ago, I'd never seen black eggs."

Her cheeks turned pink. "I'm much better at business management."

"Let's go back inside," he suggested when she shivered against him. The weather was colder than normal for February, and he wouldn't be at all surprised if they were in for some kind of frozen precipitation.

Once they were back in the kitchen, Mariah scraped the charred eggs into the garbage disposal and put the skillet in sudsy water to soak while he closed the windows. "Would you like some toast for breakfast?" she asked, her voice a bit subdued. "I know I can make that."

He shook his head. "I'll just take a cup of coffee."

"I was going to ask you about that," she said, eyeing the coffeemaker as if it might bite her. "I normally waited until I got to work to have my morning coffee. The office had one of those makers that used the little individual cups."

All things considered, he probably shouldn't find her lack of kitchen knowledge amusing. But he did. "Making coffee is pretty easy. I'll show you what to do so you can make it tomorrow morning." Once he showed her how to get the coffeemaker started, he got two mugs from the cabinet and poured them both a cup when it finished brewing.

"Thank you," she said, adding creamer to her coffee.

Walking over to the table, she slumped into one of the chairs. "I thought I would ask Bria to show me a few simple things to make, but I haven't had the chance to go over there yet."

"Don't worry about it." He sat down beside her, then reached over to cover her hand with his. "If you don't mind, I think I'm going to change your job description."

"To what?" she asked, looking as though she expected the worst. "Unemployed?"

"No." He smiled. "In light of recent events, I think it would be in both of our best interests to move you into a position that you're more familiar with. How would you like to take over as ranch manager?"

"As long as it doesn't involve getting near a stove, I'm sure I can do the job," she said, sounding relieved. "But what are you going to do for a housekeeper and cook?"

"I think the first item on your agenda as ranch manager should be to hire someone who has a little more experience in the kitchen," he teased, taking a sip of his coffee.

She smiled sheepishly. "If you want to eat more than burned offerings, that probably wouldn't be a bad idea."

He told her where to find the ranch files on his computer and gave her his password. "If you have time, you can familiarize yourself with the ranch records today. I'll stick around the house tomorrow so that we can discuss what I have planned and set goals to make it happen."

With a degree in ranch management, he could run the Wild Maverick with his eyes closed. But he had promised her a job and he wasn't going back on his word.

"I think I already have someone in mind for the housekeeping position," Mariah said, looking thoughtful. "She used to work for me at the real estate management office and when we found out we no longer had jobs, she mentioned trying to find something closer to Stephenville, where her son and his family live."

"Can she cook?" he asked, grinning at her over the rim of his coffee mug.

She made a face at him. "Reba May is almost as good a cook as Bria," she answered proudly. "She used to do the cooking for all of our office parties and everything she made was delicious. I'll give her a call a little later and see if she's interested."

"It sounds as though you have it under control."

"If she's interested in the job would you like to meet her before I hire her?" she asked.

"I trust your judgment." He set his cup on the table and checked his watch. "I need to get down to the barn. I'm helping my men repair that stretch of fence in the south pasture today."

"Will you be back for lunch?" she asked. "I may not know how to cook, but I can make a sandwich for you."

When she nibbled on her lower lip, he barely managed to hold back a groan. She wasn't trying to be provocative, but that didn't lessen the effect her action had on him.

He shook his head as he rose to his feet to take his coffee cup to the sink. "When we're working out in the pastures, the bunkhouse cook always packs lunch for us." Giving in to the overwhelming urge to kiss her, he walked back to the table, pulled her up from the chair and, wrapping his arms around her waist, drew her to him. "And don't worry about supper. I think it would be a good idea to eat out this evening."

She laughed. "Where's your sense of adventure, cowboy?"

"I think I used that up when you tried to cook breakfast," he said, unable to stop himself from pressing his mouth to hers. Giving her a kiss that left them both breathless, he motioned toward the door. "The guys are waiting on me."

"Thank you, Jaron," she said softly.

He frowned. "What for?"

"For not firing me." She kissed the exposed skin at the open collar of his chambray shirt. "I'll see you later this afternoon."

Nodding, Jaron quickly turned, grabbed his wide-brimmed hat from a peg beside the door and walked out of the house before he changed his mind about helping his men mend the fence in the south pasture. So much for the pep talk he'd given himself when he first got out of bed. It had taken less than half an hour and he'd already reverted to kissing her first and thinking about it later.

Mariah had been right about a couple of things. There was a lot more going on between them than ever before, and it appeared he was definitely fighting a losing battle. He should tell her it would be better if she found another job. But as much hell as he'd gone through the past week, he still didn't want her to leave. Just the thought of her leaving caused a knot the size of a basketball to form in his gut.

Jaron took a deep breath as he walked across the yard toward the barn. He felt as if he had jumped off a cliff into the great unknown. But there was no way to turn back the clock. It appeared that when he'd made love to Mariah, he had started something that couldn't be stopped. And, God help him, he wasn't sure he even wanted to try.

Mariah closed the files on Jaron's computer and couldn't help but be very pleased with herself. She had not only reviewed all of the ranch files and felt ready to discuss goals for the ranch with Jaron tomorrow, she'd hired her former employee to take over the housekeeping and cooking duties at the Wild Maverick Ranch. Reba May had jumped at the job offer because of the close proximity to her son and his family, as well as the idea of being able to make a living doing what she loved—cooking. That was enough to make Mariah feel a lot better after the disaster with breakfast that morning. But when she talked to Reba May and learned that the woman had won the state fair pie-making contest with an apple pie, Mariah had been thrilled with her decision to hire the woman. Given his love of apple pie, she was fairly confident Jaron would be happy with her choice, as well.

As she sat there patting herself on the back for a job well done, her cell phone rang. Checking the caller ID, she smiled when she saw the call was from Bria.

"How is my favorite sister?" Mariah asked cheerfully.

"I'm your only sister," Bria answered drily. "That makes me the favorite by default."

"You sound tired." Mariah leaned back in Jaron's desk chair. "Has that sweet little nephew of mine been running you ragged?"

"Not any more than usual." Bria sighed. "I've been battling a stomach bug for the past week that I just can't seem to shake."

"Is there anything I can do to help?" Mariah asked, immediately concerned. "If you need me, I can watch little Hank so you can get some rest." Although Bria and Sam were more than financially able to hire a nanny to help with the toddler, Bria was a hands-on mother and loved every minute of it. She wouldn't even discuss having help with her son.

"Thank you, but he's been an angel since I got sick," Bria said, her voice reflecting her motherly love. "And speaking of my little man, he's due to wake up from his nap soon, so I'll have to make this quick. The reason I'm calling is about Sam's birthday dinner. Since I haven't felt well, Taylor is going to have the celebration at her and Lane's ranch a week from this Sunday."

Taylor Donaldson had worked as a personal chef before moving to Texas and had been helping Bria with all of the family get-togethers since marrying Lane. But it concerned Mariah that Bria might have something more serious than the stomach flu. She'd never known her sister not to cook Sam's birthday dinner herself.

"Have you been to a doctor?" Mariah asked. "Maybe there's something he can give you to help you get over this."

"I have an appointment tomorrow," Bria answered. "But I'm sure it's nothing to worry about. I just wanted to let you know about the change in plans."

"I'll be there," Mariah said, careful not to mention the word *we*. Apparently Jaron hadn't mentioned anything to his brothers about her working for him. If he had, she knew her sister would have questioned her about it. Besides, she fully intended to tell Bria about losing her job and moving to the Wild Maverick when she saw her the day of Sam's birthday dinner. Some things were just better discussed in person. "Let me know what you find out after you see the doctor, and if you change your mind about me watching little Hank, don't hesitate to let me know."

"I will," Bria promised. "I'll see you a week from Sunday. Love you."

"Love you more, sis," Mariah said before ending the call. Since their parents had been taken from them so unexpectedly, they never parted without telling each other how they felt.

Mariah left Jaron's office and headed upstairs to take a shower and change. He would be back soon from working with his men and she wanted to be ready to go out for dinner.

She briefly wondered why he hadn't told his brothers about hiring her, but she had been just as reluctant to share her change of employment with Bria. Maybe Jaron was trying to avoid a barrage of questions, the same as she was.

Mariah loved her sister with all her heart, but Bria could be the overly protective big sister at times and especially where Jaron was concerned. It wasn't that Bria didn't trust him to be anything but a perfect gentleman. Mariah was certain that her sister trusted all of Sam's foster brothers without hesitation.

But Bria had known how Mariah felt about Jaron from the time they'd been introduced. Bria also knew that Jaron had never led her on or given her any reason to believe that he viewed her as anything but Bria's younger sister. Mariah was certain that if Bria got wind of her working at the Wild Maverick Ranch, she would feel compelled to caution Mariah about reading more into the situation than was really there.

Of course, her sister didn't know the entire story and Mariah had no intention of telling her. What happened between two consenting adults was no one else's business, and as far as Mariah was concerned that was the way it was going to stay. She would listen to Bria's concerns and even answer the questions she could without revealing the personal aspects of her stay at the Wild Maverick Ranch. Beyond that, no one else needed to know what went on between her and Jaron.

The following day, Jaron sat across the desk from Mariah, wondering how he was going to keep his mind on ranch business when all he could think about was taking her upstairs and making love to her. When they'd gone out for supper the night before, he'd had the same problem concentrating. Mariah had been extremely enthusiastic about the woman she'd hired to take over the housekeeping position and told him all about her. He couldn't recall a single thing she'd said other than the woman's name was Reba something or other and that she wouldn't be starting until the first of next month.

Fortunately, when they returned to the ranch, he'd received a call from his ranch foreman to tell him the calving season had started early. A couple of the prize-winning heifers he'd bought had gone into labor, and after seeing Mariah into the house, he'd walked down to the calving shed to check on them. He was sure his men could have taken care of the bovine maternity watch, but he'd used the excuse to escape what he knew now to be the inevitable. He and Mariah would be making love again—and soon.

He took a deep breath as he came to terms with that. He had reached the end of his rope and no amount of telling himself he was doing what was right had worked. His best efforts to fight his growing need for her had failed miserably and it was past time that he gave up and admitted it.

But as much as he burned for her, he was determined that it would be different than when they made love before. When he loved her again, it wouldn't be rushed the way it had been the night he'd brought her home with him from the Broken Spoke. Mariah deserved to be loved slowly, to be cherished in a way that let her know how special she was. She deserved the pampering and romance that had been lacking the first time he'd loved her.

"Are you listening to me, Jaron?" Mariah asked, looking impatient.

"Sorry." He cleared his throat. "I was thinking about something else."

"That's apparent," she said, laughing. "I asked you if you intend to raise nothing but free-range cattle."

He nodded. "That's the plan. There's a big market for drug and supplement free beef, and the demand for it is growing."

"What about the breed?" she asked, making notes on her electronic tablet. "Are you going to remain a pure-bred Brangus operation or will you be introducing other breeds into the herd?"

"I'm sticking with the Brangus," he said, amused by her questions. She'd obviously researched her job and was trying to learn all she could about being a ranch manager.

"From everything I've read about them, they're a pretty popular breed of beef cattle," she agreed, adding to her notes.

"Brangus are a cross between Brahman and Black Angus cattle and have the best traits of both." He shrugged. "They yield a good-tasting, high-quality grade of lean beef like the Angus and are more disease resistant and better suited to the Texas climate like the Brahman."

"That makes sense." She frowned as she looked directly at him. "You know your breed and why you chose it and you have a clear goal to keep the herd free-range. Why do you need me to be the ranch manager when you have all of this worked out and could easily manage the ranch yourself?"

"Because I'm a cowboy at heart, darlin'." Giving in to the heat flowing through his veins, he rose from his chair, rounded the desk and, scooping her up into his arms, sat down in the armchair and settled her on his lap. "You can take care of managing the ranch while I'm out working with my hired hands."

As she stared at him, he felt as if he could easily lose himself in her emerald eyes. "Jaron, I've never been good at playing games."

He didn't even try to pretend he didn't know what she was referring to. "I've never been any good at that, either, Mariah."

"Then, why have you been running hot and cold for the past week and a half?" she asked pointedly. "You pull me in and then push me away and I want to know why."

"I'm sorry." He kissed her soft, perfect lips. "I've been trying to do what I thought was best for you, but just having you here with me has undermined all of my good intentions."

To his surprise, she grinned. "In other words, I was right. You've been fighting a losing battle."

"Yeah, I guess I have," he admitted, smiling back at her.

"I'm glad you finally came to your senses and realized that. So where do we go from here?" she asked, her expression turning serious. "Are you going to tell me why you made love to me and then shut me out as if I was nothing more than a one-night stand? Or are you going to push me away again?"

"You don't pull any punches, do you?"

She shook her head. "I told you, I don't play games."

He knew he should tell her everything and wish her the best in life as he watched her walk away from him.

Instead, he took a deep breath and told her as much as he could without going into the revolting part about his father.

"After my mother died, I didn't have anyone who cared about me," he said, barely able to remember the woman who had given him life. "I learned early on that I always came up lacking in one way or another and it was easier not to count on anyone being there for me or caring what happened to me. It wasn't until I was sent to the Last Chance Ranch because I kept running away from the foster homes they put me in that I learned what having a family meant."

"Is that why you've always been more quiet and reserved than your brothers?" she asked softly. "You wanted to avoid rejection?"

"It's easier being a loner than setting yourself up for failure," he said, nodding. There was some truth in her assumption, and certainly where she was concerned.

"Do you think you're ready to take a chance now?" she asked, looking cautious.

He wasn't going to lie to her, but he couldn't tell her that wasn't the only reason holding him back, either. "Darlin', I doubt I'll ever be able to get past that part of my life," he said honestly. "But when we made love, it wasn't just a meaningless one-night stand and I don't ever want you to think it was." Wrapping his arms around her, he gave her a quick kiss. "Like I told you the other night, I can't offer you anything beyond the here and now. But that doesn't mean I don't want you." He knew she wasn't happy with his answer and he couldn't say he blamed her. "I know that isn't fair to you and I'll understand if you decide you want to cut your losses and leave."

"No, I'm not leaving." She gave him a smile that caused his heart to stall, then start beating like a war drum. "I'm looking forward to seeing what it's like to manage a working cattle ranch."

"It's a nice day," he said, setting her on her feet. He stood up and put his arms around her. "What do you say we get out of the house and take a ride around the ranch so you can see what you're going to be managing?"

"Ride as in on a horse?" she asked, looking a little apprehensive.

He nodded. "Is that a problem?"

"It might be, considering I don't know how to ride," she said, laughing.

"You can't live on a ranch without learning to ride a horse," he teased. "We'll ride double today and I'll start teaching you next week when we have a little more time."

"I'll get my jacket," she said, pulling away from his arms.

"Meet me down at the barn," he said as he watched her climb the stairs. "I'll go ahead and get my horse saddled."

As he left the house to walk down to the barn, Jaron felt better about telling Mariah what he could regarding his background. By no stretch of the imagination had he been transparent about his past, but his explanation seemed to be enough, at least for now.

He had no doubt the day would come when she'd

want the whole story. But he intended to put that off as long as he could and enjoy what time he had with her.

Ten minutes later, Jaron swung up into the saddle, then lifted Mariah up to sit across his thighs. Putting his arms around her, he picked up the reins and, nudging Chico into a slow walk, guided the horse out of the feedlot. They hadn't ridden fifty feet from the barn before he was wondering what the hell he'd been thinking. Her delightful little bottom rested snugly against his groin, causing him to react in a very predictable way.

He had considered putting Mariah on one of the older, more docile mares, but decided against it. She wouldn't have known what she was doing or how to control the animal on the outside chance the horse got spooked. For her safety and his peace of mind, he would rather teach her to ride in the round pen, where he had more control over her first lesson than out in an open field.

"Is that a creek up ahead?" she asked, seemingly oblivious to his predicament.

He did his best to ignore the signals his body was sending him and concentrated on answering her questions about the ranch. "There are two creeks," he said, shifting in the saddle to relieve some of the mounting pressure. "One here in the south pasture and one winding from the northeast to the western side of the property."

"Good for watering livestock," she commented. He found her determination to learn all she could about managing the ranch and all of the research she'd obviously done on the subject endearing.

He kissed her temple. "That's one of the reasons I bought this place. Besides being close to all of my brothers, it had good pastures for grazing and adequate water for the herds."

As they continued the tour of his ranch, he answered a good two dozen questions or more about the property, and by the time they turned back toward the house an hour or so later, he felt that Mariah was going to be a great ranch manager. Her questions and observations had been insightful and she'd even offered a couple of suggestions on the goals they had set.

But the ride was starting to take a real toll and he decided it was time to head back to the house before he lost what little sense he had left. Every time Mariah moved, the pressure building in the region south of his belt buckle increased, and he had enough adrenaline pumping through his veins to lift a tractor.

"I'll have to finish showing you around the northern part of the Wild Maverick another day," he said, deciding he'd had about all he could take. "It's going to start getting dark soon."

"I've really enjoyed seeing your land," she said, resting her head against his shoulder. "Thank you for showing me around."

"I'm glad you had a good time," he said as they rode into the ranch yard. "This spring we'll have to get the cook to pack us a lunch and go for a picnic down by one of the creeks."

"Can we go fishing?" she asked, sitting up to look over her shoulder at him. "When we were little, our dad took me and Bria fishing a few times. The best I can remember, we played in the water more than we fished, but we had a lot of fun."

He nodded. "When the real estate agent was showing me around the property last fall, he said that the creeks had catfish and bluegill."

"I wouldn't know the difference," she said, laughing. "But I'm looking forward to it."

She sounded as if she really meant it, and Jaron decided right then and there that whatever hell he'd gone through showing her around his ranch had been more than worth it. He might not be able to assure her that there would be a tomorrow for them, but he could do everything in his power to make her happy for as long as they were together.

And come hell or high water, that was exactly what he was going to do.

Six

When Mariah walked into her closet after her shower, she started going through clothes, wondering what on earth she was going to wear for her night out with Jaron. A few days ago, when they'd returned from their ride around the ranch, he'd been called away to help his men in the calving sheds and she hadn't seen a lot of him the rest of the week. He had apologized and explained that calving season ran for several weeks, and because the majority of the cows having calves now were first-time mothers, they had to be watched more closely for signs of trouble during the birthing process. But when he'd come in earlier than usual this afternoon, he'd surprised her by telling her to dress up for dinner because he had something special planned for Valentine's Day.

Pushing back hangers as she tried to decide on a

dress, Mariah smiled. Since their talk a few days ago, Jaron had been more at ease and now took every opportunity he could to touch her or take her in his arms for kisses that left her head spinning. And she loved every minute of it.

She knew it wasn't a commitment or even the promise of one. But it did give her hope.

It might be foolish of her to think that Jaron could eventually overcome the sadness and abandonment of his childhood. And her intuition was telling her that there were more problems in his past than what he had told her. But he had shared part of it, and that was a start. Maybe one day, he would be able to tell her all of what he had been through and the reason behind his being sent to the Last Chance Ranch. She realized that she could very well be deluding herself and opening the door for a broken heart if he couldn't. But she would never know if she didn't take that leap of faith. And not giving them a chance was simply not an option.

With her mind made up to give him the time to fully trust her with his secrets, she turned her attention back to finding something to wear. When she pushed a black cocktail dress aside to reveal the simple red minidress she'd worn the night Jaron had brought her home with him from the Broken Spoke, she grinned. He'd really seemed to like the formfitting knit jersey fabric and drop shoulders. And since it was a beautiful dark red with a little bit of shimmer to it, it would be perfect for a Valentine's Day dinner.

With her mind made up to wear exactly what she'd worn the night he'd made love to her, she slipped the dress from the hanger and grabbed her black spike heels from the built-in oak shoe rack. Walking back into the bedroom, she placed them on the bed, then opened the dresser drawer where she kept her lingerie. As she put on the matching strapless black lace-and-satin bra and panties, she hoped Jaron found them as irresistible this time as he had the first time he'd seen her in them.

Thirty minutes later, she walked out of the bedroom toward the stairs. Her makeup was in place, her hair was styled and she was ready for a night out with the sexiest man she'd ever known.

Her breath caught when she spotted the man who had captured her heart the first time she'd seen him waiting for her at the bottom of the winding staircase. Dressed in a long-sleeved white Oxford cloth shirt and dark blue jeans, Jaron looked amazing. When he looked up and saw her, the appreciation in his dark blue eyes and the smile on his handsome face caused her stomach to flutter and sent a wave of warmth coursing through her. If it was possible, he stole her heart all over again.

"You look absolutely beautiful," he said, taking her hand in his when she reached the bottom step.

She smiled. "You clean up pretty nice yourself, cowboy."

He gave her a kiss so soft and so tender it brought tears to her eyes. "I love this dress," he whispered close to her ear.

A shiver of anticipation coursed through her. "Are you going to tell me where we're going?" she asked, wondering if that throaty female voice was really hers.

"Not yet," he said, leading her down the hall. He

stopped just before they reached the kitchen. "Close your eyes."

"Jaron, what—"

He placed his index finger to her lips to silence her. "I want this to be a surprise," he said, kissing her bare shoulder.

Her skin tingled where his lips had been and she didn't think twice about doing as he commanded. "Don't let me walk into anything," she said, laughing breathlessly. As he put his arm around her waist to guide her and they continued on across the kitchen, she sensed that they weren't alone. "Jaron?"

"Just keep your eyes closed, darlin'."

Not wanting to ruin his surprise, she continued to allow him to lead her, and even with her eyes closed, she could tell they had entered the darkened sunroom. "May I open my eyes now?"

"Give me just a minute," he said, stepping away from her. She suddenly smelled the acrid scent of a lit match a moment before Jaron returned to her side. "You can open them now, Mariah."

The room was dark except for a lit single white taper in a gold candleholder sitting in the middle of a small round table along the south wall of windows. Two white china table settings sat across from each other on the red tablecloth, and when she looked up at the room's glass ceiling, the dark night sky outside was sprinkled with thousands of twinkling stars.

"Jaron, this is gorgeous," she said, turning to put her arms around his neck. "But who's in the kitchen?"

He laughed and, wrapping his arms around her waist,

kissed the tip of her nose. "The caterer and her assistant."

"How did you manage to pull all of this together in the short time I was upstairs?" she asked.

"Darlin', it takes me less than thirty minutes to get a shower, shave and put my clothes on," he said, grinning. "It takes you a good hour and a half to do whatever you do to get ready to go somewhere."

"Are you complaining?" she asked, raising one eyebrow.

"Hell no!" He gave her a kiss that curled her toes inside her four-inch heels. "I'd wait all day for the way you look tonight."

"That sounds like a line from a song," she said, laughing.

He shrugged as he led her over to the table. "I don't know if it is or not, but it's the truth." Holding her chair for her to sit down, he seated himself in the chair across from her. "I hope you don't mind not going out for the evening."

"Not at all," she said as the caterer's assistant approached the table with a bottle of champagne.

After the man filled crystal flutes with the sparkling wine and went back to the kitchen, Jaron reached across to cover her hand with his. "I didn't want to share you with anyone this evening."

His words and the warmth of his touch sent goose bumps shimmering over her skin. "I'm glad," she whispered as the waiter appeared again with their plates of food.

Sitting under the stars, they enjoyed a delicious dinner of prime rib, asparagus and rice pilaf. When they were finished, the waiter discreetly cleared the table. The chef joined them a few moments later carrying a silver tray filled with juicy chocolate-dipped strawberries. Thanking them for using the catering service, the woman bade them good-night before she and the waiter left.

"I couldn't have asked for a nicer evening," Mariah said as Jaron picked up one of the strawberries and held it to her lips. Taking a bite of the decadent dessert, she savored the mixed flavors of the tart berry with just the right amount of semisweet dark chocolate. "Thank you. This has been perfect."

He shook his head as he fed her the rest of the strawberry. "It's not over yet, darlin'."

"What else do you have planned?" she asked, marveling at his romantic gestures thus far.

"You'll see," he answered, smiling as he wiped a drop of strawberry juice from her lower lip.

Taking the tip of his finger into her mouth, she licked the droplet away and watched as his eyes darkened to navy. "I'm looking forward to finding out what other surprises you have in store for me," she said, feeling warmed all over by his heated gaze.

As they continued to stare at each other, the building tension between them was palpable and only broken briefly when he rose to his feet and walked over to a small control panel on the far wall. He pushed a button and the opening notes of a popular slow country song came from the speakers of the house audio system.

When he returned to the table, he held out his hand. "Could I have this dance, Mariah?"

"I thought you'd never ask," she said, placing her hand in his. She was well aware that he didn't care for dancing and had only made the gesture because he knew how much she loved it. Her heart swelled with emotion at his thoughtfulness.

He immediately took her in his arms, and as they swayed in time to the music, she felt surrounded by the sheer power of the man holding her close. She brought her arms up to his wide shoulders and tangled her fingers in his dark brown hair where it brushed the collar of his shirt, and stared up into the eyes of the man who had given her the most romantic, most memorable Valentine's Day of her life.

As they continued to hold each other, the song ended and another one began. Neither of them noticed. The steady beat of his heart against her breast and the evidence of his growing arousal nestled to her lower belly caused her to feel as if she would melt into a puddle at his booted feet. If she'd thought her need for him the night they made love was overwhelming, what she felt at that moment was all consuming.

"I want you, Mariah," he said, his voice low and intimate.

"And I want you," she said, feeling anticipation flow throughout her body. He kissed her and she felt as if her knees turned to jelly.

"Let's go upstairs," he suggested when he lifted his head.

Unable to find her voice, she simply nodded.

He turned to blow out the candle on the table, then put his arm around her shoulders and held her to his side as they walked out of the sunroom and went upstairs. They passed her bedroom and continued on down the hall to the master suite. Once they were inside and he closed the door behind them, Mariah wasn't at all surprised when he scooped her up into his arms and carried her to the bed.

"Why do you like carrying me?" she asked, kissing the column of his neck. "Is it an alpha male thing?"

He chuckled. "I hadn't really thought about it, but that might be." He set her on her feet beside the bed, then gently kissed her. "More likely it's because I can hold you closer and have easier access when I want to kiss you."

Mariah raised her hand to cup his jaw. "You won't get any complaints from me about that," she said, smiling.

"I know it's a little late to ask you this, but are you sure this is what you want, darlin'?" he asked, staring down at her.

"I've wanted you since we made love the first time, Jaron," she said seriously. "And I'm almost certain you've wanted me."

"Every minute of every day since," he admitted, nodding. He hesitated a moment before he added, "I still can't promise—"

She placed her finger to his mouth to silence him. "I'm not asking you for any kind of promises or declarations. All I want is to share the same beautiful experience with you that we had the first time we made love."

"I promise it will be better," he said, kissing her finger.

Moving her hand to touch the pulse beating at the base of his throat, she shook her head. "I don't see how that's possible."

"In that case, I guess I'll just have to show you," he said, slowly lowering his head.

When he captured her lips with his, Mariah knew in her heart that Jaron cared deeply for her. He might not even realize how much, but she did. No man had ever held her in his arms as if she were a rare and precious gift or kissed her as tenderly as he did. For now, that was enough for her.

As he continued to explore and tease her, she sighed from the sheer joy of being in his arms. Her pulse raced when he slipped his tongue between her parted lips and coaxed her into an erotic game of advance and retreat as he stroked and caressed.

All too soon, he eased away from the kiss to nibble his way along her jaw and down her throat to her collarbone. "Why don't we get out of these clothes so I can love you," he said, his smile reflecting his intention as he bent to pull off his boots and remove her high heels.

"I think that's an excellent idea," she agreed. She briefly wondered why he hadn't turned on the bedside lamp. But a dim light from the partially open door of the bathroom cast their silhouette on the closed drapes and she found it extremely romantic.

Forgetting about the light, she unbuttoned his cuffs, then reached for the button below his open shirt collar. "I want to touch those rippling abs of your again."

He laughed. "That's what turns you on about me? My abs?"

She grinned as she released first one button and then another. "And your pecs and your biceps and your quads and—"

"I get the idea," he interrupted when she released the button above his belt buckle.

Running her index finger along the top of it, she lightly grazed the warm skin just below his navel with her fingernail. "I also like your flat stomach and lean flanks."

He groaned when she slipped her finger beneath his waistband. "You're playing with fire, darlin'."

"You want me to stop?" she asked, glancing up at him as she tugged his shirt from his jeans.

His wicked grin warmed her all the way to her toes. "I didn't say that."

She unbuckled his belt and released the snap at the top of his fly. "What are you saying, cowboy?"

"For every action there's an equal reaction." He shuddered when she played with the tab of his zipper.

"I don't think that's exactly the way Newton's law of motion goes," she teased.

"When you get finished with your brand of torture, I'll show you." The promise in his dark blue eyes thrilled her.

"I'm looking forward to it," she said, trailing her fingernail down the metal closure holding him captive.

He suddenly took a step back. "Zippers can be dangerous to a man in my condition," he said, laughing as he eased the tab down. "I'd hate for one wrong move to ruin all of your fun."

"Aren't you having a good time?" she asked, loving their sexy banter.

"Oh, yeah." He leaned close to whisper in her ear. "But I'm going to have an even better time when I get to prove what I meant about Newton's law."

Mariah shivered with anticipation. "I'm looking forward to it."

When she placed her hands on his shoulders to brush his shirt away, her breath caught at the perfection of his broad chest and bulging biceps. "Your body is flawless."

"Like I told you before, looks can be deceiving," he said, shaking his head. Before she could ask what he meant, he shoved his jeans and boxer briefs down his legs, stepped out of them and kicked them aside. "You've got my engine firing on all cylinders and it's time for me to show you what I meant about that action/reaction thing."

As he brought his mouth down on hers, his hands came up to push her dress over her shoulders and down her arms. When it drifted to the floor around her feet, he held her gaze with his and slipped her panties over her hips and down her legs to join her dress on the floor. Once she stepped away from the pool of her clothing, Jaron unfastened her bra, tossed it aside and pulled her to his wide chest. The feel of her breasts against all those hard muscles caused her knees to wobble.

"You feel so damned good, Mariah," he said, burying his face in her hair.

If she could have found her voice, she would have

told him she felt the same way about him. But since words were beyond her capabilities, she nibbled kisses from the strong column of his neck to his collarbone then down to the thick pads of his pectoral muscles. He went completely still when she kissed one flat male nipple, then the other.

"You're trying to…give me a heart attack…aren't you," he said, sounding completely out of breath.

A feeling of feminine power coursed through her at the thought that she could instill that kind of desire in him. "I need you more now than you can possibly know, Jaron."

"I need you, too, darlin'." He took a deep breath. "Let's lie down while we still have the strength to get into bed."

Once they were stretched out on his king-size bed, he pulled her to him and kissed her with a passion that caused her to feel light-headed. When he broke the caress, he brushed his lips along her cheeks, her neck and the hollow behind her ear as he gently cupped her breast in his large palm. The delicious abrasion of his calluses on her sensitive skin sent tingles of excitement spiraling all the way to her feminine core.

Needing to touch him, to bring him the same degree of pleasure, she slowly skimmed her hand over his abs and taut stomach. When she felt the crisp hair below his navel, she traced the line with her finger until she found his persistent arousal.

She had no idea what she was doing, but as she measured his length and girth, a low groan rumbled up from deep in his chest. She took it as a positive sign that he was enjoying her exploration. But as she continued to learn his body, an impatience built deep inside her and she ached for him to make them one.

"Darlin', don't get me wrong," he said suddenly, catching her hand in his. "I love what you're doing. But if you keep that up, we're both going to be mighty disappointed."

"Then, why don't you do something to keep that from happening," she said, slightly shocked by her own boldness.

"Good idea." He gave her an encouraging smile. "I promise it won't hurt this time, Mariah," he said as he reached for a foil packet on the top of the bedside table.

When he had the protection in place, he rose above her and, taking her hand in his, helped her guide him to her. Her heart skipped a beat as he slowly moved forward and began to enter her. The exquisite fullness and the feeling of becoming one with the man who meant so much to her were overwhelming. She'd never felt more complete in her entire life than when they made love and she knew beyond a shadow of doubt that what she felt for Jaron was no longer the starry-eyed crush she'd had on him as a teenage girl. What she felt for him now went deeper and was far more real.

When his lower body rested against hers, he remained perfectly still. "Are you all right? There isn't any discomfort, is there?"

"I'm fine," she said, wrapping her arms around his neck. "Please make love to me, Jaron."

His gaze held hers as he began a slow rocking motion, and Mariah quickly lost herself to the wonderful feeling he was creating inside her. As the sensations began to build, she felt as if they were one body, one heart and one soul. She fought to prolong the connection between them as long as she could, but all too soon she felt her feminine muscles tighten as she approached the culmination they both sought.

Suddenly feeling as if a thousand stars had burst inside her, she was released from the delicious tension, and waves of intense pleasure flowed through every fiber of her being. As she floated back to reality, she felt Jaron's body surge inside her as he found his own satisfaction. When he collapsed on top of her, she kissed his shoulder and, wrapping her arms around him, held him to her as she reveled in the feeling that she was completely surrounded by him.

"I'm too heavy for you," he said, starting to lever himself off her.

Reluctant to let him go, she tightened her arms around him. "That was even more beautiful than the first time," she murmured against his shoulder.

"It's only going to get better each time we make love," he said, kissing her with such tenderness it brought tears to her eyes.

As he moved to her side, her fingers slid over his back and she felt several smooth ridges that she hadn't noticed the first time they made love. Her heart stalled when she remembered the scars on top of his shoulders that she'd asked about that night. He'd given her an excuse about all rodeo riders having their share of scars. But what she felt on his back didn't feel like anything that could have come from riding the rough stock.

"Jaron, could I ask you something?"

Gathering her to him, he kissed the top of her head. "What do you want to know, darlin'?"

With her head pillowed on his shoulder, she looked up at him in the semidarkness. "Are those scars on your back?"

His body stiffened and the smile on his face immediately disappeared. "Yes," he answered tightly.

She could tell by the shadows in his blue eyes that she'd asked him about something he'd just as soon forget. Placing her hand on his cheek, she caressed his jaw. "What happened, Jaron?"

"I don't want to talk about it," he said stubbornly.

"But—"

"You don't need to know," he said, cutting her off. There was an edge to his voice that warned her to drop the matter.

She stared at him for a moment, knowing the blemishes were tied into his reasons for thinking he wasn't right for her. "I'm sorry," she said softly. "I didn't mean to pry."

He closed his eyes a moment. When he opened them, he shook his head. "They don't matter. Let's forget about them and get some rest."

"Maybe I should go back to my room," she said, hating that she'd brought up a painful subject for him. The evening had been perfect until that point and she felt as if she'd ruined the intimacy between them.

His arms tightened around her. "I think you should stay right here."

Glancing up at him, she saw that the shadows in his

eyes were gone, and she knew as far as he was concerned the matter was closed. "All right." She snuggled into his embrace. "But you have to promise to get me up early in the morning."

"Why?"

"I need to do some laundry and I want to go over the list of supplies we need for your horses before I call the feed store to place an order for delivery," she said, yawning.

When they fell silent, Mariah couldn't stop thinking about what she'd discovered. She could only imagine what had taken place all those years ago and what Jaron had been through. He had mentioned that after his mother died no one had cared what happened to him, but she'd thought he was harboring the memory of a disillusioned child. Now she knew it was much more than that. It had been all too real.

It was clear that Jaron had suffered at the hands of someone cruel and heartless. She understood more now than ever before why he had always been quieter and more reserved than the other brothers from the Last Chance Ranch. He had been an abused child and he was still haunted by it.

Placing her arm over his wide chest, she held him close. Her heart ached at the thought of what he must have gone through as a child and, blinking back tears, she vowed not to ask him again about the scars on his back. At some point in time, if he felt ready to tell her what happened, she'd listen. But she'd rather die than dredge up such painful memories for him ever again.

But how would his unwillingness to share the rest

of what happened all those years ago—likely, the most traumatic events—affect their relationship? Would he eventually be able to open up and tell her the details of what he'd endured? Or would he try to keep them locked away from her and suffer in silence?

Mariah wasn't sure what the answers were or what obstacles she faced in trying to help him move past that part of his life. All she knew was that she had to be patient. Pressing him for the answers would only shut him down and she might never learn what happened.

She sighed as she felt herself start to fall asleep. Jaron needed her patience and understanding. Fortunately, she had an overabundance of patience where he was concerned. Otherwise, she wouldn't have waited seven years for him to finally realize they were meant to be together.

Seven

The following Sunday, as Jaron drove his truck along the road leading to the Lucky Ace Ranch, he glanced over at Mariah in the passenger seat beside him. Since asking about his scars after they made love, she hadn't mentioned them again. He knew she was still curious about what had made the marks, but if he told her how he got the lines crisscrossing his back, then he'd have to tell her about his sadistic father. That was sure to cause her to ask more questions that he wasn't about to answer.

The more he revealed about his past, the bigger the chance that she would either remember hearing about his father and the murders he'd committed or more likely, she would do an internet search and find out the whole sordid story. He felt safe that she hadn't done that already because of the judge ruling that he could take his mother's maiden name after his father's conviction. But just the thought of Mariah looking at him with fear and suspicion the way some of the foster families he'd been sent to live with had done made a knot the size of his fist form in his stomach.

"Have you told your brothers about hiring me to work at the ranch?" she asked, breaking into his disturbing thoughts.

They hadn't discussed when or what they were going to tell the rest of the family about her working at the Wild Maverick, but he suspected her reasons for keeping things on the down low were similar to his own. She looked a little uneasy and he felt just as apprehensive. He'd already gone through one interrogation with his brothers Ryder and T.J. He wasn't looking forward to another inquisition by the other three. And there wasn't a doubt in his mind that was exactly what was going to happen.

The entire family had known about Mariah's crush on him. And they weren't blind. They could tell he was just as attracted to her as she was to him. They'd also known that his insistence he was too old for her had evolved over the years from a valid reason into an excuse to keep her at arm's length. In the past few years, he'd endured their good-natured ribbing about asking Mariah out on a date, but if Ryder and T.J.'s reaction was any indication, they were also concerned that it might not work out between them. Or worse yet, that one or both of them would end up with a broken heart.

"I didn't have a choice about telling Ryder and T.J.,"

he admitted as he steered the truck onto the ranch road leading up to Lane and Taylor's house. "I ran into them the night I went to pick up our supper at the Broken Spoke. But I asked them to keep a lid on the news until we were all together."

"I had the chance to tell Bria when she called about the change in plans for Sam's party, but she wasn't feeling well and I didn't want to go into it," Mariah said, nodding.

Jaron could understand her reluctance. It was his guess that her sister would have the same concerns as his brothers, and if Bria wasn't feeling well, Mariah probably didn't want to worry her.

Of course none of them knew that he and Mariah weren't just employer and employee. Since they'd made love after their Valentine's Day dinner, she had moved into the master suite with him, and as far as he was concerned that was where she would stay for as long as she wanted.

A twinge of guilt once again settled across his shoulders. He didn't think he was leading her on. He'd made it clear that he wasn't making any promises, and she had told him she wasn't asking for any. But was it really that simple? How long would she be satisfied with that arrangement? For that matter, how long would he?

As he parked his truck by his brothers' pickups and SUVs, Jaron decided that he really didn't want to know the answers. He was afraid that if he knew for certain Mariah thought there was a chance something would come of their time together, he wouldn't have the strength to do the right thing for both of them and send her on her way.

"Time to face the family," he said, taking a deep breath as he got out of the truck and walked around to open the passenger door for her.

"I…um… I'm not telling Bria or the other women about the nature of our relationship," she stated. "Only that I'm working at your ranch."

He nodded. "It's nobody's business but ours."

"I agree." Her smile caused his heart to thump hard against his rib cage. "Besides, I like the intimate feeling of it being our little secret."

"I feel the same way," he said, wishing he could take her in his arms and reassure her.

He held her hand as she got down from the truck, then made sure there was a respectable amount of space between them as they walked side by side up to the house. Even though he would like nothing more than to hold her to his side, if any of his family was watching it would be a dead giveaway that something was definitely going on between them.

"It's going to be hard as hell keeping my hands off you today," he admitted.

She laughed. "Can you imagine the look on everyone's face if you put your arm around me or kissed me?"

"That could be dangerous." He grinned. "I thought Ryder was going to have to perform the Heimlich maneuver on poor old T.J. that night in the Broken Spoke. And all I did was tell them I'd hired you to be my housekeeper."

"I can only imagine how he would react if he learned

there was more." She smiled as she reached up to press the doorbell. "Well, here we go."

"This is going to be one hell of a long day," Jaron muttered when he heard someone approaching to let them in.

When his brother Lane opened the door, he looked surprised to see Mariah with Jaron. "It's good to see both of you." He watched Lane glance at the array of parked vehicles in the driveway before his gaze swung back to Jaron. "Come on in. The guys are babysitting the kids in the game room and the women are in the kitchen."

"I'll go see if they need help finishing dinner," Mariah said, starting down the hall.

As he watched her go, Jaron couldn't keep from noticing the enticing sway of her blue-jean-clad hips. Damned if he couldn't look at that view all day long.

"Come on, bro. I've got a beer with your name on it, and you've got some explaining to do," Lane said, grinning.

Jaron followed his brother and upon entering the game room saw T.J. down on his hands and knees, giving the kids horseback rides around the pool table. The rest of his brothers were standing at the bar watching the show.

Lane walked behind the bar and uncapped a bottle of Lone Star, then handed it to Jaron. "I think our brother has something to tell us, boys."

"Is something up?" Nate Rafferty asked, perking up.

The youngest of the Raffertys, Nate and Sam were the only biological siblings of the bunch. But all six of them couldn't have been closer if they had the same blood running through their veins. Thanks to their foster father, they had bonded into a close family, and Jaron knew that every one of them would have his back when the chips were down—the same as he would have theirs.

Taking a swig of his beer, Jaron shook his head. "Nothing going on that I know of."

"Then, why did you and Mariah arrive together?" Lane asked, raising one dark eyebrow. Being a licensed psychologist, the man had a way of asking questions that cut right to the heart of the matter and in the process got the attention of everyone around him.

"You might as well tell them, Jaron," Ryder said, grinning. "You know they won't give you a minute's peace until you do."

"What do you know that we don't?" Sam asked, giving Ryder a curious glance.

Ryder shook his head. "It's Jaron's news, not mine."

"Okay, Jaron, give it up," Sam said. "What's going on with you and Mariah besides dancing around each other like two birds in a mating ritual?"

After explaining what happened three weeks ago at the Broken Spoke and what he'd learned about her losing her job and her roommate, he finished, "I needed a cook and a housekeeper and she needed a job. I offered her the position and she accepted. End of story."

"And you think having Mariah in the kitchen is going to work out?" Sam laughed. "From what Bria has told me, Mariah isn't known for her cooking abilities."

Jaron couldn't keep from grinning. "Yeah, I found

that out when she set the kitchen on fire the first morning she tried to make breakfast."

When they all stopped laughing, Nate asked, "Are you planning on losing some weight, bro?"

Jaron shook his head. "I made Mariah the ranch manager, and the first thing I had her do was to hire someone else to do the cooking and cleaning."

"But you have a degree in ranch management," Nate said, frowning. "What do you need with—" He stopped short, then, laughing out loud, got a hundred-dollar-bill out of his pocket and plunked it down on the bar. "I've got a hundred bucks that says you'll be walking down the aisle by midsummer."

"I say it'll be sooner than that," T.J. said, interrupting the kids' rides around the pool table to fish his wallet out of his hip pocket. He plunked his hundred dollars on top of Nate's. "They'll be married by the end of May."

"You're both wrong," Ryder said, looking at Jaron as if he was sizing him up. He put his money on top of the growing pile on the bar. "They'll be married by the end of next month."

"I've got this fall," Lane spoke up, adding his bet to the pot.

"I'll take Christmas," Sam said, laying his money on top of the rest.

Disgusted with his brothers, Jaron shook his head as he finished off his beer. "You're all wasting your time and money, because it's not going to happen."

Ryder tossed back the rest of his beer, then, throwing the empty bottle in the recycle bin, clapped Jaron on the shoulder. "If you'll remember, we all said the same thing when we were the ones fighting the inevitable." He laughed. "Get used to it, brother. You're one step away from joining the rest of us in the club of the blissfully hitched."

"Were you kicked in the head by a bull the last time you worked a rodeo?" Jaron asked. Before he'd retired at the ripe old age of thirty-five, Ryder had been a rodeo bullfighter and was without question the bravest man Jaron had ever known. But at the moment, he had serious questions about the man's good sense.

"Gentlemen, I hate to interrupt your lively conversation, but dinner is ready," Lane's wife, Taylor, said from the doorway.

As he and his brothers filed out of the game room and walked down the hall to take their places at the dining room table, Jaron tried to forget about their speculation and their betting pool. Nothing would make him happier than to be free to have a wife and family like they all had. But that life would never be his, and there was no sense lamenting things that he knew he'd never have.

Even if he told Mariah about his old man and she was willing to take the chance that he hadn't inherited some kind of latent cruel streak from him, Jaron wasn't. There was no way he would ever subject his wife and kid to the kind of hell he and his mother had gone through. As far as Jaron was concerned, Simon Collier's brand of crazy ended with him.

Seated at the dining room table with Bria on one side and Jaron on the other, Mariah waited until her sister was preoccupied with her son to reach beneath the tablecloth to place her hand on Jaron's thigh. Other than clearing his throat, he remained completely stoic as he covered her hand with his.

"Bria, are you feeling better?" Lane asked.

"Now that I know what the problem is, I'm feeling a lot better," her sister said, smiling. Mariah watched Bria glance at Sam before announcing, "Sam and I are going to have another baby in the fall."

"That's wonderful!" Summer McClain said from across the table. She smiled at her husband, Ryder. "We can go to doctor appointments together."

"It looks as if the family is having a baby boom," Nate said, putting his arm around his very pregnant wife, Jessie. "We're due in a month, Heather and T.J. are due this summer and both of you are due in the fall."

Mariah felt Jaron lightly squeeze her hand where it still rested on his thigh. "I'm betting you'll both have boys."

Taking her cue from him, she shook her head. "Both of them are going to have girls," she said adamantly.

She really didn't care and she knew Jaron didn't, either. They were both going to love the babies no matter what. But she knew what he was doing. They had argued about the child's gender every time one of the sisters-in-law got pregnant. The family might realize there was more going on between them than a working relationship if they didn't continue the good-natured feud.

"They're at it again," T.J. said, laughing. "How do you two work together when you can't agree on much of anything?"

"I work inside the house and he works outside the house," Mariah said, thinking quickly.

Jaron shrugged. "I've always been happier working outside."

"I can't fault you there," Ryder said, nodding. "I think if I had to be stuck inside all day I'd end up climbing the walls."

All of the men seemed to agree and Mariah relaxed when the conversation turned to talk of the calving season and plans for improvements around their ranches. By the time dinner was over and she was helping clear the table before cake and ice cream was served for Sam's birthday, she couldn't help but be a bit envious of the happy couples. They all had what she wanted—homes and families of their own.

She hoped that was in her future with Jaron. There wasn't a doubt in her mind that if he could reconcile his past it was a possibility. But what if he couldn't? What did that mean for her?

"How are things really going with you and Jaron?" Bria asked when they reached the kitchen with bowls of leftover food.

"Just fine," Mariah answered. "He works outside and I—"

"I heard you before," Bria said. "I also noticed that you two were holding hands during dinner."

"We're—" She stopped herself when she realized she really didn't know what they were. They weren't a couple and they weren't just friends.

"I don't claim to be an expert on matters of the heart," Taylor said from the other side of the kitchen island, "but ever since I became part of this family, I've seen Jaron watch you. And let me tell you, something has changed. He looks at you now as though you're the treasure at the end of the rainbow."

Setting a platter of fried chicken on the counter, Summer nodded. "That man is crazy in love with you, Mariah."

"Summer's right," Jessie said, placing containers of leftovers in the refrigerator. "He can't keep his eyes off you."

Mariah shook her head. "I know he has feelings for me, but I'm not sure I'd call it love."

"I would," Heather interjected as she dipped ice cream into dessert cups. "He looks at you the same way our husbands look at us."

Bria put her arm around Mariah. "And you've loved him since the day you met him."

"So when should we start planning your bridal shower?" Taylor asked, smiling.

Mariah shook her head. "I'm not sure it will ever come to that."

"Why not?" Bria asked.

"I'm not really sure," Mariah answered. "There's something that happened in his past that's holding him back."

"He won't talk about it because he doesn't think you'll understand?" Summer guessed.

"How did you know?" she asked, surprised.

"I had the same problem with Ryder," Summer answered.

"Even Sam waited until it almost ended our marriage before he opened up and finally told me why he got into trouble with the law when he was a teenager and how that caused him to become so driven to succeed," Bria agreed.

"I think all of them were reluctant to tell us what they'd done to get themselves sent to the Last Chance Ranch," Jessie added. "I've never seen Nate more reluctant and nervous than he was the day he told me about the trouble he got into when he was younger."

"I don't know about the others, but T.J. didn't think I'd be able to look past what he'd done years ago and accept him for who he is now," Heather said, setting the dessert cups of ice cream on a silver tray. "Silly man."

"It's a matter of trust," Summer advised. "The guys had to get used to the idea of trusting us with their greatest source of shame."

"And that isn't easy for any man," Taylor said, nodding.

"I know Jaron is a good man," Mariah insisted. "I don't care what happened when he was a boy."

"But he does, and he doesn't want you to be disappointed in him," Heather said, picking up the tray to carry it into the dining room.

"Give him time, Mariah," Bria said, giving her a hug. "When Jaron is ready, he'll take that leap of faith and tell you everything that he's trying so hard to hide because he doesn't think you'll understand."

As she and the other women walked back into the dining room, Mariah hoped they were right. Whatever secrets haunted Jaron were keeping him rooted in a very painful past, and she wanted to do whatever she could to help him move forward and leave it all behind.

Unfortunately, her fears that he might never be able to open up with her increased with each passing day. He had made progress and told her about his mother. But she had a feeling his father was the key to the worst part of his past. And until he told her what secrets he was trying to keep hidden, all she could do was love him and wait.

"You almost caused me to have a heart attack when you put your hand on my thigh during supper tonight," Jaron said when they walked into the master suite and he turned on the light.

Turning, Mariah put her arms around his neck and kissed his chin. "You looked so yummy, I couldn't help myself," she said, smiling up at the most handsome man she'd ever known.

He laughed. "Yummy, huh?"

She nodded as she pressed her lips on the pulse at the base of his throat. "All I could think about was how sexy you are and how much I wanted to kiss you and feel you touch me."

"As soon as I get these clothes off you, I intend to do both, darlin'," he said, reaching for the hem of her shirt. Leaning close, he whispered in her ear, "And I want you touching me."

"Oh, you can count on it, cowboy," she said, tugging his long-sleeve Western-cut shirt from the waistband of his jeans.

They each removed the other's clothes and in no time

at all, their clothing lay in a pile at their feet and Jaron was pulling her to him. Mariah shivered at the feel of his firm masculine flesh touching her softer feminine skin.

When he captured her lips with his, she felt as if she would melt from the heat flowing through her veins. By the time he lifted his head, her knees had failed her completely and she was sagging against him. No other man's kiss had ever affected her that way, and she knew in her heart none ever would.

The heat in his eyes caused her heart to race and her breathing to become shallow when she gazed up at him. "I—I want you now," she gasped.

He nibbled kisses down to the hollow below her ear. "But I thought you wanted me to touch you, darlin'."

Finding it hard to make her vocal cords work, she shook her head. "Please…if you don't…make love to me now…I think I'm going to…burn to a cinder."

"I want you just as much, Mariah," he said, sounding completely winded. He surprised her when he lifted her to him and in one smooth motion entered her.

Her breath caught as she wrapped her arms around his wide shoulders and her legs around his narrow hips. Resting her forehead on his shoulder, she sighed contentedly. "You feel so good…inside me."

"I intended to go…slow," he said, sounding as if he was clenching his jaw. "But I want you too damned much."

"We can go slow when we make love a little later," she said, relishing the fullness of having his body so deeply embedded in hers. "Right now, I need you to love me, Jaron."

Without another word, he carried her over to the side of the bed and sat down with her on his lap. She loved that they faced each other and would both be free to caress and kiss while their bodies moved as one.

When he began to rock them, Mariah enjoyed the friction and urgent pace of their lovemaking. Kissing his lean cheeks, the column of his neck and his collarbone, she moved in unison with him as they raced toward the culmination of the energy building inside both of them.

Feeling her feminine muscles begin to tighten around him, she clung to his shoulders to keep from being lost as she gave in to the elegant tension holding them in its grip. Apparently her release triggered his, and when he thrust into her one final time she felt him shudder as he filled her with his essence.

As they held each other while their bodies slowly drifted back to reality, she suddenly felt him go completely still. "Dammit all to hell!" he swore vehemently.

"What's wrong?" she asked, alarmed by his obvious anger.

"Mariah, I'm so sorry," he said, hugging her to him.

"Why on earth are you apologizing?" She leaned back and placed her palms on either side of his face, forced him to look at her. "What we just shared was beautiful."

He shook his head as he lifted her to sit on the bed beside him. "I was so desperate for you, I forgot to use a condom."

As the realization of what he was saying sank in, she automatically covered her lower stomach with her hand in a protective gesture. "I doubt... I mean, the odds are that I won't become pregnant," she said, trying to come to terms with the fact that she wasn't all that upset by the possibility.

What was wrong with her? The last thing she needed was an unplanned pregnancy, and especially with a man who might not ever be able to commit himself completely to their relationship.

"I've never failed to remember to use protection before," he said, rising to pace the length of the room.

"Jaron, it's not the end of the world. I'd have to do some calculations, but I don't think it's the right time of the month for that to happen," she said, trying to think if it was or not.

When he turned to make another trip across the room, she caught sight of the ugly scars marring his back for the first time. Her breath lodged in her lungs at how many of the ugly ridges crisscrossed his otherwise flawless skin.

Although she'd felt them and caught a fleeting glimpse of them a couple of times when they made love, Jaron had been careful not to let her see the extent of the damage he'd suffered. For the past week, he had already been dressed when she woke up in the mornings and she instinctively knew he'd planned it that way. But he was so angry with himself for forgetting to use protection, he had dropped his guard, and in doing so, she'd finally seen the marks he'd been trying so hard to keep hidden.

Her eyes filled with tears and, getting up from the bed, she walked over to lightly place her hand on his back. She felt him go perfectly still before he started to jerk away from her.

"Don't, Jaron," she said, catching hold of his arm to stop him.

When he turned to face her, she wrapped her arms around him and held him to her as tears streamed down her cheeks. Groaning, he pulled her closer and they simply held each other for several long minutes.

"I give you my word that I'll stand by you if you do become pregnant," he finally said, breaking the silence.

He didn't want to discuss his scars and how he got them and that was fine with her. At the moment, she couldn't think of a thing to say that wouldn't sound as though she pitied him. That was something she knew for certain that he wouldn't want to hear.

Instead, she concentrated on what he'd said about a possible pregnancy. "It never crossed my mind that you wouldn't be there for me," she said, shaking her head.

"I guess we'd better get some sleep." He released her to pick up their clothes. "I have to be up at dawn to take my shift in the calving barn."

Half an hour later as she lay in Jaron's arms, Mariah couldn't seem to turn off her thoughts. She hated to think of what he must have gone through as a child—how much emotional and physical pain he had endured. And as bad as the marks on his body were, they were nothing compared to the scars he carried that weren't visible. As long as she had a breath left in her body, she would fight like a wildcat to keep someone from doing anything like that to her child.

Her heart skipped a beat at the thought that she might

become pregnant with Jaron's baby. She'd told him that it was unlikely. But the more she thought about it, the more she realized that wasn't the case at all. She was right in the middle of her cycle, and therefore it was her most fertile time of the month.

That should have been enough to send her into a blind panic. The fact that it didn't came as a bit of a shock.

She wanted children, but did she want one now? Was she ready to become a mother?

It certainly wasn't a good time for that to happen. Knowing Jaron the way she did, if she were to become pregnant there was a very good chance he would insist that he needed to do the right thing and marry her. And as much as she loved him, that wasn't going to happen. At least, not where things stood with them now.

There were too many issues between her and Jaron that hadn't been addressed. Unfortunately, even if they did get everything out in the open, the problems might never be resolved, and bringing a child into that would be unfair to all of them. Besides, as far as she was concerned the only reason two people should consider getting married was because they loved each other and it was a natural progression of their relationship.

Forcing herself to relax, she tried to remember what Bria and the other women had told her. They had suggested that she should be patient and wait. When he was ready, he'd trust her with his secrets and tell her what had been holding him back. She could only hope they were right.

Eight

A few days after his family's get-together, Jaron propped his forearms on the top rail of one of the enclosures in the calving shed as he waited for the newborn bull calf he'd just helped deliver get to its feet. Thankfully things were slowing down with the heifers and there were only a handful left that hadn't dropped their calves. He was glad the next wave of cows to give birth had already had calves in the past and weren't as likely to have the problems a first-time mother might experience.

Every time he thought about first-time mothers or something giving birth, his heart stuttered and he had to take a deep breath in an attempt to settle himself. What if he'd made Mariah pregnant?

He still couldn't believe he'd needed her so badly that

he'd forgotten to protect her. Not one time since he'd become sexually active in his late teens had he failed to remember one of Hank's rules for life. What was there about Mariah that had caused him to lose his head and forget something as important as using a condom when they made love?

Swallowing hard, he briefly thought about having a child with her. If things were different and he'd had a halfway decent start in life, he'd like nothing more than to have a family with Mariah. But he'd never allowed himself to contemplate fatherhood, because having a kid had never been something he ever thought would happen. Unfortunately, one careless moment sure as hell had him thinking about it now.

Of course, if Mariah did become pregnant, there was no question that he'd do the right thing and make her his wife. But he couldn't help but be concerned about taking that step. Although he would gladly lay down his life to protect her and keep her from harm, how could he be sure that he hadn't inherited some part of his father's cruel nature? Even the slightest bit would be totally unacceptable.

He had no problem being able to control his temper and he'd never been prone to violent behavior. But his biggest fear had been and always would be that he'd turn out to be like his old man.

Caught up in his turbulent thoughts, Jaron welcomed the interruption when the cell phone clipped to his belt rang. But when he looked at the caller ID he felt the icy fingers of dread squeeze his chest. The call was coming from the Texas Department of Criminal Justice. He only knew one person doing time, and he was the last man on earth Jaron wanted to talk to.

How the hell had the bastard found him? When he'd had his last name changed, the judge had ordered the court records sealed due to Jaron's age and the reason for his request. And why, after twenty years with no contact between them, was his old man calling now?

Jaron's first inclination was to ignore the call. He hadn't seen or heard from his father since he'd testified against him in court all those years ago. And that was just the way he'd like to keep it. But unless Simon Collier had changed, he'd keep calling until he got hold of Jaron. That thought was even more objectionable than taking the call now.

Answering the phone, he breathed a little easier when the caller turned out to be a prison chaplain.

"Mr. Lambert, my name is Reverend John Perkins. I'm a chaplain for the Texas Department of Criminal Justice and I'm calling to let you know that your father has been transferred to the hospital unit in Galveston. I was with him when the doctor told him that he only has a few days left," the man said, his voice sympathetic. "Simon asked me to call and tell you that he wants to see you right away. There's something he needs to tell you before he passes."

"I'm sorry you wasted your time, Reverend, but he has nothing to say that I want to hear," Jaron stated flatly.

"I understand how you must feel, Mr. Lambert," the chaplain answered calmly. "Simon told me some disturbing things about his relationship with you and that he didn't treat you as well as he should have."

"That's an understatement," Jaron growled. His irritation rising, he added, "Living with Simon Collier was a living hell and I don't care to be reminded of the experience."

"I'm sure you have a lot of anger toward him, but please reconsider, son," Reverend Perkins pleaded. "This might be your last chance to see your father and make your peace with him. He asked me to stress that what he has to say is very important and something you'll want to know and need to hear."

Jaron could tell the man wasn't going to give up, and he didn't feel like explaining the many reasons he was going to ignore his old man's request. "I'm not making any promises, but I give you my word that I'll think about it," he finally conceded, hoping that would appease the man.

He would think about it, he decided. But only long enough to reject the notion outright.

"Thank you. I'll tell your father," the man said before he ended the call.

Clipping his phone back onto his belt, Jaron reached up to rub the tension tightening the back of his neck. Mariah could very well be pregnant with his baby and he had a new ranch to run. The last thing he needed piled on his already full plate was his father's dying plea to see him.

"I'm going to call it a day," he told his men. "If you need me, call the house."

"See you tomorrow, boss," one of the men called after him as he turned to leave.

When he walked out of the barn and headed toward the house, Jaron tried to forget the phone call and concentrate on spending the evening with the most exciting woman he'd ever known. As his foster father used to say, sometimes a man had to forget the past, stop thinking about the future and concentrate on the present. And that was just what he intended to do. At least for tonight.

After sharing a frozen pizza for dinner, Mariah cuddled with Jaron on the couch in the family room. He'd surprised her when he'd come in from the calving shed earlier in the afternoon and asked her to join him in the shower. That had led to them making love, and she was encouraged that he felt free enough with her to be spontaneous. But it had distracted her from something she needed to tell him, and she knew as surely as she knew her own name that the phone call she'd taken was significant and had to do with his past.

She was a little hesitant to tell him about the call. She didn't want to remind him of something that would upset him. But it might be the motivation he needed to open up and talk to her.

"When you came in this afternoon, you made me forget something I was supposed to tell you," she said, laying her head on his shoulder.

Smiling, he kissed the top of her head, then reached for the television remote. "You didn't seem to mind the distraction."

"Believe me, I'm not complaining," she said, sliding her hand inside his shirt to caress his warm skin.

"Keep that up and I'll make you forget all over again that you're supposed to tell me something," he said, giving her a promising grin.

"There was a phone call for you not long before you came in from the calving shed," she said, removing her hand from his shirt.

"Who was it?" he asked, using the remote to search for something to watch on television.

"He said his name was Reverend Perkins. He was calling from the prison hospital in Galveston." Resting against him, she noticed an immediate tensing of his muscles.

"What did he have to say?" Jaron asked, his voice tight and controlled.

"He wanted to know if he could speak to you." She sat up to look at him. "He said it was really important and—"

"Is that all he had to say?" Jaron interrupted, staring at the on-screen television guide as if it held the secrets of the universe.

"He told me…your father is dying," she said, knowing from the look on his face that the reverend telling her the nature of the call angered him.

Tossing the remote onto the coffee table, he suddenly gave up his interest in the television and rose to his feet. "He had no right to tell you that."

"I…um, asked him what the call was pertaining to," she admitted, getting up from the couch.

Turning, he pinned her with his sharp blue gaze.
"Why?"

"When the man said it was important, I offered
to take a message," she answered, defending herself.
"That's when he told me about your dad and I immediately suggested he call your cell number."

"Don't call that bastard behind bars my dad." Jaron's
voice was more of a growl than his normal baritone and
the muscle working along his jawline attested to the
fact that he was absolutely furious. "He may have made
my mother pregnant, but he was never a father to me."

"Jaron, was he the one who caused those scars on
your back?" The dark look on his face was all the answer she needed. "At some point, you're going to have to
deal with your feelings about this and put it behind you
or it's going to destroy you—it's going to destroy us."

"Drop it, Mariah," he warned as he started toward
the foyer.

"Why won't you talk to me about it, Jaron?" she
asked, following him. "Why won't you let me help you?"

"Because it's none of your concern," he said, continuing on toward the kitchen.

His sharp words cut her deeper than if he'd used a
knife, but she still had to try. "Jaron, don't shut me out.
Talk to me. There's nothing you could tell me that we
can't get through together."

When he reached the back door, he shrugged into
his jacket and grabbed his hat, crammed it on his head.
"Let it alone, Mariah. There are things you don't need
to know—things you don't *want* to know about me."

"Where are you going?"

"Out to the calving shed."

"Please stay and we'll work through this," she said, trying again.

"No amount of discussion is going to change a single thing, Mariah," he said, stubbornly shaking his head.

Knowing they'd reached an impasse, she warned, "Jaron, if you walk out that door, I won't be here when you get back." Her eyes filled with tears, but she blinked them away. She was determined not to let him see how badly his rejection was hurting her.

When he turned back toward her, his handsome face was devoid of all expression. He stared at her for several long moments before he reached for the doorknob. "Wait until morning. The drive over to the Sugar Creek Ranch will be safer in the daylight."

Mariah's heart felt as if it shattered into a million pieces as he walked out of the house and pulled the door shut behind him. The finality of the situation was overwhelming and tears flowed freely down her cheeks as she ran upstairs to her room.

Collapsing on the bed, she couldn't stop crying as she tried to think of what she should do. She wouldn't have given Jaron an ultimatum if she hadn't been so hurt by his telling her it was none of her business. She loved him—had always loved him—and it tore her apart that he wouldn't allow her to help him. But he had made his choice and it wasn't her.

Her heart ached more than she thought was possible as she got up and went into the closet and started throwing clothes into her overnight bag. It didn't matter that he thought she should wait until morning to leave. She wasn't about to stay where she obviously wasn't wanted.

As she grabbed her purse and overnight bag, she looked around. She'd come back to get the rest of her things in a few days after she'd had a chance to calm down.

On the drive from the Wild Maverick Ranch to Bria and Sam's, she knew that it was over for good with Jaron. Keeping his secrets from her was more important to him that she was. It was a hard realization, but one that she could no longer deny.

She had held out hope that he would one day be able to tell her about his past and she could prove to him that it didn't matter to her what he'd done all those years ago. It was the man he had become that mattered— the man she loved. But she knew now that was never going to happen.

It suddenly occurred to her that it might not be something he'd done that he was trying to hide. Given his reaction when she'd told him that the prison chaplain had called, it could very well be that it was something his father had done. But Jaron wouldn't talk to her about that, either.

When she parked the car and walked up to the Sugar Creek ranch house, Bria opened the door before Mariah had the chance to knock. Reaching out, her sister wrapped her in a comforting hug. "Are you all right?"

Shrugging, Mariah could only shake her head as a fresh wave of tears slid down her cheeks. "H-how did… you know?" she asked when the wave of emotion finally ran its course.

"Jaron called Sam to tell him that the two of you had argued and he found you gone when he returned to the house. He said he figured you were on your way over here and asked Sam to let him know you arrived safely," Bria explained. "What happened?"

"I really don't feel like going into it now," Mariah said, suddenly feeling drained of energy. "Could we talk about it tomorrow?"

"Of course," Bria said, guiding her toward the stairs.

A few minutes later, as Mariah got into bed, she curled up on her side and hugged one of the pillows to her chest in an effort to ease some of her anguish. How could everything have gone so wrong so fast? Why was he doing this to them? Why couldn't he trust that her love for him was strong enough to overlook the demons of his past and help him put them behind him for good?

Just a few short hours ago, Jaron had held her in his arms and loved her with such tenderness she'd felt as if their souls had touched. Now she was at one ranch and he was at another. And the most frustrating thing about it all was that she really didn't know why.

A couple of days after Mariah left the ranch, Jaron looked at the miserable man staring back at him in the bathroom mirror. He looked like hell and felt even worse.

He'd known up front that one day Mariah would leave, but he hadn't thought it would be this soon or that her departure would cause him to feel as though he was dying inside. All of the pain his father had inflicted on him when he was a kid was nothing compared to the debilitating ache that had settled in his chest when he'd returned to the house two nights ago and found Mariah gone.

When his cell phone rang, he glanced at the caller ID and, groaning, shook his head. He didn't want to deal with any of his well-meaning brothers right now, and especially not Lane. No amount of psychology was going to change things, and he had no doubt that Lane was going to try to draw him out and get to the bottom of what happened between him and Mariah. Ignoring the call, he let it go to voice mail and walked out of the bathroom to get dressed.

As he pulled on his clothes, he once again replayed the argument he'd had with Mariah. She'd told him that he was letting the issues with his father destroy him. Was that what he was doing by trying to hide the shame of being the son of a serial killer? It had been twenty years since he'd been the victim of his father's violent temper. By not sharing the shame of his past with Mariah, was he allowing the bastard to victimize him yet again?

Besides being sent to the Last Chance Ranch and gaining five brothers he loved and could count on to be there for him no matter what, the only other good thing that had happened in his miserable life had been Mariah. Was he going to allow the old man to destroy what he had with her?

As a kid, he'd found a way to end the abuse by turning his father in to the law. Could confronting Simon Collier now put an end to the torment for good? Or would he be dredging up things that would only make him feel worse?

The last thing Jaron wanted to do was lay eyes on the monster who had ruined his life. But if there was even the slightest chance that he could salvage what was left of his life by confronting the man, then that was exactly what he was going to do.

Six hours later, as he walked out of the prison hospital, Jaron looked up at the sky and for the first time in longer than he cared to remember, he felt as though a tremendous weight had been lifted off his shoulders. He had dreaded seeing Simon again and had damned near talked himself out of visiting the man on the drive down to Galveston. But when he walked into the room and saw the frail old man lying almost lifeless on the hospital bed, Jaron knew he'd made the right decision. It would have been cruel not to give the man his last wish and would have made Jaron no better than Simon.

But Jaron never could have imagined that one death-bed confession would set him free and give him hope of being able to build a future with the woman he loved. And, God help him, he did love Mariah.

For years he'd tried to convince himself that he was too old for her or that he wasn't the type of man she needed. He'd even gone so far as telling himself he didn't believe in love. But the truth of the matter was, from the moment he'd met Mariah, he'd been fascinated with her, and he'd used every excuse he could to be close to her. And that included arguing with her over the gender of their nieces and nephews before they were born.

He needed her as much as he needed the air he breathed, and he knew as sure as the sun rose in the east each morning that he always would. And there wasn't a doubt in his mind that she loved him just as much.

But straightening things out between them wasn't going to be easy. The other night, he had done a lot of damage to their relationship when he'd shut her out and told her his past was none of her business. She might never be able to overlook that. But if he had to get down on his hands and knees to beg her forgiveness, that was exactly what he intended to do. Nothing was more important to him than making things right with the woman who owned him heart and soul.

As he walked across the parking area to his truck and got in, he checked his watch. He had a five-hour drive to get to the Sugar Creek Ranch and a stop to make in Waco before he got there.

Swearing a blue streak, he started the truck and steered it out onto the highway headed north. Waiting until morning was one of the hardest decisions he'd ever had to make. But it would be late by the time he arrived at Sam and Bria's, and what he had to say to Mariah wasn't something that could be covered in a matter of minutes.

He released a heavy sigh as he merged into traffic on the interstate. Normally he was a very patient man. But without question he was facing the longest, most frustrating night of his life.

* * *

Sitting on the window seat in the bedroom she always used when she stayed overnight at her sister's, Mariah closed her eyes as she waited to see what the stick in her hand was going to indicate. If the claim on the back of the box was true, the test she'd chosen showed the earliest, most accurate results possible.

Unable to wait any longer, she opened one eye to peek at the tiny screen. Opening her other eye, she stared at the pregnancy test in disbelief. It not only displayed the word *pregnant*, it gave the estimated number of weeks.

"Well, that explains a lot," she murmured, placing her hand over her lower stomach.

When she'd awakened feeling sick the morning after she'd left the Wild Maverick Ranch, she'd chalked it up to having cried herself to sleep the night before. But feeling the same way two mornings in a row, she'd driven to a drugstore up in Stephenville to purchase one of the tests to rule out the possibility that she was expecting. But instead of doing that, it had confirmed that she was indeed going to have Jaron's baby.

Now what was she going to do? She was not only jobless, homeless and pregnant, she was at odds with the father of her baby.

Tears filled her eyes when she thought about the man she'd loved since she was eighteen years old. Why did he have to be so darned stubborn?

As she sat there staring at the stick in her hand, wondering how she was going to tell the love of her life that he was going to be a daddy, someone knocked on the bedroom door. "Mariah, sweetie, do you mind if I come in?" her sister asked from the other side.

Swiping at her eyes, she tucked the pregnancy test into the pocket of her jeans. "Come on in, Bria."

Her sister immediately opened the door and walked over to sit beside her on the window seat. "How are you feeling today?"

Mariah shrugged one shoulder. "About the same. Disillusioned. Hopeless. Sad. Take your pick."

Bria shook her head. "I'm not talking about your emotions. I'm asking about your morning sickness."

Shocked, Mariah turned to look at her. "How did you know?"

Smiling, Bria put her arm around Mariah's shoulders and gave her a reassuring hug. "I recognize the symptoms. When the smell of bacon frying sent you running from the kitchen yesterday morning, it raised my suspicions. When it happened again this morning, I knew for sure."

"How can you stand the smell when your cook is making breakfast?" Mariah asked. "As soon as I walked into the kitchen I thought I was going to die."

"Bacon doesn't bother me," Bria answered. "It's the smell of coffee that sends me running." She laughed. "Poor Sam has to go down to the bunkhouse now if he wants his morning coffee."

Mariah couldn't keep from feeling envious. Knowing her brother-in-law, he didn't mind at all. Sam Rafferty would walk through fire for Bria and do whatever it took to make her comfortable. She just wished Jaron felt that way about her.

"Isn't it a little soon for me to be feeling sick?" Mariah asked, glad that she had her sister to talk to about it.

Bria shook her head. "It's different for every woman and can happen at any time, although mornings are the most common. Some women get sick right away, while others don't have a problem for a few weeks. And some aren't bothered with morning sickness at all."

"You might know I wouldn't be lucky enough to be in that last group." She sighed. "Please tell me it doesn't last long."

"I wish I could," Bria said, her voice sympathetic. "It's not an exact science, and each pregnancy is different. For some women it's just a few days and others it's a couple of months. But it usually goes away by the time you get to the end of your first trimester."

Mariah groaned. "That sounds like an eternity."

Bria nodded. "It feels that way sometimes." They were silent for a few moments before she asked, "When are you going to tell Jaron?"

"I don't know." Mariah reached into her jeans pocket and withdrew the pregnancy test to show her sister. "I took this a little while ago and it indicates I'm between one and two weeks along. I guess I'll tell him when I go over to the Wild Maverick to clear out the rest of my things next week."

Bria surprised her when she laughed. "Sweetie, I don't think it will take that long."

"What do you mean?" Mariah asked, confused by her sister's speculation.

"I know Jaron loves you, and it's my guess that he won't be able to wait for you to come back to the

ranch," Bria said, apparently more confident about it
than Mariah was. "I think he'll be over here within the
next few days. Remember how Sam came after me when
we were having problems?"

"This is different," Mariah insisted. "Sam was willing to talk to you and try to work things out. Jaron re-
fuses to do that. Knowing him, the first thing he'll do
when he learns there's a baby on the way will be to
tell me he'll do the right thing and we'll get married."
She shook her head. "That's not going to happen. He'd
want to keep his secrets even if we were married and
it would end in disaster."

Bria nodded. "I can understand that. Sam's reluctance to share all of himself with me almost ended our
marriage."

"I'm not sure Jaron will ever be able to open up and
tell me what haunts him," Mariah said, staring down
at her hands twisted into a tight knot in her lap. "One
of the reasons I left the other night was because he told
me that his issues were none of my business. That's not
exactly the basis for a lasting relationship."

"Give him time, Mariah," Bria advised as she rose to
leave. "I know he loves you. He looks at you the same
way Sam looks at me."

"I know he loves me," Mariah admitted. Looking up
at her sister, she shook her head. "But there are times
when love just isn't enough."

Nine

The next morning, when Jaron parked his truck in Sam and Bria's driveway, he stared through the windshield at the house for several minutes before he finally took a deep breath and got out. He'd tossed and turned the entire night, going over what he intended to say to Mariah. Nothing he'd come up with was adequate to cover how bad he felt over the way he'd handled things with her.

Knocking on the back door, he waited for what seemed like forever before Sam opened it. "Hey there, Jaron. I've been expecting you. How are you doing?"

"I'm betting about the same as you when you screwed up with Bria," Jaron answered.

Sam nodded. "Yeah, I figured you've been going through hell the past few days."

"Where is she?" he asked, looking around.

"Upstairs. First door on the left." When Jaron started to cross the kitchen, Sam stopped him. "Wait a minute. I'll be right back." He disappeared into the pantry. When he returned, he shoved a box of tissues into Jaron's hands.

"What are these for?" Jaron asked, frowning.

His brother gave him a knowing smile as he rocked back on his heels. "Trust me. They'll come in handy."

Jaron groaned. "I hate when a woman cries. But when it's Mariah doing the crying, it feels as if I've been punched in the gut."

"It's our penance for screwing up," Sam agreed, nodding. "Good luck," he added when Jaron started down the hall.

When he reached the top of the stairs, he knocked on the door. He thought about calling her name, but stopped himself. For one thing, Sam and Bria's little boy might be sleeping. And for another, as bad as he'd messed up, he wasn't sure Mariah would let him in if she knew who was knocking.

"Hello, Jaron," Bria said, opening the door. She stepped back for him to enter the room. "It's good to see you."

He nodded but didn't take his eyes off Mariah sitting on the window seat across the room. She looked tired, and he figured she hadn't been sleeping any better the past few nights than he had. But it was the sadness in her eyes that just about tore him apart. He was the cause of her unhappiness and he could have kicked himself for being such a stubborn jackass.

"I'm sure the two of you have a lot to talk about,"

Bria said, stepping out into the hall. "If you need anything, I'll be downstairs with Sam."

Jaron barely noticed when his sister-in-law closed the door with a quiet click. All of his attention was focused on the beautiful woman staring at him from across the room. She looked miserable. Knowing he was the cause made him feel lower than the stuff he scraped off his boots after a trip through the barnyard.

"What do you want, Jaron?" she asked, her soft voice quieter than usual.

"I've come to take you home, where you belong," he said, crossing the distance between them to sit down beside her.

She shook her head. "The Wild Maverick is your home. Not mine."

"That's where you're wrong, darlin'," he said, shaking his head. "Without you there with me, it's just a house."

To his surprise, she got up from the window seat and turned to face him. "You made it perfectly clear the other night that I'm not *with* you. If I was, you wouldn't have told me to mind my own business."

He shook his head. "I didn't say that. I told you it wasn't your concern."

"That's just a matter of semantics, and you know it," she retorted.

She was getting angry. Good. He'd rather have her tear into him like a cougar with a sore paw than see her looking so dejected.

"You're right," he admitted, feeling about as guilty as a man possibly could. "I'm sorry, darlin'."

"You're sorry? That's all you can say?" She was gaining a full head of steam, and he didn't think he'd ever seen her look more beautiful. "You were clearly upset by that phone call about your father, which, by the way, you already knew about because Reverend Perkins called you." She looked at him accusingly. "You blamed me for the man explaining why he was trying to get in touch with you. That was unfair and we both know it."

That was exactly what he'd done, and he couldn't blame her for being furious with him. "That was wrong, and I can't tell you how much I regret reacting like that," he said honestly. "It wasn't your fault and I had no right to blame you for it."

"At least we agree on that," she said, nodding.

"Darlin', I've got some things to tell you that I think might help you understand why I acted the way I did," he said, deciding there was no easy way to explain how screwed up his life had been up to that point.

She wrapped her arms around herself protectively and he hated that she felt so wary with him. Unfortunately, her caution was no less than he deserved. He'd been a complete ass about the matter.

"Please sit down and listen to what I have to say, Mariah," he requested.

After years of trying to keep his past concealed, revealing what he'd gone through wasn't going to be easy for him. But there were things she needed to know if there was any chance of them having a future together.

Instead of sitting beside him on the window seat, she lowered herself to the side of the bed, facing him. "Okay, I'm listening."

He took a deep breath. "You were right about my father causing the scars on my back. He had a violent temper and I was a convenient outlet for his anger." He shrugged. "It didn't matter if I had done something or not—I was there and too young to fight back."

"I'm so sorry," she said, her eyes filled with sympathy. "No child deserves that kind of treatment."

He shook his head. "I'm not telling you any of this because I want you to feel sorry for me. I want you to understand why I've spent my life trying to hide it."

"Continue," she said, nodding.

"I think I told you I lost my mom."

She nodded. "You said you were six when she died and that you didn't know what happened."

"What I said was one day she was gone and I knew I'd never see her again. I never said I didn't know what happened to her." He stared down at the toes of his boots for a moment before he looked up to see Mariah watching him. "My mom didn't die of natural causes. The bastard she was married to killed her."

"Oh, my God," she gasped, covering her mouth with her hand. "Did you witness the murder?"

Shaking his head, he explained, "Her body was never found because nobody knew to look for her. He told everyone, including me, that she took off. I didn't find out what happened to her until I was thirteen. He got pissed off about something, and while he was taking out his anger on me, he let it slip that he should kill me and do away with my body the same way he had done with my mother."

Mariah's eyes widened in horror and he hated having to share the ugliness of his life with her. But they couldn't move forward until she knew it all.

"I knew that it was only a matter of time before he carried through on it and I disappeared the way my mom did." He reached up to rub the tension building at the back of his neck. "I was the one who turned him in to the police."

"That's why he's in prison, isn't it?" she asked as tears filled her eyes. "Because he killed your mother."

"Yes and no," he admitted, opening the box of tissues Sam had given him.

She looked confused as she accepted the tissue he handed her. "You want to explain that?"

He released a heavy sigh. "At first, the cops thought I was just a kid with a grudge against my father. After I showed them the scars on my back, they picked him up for child abuse." He shook his head. "I kept trying to tell them about my mom, but they focused on the abuse that I had suffered instead of what had happened to her. When they arrested him and brought him in to police headquarters, he saw me and all hell broke loose."

"What did he do?" Unable to bear the horrified expression on her pretty face, Jaron trained his gaze on a picture of her and Bria when they were little girls hanging on the wall across the room.

"He went into a tirade and without thinking repeated his regrets that he hadn't killed me the way he'd done my mom." Jaron shook his head. "During the investigations, they weren't able to find any evidence that he killed her, but they found enough to tie him to a few other murders and suspect him of several more. Along with the charges of child abuse, they had enough to put him away for life."

"Dear God, he…"

When her voice trailed off, Jaron finished for her. "He was a serial killer."

To his relief, instead of Mariah looking at him with suspicion the way some people had, tears streamed down her cheeks when she got up from the bed and came over to sit down beside him on the window seat, then put her arms around him. "I hate that you had to go through all that, Jaron."

He wrapped his arms around her, and for the first time in three days felt the sense of contentment that he only experienced with Mariah. "Don't cry, darlin'. I survived."

"But why were you so reluctant to tell me about all of this?" she asked.

"When Simon was arrested, I was put into foster care," he explained. "You'd be amazed at the number of foster families who refuse to take in the kid of a serial killer. And the ones who did open their homes to me acted as if they thought I might be a danger to them."

She looked puzzled. "Why would they do that?"

"I guess they were afraid that I would turn out to have tendencies like the old man," Jaron said, shrugging.

"That's why you wanted to keep everything about your past hidden, isn't it?" she guessed. "You didn't trust that I wouldn't do the same thing."

He nodded. "It wasn't until I was sent to the Last

Chance Ranch that I felt accepted for who I was—just a kid caught up in a bad situation."

"But I thought only boys who were in trouble with the law were sent to live with Hank Calvert," she said, frowning.

He smiled. "I had a bad habit of running away from foster homes when I got tired of them looking at me as though they were afraid I'd kill them in their sleep."

"That was unfair," she said indignantly. "You had nothing to do with your father's crimes."

"Unfair or not, I learned that if I wanted to be treated like everyone else, I kept my mouth shut and didn't let anyone know whose kid I was." Unable to stop himself, he kissed her forehead. "I was afraid if you knew what had happened, you might look at me that way, too." He shook his head. "I couldn't stand the thought of that."

"I suppose I can understand how you felt. But I've known all along that your past was sketchy and I didn't care," she reminded him.

He nodded. "I guess I was just so conditioned to having people look at me differently once they found out who I was, I expected everyone would. Hell, I even started to fear that one day my father's cruel streak could show up in me."

"That's ridiculous," Mariah said, defending him. "There isn't a cruel bone in your body."

"Thank you for believing in me, darlin'." He swallowed around the sudden lump clogging his throat. "But the way I talked to you the other night, I don't deserve it."

"You were upset," she said, shrugging one shoulder.

He shook his head. "That's no excuse for treating you that way."

They fell silent for a few minutes before she asked, "Did you go see your father?"

"I went to see Simon Collier."

"Who's that?" Mariah asked, looking confused.

"My stepfather," Jaron said, still getting used to the fact that the man wasn't his real father. "The reason he insisted that he had to see me before he died was because he wanted to clear his conscience. He asked my forgiveness for the beatings, then told me that my mother was already pregnant when he married her and he wasn't my biological father."

"But if you didn't know that, why didn't you question your last name being different than his?" she asked, frowning.

He smiled. "Due to the nature of his crimes and the reluctance of foster families taking me in, my caseworker talked to the judge and I was allowed to change my surname to my mother's maiden name."

"I'm happy he did the right thing and told you he wasn't your father," she stated.

"I am, too." Jaron smiled. "I know now that I didn't inherit his mean streak and can't pass that on to the next generation." He picked her up and set her on his lap. "Now that you know all about me, I have something I've been wanting to ask you."

"Okay," she said cautiously. "What is it?"

"Why am I the one you chose to take your virginity?" he asked.

"Why do you think?" she asked evasively.

"I hope it's because you love me," he said, knowing that was exactly why she'd made love with him.

"I'm not saying that's the reason, but how would you feel if that was the case?" she asked, looking cautious.

"I'd be the happiest man alive," he admitted, smiling. "It makes it a whole lot easier knowing that the woman I love more than life itself loves me back."

Fresh tears filled her emerald eyes. "You love me?"

"Mariah, I've loved you since the moment we met," he said honestly. "I just didn't want to saddle you with the baggage that came along with me."

"Oh, Jaron, I've wanted to hear you say that for so long," she admitted. "I love you more than you'll ever know."

"And I love you just as much," he said, kissing her soft lips. That seemed to open the floodgates, and he hoped the tears she now shed were happy ones.

When her crying ran its course, he handed her more tissues, and while she wiped away the last traces of her tears, he pulled a small black velvet box from his jeans pocket. He'd stopped at an exclusive jewelry store in Waco on his way back from the prison hospital, and he hoped she liked the ring he'd chosen.

Setting her on the window seat, he got down on one knee in front of her and opened the box with a two-carat marquis diamond inside. "Darlin', I know I'm not nearly good enough for you, but I love you and I promise I'll spend the rest of my days doing everything I can to make you happy. Will you marry me?"

"Only on one condition," she said, her eyes filled with more love than he would ever deserve.

"What's that, darlin'?" he asked, knowing he would agree to anything as long as she agreed to share her life with him.

"No more secrets," she stated. "I want nothing but complete honesty between us."

He nodded. "Mariah, I give you my word that I will never hold anything back with you ever again." Removing the ring from the box he held, he asked, "Now will you make me the happiest man alive and tell me you'll be my wife?"

"Y—yes!" she said, throwing her arms around his neck.

When he slipped the ring on her finger, it seemed to induce another wave of tears, and Jaron was glad his brother had the foresight to send the box of tissues upstairs with him. Scooping her up, he sat back down on the window seat with her on his lap and held her while she cried against his chest.

"I—I have…something…I need to tell you," she said, sniffing back more tears.

"I'm all ears, darlin'," he said, feeling happier than he'd ever felt in his entire life. "You can tell me anything."

"I took a pregnancy test this morning," she said, causing him to catch his breath.

"And?"

Reaching into her pocket, she handed him a white plastic stick with purple trim on it. The message on the tiny screen had his heart pumping double-time.

Completely dumbfounded, he couldn't have strung words together if his life depended on it.

"We're going to have a baby," Mariah said, looking as if she was unsure how he would take the news.

"I love you, Mariah, and I couldn't be happier." Kissing her until they both gasped for breath, he grinned. "In the past few minutes, you've given me everything I never thought I would have."

They held each other for some time before she asked, "When do you want to get married?"

"Is this afternoon too soon?" he teased.

"That would be nice, but there's a waiting period, and I doubt they would waive that just because you're impatient," she said, laughing.

"I'm good with whatever you want, darlin'," he said, meaning it. "You plan it and I'll see that it happens."

"Why don't we go home, and after you make love to me, we'll start planning our wedding?" she whispered in his ear.

It felt as though molten lava flowed through his veins at her suggestion. "I like the way you think."

She gave him a smile that lit the darkest corners of his soul. "Then, take me home, cowboy."

Two weeks later, as Jaron stood in front of the fireplace in Sam and Bria's living room, he checked his watch. His sisters-in-law had insisted that it was bad luck for the groom to see the bride before the wedding and Mariah had spent the night upstairs in the room where he'd proposed. It seemed like an eternity since he'd held her, and he vowed right then and there that for as long as he lived, he'd never spend another night away from her.

"Getting cold feet, bro?" Nate asked as they faced the rest of the family.

"Not at all." Jaron grinned. "I'm just looking forward to getting the honeymoon started."

His brother nodded. "I felt the same way when Jessie and I got married. Did you ever think when we were raising hell out on the rodeo circuit that we'd be happy settling down with one woman and having a bunch of little kids?"

"No, I can't say that I did," Jaron answered.

When the beginning notes of "Here Comes the Bride" came from the house audio system, Jaron fixed his gaze on the door that led out into the foyer and waited for Sam to escort the woman of his dreams across the room to join him in front of the pastor. In just a few short minutes, he and Mariah would be husband and wife, and as far as he was concerned it couldn't happen soon enough.

As Bria walked through the doorway and across the room to stand on the other side of the fireplace, he barely noticed. His eyes were trained on Mariah in her long white wedding gown as Sam walked her toward him. She looked absolutely gorgeous, and he swallowed hard at the thought that a woman so beautiful would fall in love with a dust-covered cowboy like himself.

"Are you ready for this?" he asked, taking her hand from Sam.

"I've been waiting all my life for you," she said, smiling.

"And I've been waiting just as long for you," he said, kissing her cheek. "Let's make this official."

* * *

An hour later, as Jaron stood at the bar with his brothers having a drink to toast his and Mariah's marriage, his gaze kept drifting to his new wife. She owned him heart, body and soul, and he couldn't have been happier about it.

"Well, now that I've won the pool for when Jaron and Mariah would get married and we've all joined the club of the blissfully hitched, what are we going to bet on next?" Ryder asked.

"How many kids we're all going to have?" T.J. asked, grinning.

Lane shook his head. "We wouldn't know the outcome of that for years."

"Mariah and I were talking the other day about the Last Chance Ranch and what a difference it made in all of our lives," Jaron said, watching her and the other women laughing at something one of the kids had done. "What do you think about giving other kids the same chance we had?"

"You've got my attention," Sam spoke up.

Lane nodded. "What do you have in mind?"

"I think we should buy some land and build the Hank Calvert Memorial Last Chance Ranch," Jaron answered.

"We've got a board of directors right here," T.J. said, nodding.

"And it's not as though we don't have our own psychologist to oversee the programs the kids would need," Ryder added.

"I think Hank would approve wholeheartedly," Sam said, looking thoughtful.

"If there's a chance of giving kids the lives that Hank gave us, I say go for it," Nate agreed.

"Then, it's settled," Jaron said decisively. "We can get things set up and look for a piece of land as soon as Mariah and I get back from our honeymoon. Why don't we bet on how long it's going to take to get the ranch up and running?"

"Sounds good to me," his brothers said almost in unison.

"We'll start the betting pool and get things set up as soon as you get back from your honeymoon," Ryder said.

Jaron grinned as he set his beer bottle on the bar. "If my wife is ready, we'll go get started on *that* right now."

Walking over to Mariah, he took her in his arms. "Are you ready to leave, Mrs. Lambert?"

"I thought you'd never ask," she said, kissing his chin.

Saying their goodbyes, they walked hand in hand out to their newly purchased minivan. "I'm glad we decided on Hawaii for our honeymoon," Mariah said as he helped her into the passenger seat. "It may be the last time I get to wear a bikini for a while."

"Why do you say that, darlin'?"

"I'm going to be having lots of little Lamberts in the next several years," she said.

Staring at the woman he loved with all his heart, he grinned. "I'll be more than happy to help you with that, darlin'."

"I love you, cowboy," she said, giving him a smile that sent his blood pressure soaring.

"And I love you, darlin'. Forever and always."

Epilogue

One year later

As Jaron looked around the reception hall following the ground-breaking ceremony for the Hank Calvert Memorial Last Chance Ranch, he smiled. The turn-out couldn't have been better. Several politicians had shown up, as well as the head of the Texas foster-care system and most of her staff. There were also quite a few members of the media covering the event. Jaron wasn't surprised. Hank had been well-respected for the difference he'd made in the lives of the kids most people had given up on as lost causes. Jaron hoped that the ranch he and his brothers were setting up for troubled youth carried on Hank's legacy.

"It looks as though the ranch is well on its way to

becoming a reality," Sam said, checking the bottle he was giving to his new baby son.

Jaron nodded. "I think Hank would approve."

"I know he would," Lane said, setting his little boy on his feet to run over to his mother. "Hank would be proud to know the boys he saved from a life behind bars or an early grave were going to give other troubled kids the same chance he gave us."

Nate patted his sleeping daughter's back when she raised her head a moment before falling back to sleep. "Hank always told us to do something about it whenever we saw a need," he added quietly to keep from disturbing the baby.

They all nodded a moment before Ryder's groan drew their attention. "The smell of a clean shirt nauseates this baby the same as it did her big sister."

"I think that's true for all babies," T.J. said, joining them. He was wearing a different shirt than the one he'd worn for the ground breaking. "Heather always puts an extra shirt in the diaper bag for me the same as she does for the boys."

"Try keeping your shirt clean with twins," Jaron said, laughing. "It's just not going to happen."

Nate grinned. "Since you always insisted that our babies would be boys and Mariah argued that they would be girls, it's only fitting that you ended up with one of each."

"Our family sure has grown a lot in the past few years," T.J. said, looking around the reception hall.

"No kidding," Sam agreed. "Between the six of us, we have ten kids."

"And they're all under the age of four," Lane added.

Ryder laughed. "Who would have ever thought four years ago that we'd be standing around talking about babies instead of the merits of a Brahman cross over a purebred bucking bull?"

"Jaron, could you watch Alisa while I change Brett?" Mariah asked, pushing the stroller up beside him.

"No problem." He waited until she picked up their smiling son, then kissed her cheek and whispered in her ear, "Thank you, darlin'."

"For what?" she asked, smiling back at him.

"You didn't give up on me when you had every reason to," he said, meaning it. "You and the kids are my world and I never want you to doubt how much I love all of you."

"And we love you, cowboy." The deep emotion he detected in her emerald eyes robbed him of breath.

"How would you like to head home and get the kids down for a nap as soon as you change our son's diaper?" he asked, needing to show her how much he cherished her. "I'd really like to make love to their mother."

"I like the way you think, cowboy." She gave him a smile that sent his hormones into overdrive. "Let's hope we can stay awake long enough for that."

He laughed. "Yeah, that's something we haven't had a whole lot of lately."

"We probably can't count on much of that for another eighteen years or so," Mariah said, grinning as she headed toward the ladies' room to change their baby boy.

As he watched her disappear down the hall, Jaron

couldn't help but feel blessed. He had the love of a good woman, two beautiful babies and a band of brothers who had his back no matter what. And all because as a troubled kid he'd been lucky enough to be sent to the Last Chance Ranch.

* * * * *

THE GOOD, THE BAD AND THE TEXAN

Don't miss a single novel in this series from
USA TODAY bestselling author Kathie DeNosky!
Running with these billionaires will be one wild ride.

HIS MARRIAGE TO REMEMBER
A BABY BETWEEN FRIENDS
YOUR RANCH...OR MINE?
THE COWBOY'S WAY
PREGNANT WITH THE RANCHER'S BABY

All available now, only from Mills & Boon Desire!

"I've changed my mind."

Eva stopped in front of Kyle. Any nerves about seducing him had long since burned away. She ran a finger down his chest, igniting a trail of heat. The heady masculine scents of clean skin and sandalwood made her head spin.

His hand curled over hers. "What about?"

She boldly wound one arm around his neck, leaned in close and gently bit down on one earlobe. "The clause in our marriage agreement that prohibits sex. If anyone is going to sleep with my husband, it's going to be me."

When she would have drawn back, his hands closed on her waist, holding her against him. "I'll get my lawyer to strike it out in the morning."

"As long as we have a verbal agreement, the new condition is in effect."

"We could shake on it," he muttered, "but I have a better idea." Lowering his head, he finally did what she'd been dying for him to do ever since the wedding ceremony. He kissed her.

* * *

Needed: One Convenient Husband
is part of The Pearl House series—
Business and passion collide when
two dynasties forge ties bound by love

NEEDED: ONE CONVENIENT HUSBAND

BY
FIONA BRAND

First Published in Great Britain 2016
By Mills & Boon, an imprint of HarperCollins*Publishers*
1 London Bridge Street, London, SE1 9GF

© 2016 Fiona Gillibrand

ISBN: 978-0-263-91849-6

51-0216

Our policy is to use papers that are natural, renewable and recyclable products and made from wood grown in sustainable forests.The logging and manufacturing processes conform to the legal environmental regulations of the country of origin.

Printed and bound in Spain
by CPI, Barcelona

Fiona Brand lives in the sunny Bay of Islands, New Zealand. Now that both her sons are grown, she continues to love writing books and gardening. After a life-changing time in which she met Christ, she has undertaken study for a Bachelors in Theology and has become a member of The Order of St. Luke, Christ's healing ministry.

For the Lord. Thank You.

I am the light of the world.
Whoever follows me will never walk in darkness,
but will have the light of life.

—*John* 8:12

One

Kyle Messena's gaze narrowed as the bridal car pulled up outside Dolphin Bay's windblown, hilltop church. The bride, festooned in white tulle, stepped out of the limousine. A drift of gauze obscured her face, but sunlight gleamed on tawny hair that was heart-stoppingly familiar.

Adrenaline pumped and time seemed to slow, stop, as he considered the stunning fact that, despite his efforts to prevent Eva Atraeus marrying a man whose motives were purely financial, she had utterly fooled him and the wedding he had thought he had nixed was going ahead.

Kyle had taken two long, gliding steps out of the inky shade cast by an aged oak into the blistering heat of a New Zealand summer's day before the ocean breeze whipped the veil from the bride's face.

It wasn't Eva.

Relief unlocked the fierce tension that gripped him.

A tension that sliced through the indifference to relationships that had shrouded him for years, ever since the death of his wife and small son. Deaths that he should have prevented.

The unwanted, brooding intensity had grown over the months he had been entrusted with the duty of ensuring that the heiress to an Atraeus fortune married according to a draconian clause in her adoptive father's will. Eva, in order to get control of her inheritance, had to either marry a Messena—*him*—or a man who genuinely wanted her and not her money.

Acting as Eva's trustee did not sit well with Kyle. He was aware that his wily great-uncle, Mario, had named him as trustee in a last game-playing move to maneuver him into marrying the woman he had once wanted but left behind. Confronted by the mesmerizing power of an attraction that still held him in reluctant thrall and unable to accept that the one woman he had never been able to forget would marry someone else, Kyle had been unable to refuse the job.

A gust of wind whipped the bride's veil to one side, revealing that she was a little on the plump side. Her hair was also a couple of shades lighter than the rich dark mane shot through with tawny highlights that had been a natural feature of Eva's hair ever since he'd first set eyes on her at age sixteen.

Kyle's jaw unlocked. Now that he had successfully circumvented Eva's latest marriage plan, he was ready to leave, but when a zippy white sports car emblazoned with the name of Eva's business, Perfect Weddings, pulled into a space, Kyle knew he wasn't going anywhere.

Eva Atraeus, dressed in a pale pink button-down suit that clung in all the right places, closed the door with an expensive *thunk*. Cell held to one ear, she hooked a matching pale pink tote over her shoulder and started toward the church doors, her stride fluid and distractingly sexy in a pair of strappy high heels. At five feet seven, Eva was several inches too short for the runway, but with her elegant, curvy figure, mouthwatering cheekbones and exotic dark eyes, she had been a knockout success as a photographic model. Gorgeous, quirky and certifiably high maintenance, Eva had fascinated gossip columnists for years and dazzled more men than she'd had hot dinners, including *him*.

Every muscle in Kyle's body tightened on a visceral hit of awareness that had become altogether too familiar.

A faint check in her step indicated that Eva had spotted him.

As the bridal party disappeared into the church, she terminated her call and changed direction. Stepping beneath the shade of the oak, she shoved the cell in her tote and glared at him. "What are you doing at *my* wedding?"

Kyle clamped down on his irritation at Eva's deliberate play on the "my wedding" bit. It was true that it was supposed to have been her actual wedding day. Understandably, she was annoyed that he'd upset her plan to leverage a marriage of convenience by offering the groom a lucrative job in Dubai. The way Kyle saw it, he had simply countered one employment opportunity with another. The fact that Jeremy, an accountant, had taken the job so quickly and had even seemed relieved, more than justified his intervention. "You shouldn't have arranged a wedding you knew couldn't go ahead."

Her dark gaze flashed. "What if I was in love with Jeremy?"

He lifted a brow. "After a whole four weeks?"

"You know as well as I that it can happen a whole lot faster than—" She stopped, her cheeks flushed. Rummaging in her bag, she found sunglasses and, with controlled precision, slipped them onto the bridge of her nose. "Now you get to tell me what you're doing at a *private* wedding. I'm guessing it's not just to have another argument."

He crossed his arms over his chest. "If you think you can kick me out, forget it. I'm a guest of the groom. I manage his share portfolio."

She took a deep breath and he watched with objective fascination as the flare of irritation was replaced by one of the gorgeous smiles that had graced magazines and posters and which had the power to stop all male brain function. "That's thin, even for you."

"But workable."

"And here I was thinking you were here to make sure I hadn't pulled off a last-minute coup and found another groom."

He frowned at the light, floral waft of her perfume and resisted the impulse to step a little closer. "It's not my brief to stop you marrying."

Her head tilted to one side. Through the screen of the lenses her gaze chilled. "No, it's to stop me marrying the man of my choice."

"You need to choose better." Out of an impressive discard pile during the last few months, on three different occasions, Eva had selected a prospective groom. Unfortunately, all three had been strapped for cash and willing to sign prenuptial agreements that spelled out the cutoff date for the marriage: two years to the day, the exact time period specified in Mario's will. Kyle had been honorbound by the terms of the will to veto the weddings.

"Jeremy was perfect husband material. He was attractive, personable, with a reasonable job, his—"

"Motive was blatantly financial."

Her expression turned steely. "He needed money to cover some debts. What is so wrong with that?"

"Mario would spin in his grave if you married a man with a gambling addiction."

There was a small icy silence, intensified by the strains of the wedding march emanating from the church. "If I have to marry Mr. Right according to Kyle Messena, then maybe *you* should choose someone for me. Only I'll need to marry him by—" she checked the slim pink watch on her wrist "—next month. Since now, thanks to you, I only have three weeks left to marry before my inheritance goes into lockdown for the next *thirteen years*."

Despite Kyle's resolve to withstand the considerable pressure he had always known Eva would apply, a twinge of guilt made his stomach tighten.

Women and relationships in general had always proved to be a difficult area for him. It was a fact that he was more comfortable with the world of military operations or the clinical cut and thrust of his family's banking business. He could do weapons and operational tactics; he could do figures and financial markets. Love and the responsibility—and the searing guilt that came with it—was something he would not risk again. "It isn't my intention to prevent you getting your inheritance."

Eva's serene smile disappeared. "No," she said with a throaty little catch to her voice. "It's just turning out that way."

Spinning on her heel, Eva marched back to her car.

Kyle frowned. Eva's voice had sounded suspiciously husky, as if she was on the verge of tears. In the entire checkered history of their relationship, he had only ever seen Eva, who was superorganized with a serene, kick-ass calm, cry twice. Of course, she had cried at Mario's funeral almost a year ago. The only other occasion had been close on eleven years ago when he'd been nineteen. To be precise, it had been the morning after Mario had hauled them both over the coals for a passionate interlude on Dolphin Bay's beach.

Memory flickered. A hot, extended twilight, a buttery moon sliding up over the sea, the clamor of a family party at the resort fading in the distance as Eva had wound her arms around his neck. He'd drawn a deep breath, caught the scent of her hair, her skin. Every muscle had tensed as he'd dipped his head and given in to the temptation that had kept him in agony most of the summer and kissed her...

If Mario hadn't come looking for Eva, they would have done a lot more than just kiss. The interview with Mario that had ensued that night had been sharp and short. As gorgeous and put-together as Eva had looked at age seventeen, she had more than her share of vulnerabilities. The product of a severely dysfunctional family, Eva needed security and protection, not seduction. Mario hadn't elaborated on any of those details, but the message had been plain enough. Eva was off-limits.

Until now.

He had no illusions about why Mario had done a complete about turn and made him a trustee, when for years he had treated Kyle as if he was a marauding predator after his one and only chick. For years Eva had stubbornly resisted Mario's attempts to find her a safe, solid husband from amongst the sons of his wealthy business associates. Mario, forced to change tack, had swallowed his objections to the "wild Messena boys," and had then tried to marry Eva off to both of Kyle's older brothers, Gabriel and Nick. When that strategy had failed because Gabe and Nick had married other women and Kyle's younger brother Damian had a long-standing girlfriend, in a last desperate move, Mario had finally settled on Kyle as a prospective bridegroom.

His gaze still locked on Eva, Kyle strolled back to his Maserati. Now that he knew Eva wasn't the bride, he should drive back to Auckland. Back to his ultra-busy, smoothly organized life. If he left right away, he could even make the uncomplicated dinner date he had with Elise, a fellow banking executive he had been see-ing on and off for the past few months, mostly at busi-ness functions.

But as he approached the Maserati, which was nose to tail with Eva's white sports car, he couldn't shake the sense that something about the way Eva had stormed off had not rung true. It occurred to him that the tears he thought Eva had been about to cry could have been fake. After all, she *had* taken acting classes. She had been good enough that she had even been offered a part in a popular soap, but had turned it down because it had conflicted with her desire to start her own wedding plan-ning business.

Suddenly positive that he had been duped, he dropped the Maserati's key back into his pocket. There could be only one reason why Eva wanted him to feel guilty enough that he bypassed the reception. She had already found a new candidate for groom and he would be at-tending as her guest. Since she only had three weeks to organize her final shot at a wedding, keeping her new prospective groom close made sense, because time was of the essence.

Certainty settled in when he caught the tail end of a conversation with someone named Troy. His jaw tight-ened. Troy Kendal, if he didn't miss his guess. A flashy sports star Eva had met less than a week ago in a last, desperate attempt to recruit a groom. Out of nowhere, the jealousy he had worked hard to suppress because it was just as illogical as the desire that haunted him, roared to life.

If Eva had been crying, they had been crocodile tears.

She had been getting rid of him.

In no mood to leave now, Kyle waited until Eva terminated the call and dropped the phone in her bag. "We need to talk."

"I thought we just did."

Dropping her bag on the passenger seat, she dragged off her sunglasses and checked her watch, subtly underlining the fact that she was in a hurry to leave. Without the barrier of the lenses, and with strands of hair blowing loose around her cheeks, she seemed younger and oddly vulnerable, although Kyle knew that was an illusion, since Eva's reputation with men was legendary. "There's a solution to your problem. If you marry a Messena, there are no further conditions, other than that the marriage must be of two years' duration."

Her brows creased as if she was only just considering an option that had been bluntly stated in the will. "Even if I wanted to do that, which I don't, that's hardly possible, since Gabriel and Nick are both married, and Damian's as good as."

Kyle's jaw clamped at the systematic way she ticked his brothers off her fingers, deliberately leaving him off the list. *As if her fingers had never locked with his as they'd strolled down the dimly lit path to Dolphin Bay, as if she had never wrapped her arms around his neck and kissed him.*

"There's one other Messena," Kyle said flatly, his patience gone. "I'm talking you, me and a marriage of convenience."

Two

Eva choked back the stinging refusal she wanted to fling at Kyle. She didn't know why she reacted so strongly to him or the idea that they could marry. Mario's previous attempts to marry her off to other Messena men had barely ruffled her.

A year ago, when she had read the terms of the will and absorbed the full import of that one little sentence, she had been so horrified she had wanted to crawl under the solicitor's desk and hide. The whole idea that Kyle, the only available Messena husband—and the one man who had ditched her—should feel pressured to marry her, had been mortifying. "I don't need a pity proposal."

The wind dropped for a split second, enclosing them in a pooling, tension-filled silence that was gradually filled with the timeless beauty of the wedding vows floating from the church.

"But you do need *a* proposal. After two years, once

you've got your inheritance, we can dissolve the marriage."

Kyle's clinical solution contrarily sent a stab of hurt through her, which annoyed her intensely.

A former Special Air Service soldier, Kyle had the kind of steely blue gaze that missed nothing. He was also tall and muscular, six foot two inches of sleek muscle, with close-cut dark hair and the kind of grim good looks and faintly battered features, courtesy of his years in the military, that mesmerized women.

All of the men in the Messena and Atraeus families seemed to possess that same formidable, in-charge quality. Usually, it didn't ruffle her in the slightest, but Kyle paired it with a blunt, low-key insight that was unnerving; he seemed to know what she was going to do before she did it. Added to that, she wouldn't mind betting that he had gotten rid of some of her grooms with a little judicious intimidation.

The idea of marrying Kyle shouldn't affect her. She had learned early on to sidestep actual relationships at all cost. The plain fact was, she wouldn't have trusted in any relationships at all if it hadn't been for Mario and his wife picking her up when they'd found her on the sidewalk near their home one evening twelve years ago.

When they'd found out she was on the run from her last home because her foster father had wandering hands, they had phoned the welfare people. However, instead of allowing her to be shunted back into another institutional home, Mario had made a string of phone calls to "people he knew" and she had been allowed to stay with them.

Despite her instinctive withdrawal and the cold neutrality that had gotten her through a number of foster homes, Mario and Teresa had offered her the kind of quiet, steady love that, at sixteen, had been unfamiliar and a little scary. When they had eventually proposed adopting her, the plain fact was she hadn't known how to respond. She'd had the rug pulled emotionally so many times she had thought that if she softened and believed that she was deserving of love, that would be the moment it was all taken away.

In the end, through Mario's dogged persistence, she had finally understood that he was the one person who wouldn't break his word. Her resistance had crumbled and she had signed. In the space of a moment, she had ceased to be Eva Rushton, the troubled runaway, and had become Eva Atraeus, a member of a large and mystifyingly welcoming family.

However, the transformation had never quite been complete. After watching her own mother's three marriages disintegrate then at age seventeen finding out *why*, she had decided she did not ever want to be that vulnerable.

She caught a whiff of Kyle's cologne and her stomach clenched. And there was her problem, she thought grimly. Although, why the fiery tension, which should have died a death years ago—right after he had dumped her when she was seventeen—still persisted, she had no clue. It wasn't as if they had ever spent much time together or had anything in common beyond the youthful attraction. Kyle had married someone else a couple of years later, too, so she knew that what they had shared had not affected him as deeply as it had her.

Now, thanks to Kyle's interference, she had three weeks to marry anyone but him, and the clock was ticking…

Frustration reignited the nervous tension that had assaulted her when Jeremy had informed her he was backing out of their arrangement, but now that tension was laced with a healthy jolt of panic. Mario Atraeus couldn't have chosen a better watchdog for the unexpected codicil he had written into his will if he had tried.

She had been so close to marriage, but now Jeremy had run like a frightened rabbit. She couldn't prove that Kyle had engineered the job offer to get rid of Jeremy. All she knew was that he had used the same tactic twice before. Every time she got someone to agree to marry her, Kyle got rid of him.

Although why Kyle had stopped her marrying a man who had been eminently suitable, and whom she had actually liked in a lukewarm kind of way, she didn't know. Given their antagonistic past, she had thought Kyle would have been only too glad to discharge a responsibility that had been thrust on him, and which he could not possibly want.

Just like he hadn't wanted her.

Frowning at the thought of the brief, passionate interlude they had shared eleven years ago, she met Kyle's gaze squarely. "Thanks, but no thanks."

Dropping into the little sports car's bucket seat, she snapped the door closed. The engine revved with a throaty roar. Throat tight, still unbearably ruffled that he had actually had the gall to give her a *pity* proposal, she put the car in gear. Spinning the car in a tight turn, she headed in the direction of the Dolphin Bay Resort, where the reception was being held.

Her jaw tightened at the thought that even the location of the reception was tainted with memories of Kyle and the one time he'd kissed her. In starting her wedding business, though, she'd had to be pragmatic. The Dolphin Bay Resort was family run and offered her a great discount. She would have been flat-out stupid not to use the venue.

Still fuming, Eva strolled into the resort to oversee the gorgeous, high-end fairy-tale wedding she had designed as a promotional centerpiece for her wedding planning business. A perfect wedding that should have been hers, if only Jeremy hadn't cut and run.

Cancel that, she thought grimly. If only Kyle hadn't paid Jeremy off with a lucrative job offer in sandblasted Dubai! Taking a deep breath and reaching for her usual calm control, she checked her appearance in one of the elegant mirrors that decorated the walls. The reflection that bounced back was reassuring. Lately her emotions were all over the place, she was crying at the drop of a hat, she actually wanted to watch rom-coms and she was having trouble sleeping.

None of that inner craziness showed. She looked as calm and cool and collected as she wished she felt, her mass of tawny hair smoothed into an elegant French pleat, her too curvy figure disguised by a low-key skirt and jacket in a pastel pink that matched her shoes and handbag. The businesslike but feminine image achieved a balance between the occasion and her role as planner.

More importantly, it ensured that she did not compete with the bride or other female guests in any way. She had learned that lesson at what would have been her first wedding when the groom had gotten a little too interested in her and the bride had cancelled.

Eva walked through to the ballroom where the reception was being held and lifted a hand to acknowledge the waitstaff, all of whom she knew well thanks to the half dozen weddings she had staged at Dolphin Bay. She tensed as she glimpsed commiseration in the normally businesslike gaze of the maître d' as he mopped around an ice sculpture of swans she had recklessly commissioned because this was supposed to be her one and only wedding day.

The five-tiered extravaganza of a cake, snow-white

icing sparkling with crystals and festooned with clusters of sculpted flowers so beautifully executed they looked real, stopped her brisk movement through the room. Out of the blue, the emotion she had been working hard to stamp out grabbed at her. She had wanted to make this a day she would remember all of her life. Unfortunately, that had been achieved since it would be difficult to forget that her perfect wedding now belonged to someone else.

Stomach churning with a potent cocktail of frustration, panic and a crazy vulnerability caused by the fact that Kyle seemed intent on stopping her attempts to achieve a workable, safe marriage, she spun on her heel and made a beeline for the kitchen.

Bracing herself, she pushed the double doors open and stepped into a hive of gleaming white walls and polished steel counters. The cheerful clattering and hum of conversation instantly stopped. Eva's chest squeezed tight as waves of sympathy flowed toward her, intensifying the ache that had started in her throat and making tears burn at the back of her eyes. The jolt of emotion was crazy, given that she hadn't loved Jeremy in the least and marriage had not been on her horizon until Mario had literally forced her to it with that clause in his will. A clause designed to railroad her into the kind of happiness he had shared with his wife and which he had thought she should also have, whether she wanted it or not.

Until she'd started planning this wedding, she had thought Mario had been utterly wrong in believing he could make her want to be married. But every detail of planning her own wedding had confronted her, throwing together the stark realities of her life and cruelly highlighting the parts she couldn't have: the romance and the happy-ever-after ending that true love promised. Most of all, it emphasized the happy aftermath she would never experience: her own babies.

She had known since she was seventeen, thanks to a rare genetic disorder she carried, that she shouldn't have children. The disorder had proved fatal for her twin and two siblings, which had made her doubly wary about the whole concept of marriage. There was always the possibility that she could meet someone who didn't care about the disorder and who would be happy to adopt, but she had difficulty getting past the fact that she literally carried death in her genes.

In retrospect, it had been a huge mistake giving in to the temptation to design a wedding that patently did not go with a marriage of convenience. It smacked of wish fulfilment, and it had opened up a Pandora's box of needs and desires she had thought she had put behind her. She should have settled for a registry office ceremony. No fuss, no bother, no emotion.

Pinning a smile on her face, she breezed through the large bustling kitchen and waved at the head chef, Jerome, a Parisian with two Michelin stars. Jerome had designed the menu personally for her. He sent her an intense look brimming with passionate outrage and sympathy, even though he knew she had managed to sell the wedding on to a couple who had been desperate to marry quickly, owing to a surprise pregnancy.

Eva flinched at the concept that her pretty young bride not only had her perfect wedding, but was also pregnant. She could not afford to dwell on the painful issue that while she could not have children, other women could, and at the drop of a hat.

Keeping her professional smile firmly fixed, Eva fished her menu out of her bag and ran through it with Jerome. For once there were no last-minute glitches. Every aspect of this wedding appeared to be abnormally perfect. After dutifully admiring the exquisite mountain of cupcakes, which Jerome was decorating—her favorite forbidden snack—she escaped back to the reception room before he could toss his icing palette knife down and pull her into a comforting bear hug.

Kyle had proposed.

The kitchen doors made a swishing sound as they swung closed behind her. Eva stared blindly at the crisp white damask on the tables, the sparkle of crystal chandeliers and lavish clusters of white roses. She did not know why Kyle had the power to upset her so. It wasn't as if she was immersed in the painful, oversentimental first love that had gripped her at age seventeen. It wasn't as if she still wanted him.

As the wedding guests began to spill through the doors, she rummaged in her handbag, found and slipped on a pair of the most unflattering glasses she'd been able to buy. The lenses were fake, just plain glass, but the heavy, dark rims served to deflect the attention that her good looks usually attracted.

Fixing a smile on her face, she did a brisk circuit of the main reception room, which she and her assistant, Jacinta, had dressed earlier. Waiters were loading silver trays with flutes filled with extremely good champagne she had sourced from an organic vineyard. Trays of her favorite canapés from the five-star kitchen were lined up in the servery.

The reception was heartbreakingly gorgeous. Since it was supposed to have been her own, she had put a great deal of thought into every detail, no expense spared. The only consolation was that she would be very well paid. And, in three weeks' time, if she was still unwed, she would be in desperate need of cash in order to retain her house and keep her business afloat.

The doors to the kitchens behind her swished open as guests began to seat themselves at tables. Jacinta Doyle, her sleekly efficient personal assistant, came to stand beside her, a folder in one hand. Jacinta gave her a look laden with sympathy but, tactfully, kept things business-like. Halfway through a list of minor details, she stopped dead. "*Who* is that?"

An annoying hum of awareness Eva was desperate to ignore made her tense. Adjusting the glasses, which were too heavy for her nose, she frowned at the rapidly filling room. Her mood plummeted when she saw Kyle. "Who do you mean, exactly? There must be a hundred people in the room."

"He is *hot*." Jacinta, who was hooked into the sophisticated, very modern dating scene with a new man on her arm every week, clutched dramatically at her chest before pointing Kyle out just in case Eva hadn't noticed him. "I'm in love."

Irritation flared, instant and unreasoning. "I thought you were dating Geraldo someone-or-other."

"Gerard. His visa ran out, and his money." She shrugged. "He went back to France."

Eva pretended to be absorbed in her own checklist of things to do. "Don't let your heart beat faster over Kyle, because you'll be wasting your time. He's too old for you, and he's not exactly a fun type."

"How old?"

The irritation morphed into something else she couldn't quite put her finger on. "Thirty," she muttered shortly.

"I wouldn't call that old. More…interesting."

Something inside Eva snapped. "Forget Kyle Messena. He isn't available."

Jacinta sent her a glance laced with the kind of curiosity that informed Eva she hadn't been able to keep the sharpness out of her voice. "Kyle Messena. I thought he looked familiar. Didn't he lose his wife and child in some kind of terrorist attack overseas? But that was years ago." She pointedly returned her gaze to Kyle, underlining the fact that she could look at him any time she liked, for as long as she liked.

Even more annoyed by the speculation on Jacinta's face, as if she was actually considering making a play for Kyle, Eva consulted her watch. "We're ten minutes behind schedule," she said crisply. "You check the timing for service with the chef. I'm going to get a cold drink then have a word with the musicians. With any luck we'll get out of here before midnight."

With a last glance at Kyle, Jacinta closed the folder with a resigned snap. "No problem."

But there was a problem, Eva thought bleakly. The kind of problem she had never imagined she would suffer from ever again. For reasons she did not understand, Jacinta's interest in Kyle had evoked the kind of fierce, primitive response she had only ever experienced once before, years ago, when she'd heard that Kyle was dating someone else.

She needed to go somewhere quiet and give herself a stern talking-to, because somehow, she had allowed the unwanted attraction to Kyle to get out of hand, to the point that she was suddenly, burningly, crazily jealous about the last man she wanted in her life.

Three

Kyle strolled to the bar, although if he were honest, the drive to get a cold beer over settling for the champagne being served had more to do with the fact that Eva was headed in that direction.

Eva's expression chilled as he leaned on the bar next to her. The faint crease in her smooth brow as she sipped from a tall glass of what he guessed was sparkling water somehow made her look even more spectacularly gorgeous, despite the disfiguring glasses. It was a beauty he should have been accustomed to, yet it still made his stomach tighten and his attention sharpen in a completely male way.

She met his gaze briefly before looking away. An impression of defensiveness made him frown. Normally Eva was cool and distant, occasionally combative, but never defensive.

She placed the glass down on the counter with a small click. "I thought you had left."

The unspoken words, *now that you'd made sure I hadn't secretly gotten married,* seemed to hang in the air. Kyle shrugged and ordered a beer. "I decided to stick around. We still need to have a conversation."

"If it's about the terms of the will, forget it. I've read the fine print—"

"You've ignored the fine print." She had certainly failed to notice that he was her primary marriage candidate.

The faint blush of color in her cheeks flared a little brighter, sharpening Kyle's curiosity. Eva was behaving in a way that was distinctly odd. He was abruptly certain that something had happened, something had changed, although he had no idea what.

She sent him a breezy professional smile, but her whole demeanor was evasive. "If you don't mind, I really do need to work."

Usually, Eva was as direct and uncompromising as any man. The blush and the avoidance of eye contact didn't fit, unless… His heart slammed against his chest, spinning him back to the long summer days they had spent on the beach as teenagers. For a split second he wondered that he had missed something so obvious. But he guessed he had been so absorbed with trying to control the desire that had come out of left field that he had failed to see that Eva was fighting the same battle.

She tried to sidestep him, but the bar area was now filling up with people, lining up for drinks. Feeling like a villain, but riveted by the discovery, he moved slightly, just enough to block her in. She stopped, a bare inch from brushing against his chest.

Kyle's stomach tightened as he caught another whiff of Eva's perfume. He knew he should leave her alone and let her get on with her job. But the desire to evoke a response, to make Eva admit that she wanted him, was too strong. "The whole point of Mario's will was that he wanted you to marry someone who would actually care about you and who wasn't in it for the money."

"I know what Mario wanted, no one better. What I don't get is why you're so intent on enforcing a condition that is patently ridiculous?"

Kyle's gaze narrowed at the way Eva carefully avoided the issue of his proposal. "You're family."

"Distant and only on paper. It's not as if I'm a real Atraeus."

Kyle's brow's jerked together. "Your name is Atraeus."

Eva dragged in a breath, relieved that the unnerving sense that Kyle had seen right through her desperate attempt to seem normal and completely impervious to him had dissipated. "That doesn't change the fact that I'm adopted. I'm not blood." And that she could still remember what it felt like to wear secondhand clothes, eat cereal for dinner and fend off her mother's boyfriends. She was a very poor cuckoo in a diamond-encrusted nest.

"Mario wanted to help you. He wanted you to be happy."

She drew a breath. The clean scent of his skin deepened the panicked awareness that was humming through her. "I'm twenty-eight. I think that by now I know what it takes to be happy."

"And that would be paying some guy to marry you?"

Eva's brows jerked together. "Correct me if I'm wrong, but barely fifty years ago, arranged marriages were common in both the Messena and the Atraeus families."

"Last century, maybe."

"Then someone should have told that to Mario. And it underlines my point that a marriage of convenience is not the worst thing that could happen." And it wasn't as if she actually wanted to be loved. She had seen what had happened to her mother when she had become emotionally needy. Relationship train wreck followed by train wreck, the plunging depression and slow disintegration of Meg Rushton's life. It had all been crowned by her mother's inability to care for Eva, the one child who had survived the disorder.

A young man tried to squeeze in beside Eva. Kyle blocked him with a wolf-cold glance and a faint shift in position. In the process, his arm brushed against hers, sending a tingle of heat through her that made Eva even more desperate to get away. With grim concentration, she stared over Kyle's broad shoulder at the bottles of spirits suspended at the rear of the bar and tried not to love the fact that Kyle's behavior had been as bluntly possessive as if they had been a couple. That was exactly the kind of thinking she could not afford.

Kyle's gaze, edged with irritation, captured hers. "Let's put this in context. If a man is unscrupulous enough to take your money for marriage, chances are he won't have a problem pressurizing you until you give in to sex."

Eva's heart thumped hard in her chest at the thought that Kyle could possibly have a motivation that was tied in with caring about her, that in his own hard-nosed way, he had been trying to protect her. The next thought was a dizzying, improbable leap—that Kyle had a personal interest in stopping her from having sex with other men because *he* wanted her.

Annoyed that she should even begin to imagine that Kyle's concern was based on some kind of personal desire for her when she knew he regarded her as a spoiled, shallow good-time girl, she put the revelation in context. Kyle was gorgeous, megawealthy and successful, but the reality was that, like his older brothers and her macho

Atraeus cousins, shunt him back a few centuries, give him a sword and buckler and he would fit right in. Just because he was being protective to the point of being intrusive didn't mean he was attracted to her. It was just part of his DNA. "I know how to handle men. Believe me, sex will not be an issue."

Kyle's gaze dropped to her mouth. "Then, honey, you don't know men very well."

Her heart pounded a little harder, not at the implication that she was naive about men in general, but at the low, rough timbre of his voice and the sudden revelation that Kyle *did* find her attractive.

Eva swallowed against the sudden dryness in her throat. The fingers of her right hand curled tight against the childish urge to press the heel of her palm against the sharp pounding of her heart.

Someone else jostled her to get to the bar. Kyle said something low and curt, his arm curled around her waist as he pulled her against his side. The move was more courteous and protective than overtly sensual, but even so, another hot pang shot clear to her toes.

He released her almost immediately, but not before his gaze touched on hers, filled with unexpected knowledge. Another shockwave went through her. If she'd thought Kyle hadn't noticed that she was still crazily attracted to him, she was wrong. He knew.

"Damn, let's get out of here."

Taking her hand, he forged a path through the now-busy bar, and out of the blue, memories she'd buried flooded back. Kyle's fingers linked with hers years ago, the carefree flash of his grin as they'd escaped from the crowded party. The way the earth had stopped spinning and she'd forgotten to breathe when they had run down to the beach and long weeks of swimming and talking together had finally reached a flash point.

Breath suddenly constricted, she pulled her hand free and tried to ignore the heated tingling of the brief contact.

Kyle stopped, coincidentally, right beside the wedding cake. "You might think you can handle marriage to some guy you've only just met, but I know for a fact you've never even lived with a man."

The memories winked out with the suddenness of a door slamming. Her temper flared at the evidence that Kyle had been prying into her life. "Just because I haven't had a long-term relationship—"

"The way I heard it, you haven't had *any* real relationships."

She dragged off the glasses, her eyes flashing fire. "How can you know this stuff?" Although she knew the answer had to be Kyle's younger sisters, the Messena twins, Sophie and Francesca. Over the years she had become good friends with the twins, so of course they knew exactly how her life had played out. No doubt Kyle had engaged Sophie and Francesca in some kind of casual conversation, *gathering intelligence*. They would not have realized that telling Kyle she didn't go in for casual relationships would matter. "I knew it. You've been *spying* on me."

"Checking up on you. It's part of the brief."

And with his military background, Kyle had a certain skill set. When he had gone into the army, she had still been lovesick enough to keep tabs on him. Not satisfied with the rank and file, he had done officer training, then had gone into the Special Air Service, the SAS. When he had been sent on his first overseas assignment, she had lost sleep for weeks, wondering if he had been wounded or even killed. Then she had learned that he had come back from the mission just fine and gotten married on his days off. It was then she had decided she would never worry about him again.

She folded her arms across her chest, glad to have that salutary reminder about just how meaningless that long-ago holiday romance and kiss on the beach had been. "I am not a job."

"No." He stared at the monster cake with a faintly in-credulous gaze. "You're a pain in the butt."

Her chin shot up. "Then why do the job?"

"Believe me, if Mario had chosen someone else, I would have been more than happy."

"Ditto."

A muscle jerked fascinatingly along the side of his jaw. Bolstered by the unmistakable sign of tension, Eva delivered the only ultimatum she had. "Then unless you want to keep tabs on me for the next thirteen years as my trustee, maybe you should let me get on with the business of getting married."

"Troy Kendal will never marry you."

She should have been shocked by the flat pronounce-ment, but in a weird way, after the relentless research he had conducted into all of her other grooms, she had half expected him to find out. "You don't know that."

The resolute quality of his gaze, as if he would let her marry Troy over his dead body, sent a forbidden little thrill through her. She drew a breath in an effort to still the rapid pounding of her heart. Something was defi-nitely, seriously wrong with her. She should have been angry, desperate. She shouldn't *like* it that Kyle was sys-tematically getting rid of her grooms.

She slid her glasses back onto the bridge of her nose, suddenly needing the camouflage. "This conversation is over. I have a business to run."

Kyle dragged his gaze from the mesmerizing sight of Eva walking away, gripping her official clipboard. His frown deepened when he noted a familiar figure giving him the kind of narrowed, assessing stare he had gotten used to over the past few months. Kendal was new on the list of men Eva had dated since Mario had died. He also deviated from the pattern of older, biddable admirers Eva had approached in order to find a manageable, paid husband.

Kendal was twenty-four, which made him younger than Eva by four years. He was also a well-known professional rugby player with a list of stormy liaisons behind him. Recently, Kendal had been sidelined by injury and had missed the cut for the new season, which meant his career was stalled. According to the research Kyle had done, he was also currently strapped for cash.

His jaw tightened as Kendal slung his arm around Eva's waist. He knew exactly where and when Eva had picked Kendal up, because he had conducted the surveillance himself. It was four nights ago at a trendy singles bar in downtown Auckland.

He relaxed marginally as Eva detached Kendal's arm with the kind of brisk efficiency that spelled out loud and clear that whatever bargain she had struck with Kendal, it was purely business. Which suited Kyle, since Kendal had the kind of reputation with women that sent a cold itch down his spine.

Kyle found a seat in the shadow of a large indoor palm, where he could keep an eye on Eva and Troy. Taking out his phone, he made a call to a contact. His family's bank poured a lot of money into sponsoring professional rugby. A few minutes later, after pledging a further personal donation from his own funds, contingent on a contract offer to Kendal, he hung up.

A waiter placed a plate of food in front of him. Kyle ate without tasting, intent on Kendal as the man took a call on his cell. Minutes later, Kendal left the wedding with a pretty blonde who had been seated at his table.

Kyle's phone buzzed. After receiving confirmation that Kendal had verbally accepted a contract offer, he terminated the call and sat back in his chair.

Eva wouldn't be happy with him. She was smart and would know exactly what he had done, but Kyle couldn't regret getting rid of Kendal. He was the kind of unsavory guy he wouldn't trust with any of the women he knew, family or not.

With Kendal now out of the picture, Eva's last marriage scheme had just collapsed.

The thought filled him with relief. If Eva had picked someone she could love, he would not have intervened. Instead, she had chosen a list of controllable men who really did just want money. Losers who were not immune to the fact that Eva was drop-dead gorgeous and distractingly sexy. Kyle knew exactly how the masculine mind worked. Platonic agreement or not, it would have only been a matter of time before Eva would have found herself maneuvered into bed.

His stomach tightened on a hot punch of emotion.

Over his dead body.

Kendal sliding his arm around Eva's waist had sealed his decision in stone.

Eva had turned him down, but in the space of an hour the game had changed. She wanted him. Up until now he had been content to keep his distance and let Eva exhaust her options, but now he was no longer prepared to stand back or let any other man enter the picture. She would accept his proposal; it was just a matter of time.

Eva was his.

Four

Eva shoveled a chunk of the gorgeous wedding cake onto a plate and for good measure snagged two of the ridiculously cute frosted cupcakes and a flute of champagne. It was an undisciplined decision and the calories would go straight to her hips, but it had been hours since she had eaten. Besides, since it was supposed to be her wedding, she figured she deserved a little comfort food.

Irritated with the glasses, which were pressing hard enough on the bridge of her nose to give her a headache, she dragged them off and tucked them in her pocket. The music was still pounding in the main reception room, but the bride and groom had departed, so there was no longer any need to look nerdish. Plate in one hand, glass in the other, she scanned the room for Kyle so she could avoid him. Although, since she had acknowledged the crazy, self-destructive fatal attraction that gripped her, she seemed to have developed an ultrasensitive inner radar so that, without looking, she knew exactly where he was.

When she couldn't find him, instead of being relieved, her stomach plummeted. Taller than most of the guests, he was normally easy to spot.

A wild suspicion formed that maybe he was with Jacinta, whom she had seen chatting to him on a number of occasions. The suspicion was allayed when she glimpsed Jacinta in animated conversation with the best man, who was considerably better looking than the groom.

She strolled down into the tropical gardens, where a few guests were sitting at tables, enjoying the balmy evening. The exotic plantings looked spectacular when lit at night. Kyle was nowhere to be seen, which meant he had probably left. Jaw firming against the impossible notion that the weird, plunging feeling in her stomach was disappointment, she belatedly remembered Troy.

The last time she had seen him he had been sitting with some blonde and drinking too much. Suspicious, because he had a definite reputation when it came to women, especially blonde women, she checked the dance floor. When she didn't see him there, she made a search of the hotel lobby and loitered near the men's room while she polished off the wedding cake and sipped a little more champagne. When Troy didn't appear, she strolled to the pool area.

The patio, which was fringed with palms and drifts of star jasmine that scented the night, was dimly lit and lonely. The enormous pool was empty of bathers, its surface limpid, the lights under the water giving it a jewel-like glow. Eva checked the bathing pavilion, which held changing rooms, showers and stacks of fluffy white towels. It, too, was empty. With the way her luck was running lately, she had to consider that either Troy had left with the blonde, or they had gotten a room together.

She should have been disappointed, but the plain fact was she had not liked Troy. Sitting down on a deck chair, she finished off the last of the champagne. Instead of leaving the flute on the pavers, where it could be knocked over and shattered, she decided to store it in her bag until she could drop it back at the bar.

She stared gloomily at the cupcakes. She was halfway through the chocolate one with fudge icing and pretty sugar flowers when a deep, curt voice cut through even that meager pleasure. "If you were looking for Kendal, he left."

"With the blonde?"

"With the blonde."

Eva slapped what was left of the cupcake back on the plate and tried to ignore the dizzying relief that while Troy had left, Kyle was still here. It was an odd time to note that while every man she had handpicked and tried to organize into her life—for just a brief time, and for money—had run out on her, the one man she had been desperate to avoid and who didn't need money, had stayed. "What did you say to him?"

Kyle emerged from the shadows of the palms, where she knew there was a shell path that led to the beach. Her stomach tensed. It was a path she could hardly forget, since it was the one she and Kyle had taken years ago when they had sneaked away to share their one and only passionate interlude. The awareness that was becoming more and more acute hummed through her like an electric current. A little desperately, she picked up the lemon cupcake with white chocolate icing and a delicate sprinkling of raspberry dust, although her appetite was gone.

Kyle dropped his jacket, which he'd slung over one

shoulder, over the back of a deck chair and walked around the pool toward her. "I didn't say a word to Kendal."

She tried not to be mesmerized by the way the pool lights glanced off the taut lines of his cheekbones and jaw, investing his skin with a bronze sheen as if he really was a warrior of old. "You've gotten rid of every other man, so why not Troy?"

He undid a couple of buttons and loosened off his tie, unwittingly drawing her gaze to the muscular column of his throat. Swallowing, she looked away from that fascinating triangle of tanned skin and ended up studying a scar that made a small, intriguing crescent on one cheekbone. For the first time she noticed that he had dark circles beneath his eyes, as if he hadn't been getting enough sleep.

Join the club, she thought, firmly squashing any hint of compassion. Just because an old attraction that should have died years ago had somehow reactivated, that didn't mean her brain had turned to mush. If Kyle had let her marry any one of the grooms she had chosen, they would both be getting plenty of sleep.

He paused just feet away. "Kendal's agent made him an offer he couldn't refuse."

There was a moment of weird disorientation, where ordinary sounds and sensations seemed to blink out, and yet her heart pumped so loudly it was deafening. She looked down and saw the lemon cupcake had turned to mangled chunks between her fingers. Dropping the remains of the cupcake on the plate, she grabbed the napkin that was folded to one side of the plate and wiped icing off her fingers.

Losing her temper wouldn't get her anywhere with Kyle. As long as she could remember, he had been utterly male, as blunt and immovable as a rock wall. Crazily, that was what had once attracted her so much. When her teenage world had been in pieces, he had seemed strong and disciplined in a quiet, steady way. Special forces had suited him down to the ground. "Money. I should have guessed."

He strolled to the edge of the pool. "Kendal's got a reputation. You wouldn't have been able to handle him."

"So you decided to handle him for me." She launched to her feet, too upset to stay. But in her hurry, she forgot that she had dropped her bag by the recliner, and in the dim light she didn't see the strap lying on the pavers. One of her heels snagged in the strap and she stumbled.

Strong fingers closed around her upper arm, steadying her. Her reaction was instantaneous as she jerked free and shoved at Kyle's chest. She had a split second to register how near she was to the edge of the pool. Kyle said something curt and grabbed at her wrist, but it was too late as the glossy surface of the water came up to meet her.

The cool water was a shock, but not as much as Kyle, whom she must have pulled off balance, plunging into the water beside her. Holding her breath, she kicked to the surface and tried to ignore the fact that she had left her shoes at the bottom of the pool. Pale pink to match her suit, and superexpensive, she had loved them with passion, but no way was she diving back in to get them with Kyle watching. She would wait until he was gone then fish them out later.

Swimming to the ladder, she climbed out, trying not to be aware of Kyle boosting himself over the side in one lithe movement. She was still angry with him, but it was difficult to sustain fury when her clothes were wet and clinging, her hair had collapsed into a bedraggled mess and every time she looked at Kyle, his wet shirt plastered to his chest, her mind went utterly blank.

Kyle dragged off his tie and peeled out of his shirt. Averting her gaze from his impressive torso, Eva walked briskly into the poolroom and retrieved two towels from the nearest shelf. Tossing one at Kyle, she kept her eyes averted as she dried herself off.

Instead of using the towel, Kyle draped it over a nearby lounger and dropped back down into the pool. Seconds later, he climbed back out with her shoes. Water slid off bronzed skin and dripped from his nose as he handed them to her. "I'm sorry I pushed you so hard."

Eva ruthlessly suppressed the desire to respond to the glimpse of humor since, technically, she was the one who had done the pushing. Grimly, she concentrated on drying the shoes. She absolutely did not want to start remembering all the moments they had shared all those years ago and start thinking of him as funny or sweet. They'd had their moment, and it hadn't worked out. "I'm glad I pushed you. You deserved it."

The quick flash of a grin almost stopped her heart. "Still the same old Eva."

And who, exactly, was that? she wondered a little bitterly. Years ago she had come to the conclusion that he saw her as a messed-up adopted kid. The kind of woman no Messena male in his right mind would date, let alone marry.

To cover up the fact that she was having difficulty keeping her gaze off his torso and a smattering of scars that looked suspiciously like knife or maybe even bullet wounds, she gripped the back of a lounger to put on first one shoe, then the other. She knew Kyle had been injured twice, the second time life threatening enough that he'd been medevaced from Germany back to Auckland.

That time, she had been concerned enough that she had rung the hospital to get an update on his condition.

When they had refused to do that over the phone, she had gone there herself, brazening her way onto Kyle's ward, even though visiting hours had finished. When she had finally found him, she had used her family connection to the Messenas and her celebrity status as a model to get into his room.

She had been shocked to see him pale and still and hooked up to monitors and drips, then a senior nurse had walked in and she'd had to leave. That had been just as well, because as she'd walked out the door Kyle's eyes had flickered open.

Dragging pins from her soaked hair and finger combing it out into some semblance of neatness, she couldn't resist the compulsion to sneak another glance at the worst of the scars and, inadvertently, found herself caught out by Kyle's gaze.

"I know that was you, all those years ago at the hospital."

She froze. "Maybe."

He raked wet hair back from his forehead. "I thought I was dreaming, but the nurse confirmed it."

She busied herself picking up her bag in order to drop the pins into it, but she wasn't paying close enough attention, so some of them scattered over the pavers. Crouching down, she began gathering them up. "It was no big deal. I was in town and heard you'd been—hurt—"

"As in, wounded." He handed her a pin that had skittered over by his foot.

She straightened and found herself uncomfortably close to his naked and still-damp torso. "I didn't want to say that, just in case you had that condition—"

"Post-traumatic stress disorder. Battle fatigue." His mouth quirked in a distractingly sexy way. "No chance, since I have no memory of being hit." He hesitated. "Why didn't you stay?"

Eva, still captured by the sudden intense need to know what exactly had happened, *who* had dared to shoot Kyle, took a few seconds to absorb his question. "You were critical—they wouldn't let me stay."

"I was only critical the night I arrived. I didn't see any family until the next day. So, how did you find out?"

Despite her clothes, which were steadily dripping, and which were now making her feel clammy and just a little chilled, she found herself blushing. There was no way she was going to tell Kyle that she had practically lived on the internet, tracking down Reuters reports, and that she had made a pest of herself by calling his regimental headquarters. "I had a modeling friend whose boyfriend was in the SAS." That part was true enough. She shrugged. "I just happened to mention that you'd been hurt and she…found out for me."

"But you didn't visit me again."

She straightened, hooking the strap of her bag over her shoulder. "I was *busy*. What is this? An interrogation?" Although something about Kyle had changed. The bad-tempered tension had gone and there was an undercurrent that made her feel decidedly breathless. She tried walking in her wet heels to see if they were safe. At the same time she surreptitiously smoothed her palms down the sodden, clinging line of her jacket and skirt to press out excess moisture. As a result, water tickled down her legs and filled her shoes.

Kyle stopped in the process of wringing out his shirt, his gaze arrested. "Maybe you should take the jacket off?"

"No." Eva had routinely taken her clothes off for lingerie ads, but there was no way she was going to take one stitch of clothing off in front of Kyle. She suddenly noticed the flatness of her jacket pocket. Her glasses were gone, which meant they were probably in the bottom of the pool.

"They can stay there," Kyle said flatly. "You don't need them. You've got the eyesight of an eagle."

"How would you know what my eyesight's like?"

"Remember the archery contests?"

Dolphin Bay, two summers in a row, when she and Kyle would go head-to-head at the archery range. "You always won those."

"I'd been practicing for years. You came second."

The sudden warmth in his gaze made her feel flustered all over again. She realized that the distance she had worked so hard to preserve, and which she had been able to maintain quite well if she was angry, had gone. Burned away in the moment she had realized that Kyle wanted her.

She walked to the edge of the pool and peered in. The glasses, with their dark rims, were easily visible. "I need the glasses for work."

"Why? They're not prescription, just plain glass." His face cleared. "No, wait, don't answer, I think I can guess."

Over seeing Kyle's buff, ripped, *hot* torso, she tossed his towel at him. A split second later the sharp tap of heels on tiles signaled Jacinta's presence a moment before she rounded the corner into the pool area.

Her eyes widened when she saw that Eva was soaked. "There you are, the bride's father wants to give you a check—" She noticed Kyle. "Oops. Sorry, did I interrupt something?"

"Nothing." Eva seized her chance to end the unsettling encounter and the crazy, suffocating awareness that had crept up on her out of nowhere. "Where is Mr. Hirsch?"

"In the lobby." Jacinta glanced at Kyle's washboard abs. "I told him you'd be right along."

But suddenly, Eva wasn't going anywhere. She took the one step needed to place herself squarely in Jacinta's line of vision, so that she had to stare at her, rather than at Kyle's bronzed, dripping skin. In the moment that she moved, it struck her that she was behaving like a jealous girlfriend. Kyle did not belong to her, and yet she was ready to fight tooth and nail to fend Jacinta off. "I'm wet and my hair's ruined. You need to go and collect the check."

Jacinta didn't move. "Did you fall in the pool?"

"We both fell," Eva said bluntly.

Jacinta made an odd little noise that sounded suspiciously like amusement quickly muffled then spun on her heel and disappeared back inside.

Kyle broke the tense little silence that developed in the wake of Jacinta's departure by tossing his towel on a recliner and picking up his soaked shirt. "At least you managed to sell the wedding on. I'm guessing right about now, you're getting concerned about money."

She met Kyle's gaze head-on. "Without the backup of my trust fund, all money counts."

And that was the other reason she found this whole process of having to qualify for her own inheritance so hurtful and undermining. All of the bona fide Atraeus and Messena family members who were born to wealth received vast amounts of money, and their right to do so wasn't questioned. She understood what Mario was trying to achieve with the marriage clause, but that didn't change the fact that the whole process made her feel separated from the rest of the family, and *different*.

Stung anew by what she saw as further evidence that, despite adoption, she had never quite fitted into the Atraeus family, Eva turned on her heel, intending to make a beeline for her car, where she had a pair of jeans, a T-shirt and sneakers stashed for the drive back to Auckland.

Kyle caught her arm, halting her. "I'm sorry. I shouldn't have mentioned the money."

The tingling warmth of Kyle's palm, even through the barrier of damp silk, sent a small, sharp shock through her. She jerked free. "I suppose you think I'm a money-grubbing gold digger who doesn't deserve—"

"I don't think that." His gaze dropped to her mouth. "You deserve your inheritance."

Her chin jerked up. "Then why have you been doing your level best to deprive me of it?"

"Money isn't the issue," he muttered. "This is." Bending his head, Kyle kissed her.

Eva inhaled sharply at the warmth of his mouth, stunned by the brief caress and the molten heat that exploded from that one point of contact. When she didn't move, Kyle's palm curled around her nape. The next minute she was pressed hard against the muscled heat of his body as his mouth settled more heavily on hers.

The passion was searing and instant and this time, Eva wasn't content to just be kissed. Palms flattened against the hard muscle of Kyle's chest, and all too aware that she was making a disastrous mistake, she lifted up on her toes and angled her head to increase the contact. His taste exploded in her mouth and the furnace heat of his body warmed her, so that she wanted to press closer still, to wallow in his heat and strength.

And suddenly, it registered just how alone and isolated she had been. Since her teenage fixation on Kyle, she had simply not allowed anyone else close. She had sidestepped relationships and sex. She hadn't thought she needed either, until now.

The strap of her bag slipped off her shoulder. She registered the thump as it dropped onto the ground, and the sound of glass breaking and dimly remembered the champagne flute. Her arms closed around Kyle's neck as the kiss deepened, and suddenly the cling of her wet clothes seemed sodden and restrictive, dragging against skin that was unbearably sensitive. His hand cupped her breast through the layers of wet fabric. Eva inhaled at the sharp beading of her nipple, but it was too late as heat and sensation coiled unbearably tight and splintered.

Kyle muttered something short beneath his breath. Eva pulled free of his grasp, her legs as limp as noodles, embarrassed warmth burning through her. Not only had she practically thrown herself at Kyle like some love-starved teenager, she had actually climaxed just because he had kissed her.

Dragging damp tendrils back from her face, she snatched up her bag and noticed that the champagne flute had broken at the stem and was in two pieces. Jaw set, she found the cake napkin and wrapped the base of the flute.

Kyle crouched down beside her and handed her the rest of the flute but, with her whole body still oversensitive and tingling, Kyle helping, Kyle intruding any further into her life was the last thing she wanted.

"Eva—"

She straightened, desperate to avoid him, but he rose lithely and blocked her path.

Too late to wish that she'd searched for her compact and checked her makeup. Her mascara was probably running. She must look a total mess—

"You wanted to know why I vetoed the grooms you chose. Two reasons. None of them were good enough. And I couldn't let you marry anyone else because *I* want you."

Five

Eva stared at Kyle.

I want you.

A small, sensual shiver zapped down her spine. Not good! She should be annoyed at the way Kyle had gotten rid of all the men she had chosen, not turned on and reveling in the fact that he had done so because he thought none of them had been good enough. "Let me get this right. You proposed because you want sex?"

Suddenly irritated beyond belief, she rummaged in her handbag, found her cell and stabbed a random icon. "Wait just one second. I'm sure I have an app you need called Sex Slaves Are Us."

Impatience registered in his gaze. "I proposed because you need a husband."

Somehow that was the wrong answer. "So sex would just be an optional extra?"

There was a small, vibrating silence. "Whether or not sex would be part of the deal is entirely up to you."

The anger that rolled through Eva was knee-jerk and confusing. She had been angry that Kyle wanted sex from her. Now she was even angrier because, evidently, he could take it or leave it. In her book, that brought them back to square one. She just wasn't that important to Kyle. And didn't that just feel like a replay of the past?

She jammed her cell back in her bag. Until that moment she hadn't realized how much Kyle's defection all those years ago still hurt. He had been a friend when she had needed one. She hadn't just wanted him at age seventeen; she had liked and trusted him. He had walked away without a backward glance then fallen in love with *and married* someone else.

She should have let this go a long time ago. It was neither healthy, nor balanced. But then, balance had never been her strong point. She had always been passionate and a little extreme. Of course, letting go of the hurt of Kyle's rejection was difficult, because in her heart of hearts she had felt sure that they had been on the verge of something special.

On the heels of that thought, suspicion flared. "Did Mario suggest you should marry me before he died?"

Kyle's gaze turned wary. "He did."

Now she really was embarrassed. Mario had been convinced that, despite her disorder, as an heiress she could have the same kind of happy married life he'd had with his wife, if she would only follow the old recipe and marry someone wealthy, trusted and close to home. He had relentlessly tried to marry her off in that way to Kyle's older brothers and, to her everlasting relief, he hadn't succeeded in raising even a flicker of interest. "I know for a fact that he asked Gabriel and Nick and they both turned him down."

Kyle shrugged. "That was a given, since they were both in love with other women."

Eva swiped at a renegade trickle of water sliding down her neck, suddenly incensed. "And who would buy into that crazy kind of medieval stuff, anyway?"

Kyle dragged his gaze from the creamy line of Eva's neck and the tantalizing hint of cleavage in the vee of her suit jacket.

He would.

Although, obviously, that did not reflect well on him. "If you're so set on a marriage of convenience, then I don't get why you're so against taking the second option in the will."

"And marry you?" Eva's chin came up. "Because, while Messena and Atraeus men may look and sound like modern twenty-first century guys, they aren't. Underneath that veneer every one of you is just as medieval as Mario was. And I don't want children. Ever."

The flat certainty of Eva's statement hit Kyle in the solar plexus.

Children. He had a sudden mental image of his small son, Evan, who had been just three months old when he had died.

His stomach tightened on the kind of grief no parent should ever feel as memory flickered. Evan, soft and warm on his shoulder, well fed and smelling of soap and milk as he had relaxed into sleep. The way he had used to crow with delight every time Kyle had picked him up...

When he spoke, he couldn't keep the grim chill out of his voice. "Children won't be an issue, because I don't want them, either. But in any case, we're only looking at an arrangement that will last two years."

He logged the flare of shock in her gaze. He had been

too abrasive. But when it came to the issue of marriage and kids, he couldn't be any other way.

His own family didn't understand him. But then, none of them had seen his wife and child disappear in an explosion that had killed five others and destroyed the barracks gatehouse. None of them understood that moment of sickening displacement, the knowledge that Nicola and Evan would be alive now if it wasn't for *his* insistence that they join him in Germany for Christmas.

The shock of their deaths and the weight of grief and guilt still had the power to stop him in his tracks. It was the reason he avoided friends who had kids and family occasions that, increasingly, overflowed with babies and small children. It was the reason he steered clear of anything approaching a conventional relationship, because he knew he couldn't be that person again. Just the thought of taking on the responsibility of a wife and child made him break out in a cold sweat. His oldest brother, Gabriel, who had arrived in Germany just hours after the explosion, was the only one who had an inkling about how he felt. He unlocked his jaw and tried to soften his tone. "If you agree to marriage, you set the terms."

She crossed her arms over her chest, her stance combative. "Let me see, everything but children, and you would prefer sex as an additional extra."

His gaze narrowed at the way she phrased the same kind of straightforward marriage deal she had personally negotiated at least three times in the past six months. Except for the sex. And he couldn't help a savage little jolt of satisfaction at that fact. "Yes."

She took a half step toward him. He registered the fiery glint in her eyes as she came to a halt in front of him and trailed her finger from a point just below his collarbone to the midpoint of his chest.

"Marriage to you? Now, let me see…" Her gaze locked with his, and he knew very well that she didn't intend to kiss him. "That would be a clear…*no*."

And with a shove she sent him toppling back into the pool.

The following night Eva prepared to go to a trendy singles bar with a couple of girlfriends. She hated singles bars and normally would never go to one but, after the debacle with Kyle, she was determined to make one more attempt at locating a husband.

Kyle's proposal was an unexpected goad. The fact that she personally wanted him had somehow made the situation even more fraught. Her response to his kiss had been a case in point. She'd never been able to resist him, and now he knew it. If they married, even if she said no to sex, would she be strong enough to hold out against him?

She flipped through her wardrobe for something to wear. She needed something that was sexy but reserved enough that she could attract a man who was reasonably good-looking, intelligent and down on his luck. She doubted she would find the type of man she needed at a singles bar, since most men who went there just wanted sex, but she had to try.

She chose a little black dress and pumps that weren't too high, because she was already medium height and she didn't want to narrow her options by being too tall. After putting on makeup, she combed her hair out straight so that it swung silkily around her shoulders. Affixing tawny earrings to her lobes, she spritzed herself with perfume and she was good to go.

The bar was packed. After ordering a drink, she sat at a cozy sofa and coffee table setting. Feeling like a wallflower, Eva sipped the iced water she had ordered.

Seconds later, she had her first approach, a handsome dark-haired guy who looked like a lawyer and proved to be. She sent him on his way when she found out he was married.

Two more conversations later with men who up front admitted they were married, but had left their wives—which meant they were utterly useless to her because they couldn't remarry until they were legally divorced—she scanned the bar. Depressingly, most of the men at the bar were either already hooked up with a partner or looked older, which from experience she knew probably meant they would still be married, even if they weren't living with their wives.

She caught a glimpse of the back of a guy's head as he disappeared into a shadowy part of the bar. Adrenaline pumped, because she was certain it was Kyle. He was the right height and his shoulders were broad. He half turned, giving her a clear view of his profile. It wasn't Kyle.

Unacceptably, disappointment deflated her mood even further. Of course none of the Messena men would be seen dead in a singles bar. They were too wealthy, too macho and too gorgeous. They didn't need to go after women, because women chased them. Jacinta's reaction to Kyle was a case in point. She had practically swooned over him.

A nerdy guy approached her and asked if she would like to dance. Eva checked out his left hand and saw the pale streak around his third finger. "Why don't you ask your wife to dance?"

"Uh—she's out of town."

"And I thought this was a *singles* bar. You should go home."

His face reddened. "Who are you? My grandmother?"

She gave him a straight look. "If I was, I'd be saying a whole lot more."

After biting out an uncomplimentary phrase, he spun on his heel and strode away. All pleasure was now leeched from the evening. In no mood to date, or marry, anyone, Eva pulled out her phone and checked an app that listed nearby nightclubs and bars.

She didn't want to go anywhere else. She would prefer to go home, make a cup of tea, curl up on the sofa and watch a movie, but she couldn't give up just yet.

She stepped outside of the air-conditioned bar into the hot, steamy air of a summer's night. It was like walking into a sauna. Glancing skyward, she noticed the heavy layer of cloud that had rolled in, blotting out the night sky. Because Auckland City was situated on a narrow isthmus with the Tasman Sea on one side, the Pacific Ocean on the other, the weather could change quickly.

Hailing a cab, she gave the driver the address of a bar she'd used before that was younger and a little wilder. She'd met Troy there, and that would have worked out if it hadn't been for Kyle.

He had vetoed every other guy she had chosen, and she couldn't help thinking that if she located a possible groom tonight, he would no doubt suffer the same fate.

Kyle wanted her.

She tried to dismiss the disruptive thought, but heat flooded her at the memory of the kiss and the way she had reacted, like a love-starved teenager on her first date! She breathed a sigh of relief as the driver pulled away from the curb and the cab's air-conditioning kicked in. Something made her glance back at the entrance of the bar. A tall, dark-haired man was just sliding behind the wheel of a glossy black sports car. Her heart slammed in her chest at the thought that it was Kyle, although she couldn't be sure. There were a lot of dark sports cars in town, which all looked the same to her, and maybe she was seeing the same guy she had noticed before?

If it was Kyle, that meant he was following her. A sharp thrill jolted through her at the thought.

Determinedly, she squashed the idea along with any hint of relief that despite her saying no, Kyle might not have given up on her. Keeping her gaze fixed on the city street ahead, she tried to remember all the reasons she had to be furious with him. Unfortunately, the reasons seemed hollow when she kept coming back to the stunning fact that he had actually asked her to marry him.

And she was wondering if the offer was still open.

Craning around, she looked through the back window. The car was following so closely it was practically herding the taxi, but the windows of the sleek sports car were too darkly tinted to reveal who was driving. The driver could see her, but she couldn't see him. Her heart pounded out of control. She was suddenly certain that it was Kyle.

The taxi pulled into a space and the sports car swept past. Eva paid the fare and climbed out, all the while giving herself a good talking-to. She should be frustrated and annoyed if it was Kyle—she should be furious—so why did it feel like the evening was suddenly looking up?

In the time it took her to close the door of the taxi, the sports car had disappeared. She checked in both directions, half expecting to see Kyle walking toward her. When she realized she was loitering on the sidewalk, actually waiting for him to appear, instead of going into the bar closest to where the taxi had parked, she quickly walked a little further down the road before spotting another random bar.

Pulse rate still high, she checked the street one last

time before walking in, only to find she had another problem. Now that she was here, she had absolutely no energy or enthusiasm for finding a suitable husband. Her experience at the previous bar had literally been the last straw.

Kyle was right. She did not want a stranger for a husband.

She could still say yes to Kyle. But if she allowed the attraction that sizzled through her every time she saw Kyle to turn into actual love, where would that leave her in two years' time?

The bar she'd chosen was an Irish pub, filled with young people and a sprinkling of tourists. Feeling too put-together and conventional amongst skin-tight denim, shaved heads and psychedelic tattoos, she took a stool at the counter, dropped her chin on one hand and ordered a glass of wine.

The bartender, who looked ridiculously young and was probably a student, instantly started chatting her up. "Don't I know you from somewhere?"

Eva sipped her drink and logged the moment he recognized her.

He nodded his head, grinning. "Oh yeah. The buses. The lingerie ad."

She groaned inwardly, but managed to keep her expression bland. She'd had a lot of practice handling these kinds of conversations, since the lingerie company she had worked for had plastered images of her on the back of buses and on huge highway billboards. "That was a while ago." Two years. Although it felt like ten.

"Cool. My mom used to buy your stuff."

Eva set her glass down and checked her watch. She had promised herself she would stay for fifteen minutes. By then, Kyle should have found a parking space and gone inside the other bar and she could safely leave without him seeing her. "I didn't own the company, I just modeled for them."

He grinned again. "Still…nice. Those billboards were *big*. Most of the buses in town had you on the back of them. Pretty sure some of them still do." He leaned forward on the bar, angling for a better view down the front of her dress. "If you're still into that kind of work, I've got a friend—"

"She doesn't do charities for school kids."

The rasp of Kyle's voice sent a hot tingle down her spine as he slid onto a stool beside her. Dressed all in black, a five-o'clock shadow darkening his jaw, his gaze wintry, he looked, quite frankly, intimidating.

Eva felt like banging her head on the counter. Former Special Air Service, an assault specialist who had once belonged to some hunter-killer squad with its own scary code name… Why, oh why, had she not known he would find her?

His gaze touched on hers and her fingers tightened convulsively on the stem of her wineglass. Taking a deep breath because her heart was suddenly racing, she dredged up a dazzling smile for the bartender who, predictably, was backing off fast. "Actually, I *would* like to speak to your friend. As it happens, in about three weeks' time I'll be in the market for some modeling work."

"Uh—my friend's more into *movies*, you know? Maybe, talk to me later." His gaze flickered to Kyle, the subtext clear. *When the boyfriend's gone.*

"He's not my boyfriend."

A nervous tic jumped along one side of the bartender's jaw. He glanced around, as if willing a customer to appear. "On second thoughts, I seem to remember my friend's getting ready to go overseas…"

And if she didn't miss her guess, the bartender was getting ready to run.

Drawn by a compulsion she couldn't seem to resist, she met Kyle's gaze and tried not to notice the instant little charge of adrenaline that shot through her at the laser blue of his eyes. Trying to ignore the tension thrumming through her, she ran her finger around the rim of the wineglass. "Do you have to ruin everything? Lately, I feel like I live in some kind of Mafia family."

"If you want modeling work, there are better places to get it than over the bar of some pub, like your agent, for instance."

"What would you know about it?"

"The bank has modeling agencies as clients. I don't know how they run their businesses, but I'm pretty sure it's not at—" he looked at the sign over the bar "—Irish Jack's."

She sent him a sideways glance that was supposed to be withering, then wished she hadn't when she caught the gleam of humor in his eyes. She squashed the sudden, almost irresistible desire to smile with him. "My agent still has clients lining up. I can continue my modeling career if I want."

"In movies?"

"I don't do movies. I just said that to annoy you."

"You succeeded."

Feeling a little panicky, because she did not want to love Kyle's dry sense of humor or the possessiveness, she slipped off the barstool. Maybe if she were standing, she would feel more in control. Unfortunately, Kyle also stood, towering over her, making her feel ridiculously small and feminine.

She made a beeline for the door but couldn't suppress her automatic pleasure at the small courtesy when Kyle held it for her. In her current state of mind, she could not afford to be charmed by Kyle's manners.

When she stepped out into the balmy evening air, she spun and confronted him. "Is the offer of marriage still open?" The words tumbled out sounding a whole lot more vulnerable than she'd planned.

His gaze sharpened. "Why? What's changed?"

She swallowed at the leap he'd made, his scary insight. Because something had changed. She'd felt it in the instant he had sat down at the bar and fended off the bartender. She didn't know exactly what had changed, just that she had *liked* it that Kyle wanted to protect her. "I'm not sure. I'm confused."

"The offer is still open." He was silent for a moment. "If you want, I can give you a lift home."

She frowned at the sudden switch from aggressive pursuit to coolness. The sense of hidden depth and layers abruptly made her aware of the abyss that lay between the teenaged Kyle she had once fallen for, and the mature, seasoned man who stood in front of her now. "Okay."

The lights of Kyle's Maserati, which occupied a parking spot further along the road, flashed. A short walk later, he opened the passenger side door for her. Taking a deep breath, careful not to brush against him, she settled into the luxurious seat, stomach clenching at the subtly masculine scent of leather. The door closed and seconds later, Kyle slid behind the wheel and the car accelerated off the curb.

As they cruised through town, stopping at intersections filled with tourists enjoying the restaurants and cafés, and loved-up couples strolling, she suddenly didn't want the night to end. "I don't want to go home. Not yet."

He turned his head, and she caught the glitter of

his gaze. The tension in the enclosed space seemed to tighten. "Where do you want to go?"

"The beach." The answer came straight out of the past and made warmth rise to her cheeks, because she belatedly realized the link to their long-ago tryst. It was just that the beach had been such a carefree place for her. She'd spent long summers at Dolphin Bay swimming and sunbathing and building late-night fires. Adoptive cousins, most like Kyle—second and third times removed— and extended family everywhere, and her old life with its trouble and grief left far behind.

Kyle took a turn in the direction of the marina. Traffic slowed. Ahead, Eva glimpsed a bus and hoped it wasn't one of the ones that still had the underwear ad. And, of course, it was.

Kyle sent her a neutral look. "That's one of the reasons Mario worried about you."

Eva studied the faintly battered line of Kyle's profile, the tough jaw and ridiculously long, silky lashes. She shrugged. She wasn't about to apologize for a highly successful modeling career. "Mario was conservative."

She switched her gaze to his hands on the wheel. A scar started at the sleeve of his shirt and ran the length of the back of his hand. "How did you get that?"

He frowned. "Don't change the subject."

"You always want to talk about me. Maybe I want to talk about you."

The minute the words were out, she wished she hadn't said them, because they sounded flirtatious and provocative.

"It's a fishing injury from a couple of years ago. Nick was casting and his hook caught me."

"I thought it might be from the military."

Amusement flashed in his gaze. "Disappointed?"

"No! That last injury putting you in the hospital was bad enough. You almost died." Her stomach bottomed out at the thought. It was almost four years ago, but she could still remember how frantic she'd felt. She hadn't questioned her reaction then, she had just thought it was a leftover of the crush she'd had on Kyle. But how long did crushes last?

Kyle changed lanes and accelerated smoothly. "When I woke up, Gabriel told me that if I didn't resign, he would join up. I knew he'd keep his word, and that the family and the bank couldn't afford to lose him, so I signed the discharge papers."

"You didn't want to leave? I don't know how you could have wanted to stay in after—"

"Nicola and Evan were killed?"

She stared ahead, the stream of oncoming traffic a colorful blur. "I'm sorry, I shouldn't have mentioned it. I know what it's like losing people you love. It's hard to believe they're gone."

She registered his curious gaze, as if he were waiting for her to elaborate. But she'd said too much already. She'd found that the less she said about her past, the better she fitted in. Ignoring the past didn't make it go away, but it sure helped her to feel more normal.

Kyle took an off-ramp and stopped for lights. "It was an attack on the barracks where we were based in Germany," he said quietly. "Unfortunately, Nicola was driving past the car with the explosives when it detonated. Evan was in his car seat. It was pure bad luck. If she had been a few seconds earlier or later, they would have avoided the blast."

There was a moment of silence. "If I hadn't insisted they come out to Germany for Christmas, they would still be alive."

The words, uttered flatly, nevertheless contained a rawness that riveted Eva. She didn't know why she hadn't considered that Kyle might blame himself for the death of his wife and child, but the flat statement made a terrible kind of sense.

Kyle was an alpha male. Testosterone aside, that meant taking charge and taking responsibility. To have lost the two people most intimately connected with him, the wife and child he had vowed to care for and protect, must be unbearable. In that instant a whole lot of things she hadn't understood about Kyle settled into place. Foremost was the fact that he had *loved* his wife and child.

A sharp ache started somewhere deep in her chest. The way she, all those years ago, would have loved to be loved. "You still miss them."

The lights changed, Kyle accelerated through the intersection. "Birthdays and important dates are the worst, but it's not as bad as it used to be."

"I'm sorry." As much as she had gotten used to loss and grief, the process of losing her family over a period of years had, at least, given her time to adjust. She could not imagine what it must have been like for Kyle to lose a wife and child, literally, in an instant.

He took the off-ramp for Takapuna Beach, his expression closed. "It's okay. It hurt, but it was years ago."

She stared ahead at the road as it unfolded, feeling suddenly incredibly self-centered. She had been viewing Kyle as controlling and intrusive—the big, bad wolf—but like all the men in his family, he was a family man.

Abruptly, she understood him in a way that was unbearably and intimately personal. As the oldest child in her family, she had said goodbye to her twin and two younger siblings. She could remember holding their hands and willing them to live. One by one they had died; there had been nothing she could do. It wasn't the shock of a bomb blast, but the sense of helplessness was the same.

Kyle turned down a side street then into a park, with the sea just a few yards from a small parking lot. Now that they were alone, and at the beach, she was out of stall time.

Panic gripped her. Given that she now knew she could not marry a stranger, she needed to decide whether or not she could cope with a temporary marriage to Kyle.

Six

Kyle tossed his jacket in the space behind the driver's seat and walked around the hood of the Maserati to open the passenger side door. Predictably, Eva already had the door open, but was still seated while she unfastened her shoes. He drew in a breath at the elegant line of her legs and the tantalizing glimmer of a fine chain around one slim ankle. "If you want to walk, I don't know how long we'll have. The forecast is for rain."

It was actually for a thunderstorm. He could already see lightning flashes farther north, and from the drop in temperature the rain could start any time.

"Don't care." She sent him a fleeting look that, half hidden by a tousled swath of tawny hair, was unconsciously sexy.

His stomach tightened as he was irresistibly reminded of a seventeen-year-old girl who had trailed endlessly along the beach at Dolphin Bay in a bikini top and a pair of ragged, cutoff denim shorts, driving most of the male population crazy.

She slid out of the Maserati, the gusting breeze plastering her little black dress against the lithe curves of her body as she closed the car with a brisk thud that made him wince.

She sent him a smooth, closed smile, the kind he'd gotten familiar with lately, as if he was one of her difficult clients. "I'm tired of the city and miles of concrete. I want to feel sand between my toes."

He depressed his key and locked the car before walking to the beach. Eva was already standing on smooth, hard-packed sand, just inches shy of the water, her expression oddly relaxed.

"I love it, especially when there's going to be a storm." She sent him a slanting sideways look as he joined her, as if she was trying to assess him in some way. She smiled encouragingly. "Shall we walk?"

His jaw tightened as he suddenly got it. After months of avoidance, Eva had changed tack completely. Every muscle in his body tightened when he realized that Eva's question outside the Irish pub about whether or not his offer of marriage was still open had been for real. And that some time between that moment and the drive to the beach, she had moved on to summing him up as a potential husband. When Eva began asking him about his work hours and his interests, he realized he was being interviewed.

In a weird way, it reminded him of when he was nineteen and had spent a whole summer getting to know Eva. In a lot of ways, the process had been the exact opposite of the usual pattern. She had started out so confident and self-contained it had been hard to get close to her at all.

One day, with the summer almost over and Kyle

pushed to his limits, he had saved her from an older guy who had cornered her at the end of the beach. The tussle had been brief, but when the tourist had beat a hasty retreat, she had stared at him and blushed. She hadn't said a word, just continued on as if it hadn't happened, but from that moment on her behavior had changed. In a weird way it was as if he had passed some kind of test.

She strolled down to the water's edge, wading in ankle-deep. There was no attempt to look sexy or alluring, just a simple enjoyment of the seaside. She turned, her gaze connected with his then dropped to his mouth before she looked quickly away.

Every muscle in his body suddenly taut, Kyle waited her out. He wanted Eva, and she knew it. Last night he thought he'd blown any chance of having her in his bed, but in the space of twenty-four hours, something had changed. Added to that, the beach setting was creating an unsettling sense of déjà vu, as if they'd been spun back years.

Lightning flashed, followed by a heavy roll of thunder. Simultaneously, rain pounded down.

Eva flinched at the sudden deluge, but the rain, though torrential, wasn't cold and, besides, she loved the wildness of it. Kyle jerked his head in the direction of the car but, caught up in the adrenaline of the moment, she grabbed his hand and pulled him toward the shelter of a large, gnarled *pohutukawa* tree.

She sucked in a breath as they stepped beneath the dense overhang of the tree. With the sound of the surf and the shift of shadows as dappled light from the parking lot flowed through the leaves, in a strange way it felt like stepping back in time to Dolphin Bay and that first kiss.

When Kyle reeled her in close and framed her face with his hands, the breath stopped in her lungs. She should have extricated herself in her usual smooth, sophisticated way, but ever since Kyle had slipped onto the stool beside her in the Irish pub, she had been subtly off balance. He had been tailing her for months and had ruthlessly gotten rid of any man who had gotten too close. Now he was making no bones about the fact that *he* wanted her, and against all the odds she loved that.

And suddenly she no longer wanted to resist him. Years ago she had loved Kyle and then lost him along with the whole future she had imagined she might have as a woman, a wife and a mother. He had loved another woman, but she'd had no one. Now she had a chance at... something. If she stopped to think— But right now, with the storm pounding all around them, all she wanted to do was feel.

When she ran her palms up over his chest to his shoulders, Kyle's response was instant. Hauling her closer still, he bent his head, his breath washing over her lips. "What is it with beaches," he muttered.

Lifting up on her toes, she wrapped her arms around his neck and kissed him, the passion white-hot and instant.

Long seconds later, she wrenched her mouth free and dragged at the buttons of Kyle's shirt. He muttered something short and sharp. Dimly, she registered the loosening of the fit of her dress as the zipper tracked down, a damp blast of cool air against her skin. A split second later the dress was gone and her bra along with it.

Bending down, Kyle took one nipple in his mouth. Dizzying sensation jerked through her in waves. When he lifted his head, she remembered his shirt, but he must have shrugged out of it at some point, because she found naked skin.

Kyle groaned. "Maybe we should slow down—"

Her palms slid down over washboard abs and found the fastening of his pants. He uttered a short, soft word. Moments later, she was on her back on the sand, her dress and what she guessed was Kyle's jacket and shirt beneath her.

Kyle's fingers hooked in her panties, dragging them down. Lightning flashed, illuminating the stark planes of Kyle's face as his weight came down on her. Sucking in a sharp breath at the sheer heat of him, she wound her arms around Kyle's neck, the fierce need to keep him close momentarily blotting out coherent thought.

"Babe—there's something I need to do first." He disengaged and rolled to one side. She logged the sound of foil tearing. A condom. Thunder detonated again and the rain pattered down through the canopy of leaves, splashing on bare skin so that she shivered.

Kyle hauled her close, sheltering her with his body, and in that moment it seemed the most natural thing in the world to hook one arm around his neck and lift up for his kiss. At the same time, curious about the condom, her fingers closed around him. She felt the smooth texture, the heated satin of his skin underneath.

A split second later, he came down between her legs. She felt the heated pressure of him. There was a shivering moment of sanity, when she logged Kyle's stillness, as if, like her, he had come to the sudden sobering conclusion of exactly what they were about to do. She should say no. Kyle would stop, she knew he would, and in a crazy way that in itself was freeing.

It was a plain fact that she didn't want to relinquish him or the burning, irresistible pleasure that held her in its grip. It wasn't love. She wasn't that silly, but when set against the shadows of her past and her present loneliness—the growing fear that she would never truly be cherished—it tipped an internal balance so that she no longer wanted to think, only to feel...

She felt him tense at the tight constriction and freeze in place. She thought he was going to stop, but when he lifted his head, she clung, unable to bear letting him go, arching against the burning pressure at the center of her body.

He groaned and a second later, shoved deep. She felt the drag of the condom, an uncomfortable pinching as with each downward stroke he seemed to push a little deeper still. Her hips twisted automatically, trying to ease the discomfort, but the restless twisting momentarily dislodged him.

He cradled her closer and the next downward stroke felt smoother, sleeker, more pleasurable, and she realized that something had changed. The condom was gone, but it was already too late as irresistible sensation gripped her, coiling tight, and the damp, heavy darkness shimmered into light.

Kyle stopped the car outside Eva's house. "We need to talk. Somehow, I don't know how, because it's never happened before, but the condom slipped—"

"You don't have to worry about contraception."

The words were out before she could call them back, but she couldn't regret them. She knew Kyle would probably think she was on the pill or had some other form of contraception, but that wasn't the case. She could get pregnant.

The thought made her heart beat wildly. It was the last thing she wanted, but maybe, just maybe, she could get lucky and it wouldn't happen. If it did... She drew a swift breath, unable to imagine a scenario that was so far out of left field for her.

Fingers fumbling in her haste, she unfastened her seat belt. She still felt damp, gritty and disoriented that the night had spun so far out of control that they'd actually had sex and, in the end, because the condom had come off, unprotected sex. She couldn't wait to say goodbye and escape into the quiet refuge of her home. "Thanks," she said brightly, throwing the car door open.

It was still raining. No problem, since she was already bedraggled and her dress was most likely ruined. Cheeks burning, she searched for her clutch, which had somehow managed to slide down the side of the seat. By the time she had retrieved it, Kyle was out of the car and it was too late to make a quick getaway.

Rain was cold on her bare arms as she jogged to her front door and searched for her key. Intensely aware of Kyle beside her, she jammed the key in the lock and somehow missed.

Kyle calmly took the key from her and unlocked the door. As he pushed it wide, the tinkle of glass made her freeze in place.

"Wait here," he said softly. Kyle stepped past her, flowing into the darkened interior.

A chill went down her spine at the quiet way he'd moved, his utter assurance, and despite her dilemma over whether or not to just give in and marry him, she was abruptly glad he was with her. Burglaries were common, but this was the first time it had happened to her.

Long minutes later, lights went on and Kyle reappeared in her tiny hallway. "I'll call the police. Whoever it was, they're gone now, out through the laundry door and over the back fence. The sound of breaking glass was a vase. They knocked it over on their way out."

Eva followed Kyle into her lounge. Drawers had been pulled out and emptied onto the floor. Her one framed family photo of her mother and father in happier days was sitting on the dining table, as if whoever had broken in had paused to look at it. Immediately, suspicion flared. Her last stepfather, Sheldon Ferris, had once tried to get money out of her, but Mario had threatened him with the police.

As she checked around the sitting room, she noted that her TV and stereo were still in place, but her laptop was gone.

Kyle terminated the call he'd just made. "A cruiser will be here in the next ten minutes." He frowned. "Did you set the alarm?"

"Before I left. I always do."

While Kyle checked her alarm system, she stepped into her bedroom. Her shocked disbelief was swamped by burning outrage. If her lounge was a mess, her bedroom was worse. Her closet and every drawer had been emptied. Clothes had been dumped on the floor with hangers still attached. Shoes, makeup and costume jewelry were scattered over the bed and the floor. She picked up lacy scraps of underwear and jammed them back in their drawer. She knew she shouldn't touch anything, because the police needed to see the scene of the crime, but she drew the line at having uniformed police officers claiming her underwear as evidence.

Until that moment, she had thought a burglary was about the scariness of a stranger, losing stuff and the inconvenience of insurance claims, but she knew now that wasn't so at all. Shock and anger that someone had thought they had the right to invade her privacy and rummage through her private things kept running through her in waves. They had tossed items aside and taken what they wanted as if she didn't matter.

She didn't know what was missing other than her laptop, but suddenly the laptop ceased to matter. A chill went through her, and she found herself rubbing her arms. Her home, her sanctuary and all of the personal things that were about *her* had been violated.

Kyle, who had been quietly checking through rooms, reappeared and looked annoyed when she told him the laptop was gone. "Anything else appear to be missing?"

She skimmed the room and tried to think, although when her gaze snagged on a broken music box, a precious keepsake from her childhood, her temper soared again. If it was Sheldon, a one-time used car salesman and inveterate swindler, he would know how precious that music box was to her. "It's a little hard to say with all the mess."

His gaze was cool and very steady as he noted the damage. "Made any enemies lately?"

She frowned. "I haven't had time. I work too hard."

"What about in business?"

"I deal with hotel groups and caterers. All they want from me is a confirmed date and a check, which they get."

She heard a car pull into her driveway. Trying to keep her emotions in check, Eva looked through the rooms of her house, relieved to see that the burglar hadn't managed to get to her spare room or the kitchen. Minutes later, she opened the front door for two police officers.

Absently, she noticed that the fresh-faced detectives who introduced themselves as Hicks and Braithewaite seemed dazzled, making her aware that her damp dress was clinging and her hair was tousled. It was a reaction she'd gotten used to over the years, and which she usually managed to ignore.

As Hicks flashed his ID, Kyle stepped into the hall, his hand settling in the small of her back. The small proprietorial touch in front of Hicks forcibly brought back the passionate interlude on the beach. But, given her shakiness over the break-in, she didn't mind the context. Messena and Atraeus men were naturally protective of the women in the family. Whether it was an elderly aunt or someone much younger, the small courtesies and the masculine backup were always available if there was a problem.

Kyle kept her close as Hicks asked questions and looked around. When they walked through the rooms, he even threaded his fingers with hers. They had made love, that was intimate enough, but Kyle's possessive behavior had shunted them straight into something scarily close to couplehood.

Eva's stomach lurched as, once again, she turned over her options: marriage or stay single and possibly lose her business and house, both of which were mortgaged. She faced losing everything for which she had worked so hard over the years. She would survive; she didn't have to have the silk cushion. What would hurt, though, with Mario gone and no inheritance until she was forty, was the feeling of alienation that would go with losing that essential link. Maybe that was a ridiculous way to feel, since she was still an Atraeus by name. But it was a fact that she had always had to strive to fit in, to feel good enough to be an Atraeus.

Whichever way she viewed the future, she kept coming up against one constant: she did not want to cut Kyle out of it. That meant marriage.

She drew a quick breath at a heated flash of their lovemaking. And if what had happened tonight was anything to go on, if they married, even if they started out as a paper marriage, she didn't think it would stay that way.

After taking photographs, Hicks asked a few straightforward questions and made arrangements for an evidence tech to call in and dust for prints in the morning. Eva gave him a description of the laptop and a serial number, and promised to call in to Auckland Central Police Station with a list of anything else that was missing.

She decided against telling him right away about her suspicion that the perpetrator could have been Ferris. If it was, and he had left prints, the police would soon know, anyway, and that meant she got to hold on to her privacy. Mario had been the only member of the family who had known the whole sad and sordid truth about her past, and she preferred to keep it that way.

If Ferris had broken in, his motive would likely be the same as last time. He wanted money, and he wasn't averse to using blackmail to get it. Now that she was quite well known, thanks to her modeling career, he would no doubt threaten to release the details of her disorder and her past to the press.

After closing the door on the detectives, she walked through to the sitting room, where Kyle was examining the photo of her parents where it lay on the table. "Your mother and father?"

"Before they split up." Before her twin had died. Before her father, after finding out about the disorder, had left for Australia and a new life. And before her mother had remarried twice, having children who died to other men who left. Before Eva had discovered that she carried the same rare gene as her mother, a disorder that was lethal for fifty percent of children born to a carrier. In Eva's mother's case, the odds had turned out to be even worse, because out of four children, Eva had been the only one who had survived.

Kyle rose to his feet. "Do you stay in touch with any of your old family?"

The way he said old family, as if he saw her as part of

her new family, the Atraeus clan, was warming. "There was never much family to begin with. My mother was an only child." And the distant family that had been left hadn't wanted to know. "Why do you think I had to be adopted?"

Needing something to do, anything to take her mind off Kyle's large, distracting presence in her house and the tension that seemed to be pulling tighter and tighter, Eva began picking up cushions and stacking them on couches. Given that the cushions were cotton and linen, she figured there was no possibility that they would retain fingerprints. "I haven't seen or spoken with anyone from my mother's family since Mario adopted me."

Kyle began helping her clean up. Thirty minutes later, after picking up all of the loose clothes and underwear and putting them in a laundry basket so they didn't smear any prints that might be on the drawers or closet doors, Eva was satisfied they had done everything they could. She probably should have left everything as it was, but she had needed to restore as much as she could to reclaim her space and counter the creepy knowledge that someone had gotten into her house, even with the alarm turned on.

Kyle checked that the rear door was locked, then extracted his car keys from his pocket. "You can't stay here until you get the locks checked and your alarm upgraded. At a guess, the thief had a piece of equipment that could connect to your alarm wirelessly and give him the code—they're common enough. It would have taken him seconds to break in and then disable the alarm."

A shudder went down her spine at the brief description of how vulnerable she had been in her own home, even with the doors locked. Until she'd given the house a security upgrade, she wouldn't be able to relax, let alone sleep here.

Eva found her cell in her bag. Her first impulse was to ring one of Kyle's twin sisters, either Sophie or Francesca. Unfortunately, both of them had been out of town for a week or so. She checked through her contacts and found a number. "I've got a friend who helps me out at work occasionally. She'll put me up for the night." Annie had once had her own wedding event business, but had segued into special event planning for hotels and major corporations.

Her call went through to Annie's answering service. She tried again, with the same result. She tried Jacinta's number. Normally she never mixed business with her personal life, but she was desperate.

Jacinta's breathless *hello* was cut off by a lazily amused masculine voice, informing her that Jacinta was busy. Cheeks burning, Eva terminated the call.

Kyle lifted a brow. "No luck?"

She reached for her laptop then remembered it had been stolen. Luckily, all of her carefully managed business systems and contact lists were stored remotely so she could retrieve them, but it was still a major inconvenience. She picked up her phone and began looking online for a motel. "I could get a motel."

"Suit yourself. Or you could stay at my place. I've got a house just a couple of minutes from here. There's a guest room."

Tension zinged through her at the thought of staying with Kyle. *And continuing on with what they had started at the beach.* "I didn't know you bought a house." The last she'd heard, Kyle had lived in an ultraexpensive penthouse apartment in the Viaduct, an affluent waterfront area a stone's throw from the center of the city. Although, with all of the frustration of Mario's will and the times she'd had to spend trying to find a husband, she hadn't exactly kept up with family news.

"I bought the old Huntington place. It came up for auction a few weeks back."

Shock jerked Eva's head up. The Huntington place wasn't just a house. It was a fascinating Edwardian red brick folly situated on a rare acre of grounds that also ran down to a tiny private beach. She had caught glimpses of it from the road, through ornate wrought iron bars as she'd either jogged or walked past. But the ivy-festooned walls that glowed in the afternoon light and the lush garden possessed the kind of irresistible romantic charm that had drawn her like a moth to the flame. When she had seen that it was for sale, she had taken a risk and climbed through the gate. The overgrown gardens and the beach had been so beautiful that if she had been able to marry in time and obtain her inheritance, she would have bought it, regardless of what the house was like. "I can't believe you bought that house."

Especially since she had wanted it. From the first moment she had seen it, something had clutched at her heart. It was the most perfect family home she could imagine, even though she would not be requiring it for that, unless at some point she was able to adopt a child. Her most immediate purpose had been for her wedding business. It had everything for a perfect venue.

Kyle's expression turned wary. "What's wrong now?"

Jaw taut, Eva picked up the overnight bag she had packed and her clutch. Somehow, finding out that he was in possession of *her* house was upsetting. She couldn't quite put her finger on why. Maybe she felt so knocked off balance because for years she had been used to forging her own path, making her own decisions and doing things her way. Now, for the first and only time in her life, she had made love—with Kyle. Added to that, Kyle held the balance of power for the two things she wanted: her inheritance and the dream house.

As much as she wanted to say no about something, she couldn't deny the twisted desire to torture herself by looking around a house she knew would be beautiful and exactly what she wanted.

Seeing the house and knowing she could only have it on Kyle's terms would reinforce all of the reasons she should squash the incomprehensible, fatal attraction that had sneaked up on her.

What was wrong now?

She gave Kyle a cool stare. "Nothing much."

When Kyle tried to take her overnight bag, she kept a steely grip on it and marched to the door. "First you deprive me of my wedding. Now you've bought my house."

Seven

The crowded suburbs of Auckland seemed to disappear as Eva drove her car through the gates of Huntington House, with its stone gateposts and aged and stately magnolias arching overhead. Security lights came on, illuminating the thick tangle of rhododendrons and old-fashioned roses planted cheek by jowl with native *ponga* ferns and drifts of *reinga reinga* lilies.

The house was two-storied and peak roofed, with an array of chimneys that poked up against the night sky, adding to the old-world charm. Apart from more security lights, which illuminated the circular piece of drive before the front porch, the house sat in darkness, enclosed and secret with the thick press of overgrown trees and gardens.

Kyle drove into a garage off to the side. Since she was only here for the few hours that were left before she had to be at work, Eva parked near the front portico. By the time she had grabbed her things and locked the car, lights glowed softly in the downstairs area.

The scent of the sea and the sound of the waves hitting the shore nearby should have been relaxing after the tension of the break-in, except that it gave her another searing flashback of their passionate moments on the beach.

The portico lights came on and Kyle opened the front door wider, stepping out to take her bag from her.

Unwillingly loving Kyle's manners, Eva walked into the foyer, her heels clicking on the marble floor. Directly ahead a stairway curved away in a graceful arc. To one side there was an elegant front parlor and what looked like a series of reception and family rooms. On the other side of the staircase she knew, because she had peered through the windows when she had snuck into the estate previously, that a hall led in the direction of the kitchen and what had probably originally been the servants' quarters.

Eva let out a breath. "It's perfect." As a wedding venue. *As a family home.*

Kyle shrugged and indicated she should follow him. "At the moment it's a museum."

"You don't like it?"

"I wouldn't have bought it if I hadn't liked it. It just needs updating."

He walked into a huge kitchen, which was shabby and badly lit, but which already contained a selection of gleaming stainless steel appliances; fridge, cooktop, microwave and dishwasher. Kyle pointed out a kettle and toaster and a pantry that contained cereals and bread and a few food essentials if she needed to make a hot drink or get breakfast.

He indicated she should follow him up the stairs and showed her an array of bedrooms, finishing up with a large room with a king-size bed that was unmistakably his. He set her overnight bag down in the hallway.

Eva's cell beeped. When she took it from her bag, she saw Hicks's name flash up on the screen. When she answered the call, his voice was curt. Apparently they just had a call from a neighbor of hers to say that a man had been seen in her rear garden. They had just dispatched a cruiser to check it out. His main concern was that she was out of the house and safe.

When Kyle realized it was Hicks, he took the phone and had a terse conversation with the cop before terminating the call and handing her phone back, his expression grim. "You're not going back until whoever broke in is in custody."

"If they can catch him." She'd reached her limit for the night. She felt cold and shaky and couldn't seem to stop the tremor in her hands.

"Hicks is no slug. He's a member of the Armed Offenders Squad—he knows what he's doing."

She rubbed at her arms, which suddenly felt chilled, and couldn't keep the grumpiness out of her voice. "How do you know this stuff?"

"Quite a few former SAS end up in the AOS." He stopped. "Are you all right?"

She tried for a smile. "Of course."

"You don't look it."

A split second later she was in his arms, his hold loose enough that she could pull free if she wanted. As if sensing her tension, or more probably realizing that she was actually shaking, he wrapped her more tightly against him.

Eva took a deep breath, soaking in the burning heat that seemed to blast from Kyle as the horrible tension that had crept up on her finally began to unravel. "I guess that's what they call delayed shock. Interesting."

"You can be sure that whoever broke in to your house won't do it again," Kyle said coldly. "I'll make sure of it."

The soft, flat statement sent an electrifying shiver down her spine, and she had a moment to feel sorry for whoever it was who had broken into her house. She tilted her head back and met Kyle's gaze, and just like that her decision was made. Kyle was a powerful, in-control kind of guy, and right now that was exactly what she needed. She would probably regret it, but for better or worse she was going to marry him.

Kyle loosened off his hold slightly. "What is it?"

She drew a deep breath. "You were showing me to my room."

"You can have your own room, or you can share mine. Your choice."

She held his gaze unblinkingly. "Your room."

A hot pang went through her as he cupped her chin and bent his head, giving her plenty of time to pull free if she didn't want the kiss, and abruptly that was the final reassurance she needed. Kyle had already proved that he would never push her where she didn't want to go. Her heart slammed against the wall of her chest as his mouth settled on hers.

Eleven years ago, kissing Kyle had been the angst-filled, desperate risk of a teenager. Now it was an adult reaching for something that had been missing for more years than she cared to count, a hunger for warmth and closeness and for the no-holds-barred intimacy of making love.

Another long, drugging kiss later and she found herself being maneuvered through the door to Kyle's room and walked back in the direction of the bed. But when

Kyle tried to pull free, she coiled her arms around his neck, lifted up and kissed him again.

With a groan he pulled her close. He kissed her, his mouth firm, the feel of his muscled body pressed against hers, the shape of his arousal, the taste of him making her head spin. Another long, heated kiss and she felt her zipper open and the straps of her dress slide from her shoulders. "I'm still sticky and grainy from the beach."

"We can have a shower. Later." As her bra released, she tugged at the buttons of his shirt, dragging it open, but had to stop when he bent and took one breast into his mouth.

Her breath caught in her throat as a heated, aching tension gathered in the pit of her stomach. Somewhere in the distance she heard the lonely sound of a night bird, almost swamped by the slow sound of rain starting on the roof. She arched restlessly against Kyle's mouth, needing something more, but at that point he lifted his head and she felt the soft brush of the bed at the back of her knees. Sliding her hand down over the hard muscle of his abs, she found the top button of his pants, fumbled it open and dragged the zipper down.

Kyle's breath caught audibly, his hand stayed hers. Gaze locked with his, she lifted up and kissed him again. Attempting to step out of her shoes mid-kiss, she wavered off balance and ended up tumbling back on the bed. Kyle sprawled heavily, half on top of her, but when he would have moved, she wound her arms around his neck, tangling her fingers in his dark, silky hair and pressed herself against him.

Acting on impulse, she closed her teeth over the lobe of his ear.

Kyle's fingers closed around her wrists, his breath mingled with hers. "Babe, you don't know what you're—"

"Yes. I do." Dizzy with delight at the feminine power she had over Kyle, stunned by the sensations cascading through her and the careful way he held her close as if he truly cared for her, she kissed him again.

She felt his swiftly indrawn breath. "This time we're doing it right."

He disentangled himself and obtained a foil packet from his bedside table. After sheathing himself, he returned to the bed. A split second later, his weight came down on hers.

He cupped her face. "Are you sure you want to do this again?"

She lifted up for his kiss. "Why would there be a problem?"

She felt the scrape of lace as he peeled her panties down her legs, then his thighs parted hers. "Correct me if I'm wrong, but I think it's been a while since you've done this."

She hesitated, on the brink of telling him that before tonight she had never "done this," but then a quiet, instinctive caution gripped her. She had already given more of herself, and agreed to more, than she had planned. The urge to protect herself now was knee-jerk. Confessing that until tonight she had been a virgin would lay bare too much.

This time their lovemaking was more leisurely as he took his time kissing her, cupping her breasts and at the same time encouraging her to explore. Just when she thought she couldn't take much more play, she felt the press of him between her legs. Automatically, she shifted to accommodate him.

This time their joining was smoother, easier. She heard his indrawn breath, then his mouth came down on hers and he began to move and the heated tension turned molten.

Long minutes later, Kyle gently disengaged himself and rolled to one side, taking her with him.

There was a small vibrating silence. "The condom slipped the first time, but that's never happened before, so there's no risk of STDs" He propped himself up on one elbow. "But you also should have told me you haven't made love for a while."

She studied the stubbled line of his jaw, and the resolve not to reveal just how vulnerable she was with all things sexual settled in. She ran her palm over the damp skin of his chest, and evaded his gaze. "There wasn't exactly much time for conversation."

He cupped one breast, the intimate touch sending a tingling thrill through her. "It would have been good to know. We could have done things...differently."

She shivered as he dipped down and took her nipple in his mouth, her eyes closing as the heated, coiling tension started all over again. She tried to think, but her brain was fast becoming scrambled. "How, exactly?"

"I would have taken a whole lot more time."

Her eyes flipped open at the way his voice cooled, as if he was remembering the mishap with the condom. She summoned as much confidence as she could. "There won't be a baby."

Although the gravity of what had happened came back to hit her full force. The plain fact was that because she hadn't been sexually active, she didn't know a lot about where in her cycle was the optimum time to get pregnant. She had never before needed to keep track of her ovulation. She knew roughly when her period was, but that was about it. If by some remote chance she did get pregnant... But that wouldn't happen, she thought grimly, she would make sure of it. She would make an appointment to see her doctor tomorrow and get a morning-after pill.

And arrange contraception.

The decision made, she forced herself to relax about the whole issue of pregnancy. There was nothing she could do until the morning. "I'm sorry we didn't have a conversation before we made love, but I thought if we stopped you might...leave." She lifted up, pressing against his chest, and boldly rolled on top. "It's not as if you haven't done that before."

He tangled his hands in her hair, grinned lazily and pulled her mouth down to his. "You must be talking about leaving, since we've never made love before."

He kissed her and she felt him stir against her stomach. He rolled until they were lying comfortably sprawled, side by side.

It occurred to Eva that she had never felt so relaxed or so comfortable with a man, and she went still inside at the stunning thought that since Kyle didn't want kids then maybe, just maybe, he was the perfect man for her?

Just as long as she didn't get pregnant.

Eva woke to the sound of the shower. She blinked at the enormous old-fashioned room with its striped brown wallpaper and bare boards. She was presently the sole occupant of the huge modern bed, which sat in the center of the room.

Kyle stepped back into the room, wearing dark pants and a shirt he was in the process of buttoning. Feeling exposed, Eva dragged the sheet up to her chin before attempting to drape the sheet around her like a sarong.

Kyle strapped on his watch. "We need to have a conversation before we go to work."

Eva tried for a smile as if waking up in some man's bed after spur-of-the-moment sex was a very normal thing for her. "A conversation would be good in just a few minutes."

She found her overnight bag and lugged it through to the bathroom, which was still steamy from Kyle's occupancy. She quickly showered and dressed. There was no dryer, so she had to be content with combing her hair out straight. She quickly made up her face then checked her appearance. When she saw a faint pink graze on her neck, where Kyle's five-o'clock shadow must have scraped against her skin, the reality of what they'd done last night hit her.

When Kyle knocked on the door, she stuffed the sheet she'd worn into a laundry basket, hung up her towel and walked out into the hall. She was still barefoot, and Kyle, now fully dressed in a dark suit with a blue tie that made his eyes seem even bluer, towered over her.

She had hoped he might pull her into his arms and kiss her so they could both relax and have the discussion they needed to have, but he had his banker face on, cool, neutral and unreadable.

He glanced at his watch. "If we're going to get married, we should make arrangements."

Eva frowned at the way Kyle had casually leapfrogged the whole concept of a proposal. She guessed it wasn't warranted in her case, because she was the one seeking the marriage. Technically, Kyle was doing her the favor, but he had *checked his watch* as if he didn't even have time to talk about it.

Abruptly, she wondered if their lovemaking last night had meant anything at all to him. Annoyed enough to keep him waiting, Eva reached into her bag and found her cell, taking her time as she flicked through to her calendar, which she already knew was packed full of consultations that morning and clear for most of the afternoon, which meant she could book a doctor's appointment directly after lunch.

His gaze shifted to her mouth, and for a shivering moment the sensual tension was alive between them.

"What's wrong?"

"That would be the marriage thing. You haven't exactly asked me."

There was a vibrating silence. "I thought I had."

With careful precision, Eva checked the next month's appointments, of which, thankfully, there were a number. "I can recall something along the lines of a command, followed by a business-type proposition."

"Correct me if I'm wrong, but technically it *is* a business proposition. If you become engaged to me, the marriage can be approved immediately, since Mario made it clear his first preference for a husband was a Messena. You should have access to your trust fund within a couple of weeks. After two years, you receive the full inheritance."

When she continued to flick fruitlessly through her calendar, Kyle said something soft and curt beneath his breath. They both knew her answer had to be yes, but she was frustrated and terminally annoyed that after the searing intimacy they'd shared last night, he was now treating her as if she was an irritating pain in the rear again.

"Marry me, and you get the house."

She clamped down on the automatic burst of outrage that Kyle clearly thought she was so materialistic that he could buy her with the house. "I thought you bought the house for yourself."

He straightened away from the doorframe, but still didn't enter the bedroom, his expression oddly cagey. "For the short term. It's a good investment."

It occurred to Eva that after the passionate lovemaking last night, Kyle was now doing his level best to create some distance. Maybe it was just a masculine desire to compartmentalize. Whatever it was, it did not work for her. The last thing she wanted was to be treated as some kind of sexual convenience who could be bought.

She drew a deep breath. "Okay, I'll marry you. But what happened last night can't happen again. If you want a marriage of convenience then it has to be on the same terms I offered the others."

She hated saying the words; she had adored making love with Kyle, and she wanted to do it again but she couldn't do so under these conditions.

The hum of a cell sounded from his jacket. The cool neutrality of his expression, the same kind of expression she imagined he used at the negotiating table, didn't alter. "No sex. Agreed."

Kyle reached for his cell and slid smoothly into a business conversation, but Eva refused to let herself get either angry or depressed about it. Last night had been special in a way she hadn't expected, but this morning they had bounced back into the old, aggravated relationship. But perhaps the fact that Kyle had pressed her for marriage signaled that he wasn't as indifferent as he seemed.

It shouldn't be important, but she had to wonder exactly how Kyle had viewed their night together, her first and only night with a man. According to the gossip columnists, like all the ultrawealthy Messena and Atraeus men, he was hotly pursued and had enjoyed a number of brief liaisons. And, of course, she could not forget that he had been married. On his scale of things, having sex with her had probably barely registered.

Kyle terminated the call. "I'll apply for the marriage license today. How about having the wedding the week after next? Thursday?"

The date he wanted was twelve days away. She had already checked her calendar, so she knew that day was free. "Are you sure it has to be a Thursday?" Who got married on a Thursday?

She did. Giddy pleasure fizzed through her, which was crazy and dangerous, because she could not afford to project any kind of romanticism into this *business deal.* She could not afford to make herself any more vulnerable to Kyle than she already was.

Kyle leaned against the door, his gaze lingering on the rumpled bed. "You can change the date if you want. I'll just have to check in with my PA."

"Thursday will do." At least it would mean she would have more chance of getting a venue she liked, because all the good ones would be booked out on a weekend day.

"And Eva?"

She tried for her absentminded "I'm concentrating so hard on my schedule that I can't hear you" look, although from the piercing quality of Kyle's gaze she wasn't entirely sure she pulled it off. "What?"

"We need to keep the wedding low-key."

"What exactly do you mean by low-key?"

"I was thinking a registry office, two witnesses."

She stiffened as it occurred to her that while Kyle hadn't minded sleeping with her, he was not entirely happy at being linked with her in marriage. That maybe marrying a lingerie model did not fit so well with his conservative banker's image.

She tucked her cell back in her bag. "Maybe the word you should have used to describe the wedding is *secret*?"

"There's not exactly time for a big wedding."

"And why would we have one when it's only for two years?"

A pulse started along the side of his jaw. "Precisely."

She forced a smooth, professional smile. "No problem. We can get married *quietly*."

But it would not be in a registry office, and it would not be a hole-in-the-corner affair, as if Kyle was ashamed to be marrying her!

Eight

Shortly after nine that morning, Kyle's twin sisters, Sophie and Francesca, who had both recently returned from a buying trip for Sophie's boutique in Australia, cornered him at his favorite café. It was a neat pincer operation that could only have been spearheaded by his mother, whom he had made the mistake of ringing before he had left the house for work. Sophie, who was normally sleek and unruffled, looked haphazard in jeans and a cotton sweater, as if she'd left the house in a hurry. Francesca, the more flamboyant of the two, looked pale and still half-asleep.

Kyle braced himself. Both twins worked some distance away, and thus they did not normally frequent this café, which was close to his bank. He loved his sisters, they had stood by him through thick and thin, but they had a take-charge streak and a facility for winkling out the truth that tended to make things worse. "What do you want?"

Sophie lifted a brow. "We're family. Maybe we just saw you and wanted to say hello?"

Resigned, Kyle paid for his coffee and ordered a long black for Sophie, a latte for Francesca. "I repeat, what do you want?"

Sophie gave him a serene look. "Mom rang. We know you're engaged to Eva—we want to know why. You know we love you, Kyle. We also love Eva. Just answer our questions and we'll let you go."

Kyle paid for the coffees and joined Sophie and Francesca, who had commandeered a corner table. "Maybe we fell in love."

Neither of the twins showed a flicker of interest in his reply. Resigning himself to a longer conversation, Kyle sat back and worked on his poker face.

Their coffee arrived. After the waitress had gone, Francesca leaned forward and gave him a friendly smile. "You kissed Eva on the beach approximately eleven years ago, since then, nothing." She made a slitting motion across her throat. *"Niente."*

Kyle didn't allow his sister's Italian theatrics to do what they were designed to do—lure him into a discussion about his love life so they could really mess with his head. He had no idea how the twins had found out that piece of information, since he hadn't told anyone, including his mother. To his certain knowledge, the only people who had known had been Mario, who was now dead, and Eva. "Since I know you're not psychic, so you couldn't have spoken to Mario, I'm guessing you talked to Eva."

Sophie set her coffee down. "She rang me first thing. She needs a dress."

Kyle pinched his nose. The phone had obviously been running red hot.

A dress. That did not sound like a registry office wedding. "And since you supply a lot of Eva's brides, she called you."

"It's good business. I recommend Eva's wedding planning. She recommends my dresses. It's a marriage made in heaven," Sophie said smoothly, "while this one, clearly, is not."

Francesca put her coffee down with a snap. "We know Eva needs a husband to get her inheritance."

The hum of conversation in the café abruptly dropped. Heads began to swivel. Kyle's jaw compressed. "Eva told you that?"

Francesca blushed. "Not exactly. I saw Mario's will on your coffee table in your apartment one day. I couldn't help wondering why you even had a copy, so—"

"You read a confidential document."

Francesca's brows jerked together. "Maybe you shouldn't have left it out where just anyone could read it."

Kyle could have pointed out that his apartment wasn't exactly a public area, but he recognized a blind ally when he saw one. A little desperately he tried to recall the original thread of the conversation. "The reason I'm marrying Eva is private and, uh, personal."

A hot flash of just how private and personal they had gotten last night momentarily distracted him. He dragged at his tie, which suddenly felt a little tight, then realized his mistake when Sophie noticed the faint red mark on the side of his neck.

Sophie blinked. "You're sleeping with her. That changes things."

Francesca stared at him as if he'd just grown horns. "You're Eva's legal trustee and you're *sleeping* with her? Aside from being sleazy, isn't that against the law?"

Kyle kept a firm grip on his temper. "I'm not responsible for Eva. I'm a trustee of her adoptive father's will, that's an entirely different thing—"

Francesca gave him a horrified look. "Then she's pregnant."

"She can't be pregnant." Although the thought hit him like a hammer blow, despite Eva's confidence that she couldn't be.

He took a mouthful of coffee, which he suddenly needed. Although, Eva had not seemed to be worried about the possibility of a pregnancy, so he assumed that, like a lot of women, she was on the pill or had taken some other precaution.

Another thought hit him out of the blue as the strange dichotomy of making love with a sophisticated woman who had been at turns fiery and passionate then oddly awkward and uncertain registered. He had assumed the reason Eva had been awkward and uncertain was that she hadn't made love for a very long time.

Either that, or she was a virgin.

He drew a long breath and let it out slowly. He knew that Eva had never had a live-in lover; that was common family knowledge. They had all assumed it was because Mario was so old-fashioned and that Eva, out of respect for her adoptive father, was preserving an outward show of chastity. It had never occurred to any of them, least of all, Kyle, that she had been doing exactly what it appeared; keeping herself for marriage.

Although, technically, she hadn't saved herself for her wedding night.

"So this is going to be a real marriage?" Sophie picked up her bag, which she'd placed on the floor.

Kyle frowned as Sophie extracted her phone and made a call, speaking in the kind of low, flat voice that could have been lifted straight out of some B-grade thriller.

Apparently, something was green, not red, the 10-33 was over but in general it all still qualified as Alpha Charlie Foxtrot.

Kyle recognized code when he heard it, even if it was a crazy mix of the standard radio language used by the military for decades and the 10 Code that was in popular use by police and emergency services. At a strong guess she was relaying information to their mom, who had spent time volunteering for the local ambulance service as one of their call operators. "If you hand the phone to me, I can speak to Mom direct."

Sophie's gave him a faintly irritated look. "No need. She'll be in Auckland by this afternoon. You can talk to her at my apartment, since both you and Eva are invited to dinner at my place tonight. There's a lot to decide in a short time frame."

"Not that much, since the wedding is in twelve day's time."

Francesca gave him a pitying look. "You're marrying a wedding planner. They're Type As. And you know, Eva, she's like a double A."

Sophie set her cup down. "That means perfectionist. Aggressive. Even if you got married in a registry office, which will never happen because I know what the dress is going to be, it would be the most perfect registry office wedding imaginable. But, like I said, it's not a registry office, so you should brace yourself."

Kyle groaned inwardly. When he'd left Eva that morning, he'd been relieved that he'd gotten her to agree to the marriage. His concern had been to get the marriage done quickly and quietly. He thought he'd managed to convey that to Eva, but something must have gotten lost in translation, because now all hell was breaking loose.

But now he could see he had made a big mistake in

not factoring in the impact this would have on his family. Mistakenly, he had assumed that his mother, who had been pressurizing him to think about marriage again and find someone "nice," would be happy that he had finally decided to step back into relationship waters again.

The certainty that Eva had been a virgin when they had made love hit him anew. The anomaly of Eva choosing to give herself to him after years of celibacy and before they had even agreed to a marriage pointed to only one clear answer.

She wanted him just as badly as he wanted her.

An odd tension dissipated at the thought. At the same time, Kyle was aware that hell would probably freeze over before Eva would admit feeling anything at all for him. But then Mario had given him the distinct impression that Eva had suffered a lot of emotional difficulties as a child. He had assumed there was abuse in her past and had done what Mario requested and left her alone. He hadn't pried into Eva's history, but now that they were getting married, he resolved to find out exactly what had gone wrong.

A part of him was fiercely glad that Eva hadn't slept around, that she had waited and given herself to him. But he was aware that he would have to step carefully. He was cool, logical and disciplined. Eva was gorgeous and passionate, like rich, decadent chocolate, meant to be enjoyed in small, ruthlessly measured doses.

Francesca waved a hand in front of his face to attract his attention. "Just tell us one thing. Is Eva pressuring you to marry her?"

"No." The reason he wanted to marry Eva was cut and dried: it was the most efficient way of keeping her away from other men.

Sophie gave him a considering look. "But this is a marriage of convenience, right?"

Kyle decided there was no point prevaricating, since the twins had clearly made up their minds that it was. "Yes."

Sophie stared at him with her spooky eyes, the ones that interrogation officers would kill for and which sucked the truth out of you whether you wanted to tell or not. Clearly, she had just sucked something significant out of his brain, because she exchanged a look with Francesca. "Is there something wrong with a marriage of convenience?"

The twins gave him a pitying look.

Sophie sat back in her chair as if the case was concluded. "A marriage of convenience where you sleep with Eva? Sounds like a real marriage to us."

Eva rushed to her doctor's appointment only to find her last consultation had dragged on so long she had missed it and had to wait for an emergency appointment. Stomach churning, not least because she hadn't stopped to get any lunch, she sat down to wait.

At three o'clock, she finally got in to see Dr. Evelyn Shan, an elegant Indian woman with an impressive list of qualifications and a daughter, Lina, who had been a good friend of Eva's in her last year of school.

After a couple of minutes of catching up about Lina, who now lived in England, Eva finally managed to get to the point of her visit.

Evelyn's eyes widened ever so slightly at Eva's request for morning-after and contraceptive pills, before she began asking a crisp series of questions. "I'll prescribe the morning-after pill, and you need to take it today, as soon as possible. The results aren't one hundred percent, and given the time in your cycle…"

She scribbled a prescription. Eva, feeling about six inches tall, folded the piece of paper and placed it in her handbag. As she hurried out to pay for the consultation, her phone vibrated.

She took the call from Luisa Messena, Kyle's mother. Feeling frazzled, she agreed to meet Luisa, Francesca and Sophie at a nearby café in a few minutes, although she was certain "coffee" was a euphemism for what was about to take place. As much as she loved the Messena women and enjoyed their company, they were, each in their own way, formidable. It was also a fact that the twins knew about the clause in Mario's will.

She paid and filled her prescription at a chemist then hurried to the café. Sophie and Francesca were grinning like a couple of cats that had gotten the cream. Luisa hugged her with an odd smile in her eyes.

Feeling dazed that all three women seemed quite relaxed about the quick marriage, Eva ordered sparkling water. She intended to sip some now then cap the bottle, place it in her bag and, as soon as she got a chance, take her pill. She didn't want to risk taking the pill at the table, because she was pretty sure that if she took out the pack, the twins would recognize the medication and all hell would break loose.

Half an hour later, just as she was making her excuses to leave, Detective Hicks called. They needed to get into her house to dust for fingerprints, and they needed her to meet them there now.

After quickly explaining about the break-in to Luisa, Sophie and Francesca, she got up to leave, but Luisa wouldn't hear about her going on her own and insisted on calling Kyle.

She beamed as she disconnected the call. "He's more or less finished for the day and will drive you to your house."

Feeling just a little bit frantic because she needed a few minutes alone to take the pill, Eva found herself strolling across the road to Kyle's bank, an imposing old building with several floors and a plaster facade in a tasteful shade of mocha. She stepped through antique wood-and-glass revolving doors into the hushed echoes of a large reception area with marble floors and very high, intricately molded ceilings. She had been in the bank on a number of occasions before, but always with Mario.

Kyle stepped out of an elevator, and her heart did a queer little leap. He was dressed in the same suit she had seen him wearing that morning, *after she had gotten out of his bed*, but he looked…different. Maybe it was the understated richness of marble floors and pillars, the diffused light that shimmered through fanlights over the doors, but in that moment he looked utterly at home in the opulence and wealth of the bank and every inch the urban predator.

An hour later, they left her house, locking it behind the police team. After the short drive home, where they were changing for dinner because they were eating out, Eva finally made it to a bathroom.

Setting her bag down on the vanity, she took the morning-after pill out of her bag and read the instructions.

She needed to take the pill in the first twenty-four hours. She checked her watch. She was within the time.

Relief making her a little dizzy, she filled a glass with water, popped the pill in her mouth, took a mouthful of water and swallowed.

Nine

Ten days later, Eva walked into her office to find Jacinta rushing out, her normally magnolia cheeks bright pink. "Anything wrong?"

"Nothing." Jacinta waved her clipboard. "Just needed this. I must have left it in here by mistake. Oh, and some man called to see you. I actually found him in your office when I came in with coffee and shooed him out. I noted down his number on the pad beside your phone."

Frowning that someone had walked into her office while she'd been having a fitting for her dress at Sophie's shop, and without an appointment, Eva checked out the number, which was unfamiliar.

Eva sat down behind her desk. It was then she noticed that her handbag, which she'd left behind because Sophie's shop was just down the street, was gaping open. Mario's will was tucked inside where she had left it, but she couldn't remember it being folded open at the second page.

Feeling unsettled, she refolded the will and replaced it in her bag. It was ridiculous to think that the person in her office could be Sheldon Ferris. Picking up the phone, she rang the cell number noted on the pad.

A male voice picked up, and her stomach plummeted as she recognized her stepfather's voice. "What were you doing in my office?"

"Now, what way is that to talk to a relative? Especially with a wedding coming up."

The veiled threat in his voice made her tense. "You married my mother for a couple of years. That doesn't make you a relative."

"I suppose, now you're an Atraeus, and rich, you've got no time for the family you left behind—"

"If you want money, you can forget it." As far as she was concerned, Ferris had only ever been with her mother to benefit himself. He had lived off her sickness benefit and run up enough gambling debts that when her mother had died there had been nothing left.

There was a small silence. "You're not going to get rid of me this time." He mentioned a figure that took her breath. "If you don't want your story splashed all over the tabloids, you'd better pay up."

In that moment Eva noticed a message sitting on her blotter, from Detective Hicks, to the effect that they hadn't been able to make a positive ID on any finger-prints other than her own. She didn't care, she was now sure in her own mind who it was that had broken in. "That was you in my house the other night, wasn't it?"

The click of the disconnected call in her ear was loud enough that she wrenched the phone away. With shaky fingers, she set the phone down in its rest.

Sheldon Ferris. He popped up in her life at odd inter-vals, usually wanting money. Mario had frightened him off the last time, but Mario had failed to tell her what leverage he had used. All she could hope was that the fear of a police investigation would be enough to scare him off.

With the pleasure of trying on her wedding dress drained away by the nasty call, Eva deliberately tried to recapture her optimistic mood by checking through her wedding file.

Predictably, Kyle had not been happy when he'd discovered that Eva had not booked a registry office wedding and that she had involved Kyle's family in almost every aspect. Eva, on the other hand, had felt it was important that his family were involved, not least because in a more distant way, they were also her family.

She had invited the Messena clan to her last wedding, which hadn't happened, so why would she not invite them to this one, especially when Kyle was the groom? It just hadn't made any kind of sense to cut family out and in the process cause hurt.

It still felt faintly surreal that she was actually getting married, and that the toxic clause in Mario's will would be neutralized in just two days' time.

Two days until she became Kyle's wife.

The speed with which the wedding was approaching made her feel breathless and just a little panicky, which was not her. Usually she was in control and organized. She lived and breathed detail and was superpicky about every aspect of a wedding, which made her good at her job. She also had a huge network of contacts thanks to her family and her modeling days. She had thought twelve days was enough time to organize a small, intimate wedding, but it seemed the universe was working against her.

She'd fought tooth and nail over venues, food and music, and she was losing sleep. To cap it off, none of her bridesmaids of choice were available on a Thursday. Even Sophie and Francesca had had prior commitments that meant that, while they could come to the wedding, they just did not have enough time to do all the bridesmaid things. She was starting to get desperate. The way things were going, the wedding *would* take place in a registry office.

Jacinta strolled back in with the clipboard in her hand, this time with a couple of sheets attached. Her dark bob was perfect and glossy, her vivid pink cotton dress, cinched in at the waist, made her honey tan look even darker and more exotic. "You said you wanted to talk to me about a new wedding."

Eva slid the page with the basic plan she had arrived at across her desk. "It's my wedding."

Her eyes widened with shock. "But, since Jeremy went to Dubai, you're not even going out with anyone—unless Troy Kendal proposed?"

"Uh-uh. Not Troy." Eva tried to look unconcerned and very busy shuffling pieces of paper as Jacinta flipped the sheet around and stared at the line that contained the groom's name.

"You're marrying Kyle Messena?" There was a curious silence. "Now I am confused. He's a babe, but I didn't think you even liked him."

Eva avoided Jacinta's curious gaze and tried to look serenely in love, which was difficult because nothing she felt for Kyle fell into the "serene" bracket. "*Like* doesn't exactly describe what I feel for Kyle."

That, at least, was honest. Nothing about any of their interactions had ever fallen into comfortable friendship territory. "We had a *thing* years ago, and when he knew how close I came to marrying Jeremy, he, uh…decided we should be together."

Jacinta managed to morph surprise into sparkly enthusiasm. "Sounds take-charge and...romantic."

Eva caught the subtext, *and so not like Eva*. She searched for a little enthusiasm herself. "Like I said, we go way back."

Desperate to quit the conversation, she checked her wristwatch. Happily, she had arranged to have lunch with Kyle, so she had a legitimate out. Jumping to her feet, she hooked the strap of the sleek handbag over her shoulder. "You know," she said vaguely, "the family connection."

Jacinta added the sheet to her file, her expression vaguely horrified. "Of course. If he's a Messena, then you're related."

Eva frowned at the way she said it. "The connection is hardly close. Mario was Kyle's great-uncle, and don't forget that I'm adopted."

"It's coming back."

Eva forced a smile. "Which reminds me, I have a favor to ask. We want to get married this week, and I was wondering if you could be my bridesmaid?"

"This week?"

"Thursday." She caught another little piece of subtext. "I'll supply the dress and shoes from Sophie Messena's boutique."

Jacinta's expression brightened. "Okay." She hugged the clipboard to her stomach. "I guess you must have both discovered you're crazy in love? Like a fatal attraction, since you didn't seem to even like one another at the Hirsch wedding."

Eva's phone chimed, negating the need to answer. Clutching the cell like a lifeline, Eva answered the call, which was from Kyle. She said his name with a pleased smile and waggled her hand at Jacinta, as if this somehow answered the question of whether or not she was in love. Happy to be free from the interrogation, she stepped out of the office.

"You sound happy."

The low register of Kyle's voice brushed across her nerves as she punched the call button of the elevator. She had stuck to her resolve that she and Kyle wouldn't sleep together, but listening to Kyle's voice, which was drop-dead sexy, didn't help. Neither did the fact that Kyle was exhibiting a kind of calm, measured patience with her that was downright scary. She shouldn't like that in an utterly male way he was waiting for her to get back into his bed. "It's lunchtime. I get to eat."

"And I intend to feed you."

Eva's fingers tightened on the phone. Why did that sound so carnal? She stepped into the elevator and hit the button to close the doors. "Where, exactly?"

"It's a surprise. I'll be waiting for you downstairs."

As she stepped out of the elevator, despite giving herself a stern talking-to on the way down, her heart skipped a beat when she saw Kyle. She was glad she had worn one of her favorite dresses, a cream sheath dress that made the best of her honey tan and tawny hair. Kyle was dressed in a sleek, dark suit with a snowy-white shirt and dark red tie and looked edgily handsome and just a little remote. She tried to look breezy and casual as she walked toward him, as if making love with him and agreeing to marriage had not been earth-shattering events but, even so, her stomach automatically tightened.

He held the door for her, and she stepped through, suddenly feeling ridiculously feminine and cosseted. Since the dinner with his mother and sisters, courtesy of living in the same house, they had spent more time together than she could remember since the Dolphin Bay days, and the tension was wearing on her nerves. "Where are we going?"

He opened the passenger side door of the Maserati and named an exclusive jeweler's. A glow of pleasure infused her. "You don't have to get me a ring."

His gaze touched on hers. "The ring's nonnegotiable. My family will expect it, and so will the media."

Her jaw squared at his reasoning and the quick little dart of hurt that went with it. Just for a moment she had felt that Kyle really did care for her and the engagement meant something more to him than a business arrangement. It was the kind of dangerous thinking she knew she couldn't afford, but which somehow kept materializing. As if it mattered that Kyle should care for her.

As if she wanted this marriage to be real.

Ten

Jaw squaring, Eva slid into her seat. "You don't have to buy the ring. I'll get one for myself, after lunch."

There was a moment of silence before the door closed with an expensive *thunk*. Fingers shaking just a little because out-of-the-blue anger had piled on top of the hurt and all over a piece of jewelry. Kyle slid into the driver's seat as she fastened her seat belt.

Somewhere behind them a horn blared. Glancing in the rearview mirror, she saw a delivery truck waiting for the space that Kyle had illegally commandeered. Her cheeks heated as she became aware that Kyle, aside from starting the car, wasn't moving. "We should go before you get a ticket."

"Not until we get something straight. I buy the ring."

Taking a deep breath, she forced her fingers to loosen on the buttery leather of her bag. "No."

The delivery truck gave another extended blast on its horn.

"I'm not moving until you agree."

She frowned at his steely blue gaze and the rock-hard set of his jaw. Not for the first time, she saw the defining quality that had seen him promoted in the military and which made him such an asset in the banking business: the cold, hard-assed ability to force his own terms.

It passed through her mind that living with Kyle would not be a cakewalk. He would be demanding, opinionated and difficult; she just bet that with his military training, he probably liked to make rules. Irritatingly, it also registered that she could never be happy with a man who didn't challenge her, that a part of her relished the battle. That in some crazy, un-PC way, Kyle suited her and that she would rather argue with him than agree with any other man she knew. "What if I don't want a ring?"

"Sophie said you wanted a dress. Why not the ring?"

She thought quickly. He was right, she did want the ring.

She guessed that, in her heart of hearts, it was tied in with the reason she wanted a real wedding in the first place. She liked the enduring conventions and traditions, the beauty and hopefulness, and she wanted to enjoy the occasion. Somehow, in going through the same process that countless other couples had entered into, there was a comforting sense of being a part of something time-honored and lovely, even if the marriage was a sham.

She decided the timing was right to mention another detail of the wedding preparations. "I'll have the ring, but on the condition that we get married in a church."

Kyle pulled out and let the delivery van take the space. "Let me guess. You've already booked the church."

"Since it's difficult to get one of those at short notice, I booked as soon as I had the date."

The extended silence that accompanied Kyle's smooth

insertion into city traffic underlined the fact that he wasn't happy with the idea of a wedding in a church.

Suddenly incensed, Eva contemplated telling Kyle to pull over so she could get out and walk back to her office. Her shoes were too high, her feet would hurt and she'd probably wilt in the heat, but it would be worth it. "If you think I'm going to stand in some dusty registrar's office somewhere, you can forget it."

Eva backed her statement with a fiery glance, in that moment prepared to cancel the wedding, cancel her very important plans for her business and the gorgeous house of her dreams—all disastrous consequences. It occurred to her that somewhere between sleeping with Kyle and agreeing to marry him she had lost her perspective and was hatching into a fully-fledged bridezilla.

Kyle muttered something curt beneath his breath as he accelerated through an intersection. "Are you always this difficult?"

Eva stared at oncoming traffic, barely seeing it. "You know I am. Mario would have wanted a church wedding. It's important."

"I guess I keep forgetting I'm marrying a wedding planner."

The easy way he said the words as if, ultimately, Kyle was relaxed with the whole idea of marriage and prepared to give her her way, doused the escalating tension. The dress, the ring and getting married in church might seem inconsequential to Kyle, but they mattered to Eva. Her upbringing with Mario had always included the church. In their small family, faith had been central, deep and important. She wouldn't feel married if it wasn't done in a church.

Kyle braked as traffic slowed. "Which church and what time?"

Kyle's sudden change of heart about the church, the ease with which he had adapted, sparked a suspicion. "You knew about the church all along."

"I didn't know the details, but the twins gave me a heads-up."

Which meant, since he hadn't mentioned it before, that he had more than likely saved the knowledge as a bargaining chip. In this case, to make sure she had the engagement ring he wanted to give her.

Feeling suddenly, blazingly happy that he had gone to so much trouble for her, she gave him the details. "It's the little church just down from the house. I was lucky enough to get it at short notice."

The vicar hadn't liked having his arm twisted, since he'd had to reschedule a regular session of the La Leche League, who had their monthly meeting in an adjacent room, but she had doubled the fee, which had smoothed things over.

A bus up ahead stopped for a set of lights. Eva winced as she recognized one of her last lingerie advertisements splashed over the rear of the bus.

The fizzing happiness died a death. Just what she needed, a reminder that Kyle was marrying a woman who was more recognizable to the general population half-naked than fully dressed. And in that moment it hit her what that would mean to a man who made his living in the ultraconservative world of banking. To say that she was an unsuitable wife for a man who dealt with the stiff etiquette of that social world was a massive under-statement.

A car peeled right and, as luck would have it, they ended up snug behind the bus, with her airbrushed, overly enhanced cleavage looming large. Eva's fingers tightened on her handbag, as any hope that Kyle had not seen the advertisement faded.

When she had been modeling, the profession had been so competitive that this particular lingerie shoot had seemed a good business move. It had certainly kept her in public view, but until now she had not noticed how tacky the posters were.

Even more on edge now, she stared at Kyle's profile, the clean-cut strength of his jaw and the way his broken nose made him look even sexier. "Maybe you shouldn't marry me."

Kyle's gaze captured hers. "What's wrong now?"

The mild, patient way he asked the question, as if she was a high-maintenance girlfriend *with issues*, made her stiffen. "Won't marrying me be a problem in terms of your career?"

Mario had thrown up his hands often enough at her decision to become a lingerie model. Added to that, over the years Eva had become sharply aware that her career, coupled with the Atraeus name, had guaranteed the kind of prying, intrusive media attention she hated.

Kyle pulled into a reserved space in the crowded, popular enclave that was the Viaduct, a collection of bars and cafés and apartments on the waterfront, just a stone's throw from the central heart of Auckland. Unfastening his seat belt, he half turned to face her, and suddenly the interior of the Maserati seemed suffocatingly small. "Is this about the lingerie ads?"

She met his gaze squarely. "It could affect your business. I mean, won't there be occasions when I have to socialize with some of your clients?"

"Honey, I part own the bank. I can buy and sell most of my clients. If they've got a problem with my wife, they can take their business elsewhere."

A curious tingling sensation riveted her to her seat. As Kyle exited the car, she registered what that sensation was: the recognition that in that moment something basic and utterly primitive had taken place. Without so much as the blink of an eye, Kyle had informed her that she was more important than his business. More, he had given her an assurance that he would uphold her honor and protect her unconditionally. An assurance that was guaranteed to melt her all the way through, because he had made her feel that she belonged to him.

Suddenly, it did not seem like a marriage of convenience to Eva.

Kyle opened her door and held out his hand. Still feeling electrified by the uncompromising way Kyle had stated his solidarity with her, his intention, on the surface of things, to treat her as a real wife, Eva put her hand in his. When she straightened, for a moment she was close enough to Kyle that she could see the crystalline clarity of his irises and the intriguing dark striations, the inky blackness of his lashes.

Only one other person had done the same, and that had been Mario.

She was aware that Kyle would know some of the details of her background, but only the parts that she and Mario had agreed could be known. He did not know about the genetic disorder, the deaths of her brother and sisters and her mother's depression; the constant moves to avoid one of her mother's violent boyfriends. He could not know or guess how difficult it was for her to trust *anyone*.

She had entrusted herself to Kyle, and now she knew why. Somehow, beneath the battle lines they had drawn for so long and all the tension and clashes, she had recognized that bedrock quality in Kyle. It was the same quality that had attracted her when she was seventeen and still raw from the disintegration of her family and being handed through a list of foster homes. It explained why she had never really forgotten him, even though he had walked away.

For a split second, his gaze rested on her mouth, and she realized that in his sharp, percipient way, he had picked up on the intensity of her thoughts and was going to pull her close and kiss her. She was so sure of it that she unconsciously rebalanced her weight to lean in close.

"Kyle! I saw you from across the street. I've been trying to get hold of you."

"Elise. I was going to call you."

Eva stiffened as a tall, narrow brunette with dainty features and a simple silk shift and jacket that she instantly recognized as Chanel, stepped up to Kyle and kissed him on the cheek. The extremity of Eva's reaction was easily recognizable; she was jealous. Why she hadn't considered that Kyle had a girlfriend she didn't know.

Kyle disentangled himself, his expression neutral. His arm came around her as he introduced Elise, a financial consultant with a rival bank. In clipped tones, he introduced Eva as his fiancée.

There was a moment of stony silence, and Eva found it in herself to be sorry for Elise.

Elise recovered fast. "I know you from somewhere."

That would probably be from the back of a bus, Eva thought.

Minutes later, Kyle unlocked a private entrance sandwiched between a high-end restaurant and an award-winning café. A few seconds in a private high-speed elevator, and they stepped out into the hushed foyer of a penthouse suite.

Opening a tall bleached oak door, Kyle indicated she should precede him. A little perplexed that Kyle had brought her to his apartment, rather than a café, Eva stepped into an elegant, spare hall that opened out into a huge light space. Beech floors flowed to a wall built almost entirely of glass, with sliding doors that opened onto a patio.

The apartment was vast and overlooked the bustling Viaduct with cafés and bars and a marina filled with colorful yachts. Further out the Harbour Bridge arched across the Waitemata Harbour linking the North Shore to Auckland City. To the right the quirky suburb of Devonport with its jumble of Victorian houses was clearly visible, and beyond, in the hazy distance, the cone-shaped Rangitoto Island.

A dapper man in a suit rose from one of the long leather couches grouped around a coffee table. "Mr. Messena, Miss Atraeus."

Kyle introduced her to Ambrose Wilson, the manager of a store that was very familiar to Eva, because a branch of her family owned it. Originally Ambrosi Pearls, the Auckland branch had recently expanded into diamonds.

Wilson indicated the long, low coffee table on which were placed several black velvet display trays that glittered with an array of diamond rings.

As Eva sat down, she fought a sense of disorientation that her wedding was in two days' time.

As she stared at the gorgeous rings, words she hadn't meant to say spilled out, "Was Elise important?"

Kyle, who had shrugged out of his jacket, tossed it over the back of one of the couches and loosened off his tie. "We dated a few times. Mostly at business functions."

And they hadn't slept together, she was suddenly sure of it. Relief flooded her. She let out a breath she hadn't realized she was holding. She didn't want to feel all twisted up and jealous, but lately she seemed unable to control her moods and Elise had pushed some buttons she hadn't even known she had.

Kyle frowned. "Does it matter?"

Eva forced a smile and picked a ring at random. "Of course not."

But if Kyle had been sleeping with Elise while he had been acting as the trustee of Mario's will, surveilling her and preventing her from getting married, all bets would have been off.

The thought pulled her up sharply as she considered where it was taking her. She could only ever recall feeling like this once before, and that had been years ago when Kyle had gotten engaged to Nicola and she had been fiercely, deeply jealous. But that had been because she had been in puppy love with Kyle, and she was not in love with him now; she could not be.

A little dazed, she slipped the ring onto her finger without really seeing it.

Kyle frowned. "That one isn't right."

"How can you know that?"

"I don't spend all my time with my head buried in stocks and bonds."

She examined the ring, with its delicate bridge of three perfectly matched diamonds. It was an expensive but very conventional ring, and he was right, she didn't like it.

Kyle picked up a ring that had its own velvet tray, a classic square-cut diamond that blazed with a pure white fire. The central diamond was large but elegant and framed by tiny white diamonds that glittered and flashed. The setting was platinum, which added to the clean, classical look of the ring. "You should wear something like this. It's pure. Flawless, wouldn't you say, Wilson?"

Wilson, who had been sitting at a side table with his

laptop open, strolled over to look at the ring. "That's correct. It was originally a ten-carat diamond, but we worked with it until we achieved an utterly flawless gem."

Eva met Kyle's gaze. He lifted a brow, and she suddenly realized what he was getting at with the ring. *He knew.* He knew that she had been a virgin when they had first made love. She went hot then cold. Normally when she had a fight-or-flight reaction, her instinct was to fight. This time running would have been the preferred option.

With an effort of will, she smoothed out her expression and replaced the ring she had picked up. When she would have slipped the ring Kyle had selected onto the third finger of her left hand, he preempted her and did it himself, the brush of his fingers sending tingling heat shooting through her.

Kyle's gaze was unnervingly intent. "Do you like it?"

She was trying not to love the ring too much, but it was as perfect as Kyle's unexpected gesture in acknowledging the gift she had given him when they had made love. She cleared her throat so her voice wouldn't sound thick and husky when she spoke. "Yes, it's beautiful. Thank you."

"Good." Kyle turned his head in Wilson's direction. "We're taking the ring."

Wilson produced another box from his briefcase. "Now would be a good opportunity for you to both try on wedding rings."

Reluctantly slipping the engagement ring off, she tried the platinum band Wilson handed her for size. The band, which had been made to match the engagement ring she'd chosen, fit perfectly, so in the end the choice was a no-brainer. Returning the band to its box, she slipped the engagement ring back on her finger.

Within minutes, Wilson had packed up the cases of rings and departed. Eva had no clue what the ring cost, although she could hazard it would run into the hundreds of thousands, if not more. No money had changed hands. But, since the Messena family were bankers for The Atraeus Group and related by blood, no doubt the transaction would take place in a more relaxed way.

Kyle checked his watch. "We need to eat then I'll take you back to work."

While Kyle was taking plastic-covered plates of pre-prepared food that had been delivered by one of the restaurants downstairs out of the fridge, Eva excused herself and went in search of the bathroom. She stepped into a wide spacious hall with several bedrooms opening off it.

The hall, like the rest of the apartment, was stylish, but bare, as if Kyle had no interest in creating a home. She had noticed the lack of artwork and family photos in the sitting room, so the two framed photos gracing the wall at the far end of the hall stuck out like a sore thumb and immediately drew her.

The largest one was of a woman with long, tawny hair and a striking tan as she stood on a street in a bright, summery dress, her arms bare as she grinned and waved at the camera. Eva instantly recognized Nicola, Kyle's wife. The second frame was much smaller and showed Kyle cradling a sleeping baby, his expression intent and absorbed as he studied the small, slumbering face.

Her heart squeezed tight as she looked at the baby, and she suddenly understood why the pictures were here and not out in the sitting room, or even placed more privately in his bedroom. It was as if Kyle couldn't bear that kind of constant exposure to his loss, but neither could he bear to not have the photos, so he had placed them in the hall, an area he didn't linger.

The look on Kyle's face as he held his son briefly riveted her and, for a splintered moment, the years spun back. Her own mother hadn't coped with losing her children. And suddenly, she understood that Kyle didn't just not want more children; after what had happened, he couldn't bear to have any more.

Eva had lost her brother and sisters and, ultimately, her mother. But she could not imagine the grief of losing a child.

Feeling subtly unsettled by the window into Kyle's past, she stepped into the cool, tiled bathroom. After using the facilities, she found herself staring at her reflection and wondering how on earth she could compete with the wife Kyle had loved and chosen, and who had *died*.

On impulse, Eva took the pins out of her hair and let it fall around her shoulders, much as Nicola's had in the photo—then, feeling foolish, recoiled and repinned it.

She wasn't Nicola and never could be. Nicola had been fresh-faced, cute and athletic, while Eva was curvy and sultry and city sleek. From everything she had heard about Nicola, they were very different. There was no way she could compete. But it was also true that Kyle had never forgotten her.

Heart beating too fast, mind working overtime, Eva reviewed every conversation, the clashes and the fights, the heavy-handed surveillance, the lovemaking and the one salutary fact that couldn't be ignored. After staying away from her for ten years, Kyle had come back. And he hadn't just blended into the scenery. He had been the dominant male in her life for the past year and had systematically gotten rid of every man she had chosen.

When Eva returned from the bathroom, Kyle had set out a selection of salads, cold meats and a savory quiche on the table. She met his gaze briefly. When his scrutiny dropped to her mouth, the undisciplined tumble of thoughts coalesced into clear knowledge. Kyle had honored her condition that they did not sleep together, but at the same time he had made no bones about the fact that he still wanted her, and not just sexually. She was certain now that he wanted *her*.

Delightful warmth suffused her. Until that moment, she hadn't realized how much that would matter. But since they had made love, she felt more intimately connected with Kyle, to the point that whenever he was near she hummed with awareness.

Conscious of the weight of the ring on her finger and the flash and glitter of the pretty diamond, Eva filled her plate from a tempting selection of salads. After choosing sparkling water, she followed Kyle out onto the patio.

While she ate, Eva kept glimpsing the diamond on her finger and couldn't help the rush of pleasure that, aside from the conventional need of a ring, Kyle had been so thoughtful. Under the circumstances, she hadn't expected a ring, let alone one that was so utterly gorgeous.

Kyle caught her gaze. "I ran into Sophie and Francesca this morning."

Eva almost choked on a mouthful of sparkling water. If Sophie and Francesca had chosen lives that did not revolve around the fashion industry, they would have been CIA, FBI or some form of Special Forces covert ops, no question. As it was, within the extended Atraeus/Ambrosi/Messena family, they were a force to be reckoned with. "You ran into them or they ran you to ground?"

Kyle's mouth quirked. "We work in different parts of town, so a chance meeting isn't likely. Sophie mentioned something about a bridesmaid and a guest list."

Eva set her glass down. "Your family need to be part of the wedding—"

Kyle set his fork down. "Babe, the wedding is two days away, there's not exactly time—"

"You don't have to worry, all you need to do is turn up. All the details are taken care of."

He lifted a brow. "How many have you invited?"

Eva put her fork down. "Just close family. I know you wanted to bypass all the fuss and frills and that you probably wanted to slide the wedding through before most of your family found out, but it is still *my* wedding, probably the only wedding I'll ever have."

Kyle's head came up. "Why won't you marry again?"

She kept her expression bland. "I'm not the marrying kind. I'm just not...suited for it."

Kyle frowned, but before he could reply, his cell rang.

Eva picked at her salad while Kyle walked to one end of the patio and conducted what sounded like a business call. When he came back to the table, his expression was thoughtful, but he didn't resume the conversation.

Relieved, Eva made an effort to eat a little more. Lately, with all the turmoil, she'd been skipping meals and eating sketchily, which was bad for her stress levels. Witness the off-the-register way she kept reacting to Kyle.

When Kyle was finished, she collected their plates and carried them through to the kitchen. Carefully taking off the ring, she set it on the counter, rinsed the plates and glasses and stacked them in the dishwasher.

Kyle, who had followed her in, replaced all the food in the fridge and wiped down the counter. When she dried her hands on a kitchen towel and went to pick up the ring, he beat her to it.

Automatic tension hummed through her as he picked up her left hand and slid the ring on the third finger. Despite trying to downplay the moment, a shimmering thrill went through her at the warmth of his hands, the weight of the ring and the sheer emotion of the moment. This was what he would do on their wedding day, and they both knew it would not mean what it should. But here in the mundane surroundings of his apartment kitchen, the small act seemed laden with meaning.

Kyle's gaze connected with hers. "You're right, it is beautiful."

For a blank moment, she thought he had said, "You're beautiful." She tried for a breezy smile. "Yes. It is."

When she would have stepped back, he kept hold of her hand. If Kyle had been any other man, she would have had no problem putting an end to the tension that had sprung up. But while a cautious part of her knew she should keep things businesslike, the crazy, risk-taking part of her wanted to kiss Kyle, to pretend for just a moment that the engagement, the wedding and *he* were the real thing. Without consciously realizing she had done it, she swayed closer. "We shouldn't."

"The hell with it," Kyle murmured. "We're going to have to kiss in church, and it's not as if we haven't done it before."

The vivid memory of the passionate night they had spent together, and further back to the long-ago necking on the beach at Dolphin Bay, sent a hot flash through her that practically welded her to the spot. Seconds later, Kyle's mouth closed on hers, her arms found their way around his neck and time seemed to slow, stop.

When he finally lifted his head, Kyle studied her expression for another few seconds, as if he was contemplating kissing her again then he released her. "We need to discuss something. Why didn't you tell me you were a virgin?"

Suddenly the choice of his very private apartment for the choosing of the ring and lunch made sense, when it would have been quicker to have gone direct to the jeweler. "It's not exactly something that comes out in casual conversation."

"I thought—"

"I know what you thought." The same thing most people thought. "That I've had more men than hot dinners."

"You don't exactly put across a facade of innocence."

Eva lifted her chin. "In the modeling business, if you're tough, men leave you alone. It's a way of keeping safe."

"Now you're making me angry."

"Don't be. The strategy worked." Until Kyle.

Walking out to the sitting room, she found her bag and hooked the strap over her shoulder, ignoring the question that seemed to hang in the air.

Kyle shrugged into his jacket and adjusted his tie. "I know you're probably not going to answer, but why me, and why now?"

"You're right," she said with a trademark breezy smile, as she headed for the door. "I'm not going to answer."

Eleven

Kyle woke, uncertain what, exactly, had pulled him from yet another restless sleep. Tossing his rumpled sheets aside, he paced to the window. Opening the curtains, he looked out over the now-smooth sweep of lawn to the bay and a delicate and beautiful sunrise.

His wedding day.

Memories cascaded. Another wedding day, clear and hot and filled with family and friends. Nicola, elegant in white. She had been sweet and smart, athletic and funny. Perfect. She had fitted seamlessly into the measured pattern of his life, and when Evan had arrived, that pattern had seemed complete. Until…Germany.

His stomach tightened. Now, a marriage of convenience.

Feeling tense and unsettled, he walked through to the bathroom and flicked on the shower. The problem was, every time he looked at Eva, convenience was the last thing on his mind and the guilt that he wanted her more than he had wanted Nicola, was killing him.

Unbidden, the hours they'd spent locked together in his bed replayed, along with the uncomfortable knowledge that there had been nothing measured about his response.

And that what he had felt had somehow sneaked up on him, eclipsing the past.

His head came up at the curious clarity of the thought. Peripherally, he was aware of the sound of the shower, steam misting the bathroom mirror, the steady beat of his own heart.

He drew a breath, then another, but the tightness in his chest didn't ease. It was an odd moment to notice that Eva had done something with the bathroom. There was a new mat on the floor in a soft shade of turquoise, and brand-new thick, white towels decorated the towel rail. A large glass jar filled with soaps decorated the bathroom vanity.

The feminine, homey touches should have reminded him of Nicola, but they didn't. Somehow, they were one hundred percent, in-your-face Eva.

Moving like an automaton, he stepped beneath the stream of hot water. He considered the moment of self knowledge that had hit him like a bolt from the blue, the guilt of wanting Eva, and that what he felt was different than anything else he had ever experienced.

It occurred to him that in the years since Nicola and Evan had died, he had done his level best to lock the past away but, in doing so, he had also failed to let it go.

And in that moment he finally understood what he needed to do.

Eva stepped out on the landing just as the front door closed with a soft click.

Frowning, she walked down the stairs and glanced through the kitchen windows just in time to see Kyle dressed in jeans and a T-shirt disappear into the garage.

It was possible that he had things to do in town before the wedding, but as it was barely six o'clock, nothing would be open for hours. Dressed so casually, there was no way Kyle was going into work, either.

Feeling unsettled, not least because after the incandescent moments in Kyle's apartment, she had half expected him to follow up with a suggestion that they break the rules and sleep together, and he hadn't.

She stepped out into the hall. The Maserati cruised quietly out of the garage. On impulse, she grabbed her car keys and decided to follow Kyle. It was a little crazy and a lot desperate, but Eva couldn't help thinking something was wrong, that maybe Kyle had gotten cold feet. Given the encounter with Elise the other day, she had to wonder if Elise was the reason. It would certainly explain the cool way he had seemed to shut himself off, as if he couldn't even be bothered trying to pressure her into bed!

Eva accelerated to the end of the drive and managed to catch the taillights of the Maserati as it turned left at an intersection. Fifteen minutes of nervous tailing later, and feeling certain that Kyle would spot her, she braked outside the gates of what was unmistakably a cemetery.

Relief that she had been wrong about Elise gave way to a sick feeling in the pit of her stomach. She had chased after Kyle in a fit of jealousy and had ended up intruding on what must be a very private moment. A moment that did not include her, because Kyle was not visiting Elise or any other old girlfriend. On the day of his wedding to her, he was visiting Nicola and Evan, the wife and child he had loved and lost.

Three hours later, hours that Eva had filled by first getting her hair and nails done then sitting in the kitchen sipping tea, she finally started to get ready for her wedding.

An odd, shaky relief filled her when she heard Kyle's Maserati return. After those moments at the cemetery, her imagination had run wild and she had half expected him to walk away from the marriage.

Although, why would he? she thought flatly. After all, to Kyle it was only a marriage of convenience.

The heat of the day grew more intense and oppressive as Eva changed into the dress Sophie had designed for the simple church-and-garden wedding. A strapless gown with a tight bodice and full, romantic skirt, the dress was made even more gorgeous by the fabric, which was a soft, pale-pink-and-rose-print silk with an ivory tulle overskirt.

Unfortunately, when she came to fasten the dress, which had about thirty tiny cloth-covered buttons at the back, she could get so far and no farther.

Taking a deep breath, she checked her watch. She was running to schedule, but she hadn't considered she would need help dressing and now she was out of time to call someone to come and help her. Another one of the little details she should have thought of, but which, in the rush to get things done, had escaped her.

She glanced out the window at the smooth sweep of lawn she had made sure was mowed and manicured, to where a group of men were setting up a white tent. Walking back to the mirror, she examined her reflection. Her hair was perfect, falling loose and tousled down her back, the soft waves held with hairspray. To match the dress, she had pulled a swath back from her forehead and fastened it with a clip studded with fresh flowers.

Turning, she tried to do up a few more buttons using the mirror, but when the silk-covered buttons kept slipping from her fingers and her arms began to ache, she gave up on the job. Ideally, Jacinta should have been here to help her, but her last text had explained that she'd had car trouble and would meet her at the church.

After checking the time again, Eva stepped out into the hall and went in search of Kyle, hoping against hope that he hadn't left for the church. A door swung open. Kyle emerged from his room and she drew a breath. In a charcoal-gray morning suit, with a white shirt and a maroon silk tie that subtly echoed the deeper color of the roses on her dress, Kyle looked breathtaking.

She half expected him to say that he knew she had followed him that morning, but instead his gaze simply swept her and lingered. She found herself blushing at the soft, intense glow that seemed to make his gaze even bluer.

"I thought I wasn't supposed to see you until the church."

"Jacinta's having car trouble, so I've lost my helper." She turned and showed him the buttons she hadn't been able to reach and tried not to sound too breathless and panicky.

She had always wondered why brides got so uptight and nervous. Now she knew. There were a hundred and one things that could go wrong. Right now she was beginning to wonder if anything would go right. "If you could do the rest of the buttons?"

"No problem. I was going to break the rules and come and see you anyway."

Swallowing at the intent way he was looking at her and feeling utterly confused because she had convinced herself that the attraction he had felt for her had fizzled out, Eva led the way into the sitting room where the light was better and waited for him to fasten the last remaining buttons.

Kyle gently moved her hair aside. The backs of his

fingers brushed her skin, the small searing touch making her breath come in. She closed her eyes and worked at controlling her breathing as he systematically fastened each tiny button.

When he was finished, she opened her eyes and remembered that she was facing a mirror and that Kyle had been able to see her face the whole time. She blushed and hoped like mad that he had been too busy with the buttons to notice that she was having a minor meltdown.

He met her gaze in the mirror. "I expected you to wear white."

She stiffened a little at the reference to her virginity. "I'm over the white dress. It would have reminded me too much of my last wedding."

"The Dolphin Bay extravaganza."

"Which, luckily, paid for the dress."

He produced a case that he must have set down on a side table while he dealt with the buttons. "You should wear these today."

Still off-balance at her response to Kyle, she opened the box and went still inside when she saw a pair of diamond studs and a pendant that matched her engagement ring. "I can't accept these."

"You're an Atraeus bride and these are wedding jewels, a tradition in the Messena and Atraeus families. Mario would have given you a set if he had been alive, and Constantine will expect it." His expression softened. "Aside from that, I want you to have them."

A blush of pleasure went through her that Kyle wanted to give her a special wedding gift, even if he had tacked that bit on the end. The mention of Mario and of Constantine Atraeus, the formidable head of the Atraeus family and CEO of The Atraeus Group, made her feel even more strained. Family was important and celebrated in the Atraeus clan, even if she had never been quite sure that she had been accepted.

Kyle took the pendant from the case and unclipped it. "You don't have to wear them for me. Wear them for Mario."

"That's not fair."

"It wasn't meant to be. Turn around."

She turned and found herself once again facing the large mirror that sat over the mantel of the fireplace. As Kyle fastened the pendant, her heart turned over in her chest. Framed by the carved gilt frame of the mirror, they could have been two people who belonged in another era, another time. She touched the pretty jewel where it hung suspended in the faint hollow of her breasts. Such a small thing, yet it added an indefinable air of nurturing and belonging that made her throat close up. Like the engagement ring, she loved the pendant, not because of its value, but because of what it said about hers. "It's beautiful. Thank you."

Feeling strained and a little misty-eyed, she took the diamond studs when Kyle handed them to her. After removing the pretty pearl studs she had inserted earlier, she fastened them in place. As she did so, she couldn't help being fiercely glad that the wedding to Jeremy had not gone ahead.

Kyle had been right. For all Jeremy's plusses in terms of a convenient marriage, he had been superficial and utterly self-centered. He would never have offered to buy her even a token engagement ring, and he had expected her to pay for the wedding rings and a new wardrobe for him. "This is turning out to be an expensive wedding for you."

Kyle grinned as he checked his watch. "Lucky for me I have a bank."

* * *

Half an hour later, the limousine Eva had ordered arrived. Still feeling flustered but relieved, she attached the ivory tulle veil that slid in just above her rose clip, picked up the bouquets for herself and Jacinta that she'd ordered from her favorite florist, grabbed her handbag with her cell and strolled out to the car.

A tall dark man was leaning down, speaking to the limousine driver. He straightened and half turned and she went into shock all over again as she recognized one of her Atraeus cousins. "Constantine. What are you doing here?"

Normally, Constantine was based on Medinos, the Eastern Mediterranean island that was home to the Atraeus, Messena and Ambrosi families. Occasionally, he and his wife, Sienna, spent time in Sydney, where The Atraeus Group had an office, but he seldom came to New Zealand.

Constantine grinned. "I heard there was a wedding, so I came to give you away."

She was glad she had thought to remember her handbag because now she needed a handkerchief. Juggling the bouquets, she found one and tried to delicately blow her nose so her makeup wouldn't be spoiled. "Who told you?"

"Kyle rang a couple of days ago, so I cleared my schedule. Sienna and Amber came with me. Lucas and Carla and Zane and Lilah were in Sydney, so they hitched a ride in the jet."

Meaning that quite a large chunk of the Atraeus family, with almost no notice, had dropped what they were doing in their high-powered, fast-paced lives to be at her wedding. Eva sniffed, abruptly overwhelmed. With Mario's death, she had been feeling more and more cast adrift, and her natural instinct was to cut ties and minimize the hurt. But it seemed that the more she tried to walk away from this family, the more they found ways to tie her to them.

When she tried to thank Constantine, he gave her a quick hug around the shoulders so as not to crush the flowers then checked his watch. "Time to go." He looked around. "Kyle said there was a bridesmaid."

Eva would have crossed her fingers if she wasn't holding the flowers. "Jacinta will meet us at the church."

When they arrived there, only five minutes' drive away, the cloud cover had increased, blotting out the sun and giving the day a murky cast. Praying that the thick cloud would blow over, Eva let Constantine hand her out of the limousine. There were a few stragglers outside the church, although Eva didn't recognize any of them. She groaned when she started counting children playing around the church grounds. The Vicar had clearly forgotten to reschedule the La Leche League meeting.

A car door popped open. Jacinta waved at her, and Eva's heart sank. Jacinta wasn't wearing her pale pink bridesmaid's dress. Instead she had on a bright, summery dress, one that fairly shouted cocktails on the beach.

Jacinta looked stressed. "I'm sorry. But when I tried to fix the car, I got oil down the front of my dress and had to change."

Sienna poked her head out the church doors. When she saw Eva, she rushed over with a pretty toddler in tow. Handing Amber to Constantine, she gave Eva a hug. "You look gorgeous. Are you ready? Kyle's going nuts in there."

Eva, who seriously doubted that Kyle was going nuts, retrieved the bouquets from the backseat of the limousine. "I'm ready." She nodded at Jacinta, who gave her a relieved grin as she accepted one of the bouquets.

Sienna took Amber off Constantine's shoulder, gave Eva a last reassuring smile and strolled into the church.

Constantine held out his arm. "Ready?"

Feeling a little shaky, Eva placed her hand on Constantine's sleeve. Jacinta remembered to pull Eva's veil over her face and they were good to go.

As the "Wedding March" started and they stepped into the cloistered shadows of the church, her heart thumped hard in her chest. Someone had taken the trouble to light candles in sconces around the wall, and of course the candles on the altar were lit, the flames lending a soft glow to the wooden pews and the vaulted ceiling. There were also flowers everywhere, white-and-pink roses dripping from vases, their scent mingling with the honeyed beeswax of the candles.

Kyle, standing tall and broad-shouldered at the altar, with Gabriel keeping him company as best man, turned, and time seemed to stand still as their eyes met: his tinged with a softness she hadn't expected to see, hers brimming. A little desperately, she reminded herself that she could not afford to feel this way, and neither could Kyle.

Kyle watched as Eva walked toward him in the soft, romantic dress, which clung delicately to her narrow waist, the skirt flowing gracefully with every step. When he'd seen her standing in the hallway of his house, for a moment he'd been stunned because the dress was the exact opposite of the sophisticated gown he had expected her to wear. But in an odd way, the dress summed up the Eva he was just now beginning to know: unconventional, gorgeous and packing a punch.

Gabriel, his eldest brother, and the obvious candidate for best man, since they worked together, caught his gaze. "Are you sure you want to do this?"

Kyle glanced at Eva, noting the way she clung to Constantine's arm. She had a reputation for being tough, professional and coolly composed, but with every day that passed he was coming to understand that the image she projected was as managed as the airbrushed ads she had used to pose for. Beneath the facade the seventeen-year-old girl he had kissed on the beach was still there.

And there was the root of his problem. Somehow, he had never been able to forget Eva even though he had stayed away from her for years, even though he'd married someone else. And Mario had known it. "Yes."

Eva came to a halt beside him and Kyle met Constantine's gaze, which was as male and direct as Gabriel's challenge. Only Constantine's version carried a different message. Marrying an Atraeus was not done lightly. Mario was no longer here, which meant now he would have Constantine to contend with.

As Kyle faced Eva, he should have been painfully reminded of another wedding day, another woman, but his first wedding, as important as it had been, was now viewed through the distance of time. At some point in the past four years, he realized, time had done its work and the grief and loss, while still there, had faded.

Eva took a deep breath as Kyle folded her veil back. A little disconcerted at the steadiness of his gaze, she said her vows steadily, although when it came to the part where they would care for each other through sickness and health, she almost faltered, because that was not in the plan. Kyle placed the ring on her finger, then Gabriel handed her the ring for Kyle.

She slipped the ring on Kyle's finger and experienced a moment of fierce possessiveness. The rings symbolized the vows, commitment, belonging and the exclusiveness of the relationship.

It was not the ideal time to consider the negative implications of her veto on lovemaking, but she was abruptly aware that if she wanted the exclusivity that the rings symbolized, then sex was going to have to be part of their bargain.

Over the past couple of days, she had been brought face-to-face with the unvarnished fact that Kyle might like to have sex sometime in the next two years. She also knew from her reaction to Elise that she would not cope well if Kyle slept around.

The thought that he might have a sexual relationship with Elise or some other unnamed woman made her go still inside. That could not happen. If Kyle was going to have sex, she needed it to be with her.

In a clear voice, the priest pronounced them man and wife. Kyle took her hands and drew her close. Eva met his gaze. "We need to talk."

"Not now." Then his mouth came down on hers, and for long moments her mind went blank.

The signing of the register was a confused affair, because the adjoining room to the chapel was filled with lactating mothers and small children.

Eva signed, then Kyle. When they stepped away from the desk on which the priest had spread the papers, Sienna almost tripped over an extremely interested little person who was clutching at the fabric of her dress.

"Sorry," a pretty young mother murmured, scooping up the little girl. "She thinks you're a princess."

Eva curtsied at the little girl, who giggled. "Then she should have this." Digging in a secret little pocket at the waist of the dress, she found the little blue silk flower she had tucked in the pocket as part of the "something old, something new, something borrowed, something blue" tradition.

When the young mother tried to refuse, she insisted, pressing the silk flower into the little girl's hand. "It's just a little thing and I'd love her to have it." Words she hadn't meant to say tumbled out. "I adore kids."

The young mother picked up the child, who was already demanding the flower be sewed onto her dress. She smiled as she started back to her seat, the little girl waving happily. "Now you'll be able to have some of your own."

Blinking at the sudden wave of emotion that hit her, Eva turned back to the wedding party to find Kyle watching her with an odd expression.

"This is different," Constantine muttered, detaching a toddler from his ankle and gently turning him around so he could crawl back to his mother.

Sienna picked up a pen and signed. "No, it's good," she corrected him. "It's like a day care at a wedding. Amber can play." She moved aside for Constantine and turned to watch Amber, cute in her polka-dot dress, who was busy martialling a group of babies.

As Kyle shook hands with the priest and handed him a check, Sienna chatted about Amber until it was time to walk back into the church.

As Eva bent down to pick up her bouquet, which she'd left on a seat while she signed the register, her stomach hollowed out and her head spun. Gripping the back of the chair, she waited for the dizzy spell to pass. However, when she straightened, she was still a little off-balance.

Kyle's arm came around, steady as a rock. His expression zeroed in on hers. "Are you all right?"

"It's nothing," she muttered, although her vision was still doing weird things. "I didn't eat last night—no time. And I didn't have breakfast."

In fact, she hadn't felt like breakfast, which was un-usual. Usually, she woke up ravenous.

Sienna insisted she sit down for a minute, and once she was seated, handed her a wrapped candy. "Here, chew on one of these. I know it's sugar, but they're good when you can't keep breakfast down."

Eva unwrapped the candy and popped it into her mouth. The sugar rush made her head spin, but in a good way. "How did you know I couldn't eat breakfast?"

"The same way I know I can't eat it,' Sienna said. "You're pregnant."

Twelve

Kyle's gaze flashed to hers, his expression unexpectedly grim. "Eva?"

"I can't be." She shouldn't be.

Possibilities flashed through her mind, a mixture of joy and dread, with the dread coming out on top. She wanted no part of the grief and death that had disintegrated her family. As much as she would adore to be a mother, she could not be pregnant.

A chill went through her at the thought of what a pregnancy would do to Kyle. After years grieving for his wife and child, Eva giving birth to a child that would most probably die would literally make him relive the nightmare of his past.

Eva shook her head, regretting the sharp movements almost immediately. "I am not pregnant. No way."

She smiled brightly at Sienna, and Constantine, who was regarding her in a thoughtful way that made her wonder if he could see something she couldn't. Sucking in a breath to stop the roiling in her stomach, she called on the years of acting classes she'd taken, smiled and pushed to her feet. Luckily, thanks to the sugar, she was steady.

Relief and renewed confidence steadied her even more. "See, I'm not pregnant, just hungry."

And to prove it, she would do the one thing she had been shying away from doing as a double check that the morning-after pill had worked—she would use the pregnancy test she had bought and which was still in her handbag.

It would be negative: it had to be. Relieved that she had successfully dealt with the whole idea that she might be pregnant with a child that would most likely die, and which would break both her heart and Kyle's, she forced another smile. "I feel fine now. Really."

Kyle took her arm as they strolled back into the church to a smattering of applause and began their progress down the aisle. "Do you usually skip meals?"

"Only when I'm trying to get married on a twelve-day schedule."

"Have you done a pregnancy test?"

Eva smiled at an elderly Atraeus aunt. "Not yet, but I have one…just to confirm that I'm not pregnant." They stepped out into the vestibule. A cold breeze drifted in, making her shiver.

Briskly, she decided that discussing the whole situation about sex would have to wait until they cleared up the murky area of a pregnancy. "Getting pregnant the first time we made love would be huge bad luck," she muttered. "About as likely as lightning striking the same place, twice."

Lightning flickered as they paused at the top of the church steps.

Kyle inspected the now darkened sky. "What was that you were saying about lightning?"

Her reply was drowned by a crack of thunder, and a split second later the heavens opened. Rain poured down in a heavy gray torrent, drenching the photographer Eva had commissioned. Kyle pulled Eva back into the shelter of the foyer as the photographer collapsed his tripod, flung his coat over his precious equipment and ran for his car.

Lightning flashed again, although it was sheet lightning, she consoled herself, not the jagged fork lightning that would have been an uncanny reminder of the night they had first made love.

Luckily, there was a second venue for the photographs. After twenty minutes of snapping wedding shots at the photographer's studio, Eva dismissed the limousine driver and climbed into Kyle's Maserati.

When they pulled into the driveway of the house, which was lined with guests' cars, the extent of the storm damage was clear. A heavy gust of wind had obviously lifted a corner pole of the marquee clear out of the ground, collapsing half of the tent. The caterer's van was parked near the back door entrance, which opened into the kitchen, so he had clearly made a decision to operate from the house.

Appalled, Eva didn't wait for Kyle, but popped her door open. Dragging her skirts up, she dashed through the rain, which had dropped to a soaking drizzle, making a beeline for the kitchen entrance. As she stepped into the kitchen, which thankfully was a hive of activity and awash with lovely scents, she kept repeating the mantra that in the wedding planning business disasters happened, the thing was to have a backup plan.

Once she was satisfied that the canapés and champagne were already served and that the simple summer picnic menu she'd settled on would go ahead, just inside, she walked through into the sitting room just in time to see Kyle step through the front door. There was a thin smattering of applause, which quickly died away when the guests realized that Kyle was on his own.

Taking a deep breath to control the automatic tension and outright fear that hit her every time she considered that she could be pregnant, Eva claimed Kyle's arm. Calling on all of her acting skills, she accepted congratulations, which had been cut short at the church, and when she got the chance grabbed a glass of sparkling water and nibbled on canapés.

Kyle lifted a brow at her water. "No champagne?"

Eva immediately caught his drift. If she were pregnant, she would be avoiding all alcohol. Heat flushed her cheeks, along with another sharp jab of panic. She forced a smile and tried to keep things light. "Habit. I don't usually drink at all, I don't have a head for it, and I usually only ever drink sparkling water at weddings."

They were interrupted by Constantine, who had made himself the unofficial MC. After toasts and speeches, a late lunch was served. By that time, the summer squall had passed and the sun had come out. Jacinta, who had taken control of the indoor service, opened the French doors and dried off the outdoor furniture.

Kyle and his brothers carried over the tables from the wrecked marquee, which was now steaming in the heat; guests moved out onto the patio.

Zane Atraeus, Constantine's youngest brother, styled himself the unofficial bartender, and so the day took on a shape that kept putting a lump in Eva's throat. The things she had expected to go right had crashed and burned, but the unexpected presence of her Atraeus cousins, who had come a long way *for her*, gave her something unutterably precious; for the first time she truly felt part of her own family.

When she saw Carla, the wife of Lucas, who was the third Atraeus brother, struggling to eat salad from a plate while she held her baby boy in her lap, Eva set her own plate aside and offered to hold him.

With David in her lap, contentedly chewing on a teething ring, and listening to Carla chat about the alterations she and Lucas were making to their house in Sydney, she slowly relaxed. Although, holding David, the urgent question of whether she was pregnant or not kept resurfacing. As she talked interior decorating loves and hates with Carla, she determined that she would take the pregnancy test as soon as she got a few minutes to herself.

Kyle, who was caught in a cluster of aunts who were obviously grilling him, caught her gaze, his own ironic. The small moment in the midst of the noisy gathering was oddly heartwarming. Since the tension that had arisen over the question of a pregnancy, she and Kyle had not had one private moment together.

After the cutting of the cake, which was a pretty selection of cupcakes iced with white chocolate icing and pink sugar rosebuds and arranged in tiers, with one large cake on the top tier, someone put on a classical waltz.

Kyle held out his hand. "They're playing our song."

Eva set her plate down, pleased to do so, even though the cake was delicious. The faint nausea, which had continued, was spelling a death knell to her hopes. "I hadn't planned on dancing."

He shrugged as he drew her close, his hand warm at her waist. "It's a Medinian tradition," he said, referring to the Mediterranean island from which the Messena and Atraeus families had originated.

She inhaled, catching the clean scent of his skin edged with a tantalizing whiff of a cologne that was now heart-wrenchingly familiar. Feeling suddenly absurdly fragile and as if she had to soak up scents and sights and sounds before everything came to pieces, she placed her hand on Kyle's shoulder. Their closeness shunted her back to their night together and the shattering intimacy of lying in bed with Kyle. She could still remember the way he had smelled and felt and tasted—the way he had made her feel.

She concentrated on keeping her expression smooth and serene as heat from every point of contact zinged through her. As they began to dance to a well-known waltz by Strauss, desperate to distract herself from sensations that were just a little too intense, she breathlessly asked, "What did the aunts say?"

Kyle completed a turn as they reached the edge of the patio, in the process pulling her more firmly against him. "Apparently, Mario instructed them to make sure I gave you a proper Medinian wedding."

She frowned, caught by the oddness of the phrase. "Did they assume that you would marry me?"

He hesitated long enough for her to know that she was right. "Apparently, Mario discussed it with them before he made the will."

Thankfully now, others were dancing and the noise of the music and the general buzz of conversation was enough to create the privacy she suddenly desperately needed, when it seemed that nothing about their relationship was private in the family. She knew she shouldn't be upset, but the thought that Kyle was really only marrying her because Mario had put pressure on him struck a sensitive nerve.

Everything that happened with Kyle mattered, *because she loved him*.

She went still inside as the truth she'd been avoiding for weeks finally sank in.

Not only did she love him, she had always loved him, right from the very first moment. She had even loved him when he had dumped her, which was why it had hurt so much.

She stared at a pulse beating at the side of his throat, feeling even sicker than she had when eating the cake. "But when Mario suggested you should marry me, you didn't agree."

"I promised to see you married—"

"But you would never have chosen to marry me." A couple whirled past, Zane and Lilah, utterly absorbed in one another, both wildly in love, the complete opposite of her and Kyle. "You just had to in the end, because I ran out of time."

His hold on her tightened infinitesimally. "It wasn't exactly like that and you know it."

She stopped dancing and pulled free. "Then how was it?" She felt tense and on edge, her heart pounding. She wanted to believe that Kyle felt something more for her than duty and desire, but she also knew she had to try and be objective. No burying her head in the sand.

He caught her fingers and pulled her close again. "If I hadn't wanted you for myself, I would have let you go ahead and marry one of the men you chose." He paused. "You know I want you, and after that night on the beach, I think you know how much."

She drew a breath. "What about...love?"

His gaze cooled. "What about it?"

She tilted her head and looked into Kyle's face, the blue of his eyes, his Mediterranean heritage obvious in his olive skin, the clean cut of his cheekbones and jaw. "I love you." The words were flat and declarative, but she couldn't hide what she wanted. "The question is, can you love again, after losing your wife and child?"

Can you love me?

He did a slow turn into an alcove of the room that was private. "We need to slow this down. You agreed to a legal marriage," he said quietly, "one you stipulated would be without sex. That's not exactly a recipe for love."

Eva instantly regretted trying to lever some kind of confession of love from Kyle. She hated the enigmatic expression on his face, as if he needed to conceal his emotions in case she saw what he was really feeling. She had seen that look on the faces of social workers and foster parents when she'd been passed from home to home as a kid. It was duty, minus emotion, the exact opposite of what she wanted!

She met his gaze squarely. "Can you really separate love from passion so completely?"

"Eva—"

"No, don't say it. Don't say anything." The conversation had always been risky, but she had blown it completely, because while failing to obtain any admission from Kyle, he now knew that she loved him.

Her cheeks burned at the kind of vulnerability she had spent years avoiding. "Ask a silly question…" she said a little bitterly. "People separate love from sex all the time."

Only, she never did. She had only ever slept with the one man she loved.

Turning on her heel, she left the room. As she walked, she could feel Kyle's gaze boring into her back. As soon as she stepped out into the spacious foyer, she felt better. At times their relationship had felt like a game, but it wasn't anymore; it was serious and important, because she needed Kyle to love her. This morning it had felt as if they were balanced on the brink of that possibility, but now...

Lifting her skirts, she took the stairs to the upper level. She was hot, her feet were hurting and after possibly the most embarrassing conversation of her life she needed a moment. As she stepped into the dimness of the upstairs hall, she almost walked into Constantine who was quietly strolling along with Amber dead asleep over one broad shoulder. Eva stared at the picture father and daughter made then quietly escaped into her room.

Peeling off her shoes, she sat down on the edge of her bed. Tired of coping with the dress and its long skirt, she started on the buttons and eventually managed to ease out of the layers of silk and tulle.

She changed into a light silk shift in rich summer shades of berry red, with touches of pink, purple and leaf green. Hanging the bridal gown in the closet, she slipped on a pair of comfortable sandals that left her feet mostly bare.

After checking her makeup to make sure the dampness in her eyes hadn't smudged her mascara, she spritzed herself with perfume and walked back downstairs. As she reached the last tread, the front door, which was not locked, swung quietly open and a face from the past that she hoped she would never see again stopped her in her tracks.

Sheldon Ferris, his countenance deceptively average—the boy next door grown into middle age—smiled, his gaze taking in the rich foyer, "Nice house. You've done well for yourself."

Eva's fingers tightened on the banister. "I don't know how you found me, but you need to leave now, before I ring the police."

His gaze darted to either side, checking to see if anyone was about to disturb them. "And charge me with what? Knocking on your door?"

"I know it was you who trashed my house. I haven't given the police your name yet, but if I do, by next week there could well be a warrant out for your arrest."

Fear flashed across his expression, but it was replaced almost immediately by a hard-eyed determination. "And I know why you haven't given them my name. You don't want anyone to know about your trashy background—"

"There's nothing wrong with my background."

"Then why is it such a big secret? I checked. There are plenty of stories about your modeling success, but nothing about your past. But I guess if you don't care about your gutter upbringing, you won't mind if I splash it all over the press. I can see the headline now, 'Street kid, sex symbol rises to become Atraeus heiress.'"

"You know very well I was not a street kid, or a sex—"

"Give me what I want and I won't sell the story. I'll leave you alone for good." He named a figure that was even larger than the one he had quoted before. "Pay up, and I won't tell your new husband what's wrong with you. You'll never hear from me again."

Eva sincerely doubted that. She stared at the shifty gleam in his eyes, not for the first time wondering what her mother had ever seen in him. She guessed he had been younger and handsome in a lean way; now he was a little heavier with gray at his temples and his suit had seen better days. "I'm not paying you a cent. And if you think you can threaten me with telling Kyle anything at all about my past, you can forget it. Believe me, nothing you could ever say would make any difference to our marriage."

And that was nothing more than the truth.

The sound of footsteps made Ferris shrink back onto the front porch: the fear in his expression was palpable. Eva didn't wait to see who it was, no doubt strolling from the sitting room down the hall to the bathroom. She grasped the edge of the door and looked Ferris square in the face. "Mario had information about you. Pretty sure, if I look long enough, I'll find out what it was, and when I do, I'll take it to the police."

She closed the door firmly and held her breath as the shadow of Ferris's outline seen through the frosted glass disappeared. Feeling empowered that she had faced down her ex-stepfather, who had always been something of a bully, Eva walked back upstairs to her room and found her tote bag.

Extracting her phone, she rang Auckland Central and left a message for Detective Hicks to let him know that Ferris had called at her house, demanding money. She also stated that he had been harassing her and that she was certain he was the person who had broken into her house. The next call was to the PI she had retained. He didn't pick up, either, so she left a message asking him to forward any information he had found out about Ferris to Detective Hicks.

She hung up and considered the threat Ferris had made. She knew he would carry through and go to the press, which meant she was out of time.

Her heart squeezed tight as she considered what the disclosure of her dysfunctional background and her genetic disorder would do to her relationships with her adoptive family and with Kyle. Kyle wanted her sexually, and they had shared tender moments, but he had just not had enough time to fall for her. She had hoped they would have time, but if she was pregnant, her time had run out.

When she replaced the phone in her bag, her fingers brushed the pregnancy test kit she had bought.

As much as she needed to know if she was pregnant or not, she couldn't do the test right now, because to do so was to know the truth. And if she was pregnant, she would be honor bound to tell Kyle.

In retrospect, her decision to veto sex had been a huge mistake.

She loved Kyle; she had loved him for years. It was a depressing thought, but she had to wonder if she would ever fall for anyone else, or if Kyle was it for her. If that was the case, and she was beginning to think it was, then she couldn't let him go without a fight.

She was out of time. She needed to try one last time with Kyle, no matter how exposing or hurtful it was. She needed to change the rules and exploit the one power she did hold in the hope that Kyle would, finally, fall for her.

She needed to make love to her husband on their wedding night.

Thirteen

Kyle would have followed Eva if one of the aunts hadn't buttonholed him. After frustrating minutes of listening to a genealogy that went back to some obscure coastal village in Phoenicia, now modern-day Lebanon, his younger brother, Damian, took pity on him, clapped him on the shoulder and insisted he help him with the marquee.

Snagging a couple of bottles frosted with condensation, Damian handed one to Kyle and jerked his head in the direction of the tent, which was flapping gently in the evening breeze. "Aunt Emilia and the family tree," Damian's expression took on a hunted cast. "How far back did she get? The First Crusade?"

"Not quite. You interrupted her during the Third."

"Cool. You owe me one."

Damian bypassed the marquee entirely and stopped where the edge of the lawn dropped away to the small crescent beach below. "Although, strictly speaking, I'm in your debt."

Beginning to be annoyed, because he was certain Damian was referring to his marriage, Kyle watched the sun as it sank by slow increments into the sea, casting a brassy glow across the water. "You are not in my debt."

Damian gave him an, are-you-for-real look. "You did the deed," he said mildly. "I didn't think you'd let Mario pressure you into marrying Eva."

Kyle's jaw tightened. "Don't talk about my wife like that," he said softly. He met Damian's gaze. Damian, for all his youth, was something of a hard-ass, but Kyle had lived and fought with tougher men. "Mario applied pressure on all of us, but that wasn't why I married Eva."

"I don't believe it—you're in love with her."

Kyle frowned at the conclusion Damian had reached. What he felt for Eva was deep and turbulent. When other attractions had faded, somehow the fiery sexual connection that sparked between them when they were teenagers had held. For reasons he could not fathom, Eva was different for him. But he did not think the difference was about love.

For a start, because he'd spent so many years staying away from Eva, he didn't know about large chunks of her life. Come to that, he didn't know about almost any aspect of her life until Mario had adopted her.

His lack of knowledge about Eva made him frown. He had already engaged a security firm to put together a file for him. It was too late in the day to check with them now, but he would make it his business to check on progress in the morning.

Damian finished his beer, checked his watch and indicated they should walk back to the house. "I forgot that you once had a thing for Eva. After you lost Nicola and the baby, I guess I didn't think you'd marry again."

The mention of Nicola and Evan made Kyle's chest

tighten, although, like the conversation he'd had with Eva in the car the night they'd made love, he was actually able to think of them again without reliving the horror of the explosion. Somehow, the one thing he hadn't thought would happen had: he was finally beginning to heal.

Kyle let the still-full bottle of beer dangle from his fingers. "I miss Nicola and Evan," he said flatly. He and Nicola had had a good life together. She had come from a military family and had understood the life. They had traveled together and eventually made a baby together. "But they're gone."

He frowned as the conversation referenced the thought that had not been far from his mind for a couple of weeks now, the possibility, even if it was remote, that he could be a father again despite what Eva had said.

He examined how he would feel if she was pregnant and hit the same blank wall he had lived with for years. The raw fact was he just couldn't go there again. He couldn't be a father again.

Damian strolled onto the patio. "Nice piece of real estate."

Kyle scanned the guests, although he couldn't spot Eva. "The twins told me about it."

"I didn't know Sophie and Francesca were in the market for a house."

"They weren't," he said deliberately. "Eva was."

Damian shook his head. "I don't know why I was so worried." Shaking his head, he clapped Kyle on the shoulder and strolled off to join his girlfriend. Sky was a lean blonde, with ultrashort hair and dark eyes and who could ride a stock horse almost as well as Damian.

Kyle dragged at his tie, loosening it. Damian thought he had fallen for Eva and had bought her the house as a gift. He should correct him, but there was no way he could lay bare the truth that he had used the house as leverage in order to convince Eva that she should move in with him.

The whole business had involved a ruthless streak he had not known he possessed, although it was a fact that ruthless male behavior ran in the family. Constantine had kidnapped Sienna, and Lucas had decided not to mess with a successful formula and had done the same with his wife, Carla. Kyle's oldest brother, Gabriel, had proposed a fake engagement to keep his wife Gemma in his bed, and Nick had not been much better, luring Elena to the Dolphin Bay Resort under false pretenses then cheating on a bet to get her in his bed.

Frowning when he didn't immediately see Eva, Kyle deposited the beer he hadn't bothered to drink on a table and went to find her, but instead got caught up in a flurry of goodbyes as Constantine, Lucas and Zane, all with arms full of sleepy kids, made their way to their cars. The caterer had finished packing up his equipment and had left while he'd been talking to Damian and, thankfully, so had the bevy of aunts.

Damian, his jacket slung over one shoulder, his arm wrapped securely around Sky, lifted a hand in farewell. He was followed by the twins, who grinned, kissed and hugged him, signifying that the conclusion Damian had jumped to had spread through the family like wildfire.

By the time Kyle stepped back inside, the house seemed eerily empty, except for the kitchen staff who were busily tidying up glasses and bottles in the sitting room.

Jerking his tie from his shirt, Kyle walked to the French doors and began closing the house up for the night. As he locked the last door, he checked his watch. It had been a good thirty minutes since he and Eva had argued on the dance floor.

His stomach tightened at the thought that Eva might have been upset enough to walk out. And in that moment he realized that, despite his attempts to control the way he felt about her, he hadn't succeeded. It had been evident in his knee-jerk reaction when Damian had spoken about Eva and the way he had claimed her as his wife.

It was evident in the way he felt now. Tension coursed through him at the thought that Eva might have been upset enough after their conversation to leave him, then a footfall registered and he turned to see her walking down the stairs.

A van door sliding closed then the roar of the caterer's van heading down the drive sounded.

Kyle noticed the test kit in her hands and went still inside. "What's the result?"

Eva reached the bottom of the stairs, her face oddly pale. "I haven't used it yet. I guess I'm a coward, but the plain fact is I don't want to know until tomorrow."

She slipped the tube back into its box and placed it on a hall table and walked toward him. "There's just one other thing. I've changed my mind."

She stopped close enough that she could feel the heat emanating from Kyle's skin. She ran a finger down his chest. The heady masculine scents of clean skin and the subtle spice of sandalwood made her head spin.

Kyle's hand curled over hers, holding her palm to his chest. "What about?"

Lifting up on her toes, she boldly wound one arm around his neck, leaned in close and gently bit down on one lobe. "About the clause in the agreement that prohibits sex. If anyone is going to sleep with my husband, it's going to be me."

"There's not exactly a line." When she would have drawn back, his hands closed on her hips, holding her against him. "I'll get my lawyer to strike out the clause in the morning."

"But as long as we have a verbal agreement, the new condition is in effect."

"We could shake on it," he muttered, "but I've got a better idea." Lowering his head, he finally did what she had been dying for him to do ever since the wedding ceremony; he kissed her.

Long minutes later, the world went sideways as Kyle picked her up. When he reached the top of the stairs, instead of going into her room, he continued on down the hall and into the master suite, where he set her on her feet. The sun was down now, and the room was dim with shadows. Moonlight silvered the walls and threw light over the large bed occupying the middle of the room.

Kyle cupped her face and bending, he kissed her again. "Since we have a new agreement, this is where you'll be sleeping from now on."

She tried to both kiss him and start on the buttons of his shirt. When he finally lifted his mouth, she finished the buttons. "You won't get an argument from me."

"Can I get that in writing?"

"No chance." She caught the corner of his grin, as if he liked it that she argued with him, and out of nowhere hope flared, built on the foundation of a long-ago friendship and the mystifying strength of the connection that had always sizzled between them.

"Thought so." He shrugged out of the shirt and let it drop to the floor.

Closing her arms around his neck, she lifted up against him, loving the hard-muscled planes of his body held tight against hers. She felt his fingers at the zipper of her dress. Seconds later, it drifted to the floor. Her bra followed, and she shivered at the searing heat of his skin against hers. Kyle's fingers tangled in her hair, and she found herself walked backward in the direction of the bed.

He bent his head and took one breast into his mouth, and for long moments her belly coiled tight, the room seemed to spin and there was no air.

The first few times they had made love the sensations had been intense, now they seemed even more so and the awareness of the changes to her body settled in more deeply. She could not say for sure she was pregnant, but with every fiber of her being she felt it to be so and the knowledge added a depth and poignancy to their lovemaking, because every touch, every caress could be the last.

When Kyle lifted his head, Eva ran her hands down his torso and deliberately unfastened his pants. She heard his swiftly indrawn breath, felt his tension. A split second later, he had scooped her up and deposited her on the bed. She watched as he peeled out of his trousers, but when she would have expected him to come down beside her, he remained standing and she realized he had a condom and was sheathing himself. When he climbed onto the bed beside her, she wound her arms around his neck and pulled him close.

She felt the drag of her panties as he peeled them down and obligingly shimmied a little, helping him get rid of that last barrier. She felt his gaze on her in the dimness as he came down between her legs. Loving the weight of him, she clutched at his shoulders as slowly, gently, he fitted himself to her.

His gaze connected with hers again. "Okay?"

"I'm fine." Lifting up against him, she pulled his mouth to hers and kissed him, the passion white-hot and instant as they began to move together. Long moments later, caught in a maelstrom of sensations that were almost too intense to bear, the responses peaked, jerking through her in dizzying waves. Moments later, Kyle collapsed beside her then half rolled, pulling her into a loose hold.

The room had darkened further, so that the shadows appeared inky and the moonlight by contrast threw stark, cold light over the bare floorboards and the bed.

Kyle's fingers tangled in her hair, stroking the strands, as if he loved the feel of it. Emboldened, Eva propped herself on one elbow and studied the planes and angles of his face. She cupped his jaw, enjoying the abrasive roughness of his five-o'clock shadow. "How many times can you do that?"

Kyle's head turned into her touch. He caught her hand, bringing it to his mouth. "It depends. How many times did you want?"

"Once more, at least." Gathering her courage, Eva straddled him. Since the first night together, she'd made it her business to do some in-depth research about sex and had made some fascinating discoveries in the process. "But this time I get to be on top."

Fourteen

Eva got up just as dawn touched the sky with gray. Sliding from the bed, she walked softly to her room, found her robe and belted it at her waist. Still moving quietly, she walked barefoot down to the front foyer, retrieved the test kit and took it with her into the downstairs bathroom.

After she had used the kit, she set the stick carefully down on top of the cardboard box it had come in and washed and dried her hands. There were two windows in the stick. According to the instructions, if the smaller one showed a line, that meant she had done the test correctly, if the second window also showed a line, that was a positive result.

Taking a deep breath, she checked the stick. There were two lines.

She sat down on the side of the bath, her heart pounding. She was pregnant. The morning-after pill hadn't worked.

She had known it. Her period was late, and even though so little time had passed, she felt different. Her breasts were tender and she had gone off food. Her sense of smell had become acute, so that scents that hadn't bothered her before were suddenly overpowering.

She touched her abdomen, feeling a sense of wonder that there was a baby forming inside her. In the same instant, dread struck as she wondered if, in the lottery of genetic inheritance, her baby would lose. Her twin had died at age four. Her younger brother and sister had almost made it to five.

Just long enough for her and Kyle—if he agreed they should stay together—to fall hopelessly in love with their child before having to say goodbye.

Which was why she had to leave now. Kyle had already loved and lost a baby, but at least, as tragic as his loss had been, it had happened fast and unexpectedly.

If she left now, she could go through the pregnancy and birth alone. She could choose to have the baby tested while she was pregnant, or wait until after it was born. Once she knew the result, she would contact Kyle and let him know. If the child was healthy, she would happily share custody if that's what Kyle wanted. Given that this was a Messena child, she could not imagine that he would turn his back on his child. Kyle was an honorable man; when it came to the crunch he would be a father. But she was under no illusions about how he would feel about her for forcing the issue. She did not think they would have any chance now of a real marriage.

If the child was affected, it would break *her* heart. She didn't know how she would cope alone, but she would. Her mother had never recovered from watching three of her children die, but she was determined to be stronger than that. This child was precious. She would love it for every second that it was with her and if she was very, very lucky, maybe the baby wouldn't have the disorder.

Pushing to her feet, she put the stick back in the box and dropped it in the bin then walked quietly upstairs. She had packed last night, so other than changing into a pair of jeans and a soft cotton hoodie and slipping on sneakers, she was ready to go. Although, she needed to write Kyle a note first.

Berating herself for not thinking to do that last night, she looked for pen and paper. There were pens in her tote, but the only paper was the back of an envelope. Beginning to feel a little frantic, because it was almost fully light now and she knew Kyle was an early riser, she quickly scribbled a note, explaining that she was leaving him and that she relinquished all rights to her inheritance until she was forty and that he could have the house.

The plumbing gurgled as if the upstairs shower had just been turned on, which it probably had. Adrenaline pumped. That meant Kyle was awake.

She picked up her overnight bag and checked that the hall was empty. Walking as quietly as she could, she made her way downstairs, wincing as a tread on the steps creaked under the extra weight of the bag.

She placed the note on the hall table, along with her wedding and engagement rings and paused at the door to take a last look at the house. Throat aching, tears misting her eyes, she unhooked the chain then slowly turned the big old-fashioned key in its lock so it wouldn't make a loud clunking noise and pushed the door wide.

Cool morning air swirled around her as she gently closed the door, groaning at the audible click it made. Jogging to her car, which she had parked around by the garage so that wedding guests would have plenty of room out front to park, she loaded her tote and bag.

She glanced at the kitchen windows, her heart pounding because she half expected to see Kyle, then climbed behind the wheel, started the engine and backed out. Gravel crunched beneath the tires, preternaturally loud in the early morning air. Certain Kyle must have heard, she spared a last glance for the house, but the front door was closed and windows were blank. Depressing the accelerator, she took off down the drive.

Kyle wrapped the towel around his waist when he heard the sound of Eva's car starting. Cold knowledge hit him as he strode past her room and noted that the dressing table was bare. Cursing beneath his breath, he made it down the stairs and outside in time to see the taillights of her little sports car wink as she went down the drive.

Stomach tight, he strode upstairs, found his phone and called her. When he got her answering service, he tried again just in case she was stuck in traffic and hadn't had time to pull over and answer the call. He rang a couple more times then gave up.

He found clothes, pulled on a pair of jeans and a T-shirt then tried the phone again. Jaw tightening, he retrieved the keys to his Maserati from the top of his dresser and took the stairs two at a time. It was possible Eva had gone to work, although he didn't think so. He knew for a fact that she didn't have any weddings happening for a couple of weeks, and Jacinta was running the office meantime.

He yanked the front door open then stopped when something fluttered to the floor. He picked up the envelope, which was covered with scrawled writing, as if Eva had written it in a hurry, and read then reread the words. His stomach hollowed out.

Eva had left him.

She knew that meant that she would not receive her

inheritance, but she would manage without it. Without the inheritance she couldn't buy the house, so Kyle could keep it.

Except that Kyle didn't want the house if Eva wasn't going to be in it. He had bought it for her.

Correction, he thought grimly, he had bought it for them, in order to make marriage to him more palatable for Eva.

When push had come to shove, he had been just as manipulative as Mario in trying to entice Eva back into his life.

She had left him.

His heart was pounding, and he was having trouble thinking. The last time he had felt like this had been in Germany when he had lost Nicola and Evan, but at that point there had been nothing he could do.

He had to think. Something had happened. It had to be that Eva was pregnant.

In the moment he also understood that the secrecy about Eva's past—a past he had only just begun to probe—was somehow tied in with the pregnancy. He didn't know how, but it was a fact that Eva reacted to children in a way that wasn't normal. She adored them but had seemed to recoil from the idea of being pregnant and having her own.

Setting the note back down on the hall table, he decided there was no point in driving to Eva's house or her business premises. She wouldn't be at either place, because she knew he would look there.

He did a quick search of her room. The jewelry case with the pendant and earrings was on top of a dresser. All of the dresser drawers were empty. The wedding gown and the shoes she'd worn were in the closet, but nothing else. There was no sign of the pregnancy test kit.

He checked his bedroom and the bathroom, but the small trash can was empty. Frowning, he went back downstairs and did a systematic search of the rooms. In the first-floor bathroom, he found the pregnancy test kit discarded in the trash. When he pulled out the little stick, he noted the two lines. At a guess, that meant she was pregnant. He scanned the instruction leaflet, which confirmed it.

He stared at the stick with its positive result, took a deep breath then another. He felt like he'd been kicked in the chest. Eva was pregnant with his child. He was going to be a father. Again.

The thought filled him with a crazy pastiche of emotions—delight and the cold wall he'd hit when Nicola and Evan had died; horror and grief and self-recrimination.

One other salient fact registered. He loved Eva.

Correction, he was *in love* with her, because just saying the word *love* didn't seem to encompass the intense out-of-control emotions that kept gripping him. He was in love with Eva Atraeus, and if he was honest, by varying degrees he had been in love with her since he was nineteen. But Mario's complete veto of their relationship had closed that door.

She loved him.

There was no other reason for her to run. But he had been too concerned with guarding his own emotional safety—the protective habit that had dominated the past four years—to appreciate that love.

He had fallen for Eva, but he had ruthlessly suppressed any softer feelings and focused on the sex. He had played it safe, using the surface image Eva projected as his compass north, even when he knew it was just a facade.

Now there was a child, and in that moment, he knew that nothing mattered but Eva and their child.

The specter of the past and his failure to protect his wife and child was just that, a burden of guilt he'd hung on to for too long and which hadn't changed anything. Logically, he had always known that he could never have saved them. The terrorist attack had not been predictable.

But he would not fail again. Eva was pregnant. They were going to have a child. He needed to be there for Eva and the baby—if she would let him.

That long-ago conversation with Mario suddenly made him go cold inside. He had said Eva needed protection. Protection from what? He could remember asking Mario at the time and not getting a straight answer. He had assumed Mario had meant emotional protection, but what if it was protection from something or someone else?

Suddenly the break-in at Eva's house took on an added significance. A lot of items had been strewn over the floor, but a family photo had been set on the dining room table. Annoyed with himself for missing clues that should have alerted him to the fact that Eva had a problem, he walked through to the kitchen, picked up the phone and rang Gabriel.

Gabriel picked up on the second ring, his voice gruff.

Kyle explained he was taking a few days because Eva had run out on him. "She's pregnant."

There was a small silence. "And the pregnancy's a problem?"

Put like that, Eva running out sounded like a simple reaction to an unplanned pregnancy, but Kyle knew it was a whole lot more than that. "She knows how I feel about having a child. She's gone, Gabe. She's prepared to end the marriage and let the inheritance go into trust."

"I'm listening."

Kyle filled Gabriel in on the break-in and his suspicion that someone from Eva's past was putting pressure on her, maybe with blackmail.

Kyle heard a voice in the background, Gemma, and Gabriel's voice, muffled, as if his hand was over the receiver. "I had a conversation with Mario shortly before he died. Eva had a stepfather. Apparently, he stole all of Eva's mother's possessions shortly before she died. Not content with that, he tried to blackmail Mario. There was also a medical issue, although Mario didn't go into detail about it."

The thought that Eva could be sick made Kyle frown. She had seemed perfectly healthy, but plenty of illnesses were invisible until the last stages. "I need to know more about Eva's past. I think I need to access Mario's safe deposit box."

"Meet me at the bank in thirty minutes."

Kyle hung up. Until the moment he had seen her car disappearing down the drive, he had been able to fool himself that what he and Eva had was controllable and, for want of a better word, convenient for them both.

It wasn't. Control had been an illusion. He had wanted her from the beginning. But it was more than that now. Somewhere along the way, the wanting had turned to a need that was bone deep and inexplicable.

He had always thought that love between a man and a woman came down to a romantic cocktail of sex and companionship, but what he felt for Eva was raw and primitive. She had made him see *her* and not the savvy businesswoman, and she had stunned him with her capacity to love.

She loved him.

Until that moment, he hadn't understood what it must have cost her to say those words. Still locked into the failure and guilt of his own past, the goodbyes he had said at the graves the morning of the wedding, he hadn't been able to respond.

When he hung up, he remembered the note, which was written on the back of an envelope. Walking back to the hall, he found it and reread it then turned it over. All the hairs at the base of his neck lifted when he noted that the address on the used envelope was for a PI.

Walking through to his study, he found his laptop, Googled the PI and found that Zachary Hastings specialized in locating missing persons and covering domestic situations. Certain he was close to discovering exactly what was going on in Eva's life, he checked the time. Hastings's office wouldn't be open for an hour. Frustrated, he forced himself to make coffee while he tried to phone Eva again. When she refused to pick up, he left a message, asking her to call him.

He made one more call to the young detective, Hicks, who had been investigating the break-in at Eva's house. The information that Hicks provided, that they had a suspect and that Eva had made a statement to the effect that the same suspect had been harassing her, made his jaw compress.

Hicks wouldn't provide him with the name of the person they were investigating, because all of the paperwork was under Eva's name, but Kyle was willing to bet it was the stepfather. It was just another example of how Eva, with the self-sufficient streak she had, out of necessity, acquired as a child—and which he had seen as a hard, brassy confidence—was used to managing on her own.

Gabriel was grim faced as they stepped into the sterile vault that housed their safe deposit boxes. He produced the two keys required, and Kyle opened the box, which was filled with family jewelry and documents.

Kyle found the adoption papers with Eva's birth name and those of her parents. He made a note of all three names and their birth dates. He flipped through the documents, which were mostly investment portfolios. At the bottom of the box, he found an envelope addressed to Mario. It was filled with Eva's medical reports.

"Bingo," he said softly.

Suddenly, he was beginning to have a glimmer of what Mario had meant all those years ago by Eva needing "protection." Eva had a genetic disorder. He didn't know what the implications of the disorder meant, exactly, but by the end of the day he would.

In amongst the paperwork was a psychologist's report. Apparently, after years of trying to fix the dysfunction in her family, Eva had, at age fourteen, chosen to walk away from her mother and her latest husband, a petty conman, choosing foster care and survival, instead of hopelessness.

Kyle's chest tightened as he began to see Eva's abandonment of their marriage in its correct context. She wasn't a quitter. She was strong and resolute and she had thrown everything she could into their marriage in an attempt to get him to love her back.

For Eva to leave meant she had given up on him.

If he got her back at all, it would be a miracle.

An hour later, Kyle sat down opposite Hastings in a small, neat office on the North Shore. When Hastings refused to divulge what, exactly, he was doing for Eva, Kyle applied a little judicious pressure. Eva was his wife and she had disappeared. If Hastings wanted his bill paid, then he needed to give the report to Kyle.

With the report in hand and the addresses he needed, Kyle started searching for Eva. Two weeks later, after a series of dead ends, he abandoned trying to find Eva through her past connections.

Although, he would find her, it was just a matter of time. Eva was pregnant with his child, which meant she needed medical appointments. More important, within the next few weeks, she would most probably be having tests to determine whether or not the baby was affected by the disorder. It wasn't the avenue he would have chosen to find Eva, but it was the only one she had left him.

Fifteen

Two months later, Eva dressed in a soft cotton shift dress and a light jacket, both of which were comfortable to wear, given that her waistline was gently expanding. After locking the tiny cottage she had rented in a remote coastal village miles north of Dolphin Bay, she drove to a specialist appointment in Auckland.

As she drove, she noticed the same silver sedan had been behind her ever since she had left the small village and turned onto the main highway. An odd tension gripped her at the thought that Kyle had somehow located her and was keeping tabs on her, although she almost immediately dismissed the thought. For Kyle to go to the effort of finding her and having her followed would mean that he cared, and she did not think that was the case. Besides, she was on State Highway 1, heading toward Auckland, New Zealand's largest city. Most of the traffic in front and behind would be heading toward the same destination.

Thirty minutes later, her small car was swallowed up in city traffic. A small jolt of adrenaline went through her when she noticed that there was still a silver sedan two cars behind her at a traffic light, but as she accelerated across an intersection with light-colored cars stretching in several directions, she dismissed the thought that she was being followed.

Minutes later, she parked her car and took an elevator up to the specialist clinic where she had booked her appointment. She had tossed up whether or not to have her baby tested while it was still in the womb. There was a small risk of miscarriage, but she had decided that she needed to know sooner rather than later. Regardless of the outcome, she would love this child with all her heart. If the news was bad, it would tear her to pieces, but she would cherish each day: she would cope.

As she sat in the upmarket clinic, the classical background music that was playing changed to a soft, lilting tune. It was the waltz by Strauss that she and Kyle had danced to at their wedding, just weeks ago. Nerves already stretched thin, she searched for a tissue and blew her nose, relieved when the tune finally changed to a light and airy piece by Bach.

She checked her watch. Abruptly nervous about the long wait, she got up to get a foam cup of chilled water from the dispenser in the corner of the waiting room. The sooner she had the procedure done, the sooner she could get out of Auckland and minimize the risk that she might accidentally bump into Kyle or someone else she knew.

She drank the small amount of water she'd dispensed, grimacing at the fine tremor of her hands, a sure sign of stress. The sound of the glass door at reception sliding open attracted her attention. Shock reverberated through her when she saw Kyle, dressed in a dark suit with a snowy-white shirt and blue tie, walking toward her.

She was suddenly glad that, evidently, she was the first appointment after lunch, so no one else was in the waiting area. "How did you know I'd be here?"

"I know you're pregnant and that you would need a specialist appointment, so I hired a security firm to find out where and when."

And that wasn't all. "You had me followed!"

"That, too. It took me long enough to locate you, and once I did, I wasn't taking any risks." He came to a halt beside her, and she noticed the dark circles under his eyes, as if he hadn't been sleeping, and that his hair was ruffled as if he'd dragged his fingers through it repeatedly. "I know why you ran."

She crumpled the cup and dropped it in the nearby trash can as she desperately tried to work out how much Kyle did know. She tried for a smooth, professional smile. "I am pregnant. And if you'll remember, you expressly stated that you didn't want children."

"I said a lot of things I regret, especially that. Will you hear me out?"

Tensing against the too-rapid pounding of her heart and the one thing she had not seen coming, that maybe, just maybe, Kyle wanted to try again, she sat and listened.

In terse sentences, Kyle outlined the raw details of the grief and guilt that had consumed him, almost to the point of losing her. "You know how much I wanted you. It practically drove me crazy, but I couldn't seem to change the way I was wired until I lost you." He grimaced. "Gabriel probably thinks I went crazy. It certainly felt like it."

Grimly, he outlined how he and Gabriel had accessed Mario's safe deposit box and found her medical reports. That Kyle had even rung Hicks and found that she was

having Sheldon Ferris investigated for harassment. He
had also found Hastings and pressured him into supply-
ing a copy of the investigation she had commissioned
into her stepfather.

"You know about the disorder."

"And that we could lose our child."

Our child. She met his gaze fiercely. "I don't understand. You didn't want a pregnancy. You can't stand the
thought of having a child, let alone one that could die."

"Couldn't. Past tense."

"What does that mean, exactly?" Against all the odds,
the very fact that Kyle was here, that he had gone to a
great deal of trouble to find her, filled her with wild hope.
Hope that she couldn't afford because she had barely
survived leaving Kyle and, now that she was pregnant,
she could not accept the empty, convenient marriage he
preferred. And she would not, absolutely not, terminate
her pregnancy.

"I followed you to the cemetery the day of the wedding. I thought—"

His gaze connected with hers for a long, tense moment. "I was saying goodbye."

Kyle pushed to his feet and did a restless circuit of
the room before crouching down and taking her hands
in his. "I made a mistake, about you and the baby. And
about myself. I thought I couldn't heal, but I did—it just
took time." In grim, rough words, he told her about his
hunt for her and the research into her past that had finally
made him face his own demons. "When Nicola and Evan
died I blamed myself."

Despite her determination to keep as much emotional
distance from Kyle as she could while he spoke, her heart
broke for what he'd been through. "You couldn't protect
them from a terrorist attack."

"They shouldn't have been with me in barracks. I should have made them stay in New Zealand where it was safe." He was silent for a moment. "I was waiting for them as they turned into the barracks. One minute they were there, the next there was…nothing."

Appalled, she stared at the tight clasp of his hands. "I didn't realize you had seen it." And suddenly the small scars across his stomach and arms, the nick on his cheekbone made sense. If he'd been caught by a bomb blast, he would have had multiple injuries.

She touched her abdomen. "This baby could die." In terse words she told him the grim details of her childhood.

"I know," he said simply. "But the fact that our child may have the disorder, as bad as that would be, was never the issue."

And finally she understood. Kyle had blamed himself for the deaths of his wife and child, but it hadn't ended there. Guilt had seared so deep he thought he didn't deserve love or fatherhood.

She touched his clasped hands. "I thought you were incapable of loving either me or the baby." When the reality was that Kyle was exactly what she had first thought him to be when she had fallen for him as a teenager, a strong protector who loved deeply. The way he had responded to the loss of his family only underlined that fact.

Kyle gripped her hand. "I can love you and this baby, if you'll let me."

Dimly, she heard her name being called.

When she stood up, she pulled Kyle with her. "This is my husband," she said a little shakily. "I'd like him to come into the appointment with me."

Kyle sat with her while she had the procedure. When the clinician had finished, he ascertained the time it would take to receive the test results then made some calls. Normally it took two weeks, but a hefty donation to the lab facility, and the time was reduced to forty-eight hours.

When they left the clinic, on the advice of the clinician, Kyle insisted that Eva shouldn't drive and that she needed to spend the next couple of days taking it easy.

Kyle accompanied her down in the elevator. When they reached the shadowy environs of the parking garage beneath the clinic, Eva gestured in the direction of her car. "I could move back into my place for a couple of days."

Kyle's Maserati flashed as he unlocked it. "I want you to stay at the house."

Kyle was still looking at her in an intent way that made her heart beat faster, as if he couldn't bear to let her out of his sight.

She drew a deep breath, feeling breathless and on edge but oddly, crazily confident about Kyle for the first time ever. "Why?"

He cupped her face between his hands, and she let him pull her close, loving the soft gleam in his gaze. "Because I love you. I'm in love with you. I want you back, if you'll have me."

She felt weird and a little dizzy, but the feeling was oh, so good. "Yes."

A split second later she was in his arms. The emotions that rolled through her were too powerful and intense to even think of moving; all she could do was cling to Kyle, absorb the warmth and comfort of his presence, and the stunning fact that he loved her.

She drew an impeded breath. "I love you."

A split second later, he dipped his head, and finally he kissed her.

* * *

Two days later, Kyle, who had taken time off work to be with her, took the phone call from the clinic. He handed the phone to Eva.

Fingers shaking, she listened to the result then terminated the call.

Kyle pulled her close. "What did they say? Not that it matters. For however long we have this baby, we'll love it, and if you want more we'll adopt."

Eva swallowed, hardly able to believe what she'd heard after years of fearing the worst. "They think it's all right. There's no sign of any abnormality." Then she burst into tears.

Kyle simply held her, and when she'd finished crying, he pulled her outside down to the sunlight-filled cove at the bottom of the garden.

He loosened off his hold and handed her a clean handkerchief. "I just wish you'd told me about the disorder years ago."

"I didn't know I was affected until after Mario broke us up." She shrugged. "It was after that that he took me to a specialist and I had the tests done. I think he was afraid I'd run after you." She sent him a slanting glance, "And he was right. But when I understood I was a carrier of the disease, that changed everything."

Kyle's brows jerked together. "I would never have walked away from you because of a medical issue. Mario told me to back off. He didn't say why, exactly, but he gave me the impression you came out of an abusive home, that you needed protection, not sex."

She coiled her arms around his neck, loving the feel of him so close, adjusting by slow increments to the knowledge that her future and the baby's was going to be a whole lot different than she had imagined. "Secrets are hard to let go of—they become part of you." She hesitated, but it was time to let go of her own hurt. "Did I tell you that I love you, that I've loved you for years?"

"Not today." Dipping his head, he kissed her for long, dizzying minutes.

Eva drew a deep breath as Kyle finally lifted his head. In the time they'd been talking, the sun had slid down the horizon and the shadows were lengthening. "We should go back to the house."

"First, you need to wear these." He reached into his pocket and pulled out a familiar black velvet ring box. Holding her wedding and engagement rings in one hand, he went down on one knee on the sand and slid them onto the third finger of her left hand.

In the deep, steady voice she loved so much, because it was an expression of Kyle's character, that he, himself, was steady and true, he asked her if she would be his wife for richer, for poorer, in sickness and in health.

Her throat closed up. "I will. I love you."

When he rose to his feet, she lifted up for his kiss. As they walked back to the house together, Eva knew they would have difficulties to face but, finally, she was secure in the knowledge that whatever came, they would face it together.

Epilogue

Six and a half months later, in the midst of renovations to the house they had firmly updated while keeping all of the beautiful period features, Eva put the final touches to the nursery.

Maybe it was old-fashioned to want an actual nursery opening off the master bedroom, but since she would only be pregnant this once, she had decided she would have it exactly how she wanted. The renovation and redecorating had entailed planning, hours of online browsing and multiple shopping trips, but it had been a labor of love.

Kyle, who had arrived home unexpectedly, considering that it was only two in the afternoon and he shouldn't have been home for a whole three hours, leaned against the doorjamb and surveyed the room. "It looks good." He gave her a slightly wary look as he loosened off his tie. "Is it finished?"

Eva dragged her gaze from the electric blue of Kyle's.

Months into a marriage that had been more sublime and interesting than she could have imagined, because she had never had to share her space with a man, she was even more in love with her husband.

Her husband.

The words still gave her a thrill and filled her with a glow of happiness. She and Kyle had spent time on Medinos, a honeymoon gift from Kyle so she could get in touch with her Atraeus roots and get to know her Messena relatives. She had met more family than she could poke a stick at, but the experience had been filled with laughter and healing. Most of all, she had enjoyed doing up the house with Kyle—the house that he had bought for her—working together to create a home that was a harmonious blend of them both. They still disagreed; on occasion they argued, but Eva figured that was a healthy sign.

She critically examined the white-painted armoire stacked full of diapers, baby wipes and the one hundred and one essentials a modern mother needed. "I think it's finished."

But she had thought so before then changed her mind. It was part of the nervous tension humming through her, a bit like the bridezilla thing, only with babies.

Feeling suddenly breathless, Eva walked to the window—although with her very large bump, walking was more like a waddle—and pushed it wide, letting in the early summer air. It was so hot, she was burning up. She also felt as big as a bus, probably because labor was a couple of days overdue, and if she put on any more weight she would explode.

She tried to take a deep breath, but these days breathing deeply didn't happen, no matter how much she needed the oxygen. She attempted to give Kyle a serene, in-control look. "Why are you home early?"

"I thought I should be here, just in case." He frowned. "Maybe you should sit down, or better still, lie down."

Eva tried for a smooth, professional smile. The only problem was, deep down, she was a bundle of nerves. "I was sitting down before. I hate lying down." Who could know that even lying down would be difficult when pregnant?

Abandoning his relaxed position, Kyle came to stand at the window with her. Placing his arm gently around what used to be her waist, he leaned down and kissed her. As soft and tender as it was, it was a distinctly sideways kiss. Her stomach was so large now that any approach from the front was doomed.

"Is your bag packed?"

She shifted so that she was leaning back against Kyle, his arms around her. It was the only comfortable way to hug. She let out a breath, soothed by his presence. Somehow, when Kyle arrived, all of her fretful stressing melted away. "I've been packed for weeks."

"Good, because I'm taking you to the hospital. Now."

"You knew I was having pains?"

Kyle leaned down and nuzzled her neck. "Of course I knew," he growled.

She smiled delightedly at a phenomenon that still took her by surprise, and which she had never thought would affect a macho, manly guy like Kyle. She met his gaze in his reflection in the window. "You're having them, too."

"My secretary thinks it's hilarious."

She had a moment to consider that, as crazy as it was that Kyle was experiencing some part of her discomfort, it was just another sign of how well they fit together. She had expected to feel passion and desire and all the turbulent depths of being in love with Kyle; what she hadn't expected was the warm, close companionship that had steadily grown. They weren't just husband and wife, they were best friends.

She placed her hands over his, holding his palms spread over her stomach. Almost instantly there was a sharp kick and she held her breath, riveted by Kyle's absorbed expression. "I won't tell your family…for a price."

"Too late," he muttered grimly. "Francesca knows. That's the same as saying everyone in the family knows. Constantine rang me up today to say it was okay to feel pains. Apparently it runs in the male line."

She hesitated then decided to ask. "You didn't feel them…before?"

The look he gave her was surprised. "No."

Happiness filled her at the relaxed, neutral way Kyle had answered a question about the child he had lost, because that, too, was a sign of healing. Thankfully, the guilt that had seared him finally seemed to have been exorcised.

A pain that was sharper and more prolonged than the one before made her stiffen. Concerned, Kyle helped her to the bedroom, but she refused to lie down. The bed, as comfortable and gorgeous as it was, was her nemesis. Once she got on it, she felt like a beached whale. She practically needed a crane to haul herself out.

Another pain hit her, and Kyle went white. "That's it. I'm calling the hospital. We're going now."

It wasn't a hospital so much as a private clinic because, before the police had managed to charge Ferris after they had found her laptop in his house, he had sold a story about her to a Sunday paper, and now there was a media problem. When the original story had broken, Kyle had decided it was as good a time as any to do what they had planned and fund a charity for disabled children. Unfortunately, instead of neutralizing the story, it had only seemed to whet the appetite of the media. But in a good way, and they had begun actively following her pregnancy. Now, apparently, she even had an online fan club.

Eva tried to get comfortable in Kyle's Maserati as he drove through the gates of the clinic. Thick, subtropical plantings lined the driveway, closing out any view of the rolling hill country or the sea, which she knew had to be just a couple of miles away. They weren't that far from Auckland, but the isolation seemed eerily complete.

Kyle parked in front of the double doors of a facility that, situated as it was in a mass of towering tropical growth, looked more like the set for *Jurassic Park* than a hospital, and helped her out.

Feeling grumpy and emotional the closer she got to giving birth, Eva leaned on Kyle, because she now had weird pains shooting up her legs, although secretly she loved it that he fussed around her.

An orderly strolled down a shallow ramp with a wheelchair. Eva ignored Kyle's impatience when she didn't immediately maneuver herself into the chair. Instead, she concentrated on dragging her handbag out of the Maserati, annoyed that evidently Kyle didn't think she needed this last bastion of her femininity. Grimly, she noted that given that she was now shaped like a bubble, the bag was possibly the only verifiable sign that she was female. Hugging to herself the pretty pink leather tote with cute tassels and sparkling diamanté stuck to the side, she pretended the wheelchair was invisible and shuffled right by it.

Kyle kept pace with her, his expression carefully

blank, as if he was dealing with a mental patient. "You should have gotten in the wheelchair."

"I want to walk. I need the exercise."

A series of cramps hit her. She'd had cramps on and off for weeks now. Someone had named them Braxton-Hicks cramps, because they were supposed to be practice contractions that prepared the body for labor. The Braxton-Hicks episodes had been interspersed by two sessions of false labor but, so far, no result. As far as she was concerned, Braxton-Hicks was a liar, and she had been in labor for a month. Who knew if these were finally the real thing?

She shuffled a few more steps, aiming at the front door when one of her dizzy turns hit. Head spinning, she found herself veering into the large patch of tropical bush that loomed over the front entrance. Kyle caught her before she stumbled into the weird little forest and disappeared forever. He muttered something short beneath his breath that she was pretty sure was a curse word and swung her into his arms.

"You should put me down," she muttered fretfully. "I must weigh two hundred pounds."

"No sweat." She caught the edge of a grin. "I bench press that much most days."

She thumped his shoulder, but desisted when she almost dropped her bag. It contained her makeup, a magazine, some low-sugar snacks and her phone which, judging from this place, over the next few days could be her only link to civilization.

The front doors slid open. A cool, air-conditioned current washed over her. "Okay, you can put me down now."

"No."

Feeling disempowered because he wouldn't put her down and tired of being huge and heavy and vulnerable, she muttered the direst threat she could come up with. "That's it. You just lost any say in names."

Infuriatingly, that didn't seem to make an impact. "As long as it's not Tempeste or Maverick I can live with that."

She tried not to let the fact that he didn't care about the names get to her. "Why are you so happy?"

He lowered her into the wheelchair, which the orderly had anxiously inserted into the space below her body, but by now she was in too much pain to protest. She was beginning to think that her body had finally given up practicing and was actually going to give birth.

Kyle bent down, one hand on either rest, corralling her. His face was taut, and she dimly remembered that he was experiencing at least something of these pains himself.

He kissed her, surprising her into silence. "I'm happy because after today the waiting will be over, we'll finally be a family." His mouth twisted in a wry smile. "And because we don't have to be pregnant again."

Another sharp pain hit her as he steered the wheelchair to the receptionist's desk. The woman behind it gave Kyle a concerned look, but Eva was suddenly distracted by a suspicious warmth. She couldn't be sure, but she thought her waters might have broken. Either that or she'd had another one of those annoying little accidents. "I need to go to the bathroom."

Kyle gave her a narrow-eyed look, as if he suspected her of hiding something from him. *As if.*

He had a quick-fire conversation with the receptionist then finally wheeled her in the direction of the bathrooms. She pointed at the ladies, but he totally ignored her, wheeling her into the disabled bathroom.

She sent him an outraged look when he didn't leave. "You can't come in here."

"You're in labor. You need help."

"No. I want to do this one thing by myself."

She might have been talking to a rock. With easy strength he helped her out of the chair.

When he saw the wet patch, he said another one of his cuss words. "Why didn't you say your waters had broken?"

Face flaming, she let him help her out of the wheelchair. "How would I know? It's not as if I've ever had a baby before."

Kyle's expression was grim as he helped her in the direction of the toilet.

When she was finished, Kyle helped her back into the chair and wheeled her out into the corridor. Within seconds another pain hit, this one severe enough that she was finally glad to be in the chair.

When Kyle wheeled her into her room, both a doctor and a midwife were waiting for them. She was already in active labor, and the pain was quite intense. Eva did her best to ride through the pain, silently begging for the fastest delivery possible

It was forty-five minutes.

When Kyle, who had stripped off his suit jacket and tie and rolled up his shirtsleeves so he could pace better, realized that she was in too much pain to be even remotely interested in conversation, his face went white. Stepping out into the corridor, he snapped out a curt series of commands, including a demand for pain relief.

Within seconds the room was full of people. Another lightning examination, this time by the midwife, and Eva found herself transferred to a gurney and wheeled into the delivery suite.

With walls that were a soothing aqua, and soft background music playing, it should have been an oasis of reassuring calm, but Eva barely noticed her surroundings. All of her attention was focused on what was happening at the center of her body and how much it hurt. Somehow, all of the literature she had read had managed to gloss over this part.

Kyle's arm came around her, a hard-muscled band of strength that in those moments she desperately needed. A cramp gripped her that was so prolonged and intense she couldn't breathe. Kyle's gaze locked with hers and for a precious few seconds they were bound together in commiseration.

Her fingers tightened on Kyle's as a powerful tingling surge gripped her, wiping her mind clean of anything but the sudden, irresistible urge to push. There was a brief hiatus then another series of surges, which squeezed all the breath from her lungs until, in a rush, the baby was born.

Eva floated in exhausted silence, watching, dazed, as the midwife cut the cord, wrapped her tiny baby girl in a cuddly white wrap and placed her in Kyle's hands. His gaze bright blue and indescribably soft, Kyle cradled their daughter as if she was made of fragile spun glass and placed her in Eva's arms. Wonderingly, she looked into her baby's small, perfect face, the tufts of damp hair clinging to her head, and fell in instant love. The bed depressed as Kyle sat beside her. She felt the warmth of his arm wrap protectively around her shoulders.

Reaching out a forefinger, he gently touched his daughter's cheek. One tiny starfish hand latched around his finger, and Kyle froze in place. Eva's heart squeezed tight at Kyle's careful stillness, the way his gaze was riveted on the fierce grip of his daughter, and another wave of pure love and connection hit her, this time for Kyle.

He would be a wonderful father. She had seen it in his patience with her, his quiet tolerance of the mood swings that had hit her, his absorption with all the aspects of her pregnancy. It wasn't just that her hormones had been running riot. It had been an emotional time of processing the past, of letting go and forming a new future together.

Another contraction grounded Eva with a thump. The midwife hurriedly took their daughter. A few minutes later the unutterable gift that had shaken them when cheerfully announced by her doctor months earlier, their second child, was born. It was a boy.

The midwife placed their son in Kyle's arms and Eva gave herself over to joy.

Twins: a boy and a girl. Even though twins ran on both sides of their families, it had been so much more than they had hoped for.

Kyle called his family to let them know the good news. He asked everyone to give them some space, but that was like asking waves to stop pounding on the beach.

The Messena and Atraeus families were like a force of nature. They arrived throughout the day: Luisa with Sophie and Francesca; Gabriel and Gemma; Nick and Elena; Damian and Sky; and a little later on Constantine and Sienna, who had flown in from Sydney where they were holidaying. They had all admired and held the babies and showered her with beautiful gifts and filled her room with flowers.

Later on that evening, when everyone had left, Grace Megan woke up, her cry distinctively high-pitched. Benedict Mario soon joined in, although his cry was more of a bellow.

Kyle handed her Grace then cradled Benedict. Both babies were on the small side, around six pounds each, but they were perfect.

Closing her eyes, Eva whispered a prayer of thanks.

Somehow, out of Mario's well-meant interference, she had gained everything she had wanted and more: a perfect husband and a perfect family.

* * * * *

If you liked
NEEDED: ONE CONVENIENT HUSBAND,
don't miss the other PEARL HOUSE *books*
from Fiona Brand:

Business and passion collide when two dynasties
forge ties bound by love!

A BREATHLESS BRIDE
A TANGLED AFFAIR
A PERFECT HUSBAND
THE FIANCÉE CHARADE
JUST ONE MORE NIGHT

Available now from Mills & Boon Desire!

MILLS & BOON®

Desire™

PASSIONATE AND DRAMATIC LOVE STORIES